VEGAS

follows you home

Sadie Grubor

ISBN-13: 978-1507651285
ISBN-10: 1507651287

dedication

mike, you believed in this story when I didn't.
You pushed me to finish when I didn't think I could.
Thank you, I LOVE YOU!

CONTENTS

blurb

"We are going to Vegas. We are going to Vegas!" They used the damn Blue's Clues theme music to their lyrics.

Olivia Harlow

It's a trip with friends. A single girl's celebratory getaway. Olivia Harlow finishes the biggest job she's been offered since starting Harlow Cakes, her custom and specialty cake shop and bakery. So, it's a Vegas weekend for Olivia, the level headed, single mother, with her life scheduled.

There is no way she could guess what would happen and who would follow her home.

Damon Knyght

His search is over. After rising up from the ashes of his life and the pain, he found them. Now that he has them, there is no letting go.

 Prologue

"Olivia!" Mercedes shouted as she emerged from the office on the furthest side of the kitchen.

"Yeah?" I replied, quietly, my attention focused on creating the complicated ribbon pattern for the wedding cake I needed to finish today.

"You'll never guess the call I just had." She stopped just before crashing into my worktable.

"Ced, if you don't calm down, I'm going to ask you take three steps away from this cake before I end up wearing all five tiers of it."

Sarah, my baking assistant, giggled from my right.

Mercedes put her hands up and took two steps back.

"But, Liv, seriously, you just got the job of a lifetime!" She vibrated with excitement.

Securing the last ribbon detail, I straightened and stretched out my spine, the three pops accentuating relief. Taking a deep breath, I focused on Ced and the topic at hand.

"What are you talking about?"

"Okay, so, I was going over the books and the upcoming schedule. Because, as you know, since we were featured on that reality wedding show, our business has completely increased, and if I don't keep on top of the books and schedule, things just get hectic crazy around here. And when things are hectic crazy around here you get gar-um-pee."

Known for her ability to complete full conversations in one breath and without another person actually participating, if I didn't interrupt, we would be here for a while.

"Ced, take a breath and circle back to the phone call."

"Oh," she blinked rapidly, "yeah, thanks. As I was saying, I got a call requesting you to prepare desserts and a cake for over two thousand people." Ced's eyes twinkled with excitement. "Two thousand people, Olivia! Do you realize how big this is?"

"Wait, a wedding with two thousand people? Is it some celebrity?"

Sarah started to go over the cake details with iridescent sugar powder, giving the ribbons a glossy sparkle.

"No, no, not a celebrity. It's a corporate function." She lifted a notepad I hadn't noticed her holding. "Vivianne Lachlan will be arriving to discuss the details with you personally, but they want you to prepare all the desserts and the large cake for their company function. They are even going to pay the traveling costs."

"Didn't you tell her we account for travel and delivery costs in the fees?"

"Of course I did." She may as well have said *Duh!* "But we've never had flight costs before, so I figured we would—"

"Wait, flight costs? Why am I flying somewhere?"

"It's in New York," Ced responded. "They want you to come to New York and prepare everything there. Hotel and travel expenses will be handled by Miss Lachlan and her employer."

"Whoa, Ced, I don't fly to other states to work. We can't do it. Call her back and apologize for the misunderstanding." I began cleaning up the icing bags.

"Are you crazy, Liv?" Mercedes stepped back up to the table. "This job will be enough money to pay for half of this year's expenses. You will retain a large profit margin this year," Mercedes argued.

From Mercedes appearance — her rainbow-dyed shag hair, purple-blue contacts, and standard vintage-inspired style, along with her A.D.D. — you would never guess the girl was a numbers genius. Appearances were deceiving. In fact, Mercedes Welch graduated valedictorian at Carnegie Mellon University in Mathematical Sciences. She had been dating one of the instructors at my Pittsburgh Culinary School when I met her. Mercedes had and always would be one of the most interesting people in my life.

"I'm not going to leave Alex and go to New York. You know—"

"I believe it would be worth your while to accept."

Snapping my attention toward the unfamiliar voice, I allowed myself a moment to absorb the unexpected visitor. A very tall, thin woman with sleek, dark brown hair wrapped smartly into a bun atop her head, stood at the doorway between the kitchen and storefront of my bakery. Her skin, fair and flawless, contrasted with her dark eyes. Beside her stood Mrs. Dorn, a woman I'd hired a few years back to run the storefront.

"I'm so sorry, Olivia. She said you were expecting her, but she wouldn't wait at the consultation table." Mrs. Dorn turned her apologetic eyes from me and glared at the corporate woman next to her.

"It's fine, Mrs. Dorn. She was expected. Thank you." Forcing a smile in the new woman's direction, I turned to Sarah. "Can you finish this up and get Greg to help you carry the cake to the cooler?"

Sarah nodded and I turned back to the tall woman. A woman whose put-together, pristine appearance had me wiping my hands on my oversized, worn, and food-color-stained jeans. As if that would fancy up the old band t-shirt and knotted red mess held on my head by a bandana. I refused to wear a hairnet like a lunch lady.

"I'm sorry, Miss..."

"Lachlan." She stepped forward with her hand held out for me.

I met her halfway between my table and the door, taking her hand and shaking it.

Mrs. Dorn retreated to the front of the shop.

"Miss Lachlan, there's been a misunderstanding. I don't travel. I can send a team from the shop to put together—"

"I'm afraid Mr. Knyght is requesting you be on site to handle things," she said, matter-of-factly, as she reached into the leather bag at her side. Pulling out an envelope, she handed it to me. "You will be well compensated. Oh, and this does not include the travel. B.I.G. will make all flight and hotel accommodations on your behalf.

Slipping the check from out of the envelope, I read the amount three times to be sure my vision wasn't doubling. It held far more zeros than I'd ever seen in person. For a moment, my greedy side wanted to drop to my knees and thank the woman, but my realistic nature tampered down the impulse.

"I'm flattered to be so in demand, but I'm afraid it just simply isn't possible." Handing the check back to the shocked corporate woman, her dark eyes grew wide with what looked like worry.

"Olivia," Ced hissed, stepping in front of me, "are you crazy?" Giving me her back, she turned toward Miss Lachlan. "Give us a moment, please?"

Grabbing my arm, she pulled me across the kitchen and into her small office. In a hush, she began her reprimand.

"Are you an idiot? You'd have to be to pass up this opportunity." She sighed heavily, grabbing the financial breakdown she must have created while on the phone with Miss Lachlan earlier. "Do you see this?" She held the clipboard in front of me. "This is a ton of money for the bakery, you, and Alex."

She put her hand up, halting my protest.

"You can go to New York, take Sarah and Greg with you. You have Emily so groomed that between her, Mrs. Dorn, and Jeff, we can take care of the bakery. I'll call some of students at the culinary school to do some temp work if needed."

Before I could try to protest again, she put her hand over my mouth.

"I will stay and take care of Alex. We haven't had any Auntie Cedie time lately. Everything will be perfectly fine for one day and night."

A light tap on the half-closed door interrupted our discussion.

"Miss Harlow?" Reaching out, I pushed the door all the way open. Miss Corporate Ladder stood there looking haughty. "I just got off the phone with my employer." She raised the cell phone she held in her left hand. "He is prepared to double the offer."

"She'll do it," Ced blurted.

"Excellent." Miss Lachlan held out the same envelope holding the check.

"Mercedes," I hissed.

She covered my mouth with her hand once more and took the check with her other. I pushed her hand from my mouth.

"The other half of the payment will be given after you have completed the job." She pulled more papers from her bag. "Now, we need to discuss the details."

Mr. Damon Knyght

After all this damn time and effort, she's turning down the offer. It's enough money to give her business a major gain at the end of the fiscal year. I should know, I've seen her financial records. I clenched my free hand into a fist.

"Vivianne, offer whatever she wants," I growled through clenched teeth.

"Sir? Are you sure about this? I mean, I can arrange—"

"Don't question me! Double the offer! Give her the initial check and she will receive the other half upon completion of the job. Don't fuck this up, Vivianne!" I slammed my desk phone down and moved to the small bar in my oversized office.

As I poured the whiskey into the chilled tumbler, I caught a glimpse of the silver frame turned over on the bar. Knowing the absolute torture I would be putting myself through, I slid my fingers across the cool silver and picked it up. Inhaling deeply, I flipped it over and looked at him. Tightness in my lungs suffocated me. I slammed the frame back to the bar and the glass shattered from the force, scattering across the lacquered wood. Grasping a tumbler and filling it halfway with whiskey, I tossed back the aged smoothness in one swig.

"M-Mister Knyght?" My secretary's timid voice carried across my vast office from the partially opened doorway.

"Yes?" I replied, my voice gravelly. I cleared my throat.

"Is, uh…is everything okay, sir?" She fidgeted, well aware of my temper.

"Yes," I answered, curtly. "Could you please have housekeeping clean the glass near my bar?"

"Of course, sir." She smiled and turned to tend to the task.

"Don't let them touch the picture frame!"

She snapped her head around quickly.

"Y-yes, sir," she said, continuing her retreat.

Sitting back into the chair at my desk, I impatiently waited for another call from Vivianne. This time, it had better be a confirmation of Olivia Harlow taking the job.

When the intercom buzzed, I grabbed the phone.

"Is it Vivianne?"

"No, sir. It's your brother." My secretary's voice wavered.

"Send him through," I said with a disappointed sigh.

Our father, Damon Senior, remarried after he and my mother divorced. I had been two. He wanted a housewife and my mother, much too independent and intelligent to waste away in a house with multiple children, refused to comply with his desires.

The conflict brought about the divorce. Luckily for me, my parents worked hard to remain civil with one another, mostly for the sake of the public eye. With my father being a world-renowned surgeon and my mother residing as the CEO of B.I.G., they needed to keep a certain level of professionalism, even in their private lives.

Damon Senior remarried about six months after the divorce and soon produced Hugh with his wife, Heidi. She is much younger than my father and more than content to be a trophy housewife. Her dependence on him also made his affairs easier for him to get away with.

The phone buzzed again. "Hugh?" I answered.

"Good morning, Damon," he greeted in his usual pleasant tone.

"So, to what do I owe this call? We didn't have a call set up, did we?" Scanning my calendar, I saw nothing.

"No, I'm just calling to let you know Scarlett and I have finally set a date."

Settling back against my chair, I took a deep breath and smiled.

"That is...great news. So, when are you finally going to make an honest woman of her?"

"I heard that!" Scarlett's charming voice in the background revealed that she was in my brother's office. I chuckled.

Scarlett started with B.I.G. as an intern during her last year of college. The impression she had in the department with her imaginative and out-of-the-box marketing skills was clear from the beginning. The impression she left on my brother was also clear from the beginning.

Hugh was still enamored by her intelligence and beauty. There was no denying Scarlett's physical appeal to men and, to be honest, even certain women. Scarlett stood at about five-foot-six, but her height meant nothing when you were matched up against the ferocity of her presentations and campaigns. Scarlett was a natural force, only enhanced by her golden blonde hair, porcelain skin, hypnotizing crystal blue eyes, which were most often framed in black rimmed glasses, and her hourglass figure. Her relationship with Hugh only manifested after I pulled her into my office and demanded she go out with my brother at least once before I killed him. From that moment forward, they've been together.

"Anyhow," she feigned annoyance, "we will be getting married near my family's hometown in Pennsylvania."

"Sounds like a good idea." Realizing that would put me close to Pittsburgh, a smile crossed my face.

"So, you won't object to traveling and standing as my best man?" Hugh rejoined the conversation.

"I couldn't be more thrilled to do just that." My brother meant a lot to me and he just gave me reason to be in Pennsylvania.

"Are you sure it—"

"Scarlett," Hugh hissed.

Knowing exactly what she was referring to, I sighed.

"It's fine." I stiffened in my seat. "We can discuss more about this later." The buzz of my intercom interrupted the direction the call had taken. "I need to get this." I hung up without a goodbye and hit the button. "Yes?"

"Sorry, sir, but it's Miss Lachlan."

"Send her through," I quipped, impatiently.

The phone beeped. "Well?!"

"She agreed to the double payment and will be—"

"Excellent! Good work, Vivianne!" A happiness I hadn't felt in years filled me.

Vivianne went over the logistics and details, but I didn't care. All that mattered was that I had found them. She would be within my grasp in just a few, agonizing days.

The day of the corporate party arrived and I couldn't get through the workday quick enough. I planned to cut out of the office early, dress, and find Miss Harlow before the party began, but a last minute disaster with one of our larger clients made it impossible. My only hope was to get to her before too many people arrived.

Arriving at the venue, I groaned at how many others arrived early. There were board members and employees I had no other option but to greet and speak with. After all, this party was in celebration of the company and its employees.

Finally getting through the throng of people, I arrived at the kitchen. Upon entering, I was greeted by a tall, dark skinned man, eyeing me skeptically.

"Hello, I'm Damon Knyght, CEO of B.I.G." Holding out my hand, I eyed him up. Who was this man to her? Employee? Lover?

His eyes widened. He quickly wiped his hand before holding it out. "It's a pleasure to meet you, Mr. Knyght."

"I just wanted to come back and see...thank Miss Harlow for traveling out here for us this evening. I know it was an inconvenience for—"

The man's brow furrowed.

"Is there a problem?"

"I'm sorry, Mr. Knyght." Turning, I came face to face with a tall, thin brunette with large blue eyes. "Liv...Miss Harlow had to get back to Pittsburgh." She twisted her fingers in her apron nervously.

Looking back at the tall, dark man, I realized they were both awaiting my reaction.

"I see," I said, biting back my anger — my fury. She wasn't there. "Well, please thank her for me." Forcing a smile and a nod, I left the kitchen.

Reaching inside my dark suit jacket, I pulled out my phone and dialed.

"Yes, Mr. Knyght?" Vivianne's voice always reminded me of what a loyal dog would sound like if a dog could speak.

"Why is Miss Harlow gone already?" I growled.

Vivianne always tried to please and take care of everything, but she would never make amends with me. Not unless she finally resigned from her position and went far, far away.

"I, uh, wasn't aware she was required to stay once the job was finished. Her assistants stayed to help out during the—"

"Goddamn it, Vivianne! Where is she?"

"Uh...um..." Vivianne stuttered.

I shouldn't be taking this out on her, but she's ruined everything. She'd always been a thorn in my side. If it weren't for my mother, I would've dropped Vivianne from the payroll years ago.

"Let me find out if she's left yet, Mr. Knyght. I will call—"

"Where are you?!" I returned to the large crowd of employees and business associates and scanned the room for her dark hair.

"I'm about to walk out the front entrance to make the call privately, sir."

"I'll meet you there. Don't move!" I ended the call and snaked my way through the crowd.

A few stops to talk and a couple of handshakes later, I was out the front door. Vivianne stood, leaning her forehead against the stone wall of the building. I cleared my throat. She jumped.

"Sir, she's already on a plane back to Pittsburgh." Tears formed in her eyes as she took in the tension of my body. She knew how angry I was.

"I'm leaving." Turning to the valet, I growled, "Get my car."

His eyes widened and he moved quickly to locate my vehicle.

"Sir, you have to make your speech. You can't just—"

"Have Hugh do it. I have some business to attend."

Before she could say anything more, my car appeared. Tipping the valet for his fast work, I slid behind the wheel of the sleek, midnight blue car, spinning the tires as I pulled away.

Pulling out my private cell phone, I dialed.

"Hello?"

"Mitch, its Damon. I need you to locate someone for me. In fact, I need you to find out as much as you can about this person and I need everything as soon as you get it."

"Anything and everything?" He wanted reassurance.

"Yes."

"Does this have anything to do with our prior contract?"

"Yes."

"Name?"

"Olivia Harlow."

"So, you found her." He wasn't asking, Mitch was stating a fact. "I'll get what I can, but you have to give me some time, Damon. Pennsylvania is a bit out of my jurisdiction and there is only so much a computer can give me. I may have to contact a few people—"

"Just keep my name out of it and do what you have to do. We both know money isn't an issue." I ended the call and tossed the phone on the passenger seat. With a heavy sigh, I sped home to bury myself in whiskey and memories I'd rather escape.

Olivia

The day after the New York job, Mercedes recruited Felicity to convince me to celebrate the opportunity. Felicity Valiente, an event planner who had grown to be a close friend after so many jobs brought us together over the years, towered over Mercedes at almost six feet tall in her heels. Today, she wore her long, thick, dark hair in a braid over her shoulder. The turquoise wrap dress complimented her golden brown skin and dark brown eyes. With her Filipino and Hawaiian heritage, she was the kind of woman men wanted and other women wanted to be.

"A trip to Las Vegas for a Girls Gone Wild weekend will be help you wind down from the big job." Mercedes pushed the topic when I didn't initially respond to the idea.

"I'm a mother. There will be no Girls Gone Wild." Laughing, I stacked the third tier, out of the five, on a wedding cake.

"Come on, Olivia. Live a little!" Felicity chided.

"Your dad can watch Alex for the weekend. We can all go and let loose. Besides, I didn't get to go to New York like you did!" Ced brought out the puppy dog eyes and pouty lip.

"You two go ahead. I have a lot of cakes to get done." Waving, I tried to shoo them away.

"There are only three cakes this weekend and Sarah and Greg can handle them, plus Emily is like your mini-me. She can handle it." They both stood on the opposite side of the table, staring intently. "Come on!" Mercedes pleaded.

"It's to celebrate your success, Liv!" Felicity added.

"We all know how celebrating ended for me before." An image of Isaac flashed into my head.

"I'm sorry, Liv. You know how sorry I am that that happened, but this isn't like that. You need to get out, be a woman, and get laid!" Mercedes stated.

The room erupted in laughter.

"Hush it, all of you," I said between my own laughter. "I can't believe you just announced it to the kitchen." Heat flushed my face.

"A vibrator can only do so much." She shrugged off my embarrassment and ignored my beet red face. The chorus of laughter around us grew louder.

"If I agree, will you shut up about my sex life, batteries or no batteries?"

Felicity and Ced gave me a synchronized smile.

"Yes!" Ced hugged Felicity, and then both burst into song.

"We are going to Vegas. We are going to Vegas!" they sang, using the damn Blue's Clues theme tune.

"Get away from my table before you knock over this cake, you loons!" Laughing, I shook my head at them.

"You love, L-O-V-E, us!" Ced sang.

Damon Knyght

Two extremely long days later, Mitch called while I was in the middle of a meeting. Unable to take the call, but unable to concentrate on the topic any longer, I rushed the meeting. I wasn't going to lose her now.

"Hello," he said. His voice was always guarded when he answered.

"You got the information I requested?"

"Damon?"

"Of course."

He chuckled. "I'm sending the information to you now, by messenger."

"Give me the summary." I closed my office door a little too roughly, excitement flowing through my body.

"Well, Miss Harlow will be taking a trip to Vegas this weekend. The flight arrangements were just made this week under the name of Mercedes Bennett, but it's Harlow." A beeping noise sounded through the phone. "Listen, I have to go, but the details should be there within the hour."

"Very well." I ended the call and hit the button on my desk intercom.

"I am expecting a messenger within the hour. I need the delivery immediately."

"Yes, sir," Mrs. Shaw quickly responded.

I settled back in my leather chair, unable to think about work. Vegas was the only thing on my mind.

The messenger arrived forty-five minutes later and Mrs. Shaw brought in the large manila envelope with a large smile on her face. I took it and thanked her. Once she closed the door behind her, I tore into the envelope. It was everything I needed. A plan began to form in my mind. I hadn't been to Vegas in years.

Chapter one – waking up in vegas
Olivia

Oh my good Lord, my head hurts. It's so heavy, like it's filled with cement. Yawning, I scrunch my face. *Did a rabbit climb on my face and stick it's ass in my mouth last night?* Thanks, Mister Cottontail. Opening one eye, my matted hair is all I can see.

How the hell did I get back to my room? I'm gonna kill those two — Felicity for pushing the damn shots, and Mercedes for encouraging the drinking game.

"You need to loosen up, Liv."

"You just finished the biggest job and got paid! It's time to celebrate, so bottoms up!"

"Come on, give yourself one night. What's the worst that could happen? A hangover?"

"We've got each other's back, we promise."

Those lying bitches.

Groaning, I try rolling over.

"What the...?" My voice sounds rough, like I'd been yelling.

I can't move. *Why can't I move?* I test my arms, they move. Legs, they move, but I can't get up. A thick arm weighs down my body. *Shit. Time for an arm check. One, two, three...three?*

Oh my God! I brought some strange guy back to my room! Those bitches let me leave with some random guy? They are so dead.

Gently shifting, I try not to wake him. No such luck. His arm tightens around my waist and pulls me against him. *Well, this feels kind of...really, really, kind of...*

"Rebecca..." he mumbles, his warm breath heating the back of my head.

Had I given a fake name? Sweet baby Jesus, I'm a slut. I don't do home wrecker.

Shame tingles over my skin as I work to pull free of his embrace. Gentle isn't working, so I shove at him, trying to push the toned arm from my body. Gripping his wrist, I finally lift, but pause before pulling myself free. The sight of the shiny band of gold on his left hand dissipates any sanity and composure I was desperately holding onto. He's married.

"Crap, crap, crap!" I shout.

His body jerks next to mine.

"Holy freaking crap!" Jumping out of the bed, I begin the slutty girl search for my clothes.

"What the hell?" A growl rumbles from the strange married man in my bed.

Unable to look him in the eye, I grab for the underwear and dress I finally find tossed about the room. With quickening steps, I rush for the cover of the bathroom.

"Olivia?" he calls out.

Freezing just before the bathroom door, it registers that he said my name.

He knows my name? Oh shit, he knows my name. Rebecca must be the wife!

Taking the last couple steps toward the bathroom, I slam the door and lock it. Sinking to the floor, tears stream down my cheeks. *I can't believe I've done something like this. His poor wife.* Pulling myself to my feet, I drag my shameful ass to the large mirror above the sink.

All of the telltale signs reflect back at me in the mirror. Swollen lips, bags under my eyes, and light red marks on my neck and chest, these are a few of my disgraceful things.

What the hell have I done? Why would I do something like this? I don't do this type of thing. I would've noticed the ring before it got this far. This isn't me — at all.

"Olivia?" The door handle rattles, drawing my attention. "Olivia, are you okay?" His voice is deep, commanding. Finding his voice pleasing only makes me feel worse.

Turning on the shower, I climb in. The water drowns out his voice. Unfortunately, it doesn't wash away the shame.

My bare skin, red from the force of my scrubbing, can't stand being in the shower any longer. I climb out and silence on the other side of the door greets me. *Is it too much to hope he left?* I quickly search for my toothbrush and scrub the filmy feeling from my mouth before grabbing all of my toiletries and stuffing them into the small bag.

Slipping the dress back over my head, I stare at my appearance in the mirror. My bright red hair clings to my skin. To avoid a straight, limp look, I twist and tuck the strands into a knot at the base of my neck.

Turning toward the door with my things under my arm, I reach for the doorknob, allowing my hand to linger for just a minute while I mentally prepare myself for what's to come. Taking a deep breath, I pull the door open and step out.

My eyes focus on the wall across the room in a weak attempt not to look at him, but I fail and glance at the bed.

He lies before me, vaguely familiar, in only boxer briefs clinging to his well-toned body. Long, lean, powerful legs stretch out on the bed. His flat stomach flexes as he sits up on the edge, his eyes studying me.

"Olivia, are you okay?" His dark, left brow raises over sparkling hazel eyes.

His familiarity feels strange. Shaking off the feeling, my only response is to nod. *I need to get my things and get the hell out of dodge.* I begin looking around the room, cataloging all of the items I still need to grab.

"Oh, really?" He stands. I tense and step back. "Then why are you freaking out?"

"Okay, so perhaps I'm not entirely alright. But I'll be fine. This doesn't need to be uncomfortable or discussed. I don't even remem—"

With the smooth prowess of a feline, he moves toward me. Knowing the look of a predator when I see it, I put my arms out in front to deter him.

"We don't have to talk about anything." Shaking my head at him only makes the pain in my head from being hung over worse. "I don't remember your name and even if I did, I wouldn't tell your wife, or anyone, so let's just go our separate ways and—"

He laughs a deep from the belly laugh.

I close my mouth in a tight line and stare.

"Trust me, she already knows about last night." Cocking one eyebrow in amusement, he comes closer.

My hands press against the warm, smooth skin of his broad chest.

Wow, he's really...uh, solid.

The urge to flex my fingers against his chest, to slide over it until I wrap my body around his, pulses through me, causing a brief memory of our bare skin pressed tight against each other to flare. *Crap!*

15

He invades my personal space. Towering over me, the intimidation pouring off him brings my thoughts back above the waist. Backing away, in hopes to retreat to the bathroom again, I drop my hands and my toiletry bag. I hit the solid wall next to the bathroom door and realize I miscalculated my direction.

"I-I don't understand," I stutter.

Taking deep breaths to avoid an impending panic attack, I continue. "But it doesn't matter. I need to go."

"I think we should talk, discuss a few things you seem to be unclear about." Smiling, he grabs my hand — my left hand. Bringing it up to my face, he holds it alongside his. "See anything familiar? Perhaps something matching?"

"You've gotta be kidding me!" I exclaim. My eyes lock onto my very own matching band of gold.

"I'm afraid this isn't a joke." His intense eyes scan over my face.

"Oh, right, I'm so sorry. I don't know how this happened." Heat flushes my skin, the embarrassment and mortification doing their job well. "Well, I'm pretty sure the margaritas and shots had something to do with it, but I assure you, this isn't something I would normally do. I'll contact a lawyer and we can get this taken care of as quickly as possible." Swallowing back a tornado of emotions, I try to move around him.

His arm winds around my waist, pulling my back into his warm, solid chest.

"You aren't getting rid of me that easily," he whispers. The heat from his breath and the intensity of his words both panic and excite me.

His warm, soft lips press against the back of my neck, momentarily stunning me. Desire prickles across my skin. A brief memory of last night's activities flashes through my mind. His twinkling hazel eyes looking up at me as his tongue presses against my breastbone and slides across my skin. Snapping out of the erotic recollection, I pull away from his embrace. He loosens his hold just enough for me to turn and look at him. *He's serious.*

"I know you don't do this often. It's done now." His arm tightens around my waist once more.

"But it can be undone," I whisper.

"If that's what I wanted. But I don't."

"You can't—" His soft, authoritative lips cut off my response.

For just a moment, I lose myself in the kiss. The feeling of his tongue against my lower lip before he sucks on it almost makes me ignore the warning signals going off in my head.

I turn my face from his, breaking the kiss. With deep, head-clearing breaths, I push at his chest.

"What?" I exclaim.

He smiles at my failed attempt for release.

"You're feisty, I'll give you that," he chuckles.

"I don't think this is funny," I scoff, continuing my push at his arms and chest.

"I'm going to take a shower. Then we can discuss all of this over breakfast."

"Are you a psychopath?" I blurt.

He grins. "I assure you, I'm not a psychopath."

"Well, if you aren't crazy, you'd agree to an annulment." The overpowering presence of his proximity makes it hard for me to think. "You couldn't, as a sane person, want to remain married to a stranger."

Refusing to look back at his face, to get lost in his eyes, or another kiss, I continue to work against his iron grip.

"I'm not crazy and I will not agree to an annulment." His words are harsh and absolute. "I suggest you get used to being Mrs. Knyght." He releases his hold and steps around me toward the bathroom, shutting the door behind him.

I stand, dumbfounded for a few moments. The sound of the shower turning on snaps me out of my haze and I start hauling ass. I grab all the things I'd cataloged in my head earlier and begin throwing them in my suitcases. At the door to the room, I remember my cell phone. I look around, find it on the nightstand, and snatch it up. I quickly text Mercedes and Felicity to see where they are and if they are ready.

Turning from the nightstand, his wallet catches my eye. *I need to know who he is before I can send him legal papers, right? Going through his wallet is completely justifiable.* I glance at the still closed bathroom door and listen. The water is still running, so I flip open the soft, black leather.

How many platinum, preferred, and black cards does a person need?

Looking deeper, I find his name. Damon Knyght. I close his wallet and smack myself in the head with the flat of my hand. *Christ, Olivia!* Technically, he's not a stranger. He's the CEO of B.I.G., my recent big client. The reason I'm in Vegas celebrating.

I groan and plop my ass down on the side of the bed, mentally berating myself. Suddenly, the room becomes silent. Completely silent. Hurrying to the door, I grab both suitcases and slip out of my hotel room.

In the elevator, I finally get a text back from Mercedes.

We R in restaurant downstairs. Waiting on U.

Stopping hastily by the front desk, I check out and make a beeline to the restaurant.

Ced and Felicity are calm and relaxed, chatting over waffles, fruit, and coffee. *Bitches.*

"Hey, sweetie," Felicity greets.

"Sit down. We will get the waitress." Ced motions to a young girl in a black vest.

I shake my head, adrenaline coursing through my body. "No, no, no. We need to go now."

"But you haven't eaten." Felicity eyes me curiously.

"What's going on?" Ced asks.

"I'll explain in the taxi. Let's go. We have to move, ladies."

Knowing I'm acting like a paranoid freak doesn't stop me from looking over my shoulder until we we're safely in the cab and pulling away from the hotel. As soon as I feel safe, my phone beeps.

You can't get rid of me that easily.

The number is unknown, but it's obvious the text came from *him — my husband.*

"Who's that?" Mercedes' eyes move from my phone to my face.

"Remember how you guys said you wouldn't let me drink too much, you'd have my back, and nothing bad was going to happen? Blah, freaking blah." I narrow my eyes at both of them.

"Uh, yeah," Felicity mumbles.

"Yeah, well, this happened!" Shoving my left hand in their face, I let them register the gold band sitting on my ring finger.

"HOLY..." Felicity starts.

"SHIT!" Mercedes finishes.

"Yeah, exactly!" I growl.

"H-how?" Felicity asks, still staring at my hand. "We didn't see anyone around you."

I sigh and tell them what I remember of the night before, which isn't much.

"So, you just took off this morning?" Felicity asks, her eyes bulging out of her head.

"What would you have done? A strange man telling me I can't get rid of him that easily...I mean, what sane person would do this? What if he's going to kidnap me or something?" Putting my face into my hands, I huff.

"Well, technically, I wouldn't wake up with a man in my room."

I lift my head and glare at Felicity before dropping it back down.

"What?" She shrugs. "But, if I woke up married to a strange woman and married to the multimillionaire, why would I give that up? We should take you back to him. Think of the possibilities."

I snap my head up to look at her again. *She can't be serious.* Felicity and Mercedes break out in a fit of laughter, letting me know how unserious they are. Groaning, I drop my head back against the headrest of the seat.

"This is seriously *not* funny."

"Calm down," Ced encourages, patting my leg.

"We'll give Alfonso a call when we get back. He'll take care of the paperwork and filing." Felicity gives me a reassuring look. Alfonso, Felicity's older brother, is a lawyer and Mercedes' long time crush.

"Ooohh, just make sure I'm working when he comes to deliver the papers." Mercedes' face lights up as she bounces in her seat. "I definitely want to see his fine ass—"

"Ew! Stop, Ced. That's my brother." Felicity feigns gagging. Mercedes shrugs.

"We can make it a family affair." Mercedes winks at Felicity.

"Enough with the pseudo lesbianism, Ced. Can we please get back on topic?" I cover my face, shame and worry battling for dominate emotion.

The long plane ride back to Pennsylvania doesn't make me feel better. I thought the more distance between Damon Knyght and me, the better I would feel. Instead, last night starts to piece together like a mental jigsaw puzzle. Now the memory lingers and it's all I can think about.

He made me slightly uncomfortable when he sat without asking, but the discomfort quickly changed when he introduced himself as Damon and we started to talk about ourselves. We both enjoyed and appreciated various types of music, reading classic books, as well as food. Though, he enjoyed eating food and I enjoyed making food. I also couldn't help but feel as if I had seen him before. It was like an odd form of déjà vu.

After mentioning that I was in a relationship with someone, his demeanor changed. He began questioning me. I wasn't comfortable with the questions, so I got up to excuse myself. He stopped me and apologized for being so rude. I smiled lightly, told him it was okay, and continued toward the ladies room.

When I emerged, I noticed he was no longer at our table. I found another drink waiting on me, courtesy of Mercedes, I'm sure. I tossed it back and after a second refill, he returned. The night turned into a blur of drinks, laughter, gambling, dancing, and then him convincing me to go to a casino with him; however, along the way, was the chapel. We ended up inside, getting married and purchasing the two gold bands there. His kiss was intense and deep, even in front of the few people at the little chapel. My body flooded with heat at the memory.

We skipped the casino and ended up in my hotel room. Just as the door shut, his hands were gripping the zipper on my dress and pulling it off my body. I giggled as I watched the green dress fly across the room.

He practically ripped his clothes from his body, stalking toward me. When he reached me, his shirt was off and his pants were sagging on his hips. He definitely was built. My hands roamed from the V of his hips and moved up, over his chest.

He devoured my lip as he pushed me back onto the bed and crawled over me. My underwear and bra were nothing for him, and soon found their way on the floor with my dress. There was an animalistic way about his actions, like he craved physical connection. Low rumbles emanated from deep within his chest when he licked or nipped at my skin, or as I licked or nipped his, especially when I fisted his hair in my hands.

The moment his pants were on the floor, I felt him push my legs further apart and climb between them. The swollen tip of his erection nudged at my entrance and he growled as he thrust into me.

"Condom," I panted out, but he didn't stop and I couldn't think straight.

It felt amazing. Never has anyone made me feel as if they were completely devouring my body.

"We're twenty minutes out of Pittsburgh International. We hope you enjoyed your flight with us today…" The pilot's announcement snapped me out of the memory replaying over and over in my head.

Groaning, I cover my face. *Great. No condom.* I take deep breaths to calm the heat coursing through my body as the memories and guilt assail me.

I can fix this. I will fix this.

First, I need to talk to Erik, which will be the end of our semi-relationship. When Erik and I first met, I thought I was ready to try a relationship again. Turns out, the little time and affection I could offer was not what Erik needed. I've tried ending it before and now, he sticks around as a friend who hopes for more.

Second, I need to arrange an appointment with Alfonso to get the annulment papers prepared, sent to Damon, and then filed.

Third, I will *never, ever, ever* return to Vegas.

When I arrive at my Pittsburgh apartment over the bakery, I pay the taxi driver and take my things to my room. After sending a quick text to let my father know I'm home, I climb into the shower. Clean, dry, and dressed in a pair of jeans and an oversized sweater, I take a brisk walk to the local pharmacy.

Nothing screams slut louder than mumbling my need for the morning after pill to the pharmacist. I receive a pitiful look from the technician when she hands over the white paper bag.

"Do you have any questions for the pharmacist?" she asks, patronizing me.

"No, thank you," I bite out through clenched teeth. I snatch the bag from her hand a bit too roughly and her eyes grow wide. She has the nerve to look stunned by my actions.

I pick up a bottle of water along the way to the register and pull out the pill instruction and FAQ sheet. As soon as I step from the pharmacy, I push the pill through the foil back, twist open the water, and take the medicine. Shoving the information papers deep into my messenger bag, I toss the remnants of the medicine package in a random garbage can.

As I enter my apartment, the voice of my little angel greets me.

"Momma!" Alex runs and wraps his arms around my legs.

Slipping my hands under his arms, I pull him to my chest and hold him close.

"Hey, baby, did you have fun with Grandpa?"

My eighteen-month-old son squeezes me tightly around my neck and nods.

"How was your trip?" My father smiles warmly as he walks up and kisses the side of my head.

How do you tell your father you got some strange and married a not-exactly-stranger? Hallmark doesn't make that card.

"Liv?" One bushy, brown brow raises over his left eye.

"It was nice. Really, it was. I'm just tired from the time difference." Forcing a smile, I push by him, hoping he doesn't pick up on my mood.

"Do you want me to stick around and keep an eye on my little guy so you can rest?"

"No, you don't have to do that. I'll be fine." I place Alex onto his feet again and he runs off toward his room.

"Are you sure?" He studies my face closely, just like he did when I was in trouble as a kid.

"I'll be fine, Dad."

"You seem a little shaken." He crosses his arms over his chest.

Closing the small space between us, I wrap him in a hug.

"I'm fine. I promise." I press a kiss to his cheek.

"If you say so, but you know you can tell me anything, right?" He pulls his head back to look down into my face.

"Of course." I force a smile, feeling horrible for not telling him what's going on.

"Alright, well, I'm gonna get going. I want to get back before dark. Call me if you need anything, okay?" He grabs his keys and jacket before turning back to look at me.

"I swear, I will." With one last hug, I send him on his way.

Sometimes I forget how quickly four in the morning arrives. Dressed in faded, food-color-stained jeans and an old Bon Jovi concert shirt, I make a cup of coffee and descend the stairs from my apartment to the bakery kitchen below. With Alex still sleeping, the baby monitor hangs from my back pocket.

My morning routine is almost always the same. Pull out pre-made dough from the fridge and get the ovens going. Before I begin gathering ingredients for the large standing mixers, I grab one of the many aprons hanging in my cubby. Today, I slip *May the yeast be with you* over my head, tie it at my back, and start prepping the worktable.

With the large floor mixer and two small table mixers running, I barely hear Mercedes come through the back door of the kitchen.

"Good morning," she sings.

"Hey, sunshine." Wiping flour on the rag over my shoulder, I lean against the stainless steel worktable and reach for a sip of coffee.

"Alex still sleeping?" Yawning and stretching her long, thin arms over her head, she makes her way toward her office.

I nod in response, glancing down at my watch. Almost five-thirty. The rest of the crew will be arriving soon. Placing my mug back down, I return to hand rolling the dough in front of me.

The mixers automatically shut down as I place trays filled with cinnamon rolls and croissants into the large refrigerator to be baked once an oven is free. And then comes cleaning up the first of many messes of the day.

"Morning, Liv." Sarah, one of my baking assistants, walks in. She hangs her personal items in her cubby and then grabs an apron and slips it over her head.

"Morning," I respond, wiping flour from the table.

"How was Vegas?" she asks as she pulls open one of the ovens to check on the trays of pastries and cookies.

"It was...fun."

"Yeah, fun is one way to describe it," Ced snorts, entering the kitchen with the appointment book in hand.

I scowl.

"Liv, you have three consultations today. Sarah, you have two, and..." Ced looks around the kitchen, "where's Emily?"

I shrug, sure that Emily, my head baker, will be in soon enough.

"Well, she has two as well." Closing the appointment book, she sets it on an empty shelf just outside her office. "What can I do to help?"

23

"Come help with the bagels," Sarah shouts over her shoulder, setting the large trays on her worktable.

With much to do, I focus on getting the pies and muffins started before Mrs. Dorn arrives at seven to start stocking the bakery cases in the storefront and writing out the daily specials on the chalk board.

"Momma," Alex calls through the baby monitor.

"Time to go get the little prince," Mrs. Dorn coos. "Or I could go up?"

"No, thank you. I've missed my little guy." Wiping my hands on the towel hanging at my waist, I walk out of the storefront and into the kitchen.

"I'm going up to get Alex and feed him breakfast." I slip the apron over my head and toss it into the hamper we keep in the kitchen.

"Momma, momma, momma." Each momma is accentuated by the sound of bedsprings.

"You better hurry before he bounces out of his crib," Ced calls out just as I reach the bottom of the stairs.

"Hey, wait!" she shouts. I look back at her. "Your first consultation is in an hour. It's for a birthday. If you need me to come upstairs with Alex so you can make the meeting just call down, okay?"

"Yep," I shout over the sound of Emily starting up a mixer and walk up the staircase.

The staircase had been the final selling point on this particular building. With my lease coming up in just a few months, I really hoped to be new owner instead of just a tenant. Mr. Coleman and I have already discussed me buying the building, since he plans to move south to be near his son.

"Momma!"

"Coming, baby!"

When I enter his room, he stops bouncing and smiles. Grabbing him under his arms, I lift him from the crib and nestle him on my hip.

"You know, soon you'll need a big boy bed." I ruffle his hair and kiss the top of his head.

After years of working hard, at the age of twenty-four, I made the decision to have a baby. First, I felt as crazy as my friends and family thought I was, but it just felt right. No father, no attachment aside from my baby — it's what I wanted. At twenty-six, I gave birth to the most beautiful little boy — my Alexander. Being a mother on my own isn't easy, just as I knew it wouldn't be, but I feel so lucky to have him.

My last serious relationship had been when I was twenty. Isaac was killed right after college in a motorcycle accident. We'd both been on the motorcycle, out celebrating my completion of two years of culinary school and my decision to try to make a name for myself as an instructor at the school.

The air had been cool and damp on my face. There had been a slick spot on the road and the motorcycle collapsed onto its side. Isaac pulled my left leg up as we fell over and spun across the blacktop. Slamming into the guide-rail, I was thrown, bruised, and concussed. Isaac and the bike finally stopped in the left hand lane of the road. He was pinned under the bike, but alive. Alive until a truck rounded a corner, slammed their brakes, and slid into him. I can still hear the screech of the brakes and the echo of my screams. *Christ, I miss him. I loved him so much.*

Isaac died about an hour after reaching the hospital, where I had been trapped in a bed, hooked up to monitors, and IV drips. Tests were run and x-rays taken. Upon my release, I left with a broken wrist and several ribs, a concussion, bruises, and an unexpected pregnancy. I'd barely come to terms with finding out I was pregnant when I lost the baby. My last piece of Isaac torn away from me.

From the moment Alex was born into my gray world, he saturated my universe in bright, colorful moments. His first smile, steps, words, and watching him grow over the past eighteen months has been the largest joy in my life.

"Toast," Alex blurts, pulling me from my memories. Playing with the bananas I put on the tray of his highchair, he giggles.

"You're supposed to eat those, not smoosh them."

Grinning, I flip a piece of French toast.

"Smooooosh," he squeals, his face lighting up brighter than the sun.

With the French toast done, cut up, and placed on his tray, I start cleaning up the kitchen. The chime from my phone pulls me away from loading the last of the dishes into the dishwasher.

"That has to be your Aunt Ced," I coo to Alex. "Though, her crazy butt could just call."

Good morning, Mrs. Knyght. I trust you slept well. See you soon.

His message takes the breath from my body. My stomach knots as nausea sweeps over me.

I really need to talk to Alfonso soon. This guy may be crazy. A freaking crazy catrillionaire.

Ignoring the message, I turn my attention back to the dishwasher, then to cleaning breakfast off Alex.

"Did you get any of it in your mouth?" I tease.

"All gone," he announces, wearing a proud smile.

After a quick baby wipes bath and getting Alex dressed for a day in the kitchen, we walk the flight of stairs toward the sweet smells and normal noises.

Stepping through the kitchen, I take Alex to the baby-proofed and gated area near Ced's office. The minute he's on his little feet, he runs for his workbench and picks up the bright red hammer. With the hammer in hand, he sits on the sit-n-spin, beating the top of it with the toy.

"Liv, your consultation is waiting at the table," Mercedes yells from her office.

"Keep an eye on Alex for me, okay?"

As I walk by her office, she steps out, holding a clipboard for me to take.

"Like you have to ask," she responds, walking the few steps to look at Alex spinning and beating the crap out of the toy. "Hey there, little guy, how are you this morning?" Ced coos to Alex. "Want to come make some phone calls with Auntie Cedie?"

"No," Alex responds before starting to pound again.

"I feel ya, little man."

The door closing behind me silences the rest of Ced and Alex's conversation.

"Hey, Liv," Mrs. Dorn greets with the same warm smile that has won over all of our customers.

"Good morning," I reply. Smiling, I walk toward the consultation table.

Extending my hand, I greet the newest clients, "Hello, I'm Olivia Harlow."

After the twenty minute consultation, I step back into the bustling activity of the kitchen.

"Another Alice in Wonderland cake," I announce.

Walking into Ced's office, I slip the clipboard onto her desk.

"That's gotten popular lately." Moving the clipboard closer, she begins filling out the official order form to attach to the consultation order.

"Yeah, well, I'm sure it has to do with all the cake shows now featured on television." I sigh.

"So, um, what are you going to do about you know who?" She whispers the last three words.

"Call Alfonso." I shrug.

"Today?" she squeaks, a hint of a smile playing on her face.

"Would you like to call his office for me?" I smile.

"Mayyybe," she drawls.

"Good, try to get an appointment to take care of this mess ASAP, please." Sighing, I stand up.

"What are you going to tell Erik?" Her brow furrows.

"The truth," I answer. Taking a deep breath, I head back out to the kitchen.

The remainder of the afternoon comes and goes with the normal workflow, along with the other consultations. It's close to closing when Ced calls out from her office.

"Liv, Alfonso said he'll stop by tomorrow to discuss your situation."

"Thanks," I shout back.

"Oh, and Erik is on the phone for you."

I groan, put down the icing bag, and stretch my fingers.

"Tell him I'll call him later. I'm in the middle of a cake."

Grasping the bag, I lean back over the cake and continue piping the second layer while Emily works on the bottom.

After closing up the shop, I trudge up the stairs with a hungry Alex in my arms, wishing I could just go lie in bed. Unfortunately, dinner, bathing, and playtime are in my immediate future.

Dinner goes well and Alex's playtime giggles put me into a much better mood. In the midst of his bath, the doorbell rings.

"Who could that be?"

"Door," Alex shouts, standing in the shallow water.

Wrapping him in a large towel, we answer the door.

"Hey, Liv," Erik greets with a kiss to my forehead. "Hey, big Al." He kisses the top of Alex's head.

"Erik, I was going to call you, but—"

He pushes by us, entering my apartment.

"I know, but I figured I'd stop by to see how your trip was and check in on you guys." Erik makes himself comfortable on my couch.

Closing the door, my earlier exhaustion suddenly returns. This conversation is going to be uncomfortable, to say the least.

"I'm gonna go dress Alex," I mumble, walking down the hall to his room.

Once Alex is dressed and on his feet, he runs off into the living room.

"Rik," he announces, rushing into Erik.

Erik reaches down and lifts him fully onto his lap.

"Toons." Alex pats his hands on Erik's chest impatiently.

"Okay, okay."

Picking up the remote, Erik turns on cartoons for Alex. I take a seat in the large, overstuffed chair across from them.

"Well, at least Alex missed me," Erik grumbles, his attention focused on me.

Ignoring the comment, I stare, unseeing, at the cartoon. When Alex yawns, I start mentally preparing myself for the discussion I won't be able to put off any longer.

"Okay, baby, it's time for bed."

"No." Alex slips from the couch, ready to run.

"I really don't like that you've learned that word." Grabbing him under the arms before he can run, I lift him to my hip.

"Night, Al." Erik ruffles his hair.

It takes a few long minutes for Alex's aquarium crib toy to lull him to sleep. It takes me a few minutes longer to return to face Erik.

Erik stands from the couch as I re-enter the room and approaches me.

"I think we should probably talk—"

His lips firmly press to mine. His hands move to hold the sides of my face as his tongue grazes my bottom lip. I pull back and push on his chest to put some space between us.

"Erik—"

"I missed you, Liv. Let me stay. We can talk in the morning." His hands move down my sides, grip my hips, and pull me closer.

"We really need to talk. Now." I push on his chest again.

"Olivia," he huffs. "I really need to be close to you tonight. I missed you so much and love—"

"Stop!" With a final push, I finally get space between our bodies. "Listen to me. You know I only want to be friends. And I've tried to be just friends, I really have, but you keep pushing for more. We just aren't more than that and we won't be."

Erik opens his mouth to speak.

"Please, let me finish. I love you, Erik, but it's not in the way you want me to or in the way I should. My love is a fondness and caring. I'm not in love with you." I search his face, hoping for understanding.

"Liv, I don't care. I love you enough for the both of us."

I take two more steps back, but he follows.

"I know it's hard for you. I know you always think back to Isaac. I get it, I do. But he's gone, Liv. And he's not coming back."

I flinch at his words. I know Isaac is gone. I never meant for him to think Isaac is the reason I can't love him.

"It's fine. I can love you enough. I won't leave, or hurt you, or—"

"This isn't about him and that isn't how love works. Besides, I have a situation I need to deal with. It's one that won't make you happy at all."

"Situation?" His brows pull together in confusion. "What's wrong?"

"Nothing is wrong, per say. Something happened in Vegas that I need to deal with."

"What happened?" He steps closer and I can't retreat anymore; it would bring us too close to Alex's room.

I put my hand up, keeping an arm's length of distance between us.

He focuses on my hand. "Tell me what's going on." His eyes meet mine.

"Sit down first." I motion to the chair I recently sat in.

He sits. "Tell me."

"In Vegas, I met someone and—"

"You met someone else in Vegas?" he sneers.

"Calm down and let me finish."

"You fucked someone else in Vegas, didn't you?" He returns to his feet, anger contorting his features.

"There was a lot of alcohol involved and I ended up married." I rush the words out and stand completely still, waiting.

Erik's face instantly turns beet red, causing his typical baby face to contort further.

"You married and fucked some stranger?!" he yells.

29

"Shh, Alex is sleeping," I hush.

"Fuck you, Liv! Who are you? Are you some whore now, huh?!" His arms flail at his sides as his voice gets louder.

Anger I'll accept, I deserve it, but insults will not be tolerated.

"Get out," I growl. "You can be angry and hate me all you want. I made a mistake I have to deal and live with, but I won't be called a whore. Get out!" My own voice raises higher than intended.

"Olivia, I don't...I'm sorry, okay? I didn't mean it. I just, I can't believe you did something like this to me. Why? I love you, why would you do this to me?"

"I drank too much and didn't know what I was doing. It's a horrible excuse and I would never intentionally hurt you this way. Never. I would never plan to do something like this. Things got out of control," I reply, my voice finally back to normal levels.

"I don't know what to say to you." He shakes his head and looks at the floor.

"I'm so sorry, Erik. I..." I trail off, not knowing what else to say to him.

"Goodnight, Olivia." Turning, Erik leaves my apartment, slamming the door behind him.

Chapter two – Legalities and Intrusions
Olivia

Alfonso arrives right on time, his briefcase in hand. He stands next to Mercedes' office, talking with her while he waits for me to finish the last detail on a Scooby Doo birthday cake.

Quickly washing my hands, I go greet my soon-to-be annulment lawyer.

"Hey, Alfonso. It's good to see you."

Straightening from his leaning position, he returns the greeting. "It's good to see you, too."

"How's Noelle?" I ask, referring to his longtime girlfriend.

"She's good." He smiles, but it looks forced.

"Good to hear." I motion toward the stairs. "Let's discuss this upstairs, if you don't mind?"

He nods and I turn to Ced.

"If you need me, give me a call, okay?"

"Will do." She smiles and pushes her chair so Alfonso can't see her. Then she mouths, "He is so hot," and fans herself.

I smile and shake my head.

"Oh, don't forget, I'm taking off early today for my date." Her grin grows, brightening her entire face.

With a nod, I pick Alex up from his play area and show Alfonso to my apartment.

He sits at my small kitchen table and I take my place across from him with Alex in his highchair on my right.

"So, tell me what happened." His fancy silver pen hovers expectantly over the yellow legal pad in front of him.

"Didn't Felicity tell you what happened?" I don't want to admit my stupidity out loud again.

"Yes, but I need your official statement regarding the occurrence." His tone is professional, but the small twitch at the corner of his mouth gives away his amusement.

"Fine," I huff.

For the next half hour, I recount what I remember of the sordid experience, leaving out the details of the amazing horizontal tango with Damon.

"Alright, well, I'm sure we can easily trace his information since you are acquainted with him. I'll get the annulment papers drawn up and sent over to him." He finally stops writing and drops the pen to the legal pad. "If he isn't on board with ending the marriage, as you mentioned, then we may have to go to court."

"How fast can we file?"

"I'll expedite it, but it will still take two days to process. Mr. Knyght will receive notification shortly after it has been filed. I would say three or four days, maybe." He shrugs.

"And if we have to go to court?"

"If he contests the annulment, he will have to go through a large process and get lawyers involved. Technically, you will need to sue for divorce in order to be heard by a judge, or a mediator, at the least."

He sighs and rubs the back of his neck.

"What?"

"Olivia, I'm going to be really honest. This isn't my specialty. While I can definitely have my paralegal work on the paperwork and get this filed, if you have to go to court, you're going to need someone with more family practice experience."

I nod and give a small shrug.

"No, Liv," Alfonso leans forward, elbows to the table, "you don't understand. If Mr. Knyght is as intent as you stated, he is not going to make this easy. I can assure you that a man of his wealth and business background will have top shelf lawyers at his disposal. Sharks that will chomp at the littlest bit of blood in the water. They'll make it an expensive endeavor."

"Fu...dge," I groan. At least I remembered not to say fuck in front of Alex.

I glance toward Alex in his highchair and feel the urge to smack myself for allowing this into his life.

"Let's hope he comes to his senses and agrees to the annulment," I say to Alfonso, but I don't take my eyes off Alex as he smashes cheerios in his hand and watches the remnants float to his tray.

"What does he want from you? Any ideas at all?"

"I have no darn clue, Alfonso."

The honesty of the answer is like a slap to the face. I have no idea what he wants or why he is so adamant about staying married to someone he doesn't know.

"Maybe you should find out," Alfonso murmurs.

"Maybe I don't want to know," I counter and then groan out loud. "As much as I hate to admit it, you're right. If I find out what he's after, maybe it will be the key to getting rid of him."

After saying our goodbyes to Alfonso, Alex and I go back down to the bakery.

With the morning behind us, our afternoon is just as crazy. Mercedes cut out early for her date, a guy she met while shopping for bakery supplies. Emily and Greg, the part-time baker assistants, have afterhours clean up duty, so it's bath and play time for Alex.

After four rounds of peek-a-boo, ten games of hide and seek, and five stories, Alex finally yawns.

"Time for bed, baby boy." Sweeping him up into my arms, he lays his head on my shoulder.

"No," he responds, yawning again.

Once Alex is settled into bed, I make my way toward my own room. A knock at the door stops me just before I reach my bedroom. "Damn," I whisper, so not to wake Alex.

I glance at the clock on the wall as I go to answer the door.

"It's almost ten. Who the hell...?"

Peeking out the window next to my door, I see Erik standing with a bunch of wildflowers in his fist.

I pull open the door. "Erik it's late."

"Liv." He steps into my apartment, causing me to take a step back.

"I am so sorry for how I reacted."

"You have every right to be angry. I understand." I cross my arms over my chest. Not in defense, but because I feel more uncomfortable with him than I ever have.

"I don't want to fight with you." He smiles, sheepishly.

"Neither do I, but I can't do...this." I motion between us.

"Liv, please, just give me another—"

I put my hand up, stopping him.

"It's not like that between us. For me, anyway." Placing a hand on his arm, I inch just a bit closer. "I'm sorry, Erik. I really wish things were different, but I can't force something that isn't there."

"You mean you can't force yourself to love me?"

His fist clenches, causing the flowers to rustle and the plastic paper around them to crinkle.

I bite my lip to stop my chin from wavering and simply nod.

"Is it him? You love this stranger?" His voice rises.

"Shh, Alex is in bed. And, no, I do not love this guy. I met with Alfonso today to resolve everything. I told you, I made a mistake. That's all, but it doesn't change things between us."

I remove my hand from his arm, taking a deep breath.

"I love you, Olivia. I love Alex and you. I've never loved anyone the way I—"

"Stop, don't do this," I beg.

"But I do!" he shouts, wrapping his arms around my waist. "I love you so much. I would take care of you. You don't have to be madly in love with me."

He surprises me by crushing his lips to mine — hard. The desperation of the kiss is a bitter reminder of how awful a person I am for this.

Pulling away from him and the kiss, I place a hand on his chest to prevent him from getting close again.

"I don't feel the same way and I'm sorry that it hurts you. It's the last thing I want to do, but it will only hurt you worse if I agree to be more than friends with you."

Softly pushing at his chest, he gets the hint and steps back from me.

"I'm just asking for one more chance. Can't you give me...give us, that?" His eyes search my face.

"No. I can't. It kills me to know that you love me and I can't return the same feelings. Because you deserve that. You deserve intense, profound love. I care about you and want to be friends, but I'm not sure it's possible. At least...not right now."

"Don't say that." He grabs my shoulders. "Don't ever say that. We're friends — always. If you would just give this a chance to grow, I know it could be the best love—"

"It won't," I groan. "I think you should go and take some time away from me. We both need time away from each other if there is any hope of being friends. Okay?"

Anger, hurt, and then defeat crease his face.

"I'm sorry, Erik."

"Me, too." Tossing the flowers onto the table by the door, he exits the apartment without looking back.

I press my head against the closed door and lock it as tears fall from my eyes.

My days have been full of regular baking, cake orders, and a large, high profile wedding we landed thanks to Felicity.

"She said no cakes, Olivia," Felicity whines from the other side of the restaurant booth after seeing cream puff cake on the menu plan.

"Its puffy pastry balls, not really a cake," I argue.

"It still says cake."

"Then change it to cream puff dessert," I sigh, tired of this Bridezilla's micro managing.

"Good idea." Her eyes light up.

"Seriously?" I ask, one brow lifted

"I don't want the word cake anywhere on the dinner menu." She points her pen at me. "You know how particular she is."

I nod.

"But she's marrying into money, so she's paid for the right to be a particular pain in my ass." She smiles.

"Ah, to marry a hometown hockey player, wouldn't that be the life." I grin.

She rolls her eyes.

"You're currently Mrs. Moneybags Knyght. You have access to enough money to buy the entire hockey team for Crepes sake," she laughs.

"That is being taken care of," I glower. "But nice with the 'Crepes sake'."

35

"Thank you, thank you." She dips her head, taking a small bow. "You talked to Alfonso, right?"

I nod.

"Well, looks like you won't be able to buy a hockey team much longer and are well on your way to being a rich divorcee."

"Still not funny," I grumble.

"Yes, it is."

We dig back into the details of the wedding for a few more minutes before Felicity changes the subject once more.

"I forgot to tell you about the hotel manager." She sits up straighter, and I swear sticks her boobs out a bit. "She asked me out." A small blush colors her cheeks.

"Really? So, is that a good thing or a bad thing?"

"Definitely good," she answers. "You should see how beautiful she is, and extremely nice."

"Are you okay with dating someone you work with?"

She shrugs. "I don't think it will be a problem. We're both adults, besides she is so hot. Whew!" Felicity fans herself. "I could never pick up someone like her in any of the bars around here."

She brings her drink to her lips and drains the last of the dark red liquid. Returning her glass to the table, Felicity sees my empty one in front of me.

"You want another one?"

"No, I have to get back soon. Mercedes is watching Alex and I don't want to even think about what she is feeding him."

"True," Felicity agrees with a nod.

Saying goodbye, we head in opposite directions.

I arrive home to Mercedes sitting on the couch, her cell phone to her ear. With a flick of her wrist, she motions to the hallway.

Stepping into Alex's room, I find him on his floor with a plethora of colorful blocks surrounding him.

"What are you building?"

Dropping to my knees, I crawl to him.

"Momma," he blurts, clapping his hands.

"Yep, it's momma." Reaching forward, I ruffle his hair. "And you're my little man, aren't you?"

He squeals.

"I'll take that as a yes."

Lying flat on my stomach and propping up on elbows, we build a block tower. His chubby little fingers reach out and knock it down. I rebuild and he does it again, laughing.

His laugh is like a balm to my soul. As we rebuild once more, I look closer at my son. His skin is pale and lightly dusted with freckles, like me. His hair is more of a darker brown rather than the natural red my hair would be if I didn't dye it a much brighter shade. Where my eyes are blue, his are green with amazing gold flecks sprinkled around his pupil. The flecks always remind me of that stage during an eclipse when the sun looks like a bright ring around the moon. Alexander is beautiful, no doubt or mother's bias about it.

Sometimes it's hard to really, truly look at the features he inherited from a stranger. The only thing I know about the donor is the information provided in a folder. I'm still not completely sure why I chose him. But among the mix of all the others, there was just something about the medical student's profile.

Most thought me crazy for having a child with a stranger and to be honest, I still sometimes wonder if I made the right choice in bringing Alex into this world without a father.

Mercedes sits on the floor next to me, pulling me from my thoughts.

"So, did you get the dessert menu finalized?"

Nodding, I ask, "Who were you talking to?"

"Adam," she replies, wistfully.

"Is this Adam the new man you met?"

"Maybe," she states in a singsong voice. Suddenly jumping up from her spot on the floor, she looks down at us. "I'll see you two tomorrow, okay?"

"Sure thing. I think I'm going to take Alex to the park tomorrow afternoon. So, I'll be down a lot earlier than normal and then take off for a couple hours. I want to get him outside again before it starts getting cold."

She nods, leans over, and kisses Alex on the top of his head.

"Ced," he giggles, pulling away from her kiss.

"Later, gators," she shouts and walks out of the room.

"Bye," I yell.

Alex mimics, yelling, "Buh."

After Ced leaves, it's time to clean up blocks, bathe, and read to Alex before he goes to bed.

The next morning, I work alone for almost two hours. Mercedes and Mrs. Dorn arrive half an hour before Sarah and Emily stroll in together. Greg follows a bit later. With a normal workload ahead of us, we work hard to bust out a few cakes and other baked goods. Mercedes and I even have time to go over the menu for the upcoming event.

Retreating to my apartment, I'm a bit relieved to find that Alex is still asleep.

"Yes," I whisper, tiptoeing down the hall, "I have time for a little nap."

Settling onto the overstuffed couch I refuse to replace until Alex is older, I close my eyes.

"Momma!"

"Of course," I groan.

"Momma!" The squeak of his mattress accompanies his shout.

After yawning and stretching, I pull my body from the couch.

"I'm coming, jumping bean."

Upon entering his room, the scene is just how I expected. His hair is messy, smile super wide, dimples deeply set, and his legs are pumping up and down on the crib mattress.

"Momma!" he giggles when he sees me.

One more yawn creeps up on me as I pick him up and out of the crib.

"Come here." I kiss his head. "You want some cereal and bananas?"

"Nanas," he cheers.

After breakfast, I dress us both for the September weather. Luckily, it's a warmer fall day. Tossing my wallet into the baby backpack, we head out the door, the umbrella stroller hanging over my forearm. After one quick text to Mercedes, telling her we left and when we planned to return, I slide the phone into the pocket on the side of the pack.

Lucky to have a space located in Robinson Township, just a few minutes from the major shopping centers, we can walk the short distance to the park. And when we arrive, Alex runs for the slide.

After an hour of playtime, it's time to round up Alex. "Come on, little man. We need to get back."

"No!" he shouts, running for the stairs leading to the slides.

"I really hate that you learned that word," I growl, rushing after him. "Now, come on. We've been here for almost two hours. It's time to get back."

He's halfway up the stairs when I wrap my arm around his waist and pick him up.

"NO!" he screams, kicking his little legs.

"Alexander Isaac!"

At the tone of my voice, he stops the tantrum for a split second. "Stop it, right now."

He starts right back up, kicking and screaming bloody murder.

Using the mother of all death grips to keep him from getting free, I pop open the umbrella stroller with my free hand. I lift my foot, locking the bar between the wheels into place.

"Settle down, mister," I scold, placing his squirming body into the canvas seat.

He struggles against me, screaming as loud as possible while I strap him in with the harness. The snap of the plastic locks and he completely loses his mind, stretching his body out as far as he can in an attempt to escape the harness. With a deep, do-not-kill-my-child breath, I move behind the stroller and start pushing us away from the playground.

The walk home is unpleasant; joggers and other mothers staring at the screaming banshee I'm pushing along. Remembering the snacks in the backpack, I pull out the little carry cup that latches to the side of the stroller.

It's amazing how fruit snacks can exercise the demon from a possessed toddler. By the time we return home, he's covered in sticky fruit snack slobber and yawning. Instead of going to the side stairs to enter the apartment, we enter through the storefront doors.

"There's my favorite boy!" Mrs. Dorn exclaims, rounding the bakery case with her arms stretched out toward Alex.

"Hey there, big man," Joe, a local plumber and frequent patron, waves to Alex.

"Oh, look at you," Mrs. Dorn laughs, taking Alex into her arms and examining the stickiness on his face. "Let's get you cleaned up."

"Looks like the boy had some fun," Joe says.

"Yes, he did." I smile. "How are you today?"

"Same ol', same 'ol." He returns to his coffee and newspaper.

I fold the stroller and when I look back up, I notice a group of unfamiliar people sitting around a table at the window. I take in the laptops and books surrounding them. College students, maybe?

"Go on back to the kitchen," Mrs. Dorn says without looking at me. "I'll keep Alex up here with me for a bit."

"Are you sure? He's getting tired, which means cranky." Pausing in front of the kitchen door, I give Mrs. Dorn the chance to send him with me.

"He'll be fine. I'll feed him some soup. If he gets too tired, I'll let you know." This time, she looks away from Alex and settles her gaze on me.

"Okay, just yell when he's ready for bed." Taking a couple steps behind the counter, I kiss the side of Alex's head before going into the kitchen.

After hours in the bakery, I finally arrive, exhausted, to the apartment. Erik's voice surprises me.

"What are you doing here?"

Both Mercedes and Erik look up from the table, holding plates of pizza.

"I brought over pizza." He smiles wide and motions to the pizza box on the kitchen counter.

He stands from the table and walks toward me. "I know you said we need time apart, Liv, but you're one of my best friends," he whispers, "I can't just cut you out of my life."

"Erik, I don't think this is a good idea. I mean, we just talked—"

He puts his fingers over my mouth.

"Shh, just be my friend." With a half-smile, he walks back to his seat.

"I'm going to take a shower," I announce, still not comfortable with Erik being here.

In the shower, I try to think of a way to explain to Erik, once again, the need for time apart. It's not just for him. When the water turns cold, I shut it off, climb out of the shower, and get dressed.

Entering the open kitchen area, I lock my gaze on Alex.

"Oh, baby, don't do that." I grab a towel from the counter and try to stop him from further rubbing pizza into his eye.

He yawns large, his head lolling just a bit.

"You eat," Mercedes orders, standing from the table. "I'll clean him up and get him into bed."

"No," I counter. "You've done enough tonight, I'll—"

"Don't argue with me." Mercedes nudges me toward a chair then turns and pulls Alex from his highchair. "I haven't seen you eat since you got back this afternoon. Knowing you, you haven't eaten all day." She eyes me before disappearing down the hall toward the bedrooms.

With Mercedes out of earshot, I finally turn to face Erik.

"We need to talk." I sit down on the dark stained chair.

"We've talked enough," he grinds out, his jaw tight.

"We still need time away from each other. It's too soon to come over like this and you know it. I still need—"

"Olivia, just be my friend, okay?" Erik rubs his forehead, frustration wrinkling his face.

Just as I prepare to argue, there's an unexpected knock at my door.

"Who could that be?" Erik asks, standing.

I beat him to the door and begin to open it.

"Heck, it better be Publisher's Clearing House with a million dollar check right about now, or I'm kicking someone's butt for...what are you doing here?"

My stomach plummets and swallowing is suddenly impossible, not to mention the inability to breathe.

"Sorry, not Publisher's Clearing House." His smile is dark, yet seductive. "However, I could technically write you a million dollar check."

Before me, standing devilishly handsome with his flawless skin, dark brown hair, piercing green eyes, and lips I knew were firm and sensual, is the sole source of my current high blood pressure.

"What," I gasp, barely able to form the word. "What are you doing here? How do you know where I—?"

"Come now, Olivia, did you think I would just ignore these?" He held up a thick manila envelope.

The annulment papers.

"Actually, I was hoping you wouldn't ignore them. I'm hoping you signed and initialed in the appropriate places." Crossing my arms over my chest, I stand firm. "So, you can just return those to my lawyer."

"I guess you still don't realize our situation. Oh, and I'm sure your lawyer doesn't want to deal with me or my legal team." He stands, self-assured, waiting for my reaction.

I open my mouth to tell the psycho to get off my property when Erik interrupts.

"Who's this?" Rounding the door, Erik narrows his eyes on Damon.

The two men lock on each other, Damon looking amused with a bit of menace gleaming in his eyes. His broad shoulders square as he straightens to his full height.

"Who might this be?" Damon directs the question to me.

"I'm Erik, her boyfriend. And you are?"

I snap my head toward Erik before turning fully to face him. I'm about to tell him to stand down when Damon's arm snakes around my body, his hand shooting out toward Erik. I jump, surprised by the move.

"I'm Damon Knyght, Olivia's husband," he replies, smugness entering his voice. I look over my shoulder at him. By the anger flaring in his eyes, it's clear his words were meant to hurt.

Groaning, I drop my head into my hands. Erik growls, bringing my head back up. Two large men fighting in my home is the last thing I need. Plus, Damon has at least four inches on Erik and a dark anger simmering underneath. I don't want Erik to get hurt.

"Look, it's late." I turn, facing Damon now. "You should go." His eyes tear away from Erik to meet mine. "And you can contact my lawyer if you want to discuss the annulment."

I try to shut the door, but Damon's arm holds it open.

"We need to talk. There are things you need to understand," he says with determined emphasis.

"It can wait—"

"Momma!"

I spin around at the sound of my son's scampering feet, panic tingling my belly. Alex rushes to me, wraps his chubby arms around my leg, and squeezes.

"Liv, that boy is crazy in the tub. How the heck do you not end up drenched when you—" Mercedes stops at the end of the hall, her eyes wide and mouth hanging open. She looks from me to Erik, back to me, to Damon, and then back to Erik. "Erik, we should go."

"No," I almost shout. "Damon was just leaving."

"I'm not going anywhere until we talk." His voice is casual, stoic.

"She said she doesn't want you here, asshole!" Erik shouts.

Putting my hand on Erik's chest, I stop his progression toward Damon.

"Calm down. Alex is right there."

Erik's hand comes up and covers mine against his chest.

"You can kick him out, Liv." Erik's eyes stay locked on Damon while he speaks to me.

"I suggest you take your hand off my wife," Damon growls, menacingly.

I look over my shoulder at Damon and the look on his face shocks me. I try to pull my hand away from Erik, but he presses it tighter against him.

"Don't threaten him," I say, keeping my voice firm without yelling. Alex doesn't need to be frightened.

Damon reaches out, yanking my hand away from Erik.

Mercedes gasps right along with me.

Erik's body starts to shake with anger, so I pull my hand away from Damon's touch.

"Erik, calm down. Remember Alex."

"Come on, Erik, let's go." Mercedes grabs her coat from the back of a chair and wraps her arm around one of his. "Let's go, Erik," Mercedes growls low, yanking Erik toward the door.

"Go on, Erik. It will be fine." Sighing, I rub the back of my neck with my now free hand.

"I'm not going anywhere, and I'm sure as hell not leaving you alone with him." Erik suddenly grabs me, pulling me behind him protectively. Alex's body jerks with the movement and tears begin to fill his eyes. I quickly reach down, pick him up, and hold him close.

Mercedes pulls harder on Erik, but he doesn't move.

Damon takes this distraction as his chance to enter my apartment completely.

"Olivia?" he says my name on a whisper, his eyes locking on Alex. His face pales and he begins breathing heavily. For a minute, I think I hear him whisper DJ.

"Are you alright?" Stepping around Erik, I move toward Damon, afraid he's become ill.

He reaches out toward Alex, but I pull him away before contact is made. Suddenly, he straightens to his full height and turns those green eyes back on me.

"I'm fine, but we are going to discuss these," he announces, waving the annulment papers again.

"We can discuss those papers at a more reasonable hour. Right now, I have a son to get to bed and you are leaving," I argue.

"Fine," he half grins, "I'll be back tomorrow morning."

"I have a business to run, so we'll need to make arrangements to talk."

"I'll see you tomorrow morning, Olivia." Pushing by Erik and Mercedes, he exits the apartment.

"That's him? Are you freaking kidding me, Liv?" Erik shouts. "He's a complete asshole!"

Mercedes smacks him in the chest before turning to me. "Are you okay? Do you want me to stay?"

Shaking my head, I hug Alex to me closely. "I'll be fine, but thank you."

"Liv?" Erik steps toward me.

"Go, Erik. Just go, please," I beg.

"Night, Liv." He stomps away.

"I'll see you tomorrow," Mercedes whispers, closing the door behind her.

After locking the door and securing the deadbolt, I take Alex to my room. Tonight, we'll sleep together.

Chapter three – stalker state of mind
Damon

"You, Damon Knyght, my big brother, are going on vacation?" Hugh didn't bother knocking before entering my office.

"Yes." I don't look up from my laptop. Instead, I continue to update my calendar in preparation for my upcoming trip.

"Who are you and what have you done with my brother?" Hugh sits across from me.

Rolling my eyes and sighing, I turn in my chair to look at him.

"Where are you going?" He doesn't wait for me to answer his first question.

"I have some... personal business to attend to." Picking up a pen, I start going through proposals for Mrs. Shaw to redraft before I leave.

"What the hell is that?"

I look up from the papers and follow his line of sight. He's looking at my hand — my left hand.

"A ring," I answer.

"Damon?" Hugh pushes.

I drop the pen and run my hands over my face as I relax back in my leather office chair.

"What, Hugh?" I snap.

"That's not your old ring, is it?"

"No, of course not," I growl.

"Then what...where—"

"I got married over the weekend. You'll meet her, eventually."

"I wasn't even aware there was a *she* to meet, or one you were considering marrying." A flash of hurt crosses his face.

"Hugh, relax." Sitting forward, I place my elbows on my desk and fold my hands. "It wasn't planned. It was spontaneous."

"You, spontaneous?" Hugh snorts.

"I know it's not like me, but I have my reasons."

"Which are?" he presses.

"I can't let her get away." I grin. "And now she can't." I shrug.

His brow furrows. "You speak as if she doesn't want to be married to you."

"Perhaps," I sigh. "She just needs time to warm up to the idea."

"Marriage isn't something you warm up to, Damon." Hugh gives me worried look. "What did you do? Is this going to come back on the company? Have you stopped taking your meds? Do you realize—?"

"First of all," my words escalate to just below a yell, "don't lecture me about this company. It's *my* company."

Hurt slashes the worry off his face.

"Second, I have reasons and, for now, they are my reasons. We have a common bond, something I'm not willing to lose. We belong together. And third, I didn't do anything. She is a consenting adult who made the choice to enter the chapel in Vegas and leave legally wed to me." Having enough, and not feeling the need to further explain myself, I return to the proposals I need to have finished by this afternoon.

"I want to understand," he states, pleadingly. "I really do, Damon. Please, tell me what's going on?"

Exasperated, I look up once more, ready to dismiss him, but the confusion, hurt, and worry on his face stops me.

"I went to Vegas over the weekend. I knew she would be there and once I was actually with her, talking, laughing, feeling better than I've felt in a very long time — hell, I'm not sure I've ever felt that kind of good — I couldn't and can't let her go. Now, she belongs to me and I intend on keeping it that way."

"Belongs to you?" Hugh shakes his head at me. "What's the matter with you? You don't *own* the woman because she said 'I do' in an all-night chapel on the Vegas strip. She can annul the marriage and you can't stop her."

"She can try, but I can drag it out and make it a miserable process. Any attorney with even a small amount of intelligence will tell her the same thing." I leer at my brother. "Plus, we have a common bond which plays in my favor. I know what I'm doing."

"Make it miserable for her?" Hugh's words are filled with disgust, matching his expression. "I can't believe you would be so callous. I thought it was just the loss of Becky before, but—"

"Damn it, Hugh, don't make this about her! It's not about her." Clenching my fists and jaw, I fight the urge to pounce on my little brother.

"You need to talk to someone, Damon. You should call the doctor. You can't just take someone else's life as a possession. You don't own this woman. She doesn't *belong* to you!" he shouts as he stands, looking down at me.

"Doesn't Scarlett belong to you?" I counter, raising a brow.

"Only because she *gives* herself to me, Damon. I didn't club her over the head and drag her by the hair back to my cave. Christ, what are you thinking?"

"We belong together," I growl. "She will understand once she knows everything." I sit back into my chair once more, trying to calm my anger.

"Knows everything about what? About Becky and—?"

"It's not your concern, Hugh." Waving him off, I turn my attention back to the proposals. "She and I have a long discussion ahead of us, and it's one I will have with her before anyone else."

In my peripheral vision, I see Hugh's shoulders slump in defeat. He turns from me and leaves without another word. Though, I know this won't be the last time I hear from him on the subject. For now, it's the last chance he would have. I already received her attempt to end our marriage, which only makes my departure more eminent.

Waking at four in the morning wasn't how I envisioned starting the day, but I always have a hard time sleeping soundly my first night in a hotel, regardless of the luxury surrounding me. Anxiousness zinged over my skin as I fought to focus on my laptop, business emails, and anything else I could use to distract me for a couple hours.

It's now seven in the morning and I can't help but think about the events of last night as I drive toward the bakery currently holding my new family.

My arrival was meant to be unexpected; however, I hadn't planned on the ridiculous ex being present. The fact that my presence interrupted his time with Olivia only fueled my need to keep her. Then, the boy appeared. I really tried not to look at him. I wasn't ready. But when Olivia turned with him in her arms, it was too difficult to keep my eyes averted.

The beauty of the little boy tightened my chest and almost forced a gasp from my lips. The pain, joy, happiness, and sorrow warring within me was the only reason I left earlier than planned. I needed to get myself together and not lose my shit before I had a chance to explain and convince her that there is no way out.

As I park along the curb outside, I take in the brightly lit bakery. The hours on the door say they don't open until seven-thirty, but an older man is at the counter, talking to a gray-haired woman, so I push open the door. Chimes announce my entrance as I look around, taking in the quaint little storefront with one large table at the window, small café style tables scattered about, and four stools at the counter. Pastries, breads, cookies, and other baked goods fill the glass display cases along each side of the counter and the ones on the wall behind the gray-haired woman. Fresh bread, cinnamon, butter, and other sweet smells assault my nose.

"Good morning." The gray woman smiles brightly. "What can I get for you? Bagels? Coffee?"

Shaking my head, I step closer to the counter. "I'm here for Olivia Harlow."

Her smile falters a bit before she recovers and motions to a small table near a bright green door. "Have a seat right there." She steps out from behind the counter and stands before the green door. "Is she expecting you?"

"Yes." I nod. "She is."

The confidence in my voice, or perhaps arrogance, causes her to narrow her eyes just a bit.

"Can I let her know who's here to see her?"

I grin. She's trying her best to find out as much as she can without being unfriendly.

"Of course." Stepping forward, I hold my hand out to her. "I'm Damon Knyght."

She takes my hand cautiously.

"Her husband," I finish.

The woman's eyes round as her mouth pops open just a bit.

"Excuse me." She pulls her hand away quickly and leaves through the green door.

"Olivia." The door muffles her voice, but the panic is obvious.

"Her husband?" The older gentleman at the counter asks quietly.

I look over at him and realize he isn't asking, he's simply processing. I turn back to the door and step closer, preparing to enter.

"Tell him I'm busy." Olivia sounds annoyed.

I push through the door.

"Oh, I think we have some very pressing things to discuss." Crossing my arms over my chest, I smirk as she spins to look at me.

"What are you doing back here?" Anger flushes her cheeks. It's quite attractive on her. "You can't just come back in the kitchen. You're breaking at least three health code violations right now."

"Sir, please wait at—"

"I agreed to wait until today for us to talk." Reaching inside of my jacket, I pull out the annulment papers — the papers that would be going into the garbage today. "Now, let's talk."

"Unless you are here to sign and give them to me, we have nothing to discuss." She crosses her arms over an apron that reads *I like big bunts and I cannot lie.*

I chuckle before responding. "Of course I'm not signing them. And since you insist on having this conversation in front of your employees, I will not be signing the annulment papers, Olivia." Side stepping, I drop the papers in a large blue garbage bin on my left.

"Why are you doing this? Are you crazy?" she huffs.

"I assure you, I am not—"

"Not crazy...yeah, yeah, yeah. You say that, but you sure as hell aren't doing anything sane so far by acting like an obsessive man possessed with having what he can't." Her eyes narrow on me.

"You didn't think I was so crazy when you were under me with your legs wrapped around my waist while I—"

"Enough!" she yells, her face blushing a deep pink. "Follow me," she growls, walking toward a doorway at the back of the kitchen while wiping her hands on the apron roughly. She unties the apron and pulls it off, hanging it on a hook beside a set of stairs.

Walking through the kitchen, I take a quick inventory of the five employees standing wide-eyed. I also notice the appliances; some look a little battered while others look ancient. Reaching the stairs, I start to ascend behind her.

"Keep your voice down," she whispers.

"Why?" I ask, my voice as quiet as hers when we reach the top of the stairs.

"My son is sleeping."

She passes a door, pulling it tightly shut.

My steps falter as I walk by the room and press my hand briefly to the door where he sleeps. *Soon.*

I catch up before she notices my lingering and enter the living room I stood in last night. Before she turns to look at me, I take in the open floor plan of the kitchen, dining, and living area. A skylight allows bright natural light into the room, but the hallway is cut off from the large light-filled space.

"What is it you want, Mr. Knyght?"

She stands in the center of the room, eyes hard, and arms crossed over a purple and blue tie-dyed t-shirt. Her bright red hair accentuates the bright blue of her irises, the creamy white of her porcelain skin, and the spattering of light freckles over her cheeks and nose.

"Want?" I raise a brow. *This should be interesting.*

"There has to be some reason you are doing this. Some reason why you won't let this go. I have absolutely no idea what you could want from or with me, but I assume it's something. So, what is it? What do you want so badly? What can I give you to convince you to go away and let me get back to my life?"

The fierce intensity swirling in her eyes mesmerizes me for a moment, halting my response. A predatory desire flares inside me, pushing me to back her against the wall and make her remember how hot she has gotten for me. Licking my lips, I calm the urges enough to finally answer.

"I. Want. You."

She shifts in discomfort, furrowing her brow. "What. Do. You. Want. From. Me?"

Rubbing her face, she takes a deep breath. "I don't have anything for you. Just sign the papers," she whines, pleadingly.

I walk toward her as she stands her ground. *Such a strong woman. God, does she know how much I want her?* The heat from her body penetrates me, the smell of sugar and buttercream making me wonder if she would taste like them.

"I will not be signing anything." I move my face toward hers, staring at her lips. Less than an inch from meeting her lips, I pause. "I want you. You are mine, Mrs. Knyght."

Chapter four — gold fleck eclipse
Olivia

"I don't have anything for you to want." I step back from the tall, dark man, his scent, like open water and fresh air, wrapping around me. The smell is too familiar, jarring memories to rush through my mind. Bare chest, tongue, my fingers gripping at the soft, short hair on his head. I close my eyes and breathe deep, a sorry attempt to clear my mind.

"Olivia."

My lids flutter open at the call of my name. The intensity on his face has melted to a wry smile, amusement gleaming in his eyes. He closes the small distance I managed to put between us.

"You are what I want. You and..."

He hesitates. I suck in a breath.

"You're my wife and I want you as my wife. My life is now yours and vice versa. We have a bond you need to accept." The small shrug of his shoulders pulls me from the seduction of his overwhelming presence.

"Accept it? A bond?" I snort. "You have to be joking. Sign the papers, Mr. Knyght, or I'll contact my lawyer and sue for divorce."

His face darkens, eyes narrow, and a muscle flicks angrily in his jaw. Nostrils flaring, he reminds me of a dragon. I wait for the flames to ignite.

"You can try suing for divorce, but I can guarantee it won't be a simple or fast process," he snaps.

I swallow, hard.

"You have to realize the money and resources I have at my disposal to fight you all the way. I can bury your legal actions with things you have no idea exist." He smirks.

"You insufferable asshole," I grind out through clenched teeth.

Irritated, I straighten my back and square my shoulders. "Why in God's name would you want to be married to someone who doesn't want to be with you? Someone you barely know? Someone who cannot stand you?"

"I know you well enough." He shrugs. "And I know you can stand me. You were quite welcoming and open with me in Vegas." He grabs my hand and kisses my wrist, ignoring my attempt to pull away. "We have plenty of time to learn more about each other. We have the rest of our lives, but we also have something else to discuss." Turning my hand, he kisses my knuckles.

"Stop it!" I exclaim, pulling at my hand. He finally releases me. "You are crazy."

I step away and around him, frustration and anger battling inside me.

"Olivia," he says, his voice gentling.

"Don't Olivia me," I growl.

"I'm not crazy," he sighs. "I've found you and I intend on keeping you, make no mistake."

"Found me?" I laugh humorlessly, the craziness of the situation catching up to me. "You ran into me, by chance, in Vegas. How long had you been *cruising the strip* for a bride?"

Guilt flashes in his eyes. *He's hiding something.*

"Regardless, I'm not signing the papers. They will stay in the garbage. You are my wife, Mrs. Knyght. I am your husband, and it would be best if you resign yourself to the fact. We have other things to discuss."

"I will not," I sneer. "You are a *mistake*, not my husband."

Spinning around, I step quickly toward the stairs. I need to get away from him. It's too much.

A strong hand grabs my arm, turning me back around. Both hands grip my biceps and pull me toward his chest.

"Please don't push me, Olivia. You are my wife. Accept us and we can move on to other matters and arrangements."

"I can't," I say, my voice more fragile than intended.

"We're connected, Olivia. I will not accept you leaving me."

I tilt my head back to look up at him and his eyes bore into mine. There is a vulnerability in them I didn't see before, a deep pain and longing.

"A piece of paper and one night in bed doesn't connect us." While I still feel an unexplainable urge and pull toward him, I lash out against it.

"We are more connected than you realize, and there is nothing you can do about it. You can try to fight it, but I will not sit by and let you slip through my fingers." His lips press firmly against my forehead before releasing my arms.

The tingling sensation left on my skin from his mouth annoys me. I quickly rub at it to make it go away. He walks over and sits on my couch.

"I have multiple lawyers on hand, Olivia. I've told you this before." He gives the cushion next to him a small pat, inviting me to sit. "We have other things we need to discuss. One matter will most likely come as a—"

"What do I have to do for you to just sign the papers?" One large step brings me behind the chair across from him. My fingers grip the back of the chair, pressing firmly on the cushion.

"Nothing," he says, giving an exasperated groan. "Can we please move on now? We need to discuss you and...your son's location."

"Location?"

"Yes. I live and work in New York. How can our marriage successfully work if we are in different states?" His left brow raises slightly.

"You're right," I admit, brightly, as I take a seat in the chair I'd been standing behind. "Looks like you should just sign the papers." Settling back into the chair, I smile and bat my lashes.

"Nice try." He gives a wry smile. "You both will move to New York with me. We can pick out a home you prefer."

"Um, no, I won't," I choke.

"Yes, you will," he argues.

"I work here. My business is here. I'm not going anywhere." My hands tighten on the armrests at my sides.

"When you agreed to marry me, you made this decision. Our home can be a house or apartment, whichever you prefer. But it will be in New York." He leans back into the couch with his right arm stretching over the back and gives me a challenging look.

"I will not move to New York. Our marriage is a drunken mistake. My son and bakery come before *you*. I've worked damn hard to get where I am and wouldn't give it up for you."

He leans forward with the grace of a large feline, his elbows coming to his knees.

"You can open a New York bakery. Call it an expansion." He smirks.

"Listen to me. I am not moving. I am not your wife. I may have—"

"Keep this location, too. It's an opportunity to branch out and grow your clientele." He leans back once more. "I have plenty of money for capital."

"Let me finish," I snap. "As I was saying, I may have made this mistake, but Alex didn't! This is where his life is. I won't uproot him because you're too crazy to move on."

His eyes soften.

"We are a family now, so obviously he is my concern. I would never—"

"We are *not* a family," I spit. "Alex is *my* son. He is nothing to you." My anger propels me to my feet.

"He's my son, too," he says, his voice distant.

"No, he's not," I whisper-shout.

Damon huffs. "There are things you don't understand. He is more my son than you think."

Confusion washes over me. *What the hell is wrong with this man?*

"Don't involve my son in your crazy." Fed up, I raise my arm and point to the door. "Get out! You'll hear from my lawyer," I shout. At the volume of my voice, I flinch internally, thinking of sleeping Alex.

"Momma!" Alex calls out. The shift of the mattress springs starts slow, until his rhythmic jumping is evident. "Momma!"

"Leave now, Damon," I growl. Walking closer to the hallway, I turn and point once more to the door.

Damon stands and begins walking, but hesitates before turning in the direction of the hallway and disappearing. My reflexes kick into gear and I sprint toward Alex's room. Damon stands before his door, his hand lingering on the flat wood.

"Stay out," I hiss, slipping my body between him and Alex's door.

"Momma!" Alex shouts louder, more impatient.

"I think he's getting tired of waiting." With a smirk, he reaches around me and opens the door.

"Don't," I cry softly. But it's too late.

Damon steps closer, backing me into Alex's room.

"Momma," Alex cheers.

Twisting, I step to the crib and take him into the protection of my arms.

What is he going to do to us?

"So help me God, if you don't get away from him, I'll kill you." My body tenses and Alex struggles against my hold.

"Why in the world are you afraid of me?" Damon cocks his head to the side, his brows furrowing.

"Because you're insane," I reply, my voice wavering with emotion.

Alex stills in my arms, obviously affected by the tension in the room. I rub his back, trying to reassure him.

"I would never hurt either of you." The intense expression he wore earlier returns. "You two mean more to me than anything in the world."

"We don't want you." My voice cracks.

His face hardens for a moment and I turn so Alex is further away from him.

"I won't repeat myself again." He comes closer, until there is barely a foot of space between us. "I want you. Both of you."

He places his hand gently against my cheek, but I turn away from his touch. Hurt flashes in his eyes and he sighs. He places a hand on Alex's back.

"Don't touch him," I snap, stepping away until my back meets the wall.

"Momma." Alex leans his head on my shoulder.

Damon presses forward.

"I'll go, but this isn't finished." He turns and walks toward the bedroom door. "I'll be back for both of you, Olivia." He looks back at us, his gaze punctuating each syllable. "I'll return for my wife and son."

"He's not your son." I sniffle, tears stinging my eyes.

Pain flashes across Damon's face. With quick, determined steps, he approaches us again.

"Don't," I warn. He pauses for a moment, but doesn't stop. "Don't." There's a hidden threat in my voice as I grab the lamp from the table next to me and grip it tight. "Get out," I growl low in warning.

"I want you to look at your...*our* son, Olivia. Then I want you to look at me." He stands a small distance from us and my eyes lock to his.

"Look at him," he says, his voice soft, but alarming.

55

Swallowing, I look at my son. Alex smiles large and puts his hand on my cheek. A hot tear slips over the apple of my cheek. The suddenness of Damon's hand on my jaw, his thumb wiping away the tear, causes me to jump.

"Now, look at me."

I close my eyes tight, not wanting to play whatever this game is any further.

"Momma," Alex coos and taps my face. "Peeboo," he giggles, thinking my closed eyes are invitation for a game. More tears slip through my lashes.

"Look at me, Olivia." Damon's voice is soft, but stern. He turns my face with his hand, but I refuse to open my eyes.

"Look at me," he demands, softly.

"No." I shake my head. "I won't play into this sick game any further."

"Open your eyes, Olivia." The edge to his voice makes Alex whimper.

I open my eyes slowly and truly look at Damon Knyght for the first time. Gasping, I cover my mouth.

"Your eyes..." I choke on a sob.

I look at Alex, and then back to Damon — their eyes are almost identical. The gold-flecked eclipse around Damon's pupils is exact.

"It's a coincidence, that's all." I shake my head, but I can't stop comparing them, no matter how hard I try.

"I told you. We're connected. I've been trying to discuss everything with you, but you've done nothing but fight me each step."

His thumb rubs my cheek, the longing and want returning to his face.

"N-no," I cry.

Shoving his hand away, I push him back from us.

"Get out," I demand. "I won't entertain your delusions. Go, now."

Alex begins to sniff and whine. His tears start next and my heart aches. I wrap my arms around his little body.

Damon comes to us slowly, holding out a hand. I slap it away.

"Don't touch us," I sneer, keeping my voice low. "We are not connected. You are delusional and I'm suing for the divorce if you refuse the annulment. Stay away from me and my son or I will get a restraining order," I threaten, moving further away from him.

Damon's face goes stone still.

"I'll go, but I won't stay away. You are my wife and he is my son."

"No." I shake my head. "He's not. He's my son."

"Reproductive Health Center. Pittsburgh, Pennsylvania. Doctor Cubeck." His tone is velvet, yet edged with steel.

"Stop it," I whisper, not willing to believe.

"If you want, I can give you a copy of the letter the clinic sent to me when they informed me of the mix up."

"You're lying," I grind out. "They would've contact me."

"I didn't actually see the letter myself. Not at first. It wasn't brought to my attention until almost a year ago." He shrugs. "I'll be sure you get a copy."

"Get out. Now." A sob tears from my chest, my knees weaken, and the sound of my heart beating fills my ears.

"Olivia?" Mercedes calls from the hallway before rushing into Alex's room at the sound of my sob.

"Take Alex, please," I beg Mercedes, my eyes never leaving Damon's face.

"Come on, buddy." Alex goes right into her arms and she swiftly exits the room.

Damon twitches in Alex's direction, but I move my body between them.

"Don't," I sneer.

His eyes return to me.

"You need to leave."

Footsteps on the stairs tell me Ced has taken Alex downstairs. *Thank God!*

"I'll go, but I'll be back." His words are both a promise and a threat. "You won't file divorce papers, Olivia." I open my mouth to argue, but he continues. "If I get one notice of restraint, divorce, annulment, separation, or anything like that, I won't hesitate to counter file for custody of Alex."

"The fuck you will!" Now that Alex is with Ced, I can really unleash.

"The fuck I won't!" he shouts back, stepping close to me. "One document, Olivia. That is all it takes for me to file custody papers and a paternity test."

"Just because you resemble my son, invade my life with your delusions, and make ridiculous claims—"

SADIE GRUBOR

"Not a claim, Olivia. It's fact. You want proof? You will have a copy of the letter from the clinic by tomorrow morning. If you need more than that, let's get a paternity test. I have absolutely no hesitation."

"I want you to go away." I shove hard at his chest. "Go!"

Hurt washes away the anger on his face. He wraps his arms around me before I can get far enough away from him.

"I didn't want it to be like this. I wanted to talk to you, explain, and make you understand." I jerk in his arms, until his lips press against my head. "In Vegas, I wanted to tell you everything, but the night escalated so quickly. I never expected you to be so...captivating, so amazingly open. Regardless of the alcohol, I saw exactly who you are and in that moment, I knew I wanted you."

When I stay silent, still processing his claims, threats, and admissions, he sighs and releases me.

"I will return. We'll discuss everything later, after you have time to think."

He leaves Alex's room and a few minutes later, I hear my apartment door close.

Dropping down, I bend until my forehead rests on the plush carpet. I release all of my pent up emotions in a scream that leaves me breathless. Sobs roll from the pit of my stomach. Sure that the hard jerk of my stomach muscles would make me sick, I crawl to the bathroom and lie on the cool tile floor.

Thin arms encompass me, pulling me from the floor.

"Alex?" I croak.

"Sarah has him." Ced rubs my arms, steering me to my bedroom and lying me on the bed.

A few moments later, the sounds of the shower fill the room. Mercedes emerges and walks me to the bathroom. Helping me undress, she doesn't say a word. With a small nudge from her, I enter the shower, standing under the hot water until it starts to cool. Even as the water goes cold, I don't move. Everything is numb.

"Come on, Liv." Mercedes reaches in, shutting off the water.

She opens the curtain and stands with a large towel open for me. Once I'm wrapped in the towel, she hugs me.

"Wanna talk about it?" she whispers.

"I need to get dressed," I say, my voice deceptively calm. Inside, I'm a typhoon of emotional madness.

After dressing, I follow the sounds coming from my kitchen. Alex is in his highchair trying to spoon oatmeal into his mouth.

Seeing me, he shouts, "Momma!"

Smiling, I walk over and kiss his head. Guilt for bringing Damon into our lives assaults me. If I'd stayed away from Vegas, maybe this wouldn't have...who am I kidding? He clearly would've just shown up here.

"Let's talk." Mercedes settles into a chair at the dining table as Sarah excuses herself back to the bakery.

"Thanks, Sarah," I shout after her.

"No prob," she calls back just before I hear her feet on the steps.

Sitting across from Ced, I stare at Alex.

"Spill it." She sips at her coffee and pushes a mug toward me.

Sighing, I sit up straight, sip from the mug, and then replay the events from my confrontation with Damon. Throughout the tale, Ced's face ranges from anger, worry, shock, and disbelief.

"But, how...I mean, is it possible he's the donor?" Ced doesn't seem to know which question to ask first.

I shrug. "I don't know. He knows so much and says he has documentation from the clinic, but couldn't he falsify all of it?" I take a deep breath. "But why go through all this trouble? Why go as far as a paternity test?" Burying my face in my hands, I groan.

"Call Alfonso," she blurts.

"If I do that then he'll—"

"He said no documentation or filing. You can still talk to Alfonso and get his opinion on things. Find out what you can do." Ced reaches for her cell phone and pulls up his number. "Call him." She slides the neon yellow phone across the table.

Picking it up, I touch the screen, initiating the call.

After three hours on the phone, half an hour of which spent on hold while he cleared his schedule for me, it boils down to me being screwed.

Damon may have broken some laws, but we don't have any proof. I could get a restraining order, but he has the money and power to manipulate the system in his favor. Also, if he's willing to bury me in court for years over a divorce, I'm pretty sure he's not above further manipulation. Plus, I have to worry about a possible custody issue.

"We can still proceed, Olivia. I mean, I'm not saying you should back down. I want you to be prepared for battle, though. It could be a long one, especially if the mix up at the clinic turns out to be true and in his favor." Alfonso clears his throat. "We'll have to bring in a family law attorney for this. I've got experience, but going against a man like Damon will take some expertise."

Alfonso is doing his best to be unbiased, but I can hear the concern in his voice. If I do move forward, he isn't confident in the results.

"Thanks, Al." An unwanted feeling of resignation washes over me as I end the call.

"Liv?" Ced questions from her spot on the floor with Alex.

"I'm screwed." A humorless laugh escapes my lips.

Dropping my head to the table, I begin to bang it a couple times. Alex mimics me by banging a block on the floor.

"I'm so sorry. Can't you—?"

Before she can finish, I tell her everything Alfonso told me.

"So, you're just going to let him—?"

"I'm not going anywhere, Ced. We may be married, because of a piece of paper, but I'm not his slave or some Stepford wife at his beck and call," I snap. Then, realizing what I'd done, I say, "Sorry, I didn't mean to take it out on you."

"I know." She gave me an understanding smile.

"What's left to do in the bakery?" I ask, trying to take my mind off things.

"You aren't seriously going back to work?" She stands from the floor, looking at me incredulously.

"Um, yes. This is my bakery, it's my name on the sign, and I need to get my mind off this shit."

I walk from the table to the living space, stopping next to Alex to pick him up.

"Momma." He snuggles against me.

Pulling back, our eyes meet. Damon stares back at me through my son's face. My lungs suddenly won't hold air. I can't get enough. Desperately searching Alex's face, I try to find something to make Damon wrong, but the more I look, the more I can't breathe.

"Liv," Ced says, concern in her voice. She takes Alex from me and rubs my back with a free hand.

"Let's get downstairs," I gasp, still trying to take in air.

Once in the kitchen, everyone is quieter than usual.

"Give me a cake," I announce, wiping a tear away before slipping an apron over my head.

No one moves, except Ced who places Alex in his play area.

I stand next to my worktable, put my hands on the top, and lean forward, closing my eyes. "Someone give me a damn cake, please," I beg, fighting more tears.

"Here you go." Greg shoves an order sheet and a twelve-inch round sponge cake at me.

After looking over the order for a four-tier marshmallow fondant anniversary cake, I look up at Greg's smirk.

"Oh, nice try, but you are so helping with this monster." I laugh a real laugh, and it feels good.

The next day, I receive a certified carrier letter. There, in black and white, Mr. Damon Knyght is informed about the mix up between him and another donor. But, it also states a letter was sent to all affected parties. Since I never received any type of letter, there's still a chance, right?

Two weeks pass with no word from Damon. Feeling rather hopeful and positive about the turn of events, Alex and I sit icing cookies together. Well, I'm icing cookies. He's doing more of a lick-the-icing-off-his-finger thing.

I laugh as he makes green and blue icing prints on the tray of his highchair, but my good mood falters with a knock at the door.

"Who could that be, huh?" I coo to Alex.

"Cookie," he announces.

"You think it's a cookie at the door?" Laughing, I wipe my hands on the towel over my shoulder and stand.

As I reach for the doorknob, I notice a missed glob of green buttercream on the knuckle of my ring finger. I pull open the door and instinctively put my knuckle to my lips.

"Can I taste?" His familiar velvety voice sends warmth down my spine.

My eyes meet his and I swallow hard, quickly pulling my finger from my mouth.

"What are you—?"

"I told you I'd be back." With a crooked smirk, he leans against the doorframe.

"We're busy. You should have called instead of just showing up. Sorry." Faking a smile, I push the door closed.

His arm juts out, stopping the door halfway before pushing it back open.

"Not so fast, Olivia."

He leans down, picking up two black leather duffle bags. Straightening with the bags in his hands, he steps around me and into my living room.

"What are you doing?" I snap.

"I'm here to see my family." He turns, looking at me from over his shoulder. "Should I put these in our bedroom?"

"Um, there is no *ours*. You can take them to a hotel, or better yet, you could take them back to New York with you." Forcing a large, fake smile, I bat my lashes.

"I had hoped the lack of divorce papers meant you accepted our marriage." He drops his bags onto the floor at his feet.

"Like you gave me the option to file for divorce," I scoff. "You're blackmail tactics worked, though I'm still not one-hundred percent sure of your claims."

"I only provided you with the facts and the position you would put me in based on your actions."

"Get out," I sneer.

"No." He steps closer to me.

"Now," I demand in a hush.

My eyes shift to Alex. He's watching us with curiosity, not an iota of fear or stress on his face. *Keep your calm, Liv.* I look back at Damon.

"Make me," he goads, a half-smile playing on his lips.

He thinks this is a joke? I'll show him funny.

Grabbing my cell from my back pocket, I start to dial.

"Who are you calling?" Damon walks closer and I step backward.

"The cops," I clip, looking at him through narrow and defiant eyes. "You can't just intrude into my home, Damon." The operator's nasally voice fills my ear. "Hello, I need assistance—"

"That's quite enough." Growling, he takes the phone from my hand and ends the call.

Walking back to the door, I reopen it.

"Go." My voice is a stern command, but I keep my volume low for Alex's sake.

"Olivia," he says on a sigh, placing my cell phone on a table. "We have a lot to talk about. I know you received the copy of the letter. I'm sure you have questions and I would like time to bond with my son." He turns his attention to Alex.

"Stay away from him," I hiss, shutting the door — hard.

With quick steps, I reach Alex and take him from his highchair. Not caring about the icing he will paint my clothes in, I hold him protectively in my arms.

"I would never hurt him." Damon rolls his eyes. "You're being ridiculous."

"Me, ridiculous?" I snort. "What about you?"

"If I were going to hurt either of you, I would've done it by now, don't you think?" A frustrated sigh leaves him.

"You think your blackmail and threat of taking him from me isn't harming me? Forcing me to stay married to you and go through this delusional idea of how a relationship begins isn't harmful?" It's hard, but I manage to keep my tone level. Alex doesn't tense once.

Damon's brow furrows.

"We need to talk. I refuse to argue about the same things every time we're together. It makes sense for me to stay here so I can spend time with Alex."

He moves from the middle of the room to the couch and sits.

"Just allow the annulment," I beg.

"I'm afraid I can't do that." He shrugs.

"Why? Why can't you just go back to your life and leave us be?" Tears threaten to spill from my eyes.

He stares at me from across the room, his eyes conveying the seriousness of the situation.

"Because, now that I've found you, both of you, I could never walk away. Don't you understand? You two are everything." Dropping the intense stare, he puts his head in his hands and grips his hair. "I searched for you for almost a year. There were three," he laughs, but it's not from joy.

"Three what?" I'm not sure why I ask since I'm pretty sure I already know the answer. I think it's just to hear him say the words.

"Three women," he blurts. "But of the three, there is only you. You and Alex." I stay silent, waiting to see if he'll offer more.

"During one month, my *supply* was used in three separate procedures. Each of them a mix up with the donor you all chose." He laughs humorlessly again. "Who knew such a difficult time in my life would lead to the one thing that can save me?"

"How did you track us down?" I ask, my voice barely above a whisper.

"It wasn't easy. The records were sealed." His eyes meet mine again. "But, as I told you, I have resources." His move from the couch to right in front of me is so sudden, I don't have time to think about moving away.

"There is only you, though. You and Alex." Damon's fingers graze my cheek.

"If this is the truth, there are plenty of other women who would—"

"No," he snaps. "I want you. You and Alex are worth more than anything else. I won't lose you."

Fear swirls in my stomach, urging me to run to my room, lock the door, and call the police. My brain pushes panic induced adrenaline through my body, telling me to be afraid. But, as ridiculous as it sounds, I know, deep down, he won't hurt us.

Well, that crazy talk won't beat out my common sense.

Pulling away from his touch, I hurry down the hall with Alex in my arms. Once in my room, I close the door and lock it.

"Olivia," Damon calls out from the other side of the door, a hint of concern in his voice.

"Go. Just go, please." Cradling Alex, I slide down the door until I sit on the floor.

"I can't. I can't walk away. Not now. I need you. You have no idea how much I need you."

A muffled slump on the other side of the door is enough to tell me he, too, sits on the other side.

Chapter five - traitor
Olivia

After killing time giving Alex the bath he needed, he sits in only his training pants, playing with some of the toys I keep at the end of my bed. Watching him play, I wait for my laptop to come to life.

"Time to Google you, Mr. Damon Knyght," I say out loud to no one. "Let's see...hmm."

B.I.G. company information and accomplishments in business cover the first page of results. Page two provides an article about Mildred Banks-Knyght.

> Mildred Banks-Knyght, CEO & daughter to the founder of B.I.G., has fallen mysteriously ill, leaving the company in peril. Without a successor, the board is frantic to find a replacement. Mildred, nor the board, was available to comment.

Skimming the article, I learn Damon stepped in — to the shock of the investment world. The article made note of his educational background being in medicine, like his father.

The next article to catch my attention is full of accolades for Damon Knyght. One quote sticking out among the rest:

> "Mr. Knyght's successes come as no surprise to the board. He worked alongside his mother from child to young adult. And while Ms. Knyght is no longer in the office, she is clearly a great resource."

"Okay, impressive, but not what I'm looking for. Come on, Google, don't let me down now." I tap the keyboard and click to the next page of online articles. I scroll. "What?" I click an article that has my breath and heart rate increasing.

TRAGEDY STRIKES KNYGHT FAMILY

'Yesterday evening, the well-known Knyght family suffered a devastating loss. Rebecca Knyght, wife to Damon Knyght, CEO of B.I.G., and their young son, were in a devastating car accident. Police have determined that the driver, Rebecca Knyght, swerved for unknown reasons, causing her to lose control of the vehicle. The car spun twice before wrapping around an oncoming car. The force of the oncoming vehicle's impact propelled the wreckage into another car parked on the side of the road.

The police have disclosed the presence of a child in the car. However, due to the child being a minor, no name has officially been released. We can only assume it was Mr. and Mrs. Knyght's two-year-old son, Damon Knyght II.

No comment is available from the family at this time. Our deepest sympathies and condolences to the Knyght family during this tragedy.'

I gasp for air, having held my breath while reading without realizing it. I sit back and darkness descends as my lids cover my eyes. *What do I even say or do with this information? It's a horrible loss for him and his family, but it doesn't make us the replacement.*

With another deep breath, I lean back toward the computer.

KNYGHT FAMILY TRAGEDY CONTINUES

'UPDATE: It has been confirmed that Mrs. Rebecca Knyght and Damon Knyght II were both killed in the shocking accident on Friday evening. Speculation has spread as to the reasons Mrs. Knyght lost control of her vehicle, but no clear or solid evidence is available at this time. We send our condolences in this family's time of loss.'

Wiping away a stray tear, I sit back with my eyes closed once more. *He lost his family...his child. It was almost three years ago, given the date of the article. It's horrible.*

I glance at Alex and my chest aches. I couldn't imagine losing him, but I do know a sense of the loss Damon felt. My mind wanders to Isaac and then to our unborn child.

Shaking the thoughts from my head, I push back from the desk and walk over to Alex. Swinging him into my arms, I take a breath before opening the bedroom door and emerging.

"You hungry, buddy?" I ask, keeping myself distracted with Alex and not the man lingering somewhere in my apartment. "What do you want to eat, huh?"

Peeking around the corner at the end of the hallway, I find Damon laying on his back with his arm over his face, his chest steadily rising and falling. He's asleep.

As quietly as possible, I set Alex down and start cleaning the cookie mess from his tray. A few minutes later, I return the tray, but Alex isn't on the floor where I left him. With a scan of the room, I see him.

"Alex," I whisper-shout, hurrying to stop him before he reaches Damon.

Two steps from reaching him and everything feels like it moved in slow motion. Alex brings both hands over his head and drops them with a smack onto Damon's chest. Damon jerks up to sitting just as I grab Alex into my arms.

"Wow, little guy, you're pretty strong." Damon rubs his chest, giving Alex a sleepy smile before focusing on me. "You finally decided to come out?"

Knowing it wasn't really a question, I walk Alex back to his chair and slip him inside. I buckle the belt around him and lock his tray.

"Are you ready to talk to me?"

"Nope," I quip, keeping my back to him. "We can talk later. After Alex is in bed." I look over my shoulder and narrow my eyes at him. "So he isn't caught in the middle of another tense situation."

Guilt flashes over Damon's face for the briefest moment.

"I'm sorry about that," he sighs.

I say nothing. Instead, I turn back to the kitchen counter and begin dinner.

With Alex fed, I clean him off and take him to get pajamas. Damon keeps out of my personal space, but shadows my every step. It's annoying, but I say nothing.

"Momma," Alex calls.

"What little man?" I focus on him with a smile.

"Down." He struggles against my attempts to get his shirt over his head. I tickle under his arms until he surrenders long enough for me to finish.

Done dressing him, I let him down. He walks straight to his blocks.

"Blocks." He drags the basket and dumps the colored squares onto the floor.

Crouching next to him, we begin building a tower. I can feel Damon lingering behind us and his sudden move to sit opposite us gets both Alex and my attention. Alex's attention returns to the blocks before mine and he knocks the tower down.

"Hey," I tease and pout. Alex giggles.

"Ghen!" he exclaims.

I reach for a block at my knee and my fingers briefly brush Damon's. Warmth spreads across my hand and I pull back. Looking up at him, Damon is focused on building a block tower. I glance to Alex who is watching Damon curiously, but it doesn't take long for a smile to brighten his little face.

Bouncing in anticipation, he scoots closer to Damon's tower and squeals when he sees me start another tower, too.

Soon, Alex pushes Damon's blocks over with a large laugh and then moves on to mine.

"That's not very nice."

I tickle him and he laughs, collapsing to the floor and squirming. From the corner of my eye, I see Damon sitting stoic, watching.

Alex yawns as we put the blocks back into the basket. With Damon still observing, I tuck Alex into bed, read him a quick story, and turn on the crib toy that usually lulls him to sleep. After one kiss to his forehead, I walk out of this room.

Needing a drink before starting this conversation with my 'stalker', I go to the kitchen.

"Are we going to talk, Olivia?" His voice is just behind me.

I nod without looking back at him. Honestly, I'm procrastinating as much as possible. I don't want to bring up the things I learned from the internet, but he is leaving me no choice.

With a glass of ice water in hand, I sit in a chair across from the couch.

"Well, then—"

"Damon," I cut him off, "I'm going to attempt to talk calmly, but if you start any of that *we're meant to be* or *connected* bullshit, I will lose my mind."

He smiles crookedly. "As you wish."

"What is it you really want from me?" My voice sounds flat. I'm exhausted but determined.

"I told you what I want."

"Yes, you say you want me, but what exactly are you expecting from me?"

"To be my wife. For both of you to be my family."

When I open my mouth to speak, he puts a hand up to stop me.

"I know this situation is unusual, but I can't walk away. I need you."

"Okay, first of all, unusual is *not* the right word. This is downright insane with a sprinkle of creepy." I raise my brows at him. "Please tell me you understand that?"

He only sighs, but I don't really want an answer anyway.

"You don't know me, Damon. You can't possibly think you need me."

It's my turn to put my hand up to stop his argument.

"I have my own life, here, in Pittsburgh. You have your life in New York. I won't even consider leaving my life behind."

His eyes harden. A chill straightens my spine.

"I don't know you, either. I know what you've said, and what you've done so far." I shake my head. "You've basically stalked me and forced me into this situation."

His eyes are still hard and intense, but I don't back down.

"My insemination was confidential. There is a privacy act. How did you really find me?"

A small smirk twitches at the corner of his mouth.

"You know how I found you." He snorts. "I have money, Olivia. Things, options, are available to me."

"I can't believe you." I take a long drink from my glass. "Okay, you said there were others. What exactly does that mean?"

He clears his throat.

"The clinic mixed up my file number with an anonymous donor. There were three others involved in the mix up, but only your insemination resulted in a pregnancy."

"You tracked them all down?" I choke out.

He nods.

"I'm just the lucky one, I guess." With a huff, I slouch back into the chair.

"I only had to gain access to the full records to see that those women did not conceive." He waves toward me. "Obviously, you did."

"How are you so sure Alex is yours? Maybe the mix up is an error." I raise a brow in challenge.

"Just seeing him, I knew." A smile spreads across Damon's face. "He resembles me as a child."

Our eyes lock together.

"Not identical, of course. I can see you in him, too. But I see and feel me in him."

Burying my face in my hands, I ask, "How did this even happen? There are supposed to be security measures in place for this."

I didn't truly expect him to answer the question.

"I'm not exactly sure of the how, yet." He pauses and I look up from my hands. "The moment I found out about the situation with the clinic, I was more focused on finding out whether there was a child out there. Now that I know there is, I'll focus on how it all happened."

"I don't even know what to say right now." Dropping my head back against the chair, I close my eyes and take a deep breath.

"I never said I'm a rational person, but I do need you, Olivia. More than you realize."

Releasing a heavy breath, I steel myself to say exactly what just passed through my mind.

"Does this have to do with Rebecca?"

At this, silence meets me. I'm too afraid to open my eyes just yet. *Did I go too far? Should I have asked in a different way?*

"Damon?" I'm finally brave enough to lift my head and look at him.

His face is flush, eyes watery. A pain pierces my chest. I know that look. I've seen that look on my own face. I remember looking into a mirror at the hospital right after I lost Isaac's baby.

"I'm sorry," I blurt.

"You know?" he whispers.

I nod.

"I was worried and did my own research online. I just—"

"I understand." He cuts me off and inhales deeply. "I'm surprised you didn't do it sooner," he says, his eyes focusing on nothing.

"You didn't answer me," I still push. *What the hell am I doing? Clearly, he is grieving and I'm being a bitch.*

"No. Yes. No. I don't know, Olivia." With a heavy sigh, he meets my eyes. "I need this, Olivia. I need you and Alex. There is no way for what happened not to be a part of what I've done, but I can't go back now. I can't."

"We can't replace what you lost," I say, my voice strained, trying not to sound a total bitch.

"*You* are not meant to replace them," he growls.

"I'm sorry, but it seems like you want an insta-family to fill the—"

"I'm trying to get my life back, Olivia!" His voice rises. His eyes flit to the hallway and he gets himself in check. "I'm trying to bring something good into my life, something good to live for again. I refuse to go back to the empty existence I've been living."

His fists clench and unclench.

"You are my wife." He points toward the hallway. "And that is my son. Regardless of what the clinic promised you, they also made promises to me. It's not my fault you gave birth to my son, but I won't be denied involvement in his life. This is what it is, Olivia."

Intense eyes penetrate mine, like a dare to defy him.

"Calm down," I hiss.

Astonishment softens the hardness from his face.

"How long has it been since you lost them?" I already know from the internet, but I need to hear it from him. *Can he acknowledge their death? The loss? If he refuses to answer, then he definitely needs to see someone about letting go of his past.*

"Why?" he growls.

Ah ha.

"It seems like you're still deeply grieving. You should talk to someone about it and get help to deal with the loss. I think—"

"I don't need a shrink, Olivia," he grinds out, his jaw tight. "I've talked to enough of them. I'm very aware that Rebecca and DJ are gone." He chokes on the last words and my heart breaks. "What I need is you and my son! Now, I think we should get back on track with discussing your move to New York."

"I'm not moving to New York," I say through clenched teeth, crossing my arms over my chest.

Pinching the bridge of his nose, he takes a deep breath.

"Olivia," he growls, "I will not have my wife and son so far away from me."

"You should have thought about that before inserting yourself into *my* life and making demands. I won't follow your orders just because you want something," I snap.

"Damn it, why are you so stubborn?" he exclaims.

"Stubborn? You think *this* is stubborn?" I snort. "Regardless of the marriage certificate, you are not my boss. I don't take orders from you and will not uproot my life for a man I barely know."

Sighing, he sits back on the couch across from me.

"I am your husband. It isn't just a piece of paper." His eyes narrow and I roll mine. "We'll come back to this." He rubs his face. "I need you to sign some legal documents." He shuffles through some folders on the coffee table and pushes them toward me.

"Are you going to order up some more drinks to convince me to sell my soul to you?" A humorless laugh bubbles from my chest.

Ignoring me, he levels a look that says he clearly doesn't find me funny.

"Your signature is needed for you to access my accounts and—"

"I don't want your money," I blurt, sitting up straight and wide-eyed.

"It's our money now and you will have access to it for whatever you and Alex need," he snaps back at me. "Don't deprive my child because you are stubborn," he accuses.

I gasp, my mouth opening and closing three times before finding the right words.

"*My* son is never deprived of anything." My voice hardens.

"You're trying to deprive him of his father," he counters. "Besides, you're taking it the wrong way. I didn't say he's not taken care of."

"Well, I still don't want it, so you can shred those. I'm not signing them." I dismiss the papers with a wave.

"I'll get you to sign them eventually."

I open my mouth to argue further, but he continues.

"This one needs to be signed so we can take care of your last names."

"Our names?"

"Yes. You both will take my last name." He pushes a long, white paper toward me.

"Ha!" I shout, but quickly lower my voice. "Our names are just fine, thank you," I remark, pleased with how nonchalant I sound.

"You won't take my last name?" he asks, clearly frustrated.

I shake my head.

"And you'll deny our son his father and right to be a Knyght officially?"

I groan.

"He's growing up just fine as a Harlow. Alex and I will keep our last name."

The flare of his nostrils gives away his attempt to stay calm. Part of me hoped he would explode so I could kick him out.

"I understand the business need of your name. But, legally, your name should be changed to Knyght, both of your names."

"Not going to happen." I keep my nonchalant facade going.

Staring at each other, it becomes a contest of who will give in first.

"You're impossible." His voice raises an octave.

Ha, you blinked first, stalky! I win!

He stands and begins to pace.

"Well, you're ridiculous. Looks like we are match made in hell."

"Why? What is so ridiculous about these things?" He motions to the papers spread out on the table.

"What's ridiculous?!" I sit up to the edge of the chair. "Damon, we are a one night stand, drunk marriage in Vegas cliché. You want to change our lives for one night. We barely know each other and you want to hand over access to your money, your name, and everything. You don't want me. You want this new identity you're creating for Alex and me. Can't you see this won't work? You need to let go of your past and let this crazy idea of us go."

Before I can scramble out of the chair, he's standing before me. Leaning forward, he braces his hands on either side of my slouched form.

"I will not let you go, either of you," he sneers. "So, get used to me being around, Mrs. Knyght."

Anger boils up from inside me, filling my limbs. I shove at his chest enough to make him sway, but not for him to release me from my chair prison.

"Move," I growl.

His right knee moves between my legs, pushing them apart.

"What are you—?"

I push at him as he drops to his knees between my parted thighs. His arms encircle my waist and his head falls into my lap.

"Please," he begs, a possessive desperation in his words.

"Please what?" I ask without moving, unsure of what he'll do next.

"Just let us be." His arms tighten around me.

My body starts to ache from the stiff posture I'm currently sitting in.

"If you are Alex's father," he tenses, "we can arrange visitations. You can be a part of his life. We don't have to be married for you to have rights to see him. That's if you are—"

"I am his father, Olivia." His voice is cold, exact. "And I don't just want visitations with him."

"Damon, please, I don't want—"

His arms tighten almost painfully.

"No, Olivia. This isn't just about Alex. It's about you and me, too. I want us. I want you to at least try." Though my thighs muffle his voice, they don't hide the desperation.

I shift uncomfortably, the heat of his breath causing unwanted reactions from my body. He eases his hold, but doesn't let me go.

"It is about Alex. I could've easily been one of the other women. If I hadn't been the one to give birth, you wouldn't even be here right now."

"If I had met you, just you, without any of this, I would still want you."

"You only say that because—"

His head lifts from my lap. A coldness caresses where he'd been and for a tiny second, I miss his warmth.

"Why can't you believe what I'm saying? I have no reason to lie, Olivia. If I only wanted Alex, I could have easily gone to a lawyer and gotten my rights instated. In fact, I'd initially planned to do just that, but then came you."

His hands flex against my body.

"Can't you just try?" Desperation darkens his eyes.

I shake my head, slowly.

This is crazy. People don't do this. At least, sane, normal people don't agree to things like this. He's a stranger who tracked me down because of sperm. And I'm not so sure about the state of his sanity and grief.

"Don't say no. Not yet," he blurts before crashing his lips to mine.

The kiss is brutal, demanding, yet conveys all the desperation and desire he thinks he feels. The warmth of his mouth is familiar and I unwittingly think about our night in Vegas. His lips warming other bare parts of my body.

I just barely open my mouth for his probing tongue when reality comes crashing back.

"Damon—"

I try to mumble a protest, but he plunges his warm tongue into the depths of my mouth. The magic of his slick tongue massaging my own entrances my body. Heat, lust, and desire pulse from where our mouths meet, causing my entire body to ache with need.

His hand cups the back of my head and fists in my hair. Memories of his grip on my hair while he took me from behind in a Vegas hotel room gets my juices flowing.

Needing air, I turn my head and gasp.

Damon's mouth travels over my jaw and toward my ear. His tongue and teeth play along my heated flesh.

"Damon..." I try once more to protest.

"Olivia," he moans, pressing his full body against mine.

I catch my own moan before it falls from my panting mouth.

"Stop." I force the word. "You need to stop."

He continues to cloud my mind and rile my body with his teeth and tongue.

"Damon!" I shout. "You need to stop."

He freezes. I try clearing my mind with gulps of air as I push his body away from mine.

He leans back onto his heels, his chest rising and falling heavily.

"I'm sorry." He drops his head. "I thought you—"

"You just..." *What the hell! It wasn't just him.* "WE got carried away." Swallowing, I sit up straight. "That can't happen."

I try to stand, but he's right back with his head in my lap.

"We have a connection and chemistry. I felt it the first night, Olivia. You felt it then and you feel it now."

His arms slip around my waist again.

With his mouth so close to still aching places on my body, I squirm.

"Please, let go."

Closing my eyes, I try not to feel the lingering tingle he left across my skin.

This is not normal, not sane. Damon Knyght is an obsessive stalker.

"Please, don't make me leave," he bargains, agreeing to release me.

"It would be best if you stayed somewhere else."

"I want to be here with the two of you," he pleads.

"Damon," I groan.

"You know I would never harm either of you. Let me stay."

His head lifts and he stares longingly into my eyes.

"Fine, but you stay in the spare bedroom." I narrow my eyes.

"Now who's the ridiculous one?" He sits back once more. "You're my wife. I've seen you naked, had you under me, screaming—"

"Okay, hotel for you. Have a good night." I push to standing. He stands with me.

"Fine," he grumbles. "Spare room."

"I don't want you thinking this means something, Damon. I meant what I said. We can work out something where Alex is concerned, but I don't want this marriage. I also don't want you to confuse him by calling yourself his father."

His face hardens.

"At least, not yet," I hurry to amend.

Hurt flashes across his face.

"I'm here for two weeks, Olivia, and, as you already know, I can be very persuasive." Before I can respond to his smug ass remark, he continues, "The spare room is this way, right?"

He disappears down the hall.

That bastard!

Exhausted, I turn off the lights, make sure the door is locked, and make my way to my bed for the night. Unfortunately, the events of the night are on replay in my head.

His demands and requests, how horrible his loss must be, and my own insanity for allowing this to continue. *I've become part of the problem.*

"He needs to find a hotel tomorrow," I say out loud to the darkness of my room before finally falling asleep.

Four in the morning blares its ugly arrival on my alarm clock. I dress and head to the bakery. My personal problems can't interfere with my business any more than they already have.

Mercedes breezes in with sunglasses on and an extra-large coffee in her hand.

"Rough night?" I laugh.

"Shh, not so loud," she whispers and slips into her office, without turning on the light.

Giggling, I start the muffins, breads, and cookies. Once I'm done with the initial baked goods, I get the urge to change the special for the day.

I grab the ingredients and start up the food processor, adding pepperoni, ham, smoked mozzarella cheese, and just a bit of smoked cheddar. In the mixer, I attach the dough hooks and place in the ingredients.

By the time Sarah and Greg arrive, the dough is on its second rising.

"Morning," Sarah smiles and Greg mumbles in unison.

"Good morning, guys." I focus on Greg. "You look like you're in the same shape as Ced."

"What are you making?" Sarah asks, pulling an apron over her head. It's the one I gave her last year that says *if you like these cookies, you should taste my muffin.*

"I changed the special." I shrug. "I'm in the mood for pepperoni and ham rolls."

"Need any help with them?" Sarah rolls up the short sleeves of her bakery shirt the way she likes them.

"Sure, if you don't have anything else to start."

She steps next to me and starts cutting pieces of dough before flattening, filling, and rolling. She inhales deeply.

"What did you put in the dough? Garlic?" she asks.

"Yeah, that and parmesan cheese," I answer.

"I will love you forever if you say I can have one this afternoon." Greg stands opposite Sarah, his hands clasped in prayer.

"You will love me no matter what," I counter.

"True, but come on. Please?" He smiles and bats his lashes.

"Oh God, tell him yes so he'll stop that." Sarah cringes, teasing.

"Okay," I laugh.

"Yes!" Greg fist pumps.

"You realize you look like a demented bobble head when you do that, right?" Sarah calls after Greg's retreating form.

"Don't be jealous!" he shouts before disappearing into the large cake fridge.

With Sarah's help, I get the rolls done in half the time I thought they would take. We place them on top of the ovens, so they can rise one last time before baking.

Sarah walks to the radio. Her hand hovering over the flour, sugar, and icing covered device on one of the shelves along the wall.

"Sure," I agree, walking toward Mercedes' office.

I grab the baby video monitor off the table along the way and then lean into her door.

"You feeling okay?" I raise a brow at her.

"Better now. Just had a hard time waking up today. I'm getting too old for long nights."

"You wanna trade nights?" I mumble, sitting in the chair opposite her.

The look of confusion on her face prompts me to tell her about the events of yesterday evening.

"He's upstairs right now?" She bites her bottom lip, her eyes wide.

"Unfortunately," I agree. "Though, he will be finding somewhere else to stay while he is in town. I already feel stupid crazy for allowing a stalker to spend the night."

Huffing, I set the monitor onto Mercedes' desk. "Can you keep an eye on him while I start on some orders?"

"Of course." She smiles. "Maybe you should get one of these put in your husband's room," she giggles.

"Not funny," I say flatly.

"Oh, come on! I'll watch that monitor for you." She winks. "Say what you will, that man is fine. I wonder if he sleeps nude or perhaps in his boxers. Wait! What kind of underwear does he wear?"

She seriously wants me to answer.

"I'm done with you," I state and turn away, heading back to the kitchen.

"Come on, Liv! Give a girl something!" Ced yells.

Ignoring her, I watch Sarah and Greg work at their tables.

"Someone cake me," I shout.

"Over here!" Sarah shouts before Greg can. "Hush it, Greg. You got her last time."

To Greg's approval, Emily arrives shortly after I begin working on a company function cake with Sarah.

"Liv, Alex is awake," Mercedes calls from her office.

78

Looking up at the clock on the wall, I stretch my neck and back. "Where did those hours go?"

Sarah snorts in response.

"Want me to go get him?" Mercedes leans against the doorframe of her office.

"I've got him." Waving her back into her office, I remove my apron and head upstairs.

"What am I gonna make for breakfast?" I whisper the question to the empty hall, flexing my fingers. *Those little fondant pieces are really making my hands sore today.*

Mid finger flex, I step into Alex's room and clench my hands into fists.

"What are you doing?" My question sounds more panicked than intended.

Damon looks up from Alex, who he is holding in his arms.

"He was yelling for you and I was already awake, working on my laptop, so—"

I barely comprehend what Damon is saying to me. All I can focus on is how relaxed Alex is in his arms. Curious, but relaxed, all the same.

"I've got him." I quickly take him from Damon and start toward the kitchen.

"Olivia," Damon sighs heavily. "I'm only trying to help."

His footfalls so close behind me, tell me he is following.

"He doesn't know you," I bark.

"He didn't seem to have a problem with me." His smugness irritates me more.

"You could have scared him. Did you think about that?" I glare at him from over my shoulder.

He snorts.

"Please, I'm not stupid. Of course I thought about it. I stepped in slowly and kept my distance. And do you know what he did, Olivia?"

Securing the final latch on the high chair, I turn toward Damon with my arms over my chest.

"What, Damon?"

"He smiled and said, 'Up!'." Damon leans against the kitchen island, looking way too just-woke-up-this-hot. "I'm pretty sure he's okay with me."

Dropping my arms in defeat, I go get apples and start slicing up tiny pieces for Alex.

"Shi...er, crap," I groan.

"Are you okay?" Damon is standing next to me before he finishes the question.

"I'm fine." Putting my cut finger into my mouth, I side step to the sink. *Damn it! Take the irritation out on him, not yourself.*

"Let me see it. Is it deep? Do you think you need stitches?" He presses close to my side, watching intently as I rinse my finger in cold water.

"I'm. Fine," I placate, raising an eyebrow at his overreaction.

"Let me see your damn finger," he growls, grabbing my hand from the water stream. He studies my finger. "You at least need a butterfly bandage for this. Do you have one?"

"No." Shaking my head, I pull my hand away and wrap a paper towel around the finger. "It will be okay. It's not the first time."

Scooping up the pieces of apples with my healthy hand, I take them to Alex's tray. Turning back to the kitchen, I pause. *Where the hell did he go?* Ignoring Damon's sudden absence, I move onto toasting some frozen waffles.

"Where is your first aid kit?" Damon's voice carries from my hallway.

"Damon," I groan, "my finger is—"

"Fine. I know, I heard you. Where's the kit?" he shouts over clanging and rustling.

"It's in the hallway closet."

Alex's waffle pops up, so I prepare and serve little man before he starts slamming his fists on his tray.

"Give me your hand." The screech of the barstool accompanies Damon's demand.

Damon has the kit open and items spread out in a very surgical fashion on the marble countertop. His hand extends out expectantly for mine.

"Just give me a bandage. I can put it on." I reach out, palm up.

He grabs my wrist and pulls me toward him, examining the cut and then his supplies.

"Will I lose it, Doc?" Feigning fear, I press my good hand to my chest.

He rolls his eyes in my direction and presses his lips tightly together.

"It could get infected if you don't take care of it properly."

Now it's my turn to roll my eyes.

"I've done worse to myself, and look," I hold up both hands and wiggle my fingers, "I still have them all."

Not amused, he grabs my hand back and begins cleaning out the cut before placing a bandage over the injury.

"Thank you," I mumble and pull my hand away.

"No need to thank me." Smiling, he stands and kisses my forehead before I can back away.

The gesture warms me, which irritates the shit out of me.

"Damon, you need to figure out where you're going to stay."

"I have." He cleans up the first aid kit, putting things away in better order than he found them.

"You have?" Part of me is disappointed. I quell the warm fuzzy feelings and replace them with indifference.

"Yes. I'll be staying here." First aid kit put back together, he faces me with a smile, propping his hip against the counter.

"You can't stay here," I blurt. "It's too awkward and—"

"Awkward how?" He studies me with one brow raised.

"You're my...stalker?" The answer came out more like a question. *What is wrong with me!*

Annoyance washes away the amusement from moments ago.

"I'm not a stalker." His words are hard, determined.

"Your actions have suggested otherwise," I mumble while I start cleaning up the kitchen.

"My actions only prove I am determined, especially when I know what I want."

I tense and my body warms, but not from his words. He stands so close behind me, his breath brushes over the back of my neck. His hands plant on the counter, trapping me. My traitorous body kicks into hormonal overdrive, every nerve-ending coming to life.

Inhaling deeply, the masculine smell of him almost melts my resolve. To clear my head, I clench my hand, causing the cut on my finger to throb.

"Stalker," I repeat.

"Liv," Mercedes calls, stopping short to take in Damon and my position. Her lips curl up on one side. "Am I interrupting?"

"What's up, Ced?" I take the moment of distraction to pull away from Damon.

"Uh, you have some fondant down there that Sarah's not sure what you were doing with and it's drying. She was going to put it away, but I told her I'd ask you about it first." Ced leans against the wall, her arms crossing over her chest. "I can finish up with Alex and then bring him down."

"I've got him," Damon interjects.

Releasing a breath of annoyance, I turn to him.

"He usually spends the day in the bakery with us."

Turning back to Ced, I ask, "You sure you can bring him down?"

"Yep." She straightens from the wall and slips into the kitchen. By the tightness of her lips, she's trying not to smile, still amused by the position she found us in.

As I pass by, I shoot her a glare.

Fifteen minutes after my return to the bakery, and the fondant, I hear one too many sets of feet on the stairs from the apartment.

Glancing up, Mercedes enters and Damon follows with Alex in his arms. The sounds of the bakery kitchen fall silent, everyone's eyes on Damon and Alex.

"Right here." Mercedes points out Alex's play area.

Damon takes a moment to look at the area before setting him down within the gate.

"This is set up really well," he comments and nods to Ced.

"We hired a safety specialist to create the space." Ced's eyes come to mine, though she is speaking to Damon. She gives me a wavering smile and quickly turns away.

"Up," Alex demands. My eyes go back to my son, who is currently holding his arms toward Damon. "Up," he demands again with a little hop.

Sitting down on the stool next to my worktable, I drop my forehead to the cold steel.

My own son, a traitor.

Chapter six — destination hospital
Damon

She watches everything I do as if I'm going to run away with the boy. Perhaps my methods have been a bit unconventional, but not once have I given her reason to think I would harm either of them.

"Up," Alex calls out.

Looking down, my chest squeezes tight. *He wants me. He's asking me to pick him up.* Quickly, I lift him into my arms. A feeling of contentment I haven't felt in so very long relaxes my tense muscles.

His hands press over my eyes, then pull away quickly. A large grin meets me as he shouts, "Boo!", and giggles. My own loud laugh encourages him to repeat the game he's playing.

We play the game until I catch sight of Olivia watching us. Again, she looks nervous. Ruffling Alex's hair, I give him a quick hug before placing him back in his play area. He walks over to a box full of toys and my resolve solidifies. *There's no way I'm giving this up.*

I turn back toward the kitchen. Olivia has turned her attention to a cake and no one is directly staring, though a couple sets of eyes slant in my direction every few seconds before shifting away.

For a moment, I don't know what to do with myself. There are no conference calls, board meetings, client visits, or any of my mother's demands to be concerned with. *What the hell do I do with myself?*

I'm contemplating climbing into the play area with my son when the phone in my pocket vibrates.

"Hello?" I answer, feeling lighter than I have in a year.

"Damon?" Hugh sounds unsure.

Turning from the bakery kitchen, I go back up the stairs to speak to my brother.

"Of course it is. Who else would answer my phone?"

"You don't sound like yourself," he states.

"Don't I?" I smile, knowing Alex, and even Olivia, are the reason.

"No. You actually sound... I don't know the right word for it." He pauses. "Let's just say you aren't barking hello and using your typical clipped tone."

"What can I do for you, Hugh? I'm on vacation, as you know." I follow my teasing words with a laugh.

"Now you're scaring me. Who are you and what have you done with my brother?"

"Hugh, what's the problem that couldn't wait until my return?"

"There is a complication with the Proneau Investment," he states, his voice returning to his familiar business tone.

"What complication?" I move to Olivia's living room where I've set up my laptop.

Hugh launches into the problems with Proneau. Apparently, the CFO has been accused of embezzlement.

Growling, I move my laptop to the kitchen island, push the button on my cell to activate the speaker, and begin pacing the length of the room.

"Is my mother involved?"

"Not that I know of. I haven't talked to her, but you know she has her spies around the office."

"Yes, I know. Well, if you get wind that she's meddling, let me know and I'll take care of her." Sitting on a barstool at the island, I bring up my email and start going through the documents Hugh sent.

"Did you receive the file?" Hugh breaks the short silence.

"Yes, I'm reviewing your highlights and notes now."

"So, are you with her?" Nervousness laces Hugh's question.

I sigh.

"It's not really any of your business, but yes, I am with my wife."

"Damon—"

"Don't," I warn. "I am not up for another lecture."

"I'm just concerned. Scarlett and I both think—"

"You've discussed my business with Scarlett?" Annoyance courses through me, washing out the contentment I felt just moments ago. "Why is my personal business a topic of gossip for you two?"

"It's not like that and you know it. We love and care about you, Damon." Hugh's voice raises a bit with concern. "It wasn't so long ago when you were simply trying to make it to the next day without a breakdown in your temperament. Now...now you're married to a stranger. And you've made it sound like she's your wife by force." He sighs heavily. "You cannot replace Rebecca and DJ with a new wife."

"Damn it, Hugh!" Grabbing the phone from the counter, I put it to my ear. Anger charges through my body, bringing me to my feet again. "Mind your own fucking business!" Fury seethes out of my every pore.

"Bullshit, Damon! You've been a mess since losing them. I've only just seen a scratch in the surface of who you used to be before they—"

"Shut the fuck up and listen to me, because I will only say this once, little brother." Before he can interrupt me, I continue my rant. "I am not trying to replace my son! Nothing could ever replace him or the love I have for him. And as for his poor excuse for a mother, I am definitely *not* trying to replace her."

My fingers dig into the skin just above my heart. It's beating rapidly and a vision of DJ fills my mind. Hair the color of mine, eyes a cool blue like his mother's, and his laugh...*God* his laugh.

"The hole they left when I lost them has never gone away, regardless of the head doctors you and our father thrust upon me and all the dates you and my mother attempt to set up. Nothing, except this, makes the throbbing ache ease. They make me better."

Closing my eyes, I take a deep breath.

"They?" Hugh chokes. "Damon, you didn't...I mean, you didn't marry this woman because she has a child, did you?" His frantic questioning flares my defenses back up.

"No, of course not! I found *my* son, Hugh. He's *my* son."

"What? Damon, where are you? I'm going to come get you."

He wants to fetch me home and to the asylum we will go.

Rolling my eyes, I sit back on the stool.

"I'll be back in a couple weeks. I know you don't completely understand and it's my fault for not explaining. There's no need to *collect* me or break out the straight jacket," I snort.

"Damon, please," he begs. "Don't turn me away. I want to help. You need to understand that your son is gone. He died, Damon. This boy isn't DJ."

Anger boils inside until the flesh on my face tingles from the heat of it.

"You don't fucking think I know that?! Christ, Hugh, you're not the one who has spent the past years running from memories." I slam my fist onto the counter. "I have! I know DJ is...gone. But Alex is alive and magnificent."

"Who is Alex, Damon?" Hugh's voice calms, trying to soothe the crazy by using one of the many tactics the doctors taught my family. This question is designed to show me the difference between real and delusion.

"He's my son, Hugh. The woman I married gave birth to my biological son," I explain as clear as I can.

"You...you had an affair?" He coughs. "When did you...how...?"

I can't help but laugh.

"I didn't have an affair. More like fate dealing me a second chance to be alive again."

"What the hell are you talking about?" Defeat weakens his voice. "Just tell me where you are, Damon."

"I'm with my family." As I answer, the sound of walking catches my attention.

I glance over my left shoulder with the phone still to my ear as Hugh rambles on about needing an explanation. Olivia is standing in the room looking at me from under her furrowed brow.

"I need to go." I cut off Hugh's diatribe. "I will call you later after I've looked over the Proneau situation." I hang up on Hugh's protest and slide my phone back onto the counter.

"We need to talk." She walks stiffly, standing in front of me with her arms defensively crossed over her chest.

"Alright." I turn around on the stool, facing my body toward her.

"You need to find somewhere to stay. I can't...I'm not comfortable with you being here."

Her eyes roam over my face, searching for my reaction. I know she's waiting for my temper to flare, but nothing can kill the happiness brought back to me today by Alex. And while I'm happy and content, there will be no leaving.

With one brow raised, I purse my lips in feigned contemplation.

"No." I shake my head.

"No?" The exasperation is evident in her question.

Standing, I walk toward her. She backs up until she's next to the chair in the living room. I pass by her, close enough to brush my arm against hers, and sit on the couch. She turns to face me.

"That's what I said." Sighing, I lean forward, placing my elbows on my knees. "I can only be here for a couple weeks and I want as much time as possible together."

Relief washes over her face.

"So, you're leaving in a couple weeks?"

I don't like the hopefulness of her question.

"Yes, however, I would like for you and Alex to join me." I raise my hand, stopping her protest. "I want you both to meet my family and see what New York has to offer."

"No," she answers, giving me a *go ahead, argue with me* look.

"No?" My frustration begins running higher, leaking into my words.

"That's what I said." She kicks my words back at me.

Narrowing my eyes, I sit up straight and frown.

"You won't allow me to introduce Alex to *his* family?"

She sighs and walks around, slouching into the chair across from me.

"Damon, I said I would allow you to know Alex. You know I won't go to meet your family. And you should realize I won't allow you to take Alex either."

Allow me? She won't allow me to introduce my son to his family?!

I inhale deeply and exhale the large breath, hoping it will quell some of my anger.

"My family will meet my son and I will take him to meet them."

"I want proof you're really his father," she snaps, sitting up straight on the edge of the chair. Her hands grip the arms of the chair so tight, her knuckles turn white.

"You want a paternity test?" I smirk.

"Damn straight I do. Like I'll just take your word as fact. We both know you have deceitful tendencies," she sneers.

I can't keep my laughter at bay.

"Oh, Olivia, if you think I'm lying and this is the way to rid yourself of me, you are sadly mistaken."

Her body tenses at my words.

"Ah, so that's what you're hoping for?" I ask, rhetorically.

Standing from the couch, I walk to my phone and put it to my ear.

"What are you doing?" She pushes out of the chair and stands.

Putting up a finger, I silence her while I wait for my call to be answered.

"Damon?" His voice is as professional as always.

"Good afternoon, Father. I need to ask a favor."

"Of course, what can I do for you?" He sounds distracted. Maybe I interrupted him during his rounds.

"Can you call in a favor from a doctor in Pittsburgh? I need a blood test." My eyes meet Olivia's anxious, wide eyes.

"A blood test? Are you okay? Did something happen?" Going into full doctor mode, Dr. Knyght has taken the place of my father.

"Everything is fine, I assure you. Actually, it's quite better than fine." I keep my eyes locked on Olivia's. "I need a paternity test done. Today would be great, if we can."

"Damon..." Olivia hisses from her gaped mouth.

"A, uh, um...a paternity test, you say?" Confusion is quickly replaced by intrigue. "Is there something I should know about?"

"Well, pending the unnecessary test results, congratulations, you're a grandfather."

"Damon," his voice now matches the same concern Hugh had.

"Can you call in the favor for me or not?"

"Yes, I can, but I think you need to explain."

"I will, and once she is satisfied with the results, you will meet him as well."

I raise a challenging brow at her. She purses her lips in anger.

"You aren't taking him anywhere," she grumbles, her hands going to her hips.

I grin.

"Very well. Let me make a couple calls and I'll let you know what I can arrange." My father is still confused, but will be patient for an explanation.

"Great. Thank you."

"I will talk with you *soon*," he replies, accentuating the last word.

"Sounds good."

Hanging up from the call, I drop the phone back to the counter.

"Once you have your proof, because we both know it will be a match, you will both come with me to New York and meet my family."

"We are not going to New York. I have a business to run." She glares.

"You have a couple weeks to make arrangements. I'm sure you can leave for a couple of days." I step closer, until she's only an arm's length from me. "Please?"

"I..." she falters. "This is never going to work. Please, just let us go. We wouldn't even matter if..." She quickly stops, her eyes widening as she bites her bottom lip.

"Go ahead, say it," I urge, narrowing my eyes.

"Nevermind." She shakes her head. "I didn't mean to—"

"You wouldn't matter if they weren't dead, right?" I finish for her. Keeping my anger under control is practically impossible.

Her eyes, wide as saucers, stay fixed on mine when she gives a short nod.

"They were already gone," I growl.

"But if they weren't, then you wouldn't be sitting here right now," she argues. "Alex and I wouldn't matter."

"You don't know that," I growl. "How do you know anything about my marriage?"

Her mouth opens, but then snaps shut.

"Exactly, you don't. You have no idea, so don't presume if they were still here, alive, that I wouldn't be standing exactly in this spot."

Defeated, she sinks down into the chair, closing her eyes.

"I know what you're trying to do." I wait for her to look at me again. "You're trying to make me lose interest, but that isn't going to happen. I'll never know for sure how this situation would play out if they were still here, but I'm pretty certain my interest would be just as fierce."

"We aren't them," she whispers.

"I don't want you to be them." Dropping to the floor, I kneel before her.

"You don't realize—"

"I know you aren't them."

"I don't think you do." Shaking her head, she continues. "Have you considered talking to someone about this obsession?"

"I've talked to a lot of people," I answer honestly.

"About this?" She motions between us.

"Sort of." I tilt my head. "I discussed this situation with my current doctor. He's well aware of the letter I received and my plans to look into it."

"It's not healthy, Damon. *This* isn't healthy," she states, her voice taking on a soothing tone.

"Did you even consider that you, both of you, are the only thing keeping me sane?"

Her eyes stare into mine as my admittance registers. Her mouth gapes open, but then closes.

"After they...died, I had a breakdown. I was distraught and angry."

"Angry at whom?"

"Myself, Rebecca, God. You name it, I was angry at it." Rubbing my chest, I try to ease the familiar twinge.

"It wasn't your fault. It was an accident," she whispers, our eyes still locked.

"Yes, it was. I wasn't driving, but I should have been." Tears sting the back of my eyes. "I, at least, should have protected DJ."

"Protected him?" Confusion wrinkles her face.

"From the accident. It wasn't... they shouldn't have been out. *She* shouldn't have had him out." Anger begins to burn in my chest, replacing the twinge. Dropping my head, I close my eyes and try to take calming breaths.

Olivia remains quiet, giving me time to collect myself.

"We aren't the answer to the guilt you feel," she says a few moments later, breaking the silence.

I clench my fists and turn my blazing eyes on her.

"Why can't you understand that you and Alex are not about guilt or replacement?" My voice rises. "The two of you are my sanity in this life I'm left to live. *You* are my happiness."

"I don't want that responsibility." Shaking her head, she remains stern against my anger.

"You don't have to do anything, but be with me. Try." My words taper to desperation.

"You need to get help. I'm not a remedy or anyone's sanity. Alex and I are not a bandage for your sadness."

Anger brings me to my feet and I begin to pace.

"You are not a God damned bandage! You make me better. You and Alex make me feel goodness. And I know you feel the connection between us. It's been obvious since that first night in front of the damn chapel in Vegas that—"

She jumps to her feet.

"That I was deliriously drunk and taken with an extremely attractive man! That is all that's obvious."

At my quick approach, she flinches back. Lifting my hand, I cup her face and pull her to look at me.

"I would never, ever, hurt you," I whisper against her lips before pressing mine to hers firmly.

Fire ripples through my body. From my lips to my toes, lust courses in every vein as her body presses to mine. Pulling back, I look down into her face.

"I know you feel that. You have to." Staring into her eyes, there's a moment when I think she's going to give in.

My phone breaks the silence, vibrating across the counter.

"Fuck," I growl, releasing Olivia and retrieving the phone. "Hello," I bark.

"Well, your mood has soured," my father responds with distaste. "Anyhow, if you can get to UPMC by three today, then you can meet with Dr. Fillman. He'll escort you to the lab and rush the test."

"How long for the results?" I question my father, but turn to look at Olivia.

Back in the oversized chair, she keeps her eyes away from me.

"I would say about two days, maybe."

"We can't get it any quicker than—"

"This isn't a pregnancy test, Damon. This is DNA testing. It takes a little more time." He's clearly annoyed with me now.

"I understand."

"Well, Dr. Fillman will draw the blood and saliva samples."

"Okay."

"Alright. I expect to hear from you soon with an explanation." He pauses, taking an audible breath. "You should probably tell your mother before—"

"She already knows."

He gasps.

"You...she...but you didn't feel the need to tell me?"

I don't need the divorced parent hurt feelings right now.

"Dad, thank you for helping. I appreciate the favor. And Mother knows because she knew before I did."

"Well, I expect to hear from you."

"Of course, I promise."

We say our goodbyes and I look at the time. I turn to Olivia and she finally looks up at me.

"We need to be at the hospital before three."

"For the test?" She begins fidgeting.

"Yes. This is what you wanted."

"I figured it would take time to get an appointment for—"

"I have connections, remember?"

"Unfortunately, I know all too well about your connections, don't I?" she grumbles, but there's a small curve at the corner of her mouth.

Standing from the chair, she looks at me briefly before walking away.

I want so badly to go back to the moment before my father's call. But the sound of her feet on the stairs tells me the moment is gone and our conversation is over — for now.

An hour later, I'm sitting at the island, working on my laptop, when Olivia and Alex enter. Abandoning the email I was typing, I watch Olivia in action.

She places Alex into his chair before moving about the kitchen. While she searches in a cabinet, I turn to Alex and give a small wave. He smiles and lifts his hand before slamming it down onto his tray.

"Momma," he calls out.

Olivia stops, looks around the cabinet door, and smiles. "Yes, sir?"

He smacks his tray again.

"Hold your horses, mister."

She pulls a jar from the cabinet and twists off the lid as she returns to him. With a small spoon, she scoops a chunky orange food onto his tray.

Alex sticks his fingers into the paste before shoving them into his mouth and sucking. *Carrots. That's what it is. Baby food.*

Olivia sits a small bowl and spoon on his tray before taking a seat in front of him. Alex tries to feed himself for a couple minutes, until she picks up a second spoon and helps get some of it into his mouth.

They're beautiful. So beautiful. They heal my wounds, balm my soul, make me feel alive again. She and Alex have replaced the meaningless nothing and anger. She needs to know, to understand.

I open my mouth to tell her when Mercedes interrupts. Her vibrant hair, makeup, and dress brighten the room.

"Liv?"

Olivia turns in the chair. Mercedes walks until she stands next to me at the island.

"There is a consult that will only speak to you downstairs." Mercedes rolls her eyes.

"Okay, um, they're going to have to wait until I finish."

"I'll watch him," I blurt as I stand and walk toward Alex's chair.

"That's so thoughtful." Mercedes gives a sarcastic smile before turning to Olivia. "I'll finish."

Olivia stands to go, handing Mercedes the spoon.

92

"I'm starting to get offended," I growl.

"Says the crazy stalker," Olivia practically sings as she leaves.

"I'm not a stalker," I grumble, sitting back on the stool and going back to my email.

"What was that?" Mercedes asks from where Olivia sat minutes ago.

"Nothing," I murmur.

Mercedes pulling Alex from his chair takes my attention away from the contract proposal I'm reviewing.

She wipes him down with a large washcloth before picking him up and carrying him out of the kitchen.

I wait to hear her walk down the steps, but instead, I hear a door. Turning at the steps coming back, I lock eyes with Mercedes.

"Where's Alex?"

"It's his naptime." She shrugs and gives a small smile.

With the same cloth, she starts wiping down the tray and chair.

"Have you always been here for her?"

My question catches Mercedes off guard for some reason. She nods.

"They're the only family I have."

There's a touch of sadness in her eyes, but I don't pry. I have another question on my mind.

"Why did she have Alex the way she did?"

Mercedes tilts her head, confused.

"You know, instead of with a boyfriend or husband?"

Realization rounds her eyes.

"That's Olivia's tale to tell."

Nodding, I respect her loyalty to Olivia.

I keep to myself the rest of the time Mercedes cleans up before heading back to the bakery.

A half hour passes before I hear footsteps again. When no one enters the living space, I climb off the stool and look down the hall. No one.

"Hello? Olivia?" I whisper, not wanting to wake Alex.

With no response, I walk down the hall and look in on him.

Jesus, he's beautiful.

Leaning back out of his room, I pull the door closed, and then continue down the hall toward Olivia's room.

Her door is open a couple of inches, so I peek inside.

From the mirror over her dresser, I can see Olivia curled up in her bed. *Must be naptime for her as well.* The urge to be close to her comes over me and it's too powerful to fight.

Pushing open the door, I step silently to her bed. Her even breaths assure me she's asleep.

Standing at the edge of her bed, I look over her. *What I would give to be able to crawl in next to her, to hold her, or to know she wanted me to do it.* Closing my eyes, I let my imagination run wild.

Eventually, I talk myself out of climbing into the bed and leave. I go back to my laptop and call Hugh to discuss the Proneau deal. He doesn't press any further about things, but I know I haven't heard the last from him or our father. In fact, I'm sure they already spoke to each other. *Worse than damn gossiping women.*

Around one in the afternoon, sounds of dresser drawers, doors, and water running echo down the hall from Olivia's room. Taking that as my cue, I put away my laptop and papers so I, too, can get dressed for the trip to the hospital.

I strip out of my clothes and pile them at the end of the guest room bed. While I wait for the water to turn off in Olivia's bathroom, I pull out a pair of dark jeans and a blue, striped V-neck sweater.

The shower quiets and my imagination runs wild, picturing her long, lean leg slowly slipping out. Still wet and flush from the warm water, tiny goose bumps covering her skin from the change in temperature. As if in slow motion, the rest of her abandons the steamy shower.

"Momma!" Alex calls, jerking me from my fantasy. "Momma!"

The squeak of his mattress hopping brings a smile to my face, but makes my chest ache.

She doesn't want him to call me dad, but once this test is complete and he's proven to be mine, it will be the end of that demand. *How I long to hear dad fall from his perfect little mouth.*

Emerging from the spare bedroom, showered, shaved, dried, and dressed, I watch Olivia buzz around the apartment, gathering different items into a blue backpack.

"Bye, bye." Alex's words draw my attention to him playing on the floor.

His bright eyes are on me. A smile deepens the dimples on each of his cheeks.

I smile back before turning my attention to Olivia.

"Is there any way I can help?"

"No thanks. You would just get in my way." She slips the backpack on before grabbing a folded up stroller hanging on a hook by the door. "We need to get going in order to make it to the bus stop in time."

"Bus stop?" I ask.

"Yeah, I don't have a personal car." She shrugs.

"I have a car," I state, putting on my jacket and taking the keys from the pocket.

"You don't have to drive."

"We're taking the car. Stop being stubborn."

Taking a couple steps, I reach down and pick Alex up. Olivia quickly appears, taking him from me.

"I wish you wouldn't be so worried about me touching him. I'm not going to hurt him. Ever."

"He needs his coat," she snaps.

Olivia opens a closet and pulls out a small green coat. With the door open, I can see a car seat stored on the floor just inside. In two quick strides, I'm at the door, pulling the seat out. Her head snaps to me, watching my actions.

"I'll just go install the seat and warm the car."

Without giving her a chance to say anything else, I walk out the door. Commotion from the stairs draws my attention and I quickly go to them.

"Here, let me take that." I grab the stroller and bag from her full arms.

She tenses for a moment, but allows me to take the items. While I load the things into the back, she buckles Alex into his seat.

"You ready to go bye-byes?" Olivia coos.

"Bye, bye," Alex giggles, opening and closing his fist at Olivia and then me. She laughs. My heart thunders behind my ribs. *I can't wait to have this all the time, every day.* I shift my eyes to Olivia, who's climbing into the passenger seat. *There is no stopping me after this test. Not when it will irrefutably tell her Alex is my son and both of them are mine — till death do us part.*

Arriving at the hospital, Olivia quickly exits the car and gets Alex from the backseat. I climb out and retrieve the backpack.

"Do we need the stroller?" I ask Olivia over the roof of the car.

She shakes her head. "I don't think so."

Once inside, we're instructed to follow a yellow line on the floor leading to the lab.

Reaching the small lab waiting room, a nurse pages Dr. Fillman, registers us, and secures plastic hospital bands around both my and Alex's wrist.

Sitting in the empty room, silence looms, like we're awaiting execution. Olivia's foot shakes, nervously. Her cheek is pressed to the top of Alex's head as he sits calmly in her lap and her fingers twist together in painful looking contortions.

"Are you okay?" I ask just above a whisper.

Her head lifts, revealing watery eyes.

"He's going to cry." She takes a deep breath. "I hate that part."

Frowning, I hadn't thought about Alex's reaction to the needle.

"Mr. Knyght?" A large, round man in green scrubs stands in a doorway across from us, his hand out in greeting.

"Dr. Fillman?" I ask, standing and taking his hand as he nods.

"You're the image of your mother, aren't you?" He grins large, his eyes twinkling.

Feeling uncomfortable by the comparison, I clear my throat. I'm well aware of the resemblance I hold to my mother, but I strive to be nothing like the cold, meddlesome, overbearing monarch in my family.

Dr. Fillman holds a door open. "This way, please."

Olivia follows the doctor and I follow her and Alex. Once in the cream and pale green room, I see syringes lying on the counter.

"Dr. Fillman?" I wait until he looks at me. "Is it possible to do the mouth swab test without the blood testing? It would still be an accurate result, correct?"

He nods.

"Yes, if that's what you prefer. Your father stated—"

"Dr. Knyght is nothing if not thorough," I chuckle.

The doctor grins and nods in agreement.

"I think, for Alex's sake, we should just do the swabbing."

"Of course." Dr. Fillman turns back to the counter and begins pulling out three plastic baggies.

I glance to Olivia and my heart skips about five beats. The smile she is giving me warms my chest. When she mouths, "Thank you," I want to press my lips to hers.

The snap of plastic pulls both our attention back to the doctor. He approaches me with a long cotton swab in his latex gloved hand.

"Open up."

Resting his fingers against my face, he inserts the swab, rubbing firmly against the inside of my cheek and gum line. It's a bit uncomfortable, but there's no pain.

He pulls the swab out and slips it into a plastic tube. Sealing it in tight, he wraps a label around the tube and writes a few things on the side in dark red before stuffing the tube into one of the plastic baggies.

Dr. Fillman preps the next swab, tube, and changes his gloves.

"Next." He turns to Olivia. "Let's show this little guy how it's done, okay, Mommy?"

Olivia nods, opens her mouth, and goes through the same process I did moments before.

"Okay, we saved the best for last." The doctor smiles at Alex, who buries his face in Olivia's chest.

"You may want to hold his arms while I secure his chin. Most children don't like the swabbing, but it doesn't hurt."

Olivia nods.

"Hey there, big boy. Can you look at me and say 'ahh' really, really loud?"

Alex squirms in Olivia's arms, but she holds tight and Dr. Fillman is able to secure his chin. When the swabbing is complete, the doctor studies Alex for a moment.

"Who is questioning paternity?" His eyes land on me.

We both stay silent, but I can't keep my lips from curling up just a bit at the corners.

Olivia sighs and the doctor smiles and nods.

"He really is a perfect mixture of the both of you."

No longer fighting it, I grin wide. Olivia scowls.

"So, my father said it would take about two days for results?"

Dr. Fillman nods. "Yes, I'll put a rush on the lab work and get the preliminary results back as quickly as possible." He begins to chuckle. "Though, I don't think you should doubt he's your son, Damon."

"Oh, I don't," I say firmly.

The doctor's eyes widen and move to Olivia, who blushes.

"Oh," is the only response he provides before signing our release papers and saying his goodbyes.

"You still need the test?" I ask as we exit the lab.

"Shut up," she growls.

My smile remains until we are back in the car and on our way to the apartment.

"Would you like to go out to dinner tonight?" I know I'm pushing it. After the stress of the day for her, I'm pretty sure the last thing she wants is to be out with me.

She gives her head a shake. "No, thank you."

"Olivia, please allow me to get you two something to eat. You need to eat."

"I need to get back to the shop." She keeps her eyes focused on the road before us.

Taking a deep breath, I try one more time.

"I realize you're upset, nervous, and mostly annoyed, but I'm only asking to get something to eat."

She remains silent as we stop at a red light. When she still shows no signs of responding, I turn in the opposite direction of the apartment.

"Where are you going?" she snaps. "I said I need to get back."

Turning in the front seat, she now faces me.

"You need to eat. I think we should go somewhere neutral to talk over dinner."

Keeping my eyes on the road, I continue to scout for a decent restaurant.

"Damon, don't do this. Not right now. Today has been emotional enough."

Parking at the curb in front of an Italian restaurant, I climb out and round the car quickly to open Olivia's door.

She just sits there, unmoving.

"Please?" I beg.

With a sigh, she exits the passenger seat. I move to the backseat, open the door, and get Alex from his seat.

"I can take him." She stretches her arms toward me.

"He's fine."

Her brow furrows as her arms slowly drop.

"I've got him. Quit acting like I'm going to harm him. I'm his father."

"I asked you not to—"

98

"When that test returns positive, and we both know it will, he will know I'm his father. I won't allow my son to grow up thinking he doesn't have one, no matter what you consider to be good enough reasons."

Before she can further argue, I start walking toward the restaurant. The sound of a slamming car door fills the air behind me before she catches up to us.

Once Alex is secured in a highchair, Olivia and I sit across from each other in a booth. Digging through the backpack, she pulls out some toys and lays them before him. A moment later, Alex starts banging plastic cars against the tray.

"Alex, honey, no, no." Olivia shakes her head, placing a hand on the one doing the banging. Like the good kid he is, he stops. Turning her attention to me, Olivia's face is lined with seriousness. "So, this is neutral territory, what do you want to discuss?"

"You know what we need to discuss."

"We've already covered quite a few things, so I'm not exactly sure what you want to talk about now." She rests against the back of the booth, her arms crossed over her chest.

"I want my name on his birth certificate once the results are back." Leaning forward, I bring my elbows to the table and fold my hands together. "With the confirmation, I can have my lawyers file the paperwork to update the document," I add before she can start protesting.

Just as Olivia's mouth pops open, the waitress arrives and requests drink orders. The minute the young girl walks away, Olivia snaps her head in my direction.

"No."

"Why?"

"You weren't even supposed to be...around. I was ensured confidentiality and anonymity. You've broken all of that. There isn't supposed to be a *you* in his life."

As soon as she finishes, I launch my counter argument.

"But I am around. So things have changed. And—"

The waitress returns with my iced tea and Olivia's water, requesting dinner orders. When she walks away once more, I continue before Olivia can interrupt.

"And I signed documents of confidentiality as well, assuming those same documents would ensure the safety of my sperm." Mimicking her position, I sit back in the booth, crossing my arms over my chest.

"I didn't ask for your...sperm. I requested an anonymous donor's profile," she snaps.

"Neither of us asked for the situation. However, it happened and I wish to be around."

"I didn't ask for you to be around."

"You married me." I smile, giving a one shoulder shrug.

"Under the influence," she blurts, a little too loudly.

"Regardless, I am Alex's father. I want to be a part of my son's life."

"You can be a part of his life, but that doesn't mean you get to be his father." Her voice drops to a hush.

"Why would you deny him a father?" Furrowing my brow, I search her face. I don't understand why she is so determined to keep him from a father.

"It wasn't supposed to be like this," she groans, covering her face with her hands.

"Did you ever stop to think that maybe it *is* supposed to be like this?"

She peeks at me through her fingers. "Are you talking about fate?"

I nod.

"This is a very big and very unacceptable medical mix up. Don't spout fate and meant-to-be prose at me." Dropping her hands to the table, she leans forward, letting it carry part of her weight. "I only wanted him." She looks to Alex, who is now making car sounds and pushing the toy around the tray.

"And I want to be his father."

Huffing, she slumps back into the booth.

"*If* I allow you to be in his life as his father, will you sign the annulment papers?" She raises one brow in challenge.

"No," I growl.

With a sigh of defeat, her shoulders drop. "Why? I'm giving you the opportunity to be his father, officially. All you have to do is agree to end this." She motions between us.

"I want both of you in my life. You would never allow me into your life if we weren't together. You would only treat me as 'Alex's father'. I don't want to be compartmentalized in your life." Elbows back on the table, I lean forward, making sure her gaze is locked with mine. "I want to be more than that, for both of you."

I settle back into my seat when the food arrives. We eat in silence, except for Olivia talking to Alex and her mumbled thank you to me when we leave the restaurant.

The car ride is also silent, aside from Alex playing in the back seat. Once we arrive back to the apartment, Olivia heads to the bakery with Alex in her arms. I settle onto the couch for about twenty minutes before following down to the kitchen.

Halfway down the stairs, I hear the music playing. When I reach the last step, I see Olivia working at a stainless steel table. Only Olivia. The kitchen is empty. Taking a step in her direction, a hand with multi-colored fingernails grips my arm, stopping me.

"Let her be." Mercedes gives a small smile.

I look back at Olivia and sigh.

"When she's stressed or in an emotional state, this is what she does." Mercedes answers my unasked question.

Standing stock-still, I watch her fluid movements around the table.

"She's almost dancing," I whisper.

"It's her element," Mercedes responds.

Alex whimpers and then cries from behind me. Turning, I see him reaching toward Mercedes and me from his play area.

"I'll take him upstairs." Mercedes quickly lifts him from the gated area.

"But you were just about to leave." Olivia wipes her hands on an apron.

"Go ahead and work on whatever you're doing. I can take him upstairs. I don't have any plans this evening." Mercedes disappears up the staircase.

When I turn back to Olivia, she is once again focused on her creation.

It isn't until I'm close enough to smell the buttery vanilla cloud surrounding her that I realize how close I've walked toward her. Licking my lips, I press the front of my body to the back of hers. She gasps and straightens. In a swift motion, before she can turn around, I swipe stray hairs from her neck and latch my mouth onto her skin. The taste of her explodes on my tongue and I murmur against her skin.

"You taste like buttercream and vanilla."

Chapter seven — Let's make a deal
Olivia

The moan slips out before I can stop myself. His lips bring back memories of exactly how talented his mouth can be. His hands slip over my hips, pulling me closer, letting me feel every warm aroused inch of his body. When his tongue grazes the crook of my neck, I inhale sharply.

"I could taste you all day long," Damon groans, rubbing his body against mine.

The sound of his voice, though muffled by my skin, snaps me back to the reality of our situation. Pushing away, I spin. In a flash, my palm connects with his cheek.

"What the fuck, Olivia?" he yells, cupping his face.

"I should ask you that question," I shout. "What do you think you're doing?"

Narrowing his eyes, he drops his hand from his face. "You enjoyed it."

"You don't get to touch me," I growl.

"I'm your husband. You are my wife."

Shaking my head, I shout, "It doesn't matter what some paper says! You don't touch me unless I say you can, do you understand me?"

Damon's jaw unclenches and the hardness melts into a softer, apologetic expression.

"I apologize. Never again without your permission, I swear." His eyes search my face for what feels like hours before he turns and walks away. "Good night, Olivia."

The instant he's gone, I exhale and lean forward, palms down, on the table. My deep breaths don't stop the spasm that rocks my body. My chest heaves and tears trail down my cheeks. Collapsing to my knees on the floor, a sob rips from my soul and out of my mouth.

It's too much. It's all too much. I'm not supposed to react — to want — the man who shouldn't be here. A man who is invading every part of my life.

"Shh," Mercedes consoles, taking a seat on the floor beside me. Wrapping her arms around me, she rocks us. "Calm down, honey. It will all work out, I promise."

"No, no it won't, Ced," I sob. "I've messed everything up. He'll never leave us alone."

"Come on, Liv. It will all be fine."

She holds me until I calm and then helps me up the stairs and into my room. Ced excuses herself to clean up the kitchen and lets me shower.

Pressing my palms into the white tile with my head bowed, I revel in the hot spray hitting the back of my neck and running over my exhausted body. The hope of hot water therapy helping me process everything is proven to be a lost cause. Stepping from the shower, my mind still swirls like it's stuck on the tilt-o-whirl ride at a carnival. Once dry and in pajamas, I throw myself into bed, letting the exhaustion take over.

The next morning, I wake to cramps. Groaning, I roll out of the bed and go to the bathroom. Low and behold, Aunt Flow is visiting. Cleaning up, I slip into menstrual approved comfy clothing. As I dress, I realize the time. I haven't heard Alex. Panic grips my chest and I dart for his room.

Empty. My chest heaves and I lunge toward sounds in the kitchen.

Alex is sitting in his highchair, shoveling handfuls of scrambled eggs into his mouth. Damon stands at the stove, his broad shoulders encased in a simple white t-shirt. Unable to stop myself, I take in the line of his tall, fit body, paying extra attention to his spectacular ass covered in gray sweatpants.

Internally groaning at my behavior and thoughts, I look back to Alex, who finally notices me.

"Momma!" he calls out.

I grin at my beautiful boy.

"Hungry?" Damon's question draws my attention back to him.

He stands on the other side of the island with a plate of eggs, bacon, and toast held out to me. I start to decline when he places it onto the counter between us and shoves it closer.

"It's just eggs, Olivia. I'm not asking for your soul." He motions to the plate. "Go on, I'm working on mine now." He turns back to the stove.

"Thank you," I speak softly.

Taking the plate to the table, I sit next to Alex. Damon joins us, sitting across from me. As we eat, I feel his eyes on me.

"Why didn't I hear Alex this morning?" I question, my fork dangling from my fingers against my plate. I finally look at Damon.

He clears his throat.

"I was already awake." He shrugs and reaches for his glass of orange juice. "I heard him moving around, so I checked on him. He was awake, so I brought him out here, watched cartoons, and then began breakfast when he got a bit fussy." Putting the glass to his lips, he keeps his eyes on mine while he drinks.

I'm not sure why it's such a sexy act, but it's doing crazy things to me.

"And my alarm clock?" Taking a bite, I raise a brow at him, holding the eye contact. *Am I flirting with him?* I quickly drop my eyes to my plate.

"You needed sleep."

I look back up at him.

"I have a business to run," I counter, coldly.

He sighs, running a hand through his hair.

"Mercedes arrived early and said she could take charge of things downstairs."

"It's my responsibility, Damon. Not Mercedes'. And it's not your decision to make." Standing, I walk my plate to the sink.

Taking a deep breath, I walk back to clean Alex up for the morning. Damon's hand lightly grips mine.

"Please?" he pleads. "Please, let Alex stay up here with me."

Seeing the emotion swimming in his eyes, I cave. With a defeated sigh, I nod in approval.

"Thank you, Olivia. I appreciate it." He raises my hand to his lips and kisses my knuckles.

I jerk my hand away, the pleasure of the simple act shocking my entire being. Fearing he will see the effect he has, I kiss Alex and hurry to the bakery.

For the next two days, I attempt to 'race' Damon to Alex in the morning. I fail each time. By day three, I forgo trying and go with what is now the morning routine. Damon takes care of Alex, he makes us breakfast, and I return to the kitchen down in the bakery.

Sarah and Mercedes aren't shy about the looks they've been giving me or the small smiles playing on their lips. I ignore them, not ready to address how things have evolved.

"Liv," Mercedes shouts from her office.

"Yo," I shout back, my attention still focused on the pale green piping.

"Felicity is on the phone. She needs to discuss some details for an upcoming wedding she's taken on," Mercedes shouts again.

"Get a time to call her back. I've gotta finish this detailing."

After twenty minutes of piping, I enter Mercedes' office, working the kinks out of my fingers and wrist.

"Can you dial Felicity for me?" I sit into the chair before her desk and hold out my hand for the cordless.

"It's ringing." She hands it to me.

"Hello?" Felicity's voice chimes.

"Hey, Felicity, it's Liv. What's up?" I cradle the phone between my ear and shoulder as I pick food coloring out from under my nails.

"Hey, lady, where the hell have you been? I tried to call you a few days ago and texted you," she scolds.

"Sorry, I've been going through some...things," I explain.

"Still married to the stalker?" She giggles.

"Not funny," I groan.

"Shit, you're still dealing with him? Jim-a-nee-Christmas! Didn't Alfonso work that out for you?" she asks, concern lacing her voice.

"He did, but resolving the situation has become a bit more difficult and I'm trying to do it without too much legal involvement." I sigh. "It's a long story."

"One you are going to need to tell me over drinks. So, let's make that happen soon, okay?"

"Okay, name the night."

"How about tomorrow night? Lorna and I don't have plans."

"Lorna and you, huh? Well, well, well, Felicity Valiente, what have you been up to? Are you getting serious with Miss Lorna?" I giggle.

Mercedes comes over to me and presses her ear to the phone to listen in on the response.

"I told you about her." Felicity acts casual.

"So, how serious is this 'thing'?" I tease.

"Looks like you will have to meet me tomorrow night and find out," she quips. "Now, back to wedding business, I have a new client."

"Lame!" Mercedes shouts at the phone before returning to her chair.

"Tell her to come with," Felicity responds.

"Will do. Now, tell me about this client." Grabbing the clipboard Mercedes holds out, I take a pen from her desk and get ready to write down the information.

"I have a mother who contacted me on behalf of her daughter. She's helping arrange the wedding since the daughter lives in New York."

I stiffen at the mention of New York, but push away thoughts of Damon so I can focus on the order.

"So, the mother is apparently acting as the bride's surrogate planner. Lucky me," Felicity grumbles. "Anyhow, they will be coming to Pittsburgh in six months to get married and I'm hoping my favorite custom cake maker will be so kind as to schedule us a consult."

"Good luck with that," I snort.

"Olivia Harlow, you damn well know I'm talking about you! Smartass!" Felicity shouts.

"Oh, I know, but good luck getting an appointment," I tease, again.

"Come on, Liv," Felicity whines. "Don't make me beg."

"But it's so hot when you beg," I giggle.

"Liv," she continues to whine.

"Okay, for you, darling, of course." I drawl out darling.

"Thank you! I will let the bride...well, the mother, know. And try to keep some extra time open for this one. It's looking to be a mighty tall order, as far as weddings go," she adds before we confirm our dinner plans and hang up.

The rest of the day goes by smoothly until I get back upstairs.

"Do you have a fax machine?" Damon asks as soon as I step into the living area.

Ignoring his question, I look around for Alex. "Where is—?"

Before I finish my question, Damon points to the floor next to him.

Taking a couple steps closer and looking over my coffee table strewn with Damon's papers and such, I see Alex sitting on the floor with his back against Damon's leg.

"What does he have?" Worried, since it looks like a cell phone, I walk quickly around the table.

"It's just my Blackberry," Damon responds.

I look up as he shrugs.

"He can play with it."

"But what if he—?"

"He has already called two people." He shrugs again. "I assume you have a fax."

I nod, amazed at his lack of concern over his phone.

"What's the number?"

As I spout off the number for the fax machine in Mercedes' office, he puts an iPhone up to his ear and starts making calls. *How many cell phones does he need?*

"I'm going to go start dinner," I mumble, walking to the kitchen.

"I already ordered Italian from the restaurant down the street."

I turn toward Damon's announcement. He stands with Alex in his arms.

"It should be here soon."

"Momma!" Alex shouts, reaching his arms out to me.

My chest warms and my heart skips a beat. Taking a couple steps, I reach out and take Alex into my arms, hugging him tightly to my chest. He squirms under the pressure of my embrace and I relax my hold.

"Where's your machine?"

"It's down in Mercedes' office." I look toward Damon when I respond. He's already started down the hallway. "Why?"

He doesn't respond, only disappears.

I place Alex in his highchair, getting him ready for dinner.

"Did you have fun today?" Smiling, I pinch his cheek.

"Momma," he giggles.

Ruffling his hair, I lean forward and kiss the top of his head. "I love you so much, little guy."

"Mon," Alex calls out.

"What?" I wrinkle my brow, confused.

"He calls me Mon." Damon's smooth voice sends tingles across my skin.

I turn toward his voice.

"I..." I don't know what to say.

Damon ignores my speechlessness and holds out the fax for me to take.

"I think we both know what these will say, but I assume you want to see the official results for yourself." His crooked smile does bad, bad, wonderful things to me.

Damn him!

"What are...?" When I see the bold print in the top left corner of the page, I swallow hard. The possibility of hyperventilation swarms over me as I look at Damon, who's still smiling. I look back down to the black and white evidence in my hand.

Parentage Testing Procedure Report
Report for Case AHarlow262.619

I take a long breath in through my nose.

DNA Solutions has undertaken a parentage testing procedure using DNA testing methods on the bodily samples identified to us as:

Alleged Father: Damon Patrick Knyght

Child: Alexander Isaac Harlow

Mother: Olivia Jean Harlow

Tests using DNA technology were carried out on the DNA extracted from the samples, analyzing multiple short tandem repeat (STR) regions of the DNA. The following results were found for each of these tested regions:

STR REGION - RESULT
D5S818 — MATCH
D18S51 — MATCH
vWA — MATCH
D3S1358 — MATCH
CSF1P0 — MATCH
D21S11 — MATCH
D13S317 — MATCH
TPOX — MATCH

D2S1338 — MATCH
D8S1179 — MATCH
D16S539 — MATCH
AMELOGENIN — MATCH
ACTBP2 (SE33) — MATCH
D6S366 — MATCH
D1S1656 — MATCH
D22S1045 — MATCH

DNA Solutions reports that the results of the parentage testing procedure carried out on the bodily samples of the donors specified above show that Damon Patrick Knyght is the biological father of Alexander Isaac Harlow.

The tears filling my eyes prevent me from truly seeing any more of the results or the signatures and certification stamp.

"You can't be that surprised?" Damon's voice causes me to look up from the papers, showing him the tears in my eyes. "Olivia," he breathes out, pain etched in his features.

The doorbell rings, saving me from his pity. Damon moves to take care of the food delivery while my mind reels. He would press for the visit to New York, the birth certificate, and every last one of his demands.

The sound of the door closing and smells of food pulls me out of my spiraling thoughts. Damon places the white bags on the counter, turns toward a cabinet, and begins pulling out plates. When he turns back around, he stops and stares at my frozen form.

"Are you okay?" he asks, setting the plates on the counter.

I can only nod.

"Well, the food is here."

One by one, Damon reaches into the bags until he finds what he's looking for.

"Aha, buddy! Here it is." With a small plastic container in his hand, he walks to Alex, who's still sitting in his chair, and dumps some macaroni noodles with plain red sauce onto his tray. "Are you going to sit?"

His question draws my attention from the tray of the high chair to him moving back to the counter. Our eyes meet and he cocks one eyebrow. Gathering the food containers and plates, he takes them to the kitchen table.

I finally unfreeze and move to sit across from him.

"What would you like?" He motions to the containers.

"I'll get it." My voice, barely above a whisper, falters.

It wasn't that I hadn't known Alex could be his son, but to see it in black and white and so official...I try to process everything and prepare for what Damon will throw at me next. I reach for the linguini, but Damon takes my plate.

"Allow me," he offers with a cocksure smile.

I don't even want to imagine what is going through his mind now.

I take the plate full of linguini from him and we eat in silence. Well, he eats. I mostly shove my food around the plate.

"Olivia?"

My eyes snap up at his voice.

"Are you not hungry?"

I clear my throat. "Not really, I guess."

"Well, then, how about we discuss your trip to New York with me?"

He sits back in the dining chair and takes a long drink from his glass.

"We will leave Sunday and—"

"I never said I was going to New York with you." I place both palms on the table.

Damon's face hardens. "Olivia, you have the results. I want my family to meet the both of you. My wife and son."

"Damon," I sigh, "I can't just up and leave. I have a schedule and a business to run."

Annoyance saturates his movements as he rubs his hands over his face.

"Fine," he growls. "When is a good time?" His eyes come back to mine, challenging.

"I'll have to look over the schedule with Ced." I shrug.

His mouth opens to protest, but I put up my hand.

"Tomorrow," I add, quickly.

"Why can't you look tonight, so I can make proper arrangements?" Irritation pours off him.

"Because Ced knows that schedule better than I do. She even remembers things that aren't written down on it or pending." I push my still full plate away from me.

"Fine, but I need to know tomorrow so I can change my arrangements." Standing, he takes his plate to the sink.

"Why do you need to change your arrangements?"

Damon leans with his palms down on each side of the sink and lowers his head.

"If I leave without you, you won't come at all, Olivia. I'm not an idiot."

"I-I wouldn't do that." As soon as I say it, I know it isn't completely true. Eventually, I would go, but I would procrastinate for much longer with him gone.

"Wouldn't you?" Turning, he narrows intense eyes on me.

"Not if I agree to do this."

"Well, I'll stay here until you agree." Pushing away from the counter, he walks back to the table.

Out of nowhere, inspiration strikes.

"Fine," I blurt, "we'll go. But there are conditions."

He stops two feet from the table and eyes me suspiciously.

"What are the conditions?" His eyes bore into me as he pulls out the chair and retakes his seat.

"Alex and I will come to New York and meet your family. We will also make arrangements for you to be in his life. But you have to sign the annulment papers, dissolving our marriage."

Leaning forward, my elbows on the table, I return his intense stare.

His eyes narrow. "No."

"Take it or leave it, Damon." Sitting back, I cross my arms over my chest.

Damon sits silently, his eyes never leaving mine. We stay locked in a staring battle until Alex throws his spoon on the floor, giggling.

"You aren't allowed to throw silverware, mister giggles." Giving him a scolding look, I pick up the spoon and set it on the table. "Are you all done?" I ask Alex.

He raises his arms and grunts, "Up." I loosen him from his chair and take him straight to the bathroom, leaving Damon at the dining table.

Once Alex is bathed and dressed, we play on his floor for a while. Damon does not join us, nor do I hear anything from him.

The hour gets late and Alex starts yawning. I begin his nighttime routine and settle him into bed. It's at this time that Damon appears. He brushes his fingers over Alex's head and whispers good night to him before walking back out of the room. Turning on his crib toy, I watch Alex for just a moment as the music lulls him to sleep.

Quietly closing the door, I back out of his room.

"Olivia?" Damon whispers.

His voice causes me to jump and turn around. Not realizing how close he is behind me, we now stand less than an inch apart. I try to step back, but I just end up pressed against the wooden door. Damon's eyes gaze hungrily at my mouth. Unintentionally, I part my lips, feeling breathless. My eyes trace the soft curve of his mouth.

Is it wrong to want to jump your stalker? I mentally slap myself from this stupor.

"I have my own conditions as well." His face moves closer.

I try to speak, to protest, but my mouth is too dry. Instead of speaking, I slide myself out from in front of him and motion for him to follow. As I turn around in the living room, he is just entering.

Taking a deep breath, I try to calm my raging hormones and breathe air untainted by his enticing, masculine scent.

He smirks, knowing he's affecting me.

"What conditions?" I quickly ask.

"First, you and Alex come to New York and stay for a week. Second, you will stay with me, in my home, as a family."

He puts up a hand, stopping me from protesting.

"Let me finish."

Crossing my arms over my chest, I huff. He smiles, amused by my pouting.

"So, where was I? Ah, yes, that's you both staying for a week, living with me as a family, and you agreeing to go out on two dates with me while you are there."

My eyes widen.

"Dates alone," he clarifies. "No Alex, just us."

Just when I thought I had leverage, he takes it away. Damn him! Oh, and there is that fucking cocksure smile again. Double damn him.

Taking a deep breath, I fight the urge to kick him out of my apartment, but it's not like he would go.

After taking a moment to mull over his proposition, I decide this may work in my favor. I could agree to this. It's just a week and then I would be free from this marriage.

"One week, live in your home, and two dates?" I question, ticking them off on the fingers of my right hand.

He nods, giving a victorious smile.

"And you will sign the annulment papers if I agree?"

"I will sign *after* you meet the conditions."

My mouth pops open in surprise. "How do I know you won't change your mind after the week?"

He shrugs. "How do I know you won't back out of New York if I sign now?"

He has a point, but I wouldn't do that.

"I told you I wouldn't do that," I argue.

"What can I say? I'm cautious." He lifts one shoulder in a half-shrug.

"Fine," I growl before thinking too much about it.

"Fine?" The shock in his voice is clear. "That's a yes?"

I nod and close my eyes. Before I can open them again, he wraps his arms around my waist and lifts me from the floor.

"Thank you," he says, his voice turning jovial as he spins me around.

"Put me down." I try not to laugh. He does as I request. "I'm going to bed."

"You'll let me know when we can go to New York tomorrow, right?"

"I said I would," I respond without looking back at him.

Padding softly down the hall, I run my hand over Alex's door. I brought this into our lives and it would never be the same again. I close my door and head straight for the shower, the promise of steamy hot relaxation calling out to me.

Relaxation doesn't come immediately. My brain won't stop turning over what I just agreed to do. It's a risk to go to New York without him signing the papers, but I need to try this before attempting a legal battle with Goliath.

Mercedes arrives to the bakery around five-thirty. Once she's settled into her office, I square my shoulders and prepare for the onslaught of questions to come.

"Hey, Ced, can you tell me what we have on the schedule for next week and the week following?" I ask, sitting across from her.

"Sure."

She reads off the three upcoming consultations and four cakes I need to personally work on. *So, next week is out of the question.*

The following week only holds two pressing orders, which I could have done by Monday night. I could leave Monday evening and return on Sunday. It's not the whole week he's asking for, but it's as close as I'll be able to do.

"I need to keep my schedule clear from Tuesday of that week until the following Monday."

I keep my eyes on the planner laid out before her, refusing to make eye contact.

"What's going on?" Suspicion saturates her question. I peek up and meet her eyes.

"I'll, uh, be in New York."

I drop my eyes back down to the planner.

"So, I need you to make sure I'm all clear and that we only take on what the rest of the crew can handle. I'll adjust the—"

"Oh my lawd!" she shouts before dropping down to a hush. "You're going with him, aren't you?"

Rolling my eyes, I look back at her and shrug.

"Wow, this is...unexpected."

"It's a means to an end." I sit back in the wooden chair.

"What?" Her brows knit together.

After providing her with the details of the deal I made with the devil upstairs in my apartment, we sit silently, just looking at each other.

"Do you really think he'll stand by his part of the deal?"

Rubbing the back of my neck, I tilt my head and crack the right side.

"I just have to hope he will."

"But, what if he doesn't, Liv?"

"Then it looks like I'll return home and give Alfonso the call to proceed with legal action."

Sighing, I push up from the chair.

"Well, I hope he keeps to his end of the bargain for your and Alex's sake."

"I hope so, too." Giving a small, forced smile, I go back to work.

As I consume myself in my work, a much needed distraction from all things Damon, my mind becomes clear and focused. While multi-tasking on three different specialty cakes with Sarah at my side, I realize just how great she's become. It's time to push her to do more of the things I normally take the lead on. If I can get her comfortable with a role similar to mine, she could easily run the bakery when I'm not available.

After talking to Ced about my thoughts on Sarah, something Ced fully agrees with, I close down the bakery and head upstairs.

"Momma!" Alex runs down the hall and captures my legs in his chubby arms.

A wave of comfort washes over me. I hadn't even realized how tense I'd become spending the day without him in the bakery. I lift him into my arms and squeeze him to my chest.

"Hey, little guy." I tickle his sides, causing him to giggle. "What have you been up to all day?" I blow a raspberry kiss on his cheek. "I missed you today."

"Down," he demands.

I place him back on his little sock covered feet and follow him into the living area. Crayons and large pieces of white paper litter the floor.

"What the heck happened in here?" I blurt.

Damon looks up from his laptop. "I got some crayons out for him."

"Where did this paper come from?"

"I found it in the hall closet." He shrugs.

It feels like someone punched me in the stomach. The paper scattered across my living room floor was the left over sheets from a sketchpad I'd stored in the back of the closet. The last sketchpad Isaac used. There were a couple of full sketchpads stored back there as well.

"Are you alright?" Damon sounds concerned.

My chest tightens as vomit rises into my throat. Without asking, he went through my closet and just ripped them out of the sketchpad like scraps of paper.

Turning, I hurry to my bathroom and splash water on my face. Once the cool water calms me, I pat my face dry and walk into my bedroom. Damon stands just inside my doorway.

"There were some drawings in there. Did you do them?" he asks with narrowed eyes.

He knew damn well I hadn't drawn them. Isaac always scrawled his initials in the lower right corner in messy calligraphy.

"No," I quip. "Where are the drawings?"

"Who is I.A.M.?" Damon questions, stepping closer.

"An old friend." I choke back a sob — thinking about Isaac brings back memories of losing him and our baby.

"A *friend*?" His emphasis on friend makes it clear he doesn't believe me.

"Yes. I lost him in an accident." My words are barely loud enough for my own ears. I close my eyes and take a deep breath.

"I see." This is all he says before turning and walking away.

Once I collect my emotions, I go to the kitchen to begin dinner. Halfway through my cooking, Damon decides it's time to talk about New York.

"Did you speak with Mercedes about the schedule?" He leans onto the counter, watching every move I make.

"Yes." I nod. "I can't next week, but the following week we can leave Monday evening and—"

"Why can't you miss Monday?" he asks, annoyance lacing his words.

I plant my hands on the counter and turn to face him. "Because, Damon, I have work obligations. If leaving on a Sunday or Monday morning is more important, I'm sure I can put the trip on hold for another week and arrange that instead."

If my words could have physically manifested, they would be flaming with anger.

"Fine." His response surprises me. I expected a bit more of a fight from him. "I will make arrangements for you to fly to New York Monday evening and return the following Monday."

He pushes away from the counter and walks toward his laptop.

"Sunday," I state before returning to the pork chops waiting to be finished.

I can feel him tense before I peek up to see his shoulders bunched together.

"Sunday?" he growls.

"Yes, Sunday," I reply, keeping my eyes focused on dinner. "And before you argue, I need to get back for work. There are a lot of upcoming events. This is the best I could do."

"Last I heard, this time of year is not a busy wedding season," he huffs, sitting down on the couch.

"And the last time I checked, you don't know shit about my business or regular clientele. Don't question what you don't know," I spit before turning my back on him to finish dinner.

He says nothing else until we're sitting at the table, eating dinner.

"Your e-tickets are on the counter," he states without looking at me.

"Thank you, but I could've made our arrangements."

"Can't you just stop at thank you?" His eyes finally lift and bore into mine.

"I just don't want you to think I expect you to do things or pay for—"

"I am well aware that you don't want or need me for anything, Olivia. You've made it quite clear," he snaps and pushes away from the table. "Unlike me."

My mouth pops open, as if to argue. Unsure of what to say, I close it and remain silent as he retreats down the hall to the guest room.

The rest of the evening is calm and silent. I clean up dinner, the crayon mess, and Alex. Damon surprises me by showing up to tell Alex goodnight before I put him into bed. Once he is tucked in and the crib toy is lulling him to sleep, I follow Damon out of Alex's room and head for my own. A hand on my arm stops me.

"I want Alex to call me dad," Damon states before I can even fully turn around.

"I don't want to confuse him," I say, keeping my voice in a whisper.

"How would he be confused about me being his father?" His grip on my arm tightens, not painfully, just firmer, and he steps closer to me.

"Because you are here now, but you'll be back in New York soon. You aren't and won't be an everyday fixture in his life. I'm just worried about it," I explain.

"I will be a part of my son's life every day, Olivia." His features harden.

"You know what I mean. We will be here and you will be in New York. I'm just not sure if it's a good idea to—"

"If I have to call him every day or get him his own webcam, I will. I will also, no matter what, be with him more than I will be away."

"He's eighteen months old," I remind, "I doubt he knows how to use a webcam."

"I don't' care. I won't lose y...him." Sadness flashes across his face before he releases my arm and walks back into the guest room.

I release a large breath and my shoulders sag. *Time for some hot, steamy water therapy.*

The next day passes in similar fashion since the day Damon arrived at my home. However, when Mercedes comes upstairs with me at the end of the day, talking about spending time with Alex, I remember Damon doesn't know about my evening plans.

"You ready for an evening of junk food, cartoons, and toys?" Ced sits next to Alex.

Damon raises a brow at me.

"I have plans this evening and Ced knows his routine." I shrug and walk to my room.

As I enter my bathroom, I hear my bedroom door open. Sighing, I turn and meet Damon in the center of my room.

"What do you mean you have plans tonight?" He narrows his eyes and tightens his lips to form a hard line.

"I have dinner plans. I was distracted, so I didn't get to tell you about—"

"Dinner plans with whom?" He steps closer, leaving only a foot of space between us.

I take a step back.

"A friend," I growl.

"Olivia?" My name parts from his lips as both a question and a warning.

"You don't know her," I snap and turn for the bathroom.

Once inside, I close the door and lock it.

After my shower, I start doing my hair and make-up. Being in a bakery all day, I typically don't wear more than waterproof mascara and some chap stick. Though I'm not a high maintenance kind of girl, I still like to do a little more with eyeliner, blush, eye shadow, and gloss when going out.

Satisfied with my appearance, I step out of my bathroom to get dressed.

Damon sits perched at the end of my bed. His head snaps over to me. Fully aware I'm in nothing but a towel, I tighten the knot at my chest and fight the stupidest urge to drop it and let him watch me walk around naked.

"I'm sorry." While his mouth speaks the apology, his eyes roam every inch of my body.

Under his stare, heat flushes my body.

"Okay," I mutter, moving to my closet to get my clothes.

I grab a pair of black skinny jeans, a baby pink silk top, black heels, and make a stop at my dresser to grab underwear and a bra before disappearing into the bathroom to dress.

As I slip into my clothes, the brush of the fabric against my skin makes me think of his hands running along my body. The way his fingers curled around my knee that night in Vegas, pulling my leg up and opening me wide for him.

"This is ridiculous," I groan as my lady parts tighten, reminding me of how he made me feel something I'd lost years before. With one more groan for allowing this crazy attraction, I force the memories away and finish dressing.

I step from the bathroom and glance over to the small hooks lining the wall next to my dresser. When I find the small clutch purse I'm looking for, I start toward the item and ignore the firm, wide, sexual maestro still sitting on the bed like an invitation to debauch him.

"You look very lovely." His compliment pulls my attention toward him.

His eyes rake over my body, causing a shiver to tingle over my spine.

"Thank you," I breathe.

He stands and approaches me, moving until our chests almost touch.

"This shirt. It is quite magnificent on you."

His fingers graze my collarbone, just under my chin, and slide across the silk, until reaching my shoulder left bare by the halter-style top. My lady parts tingle, pulse, and clench as he licks his bottom lip.

Stop thinking dirty thoughts about the stalker, my internal warnings scream at me.

Stepping back, I grab the clutch and hurry to the living room for my jacket, keys, and wallet. I quickly kiss Alex's head and ignore Ced's look of curiosity as I make a mad dash out the door to meet Felicity.

The evening with Felicity is mostly a discussion about how Lorna and she came to fruition. One date led to a lunch, which led to another date, which led to breakfast in bed.

"I can't help it if I know what I like." She winks.

I laugh. Felicity is never one to shy away from something she wants.

"So, tell me about your Billionaire Stalker." She settles back into the booth and puts her drink to her lips.

Getting her caught up on the situation was like verbally vomiting all over her.

"You are going to New York with him?" she asks, concern lacing her voice as her eyes round with worry.

I nod and shrug. "If it will get the papers signed, then I'm going to try it."

"What if he chains you to his bed, fucks you into submission, and keeps you as his house pet?"

"You have read way too many Erotica novels."

She shrugs.

"It could happen." She grins. "So, what if he won't sign the papers?"

"Then I'll make a call to your brother and have him start the proceedings through the court. This is my final civil attempt to resolve this." Sighing, I down the last of my drink.

Felicity waves a hand, hailing a waiter to refill our drinks.

"Christ, Olivia." She shakes her head. "What are you going to do about him wanting Alex to call him daddy?"

I bury my face in my hands.

"I don't know. I mean, do you think it will confuse Alex or cause more problems?"

"He's only one, Olivia." She drinks from her fresh dirty martini.

"He's eighteen months, Felicity," I respond, sarcastically.

She rolls her eyes.

"Look, he's young and probably won't even remember when Damon entered his life. Hell, the first memory I have as a kid is when I was like four or five years old. I doubt you're traumatizing him by introducing him to his father." She takes another drink. "He gets a dad. A rich daddy, at that. How is that a bad thing? I know a lot of people who wish they had fathers as kids."

"He's crazy," I choke.

She wobbles her head from side to side in contemplation.

"Maybe, but I don't let anyone stand in the way of what I want. Does that make me crazy?" Her brow rises.

"Sometimes, yes." I laugh. She throws a balled up napkin, but misses me.

"Plus, he's really, really fucking rich." She wiggles her brows this time. I throw the napkin back at her.

"Felicity, this is not about money."

She winks.

"Enough serious talk. You need to unwind." She slips from the dark red booth. "Time to dance the stress away."

Extending her hand out to me, I take it and allow her to lead me to the dance floor. Along the way, a couple of women who date in the same circles as Felicity glance at her longingly. When they see me, annoyance graces their features. I puff out my chest and proudly let them think I could land a woman as hot as Felicity.

As we step onto the dance floor, Felicity releases my hand.

"Let's shake it, Mrs. Knyght!" Giggling wildly, she starts to dance.

"That's not even funny," I shout over the music.

She laughs harder, bumps her hip into mine, and we both begin moving in time with the heavy beat.

After a couple songs, two men try to join us. Felicity plays along, dancing with a tall blond. The dark haired man attempts to move up close, but I try to keep distance between us. *I have enough man problems, buddy. I don't need you around right now.* But this guy doesn't want to take no for an answer. Grabbing my waist, he pulls me to grind against him. I shove his chest hard and open my mouth to curse the asshole when I hear a roar from behind me.

"Get your hands off my wife!"

"Sorry, man, didn't realize she was someone's. She's not wearing a ring." The guy releases me.

Turning, I come face to chest with Damon. His smell surrounds me and calms me for just a moment before the shock of him being here settles. How did he know where I was? We ate somewhere else before arriving at Felicity's favorite club. *He followed me!*

"Did you follow me?" I shout up at him.

His eyes meet mine, but he stays stoic.

"You did, didn't you?" I shove at his chest.

"I kept away so I wouldn't interrupt your night. I just wanted you to be safe," he starts to explain.

"So, you followed me! Why does this NOT surprise me?"

Felicity appears next to me and I turn to her.

"He followed me," I shout, disgusted.

She flinches at my loudness and I look back to Damon.

"Quit stalking me!" Growling, I stomp back to the table, Felicity on my heels.

"He's pretty hot when he's worked up."

Grabbing my purse, I give her my best *are you fucking kidding me* look. She puts her hands up in surrender. I kiss her cheek.

"I'll talk to you soon," I promise her.

"You sure you don't want me to come with you?" She grabs her purse.

"No, go home to Lorna and have a good night. I'll be fine."

I wave as I hurry toward the door, trying to lose Damon in the nightclub crowd.

"Olivia, wait!" Damon shouts over the crowd. He isn't far enough behind, so I pick up my pace.

My heels hit the concrete of the sidewalk and I immediately wave down a cab.

"My car is right here." The heat of his body presses against my back.

I ignore him and continue to wave at taxis.

"Quit ignoring me. My car is right here and it's safer than a taxi."

Spinning on my heels, I wobble for a moment before steadying myself.

"You think it's safer for me to climb into a car with a man who stalks me, is crazy obsessive, and possessive?" I shout, causing passersby to turn and look at us.

"I am not crazy," he growls. Wrapping one long, lean arm around me, he lifts and begins carrying me to his car.

"Put me down!" I scream.

His hold tightens.

"Help!" I shout. "Someone help me!"

"Will you stop making a spectacle of yourself?" he grumbles.

"Hey, put the lady down." One of the bouncers shows up as we near Damon's car.

"Stay out of this," Damon snaps at him.

"The lady doesn't want to go with you, so why don't you just set her down and—"

"Don't tell me what do to with my wife," Damon shouts.

"I'm not his wife," I yell.

"God damn it, Olivia!" Damon sets me down on my feet and holds me by my arms. "Stop this and get in the car," he demands, looking intent and severe.

"No, leave me alone!"

Suddenly, a wave of dizziness hits and I sway.

"You're drunk," he groans.

"I am not."

"I have a cab right over here she can take." The bouncer walks toward us, taking my arm. "If you do know her, then you will be able to find her where she lives."

As the bouncer leads me away, I look back at Damon and smirk. With a little wave at him, I climb into the taxicab and head home.

By the time I pull up to my home, the alcohol is in full effect. *What the hell was I thinking?*

After paying the driver, I stand at the bottom of the steps leading to my apartment. I groan. The thought of climbing those stairs in this condition is not ideal, especially in heels. Holding the railing, I pull my heels off each foot with my free hand. Heels in hand, I prepare to tackle the climb when the feeling of weightlessness takes over.

"What are you doing? Put me down," I growl.

"I'm helping you get up the steps without falling and breaking your neck," Damon grumbles, carrying me bridal style.

"Why can't you just go away?" I whine.

"You're my wife and I'm taking care of you," he states, his voice barely above a whisper.

He sets me on my feet by the door and looks down at me. Our eyes lock, his breath warms my upper lip, and he presses closer. My breasts warm as his chest presses against me. His head dips close.

"I'll show you, prove to you, that we belong together."

The closeness, his scent, the pure sexuality pouring off him in waves, messes with my head. Dropping my heels to the ground, I wrap my arms around his neck and pull his lips to mine. My fingers find their way to his hair, the tips of each clawing into his scalp and pulling him closer. His arms embrace my waist, bringing me firmly against his body. We devour each other's mouth and my back lands hard against the door. The sudden hit jars my intoxicated ass back to reality. I push at Damon's chest and he steps back.

"Oh my God," I gasp. "I'm so sorry. I shouldn't have...that was...oh my God, what is the matter with me?"

I cover my mouth with my hand.

"Don't apologize." Damon leans closer.

"No, no, no. That shouldn't have happened. I don't want to give you the wrong impression." I shake my head.

My hands press against his chest once more as he leans down. His lips graze my ear.

"Feel free to give me the wrong impression." His lips press against my neck, causing a shiver to form at the base of my spine. I fight it.

Pushing him back, I put at least a foot of space between us this time.

"It won't happen again."

Turning, I open the door and enter the apartment, leaving his grinning ass outside.

Chapter Eight — new york, here we Come
Olivia

I roll over in my bed and the movement makes my stomach swish, causing me to moan in discomfort. The tap on my door is not welcome.

"Go away," I grumble.

I hear him chuckle before I feel the shift of my mattress.

"How are you feeling?" he asks quietly, yet with a hint of smugness.

"Shh."

His silent laughter shakes the bed, causing me to groan. I open one eye and he smiles, motioning toward two white pills and a glass of water on my nightstand.

"Those will help."

"Thanks," I mumble.

"Finish off the water and I'll bring you coffee." He stands from the bed and leaves the room.

Pulling myself into a half-sitting position against my headboard, I chase the two white pills with a sip of water. After a few more minutes, I chug down the full glass. Waiting about five minutes, I finally drag my ass out of bed and haul it to the bathroom. The hot water feels good, but doesn't fix my wretched nausea.

Trudging into the kitchen, the much appreciated smell of coffee fills my senses. I quickly pour a cup and I start to sip before it's cooled, burning the tip of my tongue.

Alex sits in his highchair, chewing on lumps of toast and humming. Damon sits reading a newspaper at the table. Being sure not to make eye contact with Damon after my actions last night, I kiss the top of Alex's and head for the bakery stairs.

"What, no impressions to give this morning?" he calls at my retreating form.

I quicken my pace and stop midway down the steps. Groaning, I lean my forehead against the wall. "Stupid, stupid, stupid," I chant before calming the embarrassment flushing my heated face.

Thankfully, my work schedule keeps me busy enough to prevent me from thinking too much about my stupidity. About the feel of his soft, full, mouth on mine. About the way his body, firm and strong, felt pressed against me. *Damn it!*

When the day is over, I stick around to help clean up, even though it isn't my turn. Greg gives me curious glances, while Sarah smiles knowingly.

"I'm just helping out," I answer Greg's unasked question.

With nothing left to clean, I slowly walk up the stairs. On the top step, I pause and take a deep, fortifying breath before pushing myself to enter.

Olivia

The next few days fly by without him saying anything else about 'the doorstep incident'. Sure he'll use the moment of weakness against me, I've been tense and on edge each day. I find it more unnerving that he hasn't.

Finally, the morning of Damon's departure is here and I'm anxious to get Alex and my home returned to normal. A thud by the front door snaps me out of my thoughts.

"Well, that's it."

He sighs and looks to Alex, who's sitting in his highchair, eating banana pieces. Then, his gaze locks on me. His eyes reveal a storm of emotions, causing a pang of guilt and pity in my chest. When I say nothing, his shoulders drop.

"I need to get going if I'm going to make my flight in time." Raising his chin, he looks longingly at me.

Nodding, I give him a small smile, but I don't move from my spot against the kitchen island.

"Have a safe trip," I finally say.

"Mon!" Alex shouts and giggles.

Damon walks to Alex and kisses his forehead.

"I'll see you soon, little buddy." His large hand cups the side of Alex's head.

The pang strikes me again and I have to look away.

"Do I get a kiss goodbye?" Damon surprises me by being so close. "Or, can I at least get the impression you left me on your doorstep?"

And there it was, the bastard.

"Ha-ha." My words are laced with sarcasm. "Have a safe trip," I repeat and smile small.

His hand cups my face, causing me to stiffen.

"What?"

Swooping in fast, he presses his lips to mine and lingers there for a moment before pulling back.

"I'll see you soon?" It was more a question of reassurance than a statement.

Fear, sadness, and pain swirl in his eyes. He drops his hand from my face and walks toward the door. Pausing only to pick up his bags, he leaves without looking back.

The click of the door closing sends a wave of emotion through me. It wasn't only the relief I'd been expecting.

"Mon?" Alex calls out. "Mon?" He tries to push out of his chair.

I set my mug on the counter and calm him into sitting back down.

"It's just the two of us again, little man."

I thought I would feel more satisfaction by saying the words out loud; instead, there was sorrow and guilt I didn't understand. Panic set in, but I couldn't comprehend what I was panicking about.

My cell phone beeps. Grabbing it from the counter, I open the new text.

Damon: Please don't back out.

He's so afraid we won't show in New York. I'm scared he won't sign the papers and this is all a ploy to keep us in his life.

The week without Damon passed by in a blur of Alex making monumental strides in life, bakery orders, and an oven disaster. I almost cancelled the trip to New York, but Mercedes assured me things were covered.

So, here Alex and I stand, trying to get through airport security. Alex didn't want to stand still and wouldn't stay in his stroller. In an attempt to occupy him, I convinced him to help me push the stroller. He swiped two strangers' legs, rammed three ankles, and even pulled the stroller until it laid wheels up on the floor.

"Alex, baby, please. You need to stay still for Mommy right now. Okay?" Kneeling down to his level, I try pleading.

"I tired," he yawns.

Alex had taken his time to start talking, but now it was hard to get him to be quiet.

"Climb into the stroller." I motion to the seat.

Finally, he sits down. I strap him in and give him his favorite picture book.

We reach the checkpoint and I place our carry-on bags on the belt. I push the stroller toward the metal detector when the security officer holds a palm up before I can step onto the black mat.

"I'm sorry, ma'am, but you need to collapse the stroller so we can scan it."

I just got him back in it, I groan, internally.

After taking Alex back out of the stroller, I fold it up and place it on the belt. The officer motions for us to walk through. I nudge Alex to go first and I follow.

Once we clear the scan, I gather our things, put our shoes back on, and unfold the stroller. Luckily, Alex climbs back into the seat without much fuss, so we are able to catch the next transport to the terminal.

The gate attendant announces boarding will start in about twenty minutes, so I make the mad dash to the restroom. I clean Alex up from his snack and sit him on the potty. While keeping a hold of Alex's shirt, so he doesn't try to peek or crawl under the stalls, I hurry to use the restroom. I have to hiss out his name a couple times and give him a *don't make me beat you* look during one escape attempt.

Once we are both washed up and back at the gate, I see people lining up and waiting for further instruction from the gate attendant.

"Would any families with children please approach the gate for boarding?"

At the announcement, I usher Alex in the direction we need to go. Still holding onto his shirt, we inch closer to the attendant taking the tickets.

Once the stroller is tagged and left for loading, we step onto the plane. The flight attendant takes our tickets and motions to the seats in first class.

"You're right here." Smiling brightly, she offers assistance with loading our carry-ons in the overhead space.

"What?" I choke, grabbing the ticket stub back and really looking at the seats. Knowing we would board early, I didn't even pay attention to the seating.

"I can't believe him," I mutter, placing Alex in his own first class seat.

Still grumbling about the expensive seats, I sit down and place the backpack under the seat in front of Alex.

Of course, Alex doesn't want to sit still. Instead of sitting, he is standing and looking at the people behind us. Begrudgingly, I have to be thankful for the first class spacing.

Alex is less than thrilled about take-off and begins to cry from the cabin pressure change. However, once we are able to use electronic devices and he can watch his Scooby Doo DVD, everything is better and I am able to relax for the rest of the short flight to JFK.

"We are about fifteen minutes from JFK and will be arriving on time. It is currently four-twenty in the afternoon and seventy-two degrees. Thank you for flying with us and enjoy your time in New York."

The captain's announcement rouses me and the rest of the cabin, except Alex, who is still sleeping soundly.

He's going to be so pissed when I wake him up.

Sighing, I start packing up the DVD player, books, and toys.

We are instructed to return to our upright positions and prepare for our final descent. The plane hops a couple times, but it's a smooth landing overall. Screeching tires wake Alex from his nap, his eyes wide. I wrap my arm around him and he burrows into my side.

As we wait to exit the plane, I check my phone for messages.

"Holy crap," I mutter as the phone blinks and buzzes in my hand.

"Crap," Alex mocks. Yet another wonderful habit he picked up — mimicking.

"That's not a nice word, Alex. Mommy is bad for saying it."

He just smiles.

Turning my attention back to the screen of my phone, I scroll through the messages.

M: Hope the flight went well. Let me know when you've made it.

I sent a quick text letting Mercedes know we were good.

Damon: Let me know before you take off.

Damon: Have you boarded the plane?

Damon: Please answer me.

Damon: Are you coming? Mercedes said you left for the airport.

Damon: Let me know when you've arrived.

Damon: Have you landed?

Rolling my eyes, I quickly let my stalker know we are about to get off the plane and he needs to provide directions to give the cab driver. The plane door opens as soon as I hit send.

We collect our bags and exit the plane, the flight attendant thanking us for flying with them on the way out. I grab the stroller just outside the plane door, but Alex refuses to ride in it. Holding his hand, we follow the crowd into the main terminal. Once there, I look for signage leading us to baggage claim.

My phone buzzes, but my hands are too full, so I ignore it until Alex and I get on the transport to baggage.

Pulling out my cell phone and trying to keep Alex close is not an easy task, so when I get a short text simply stating, '**Don't be foolish**', from Damon, I become a bit irritated.

Knowing him, he sent a car to pick us up, which I asked him not to do. Sighing, I slide my phone back into my pocket just as we arrive at our location.

Always a ball of energy, thanks to the powernap, Alex wants to skip and run. After securing the backpack and other bag to me, I grab his hand and we begin to skip and act crazy.

"Mon!" Alex screams, excitedly, pulling his hand out of mine and running.

My head snaps up in the direction Alex takes off in. There Damon stands, in a dark suit with sunglasses on top of his head. He kneels down and lifts Alex into his arms. I freeze for a moment, unsure of how I feel about seeing Damon again and how much he already means to Alex.

Alex's little mouth is moving a mile a minute and Damon is smiling large as I approach.

"Look, Momma. It Mon!" Alex smiles widely.

I smile and nod.

Damon watches Alex in what looks like amazement.

"We see you," Alex states to Damon.

"I've missed you, little buddy." Damon plants a large kiss on Alex's forehead.

"Olivia." He turns from Alex and smiles at me.

"Damon." I nod and head toward our baggage claim area.

"You don't need to worry about that."

I turn at Damon's announcement.

"Douglas is getting the luggage."

"Who is Douglas and how does he know which bags are ours?"

"Douglas works for me and I have my ways." Damon winks.

I scowl.

He chuckles.

"I've missed that scowl." He grins wide.

I fight not to scowl again.

"This way."

He carries Alex in the direction opposite of where we'd been heading. I follow his lead to a sleek black car with tinted windows.

"This is us." He opens the back door and places Alex inside.

"We need his seat," I object.

"I've got it."

I look back at the voice and see an extremely large man with dark brown hair and eyes. He carries our luggage — every single bag — and Alex's seat.

"Perfect timing, Douglas. Thank you." Damon takes the seat, climbs into the car, and secures Alex in place.

Douglas loads the luggage.

Damon slips out of the car, catching my attention, and motions for me to get in.

I slide into the car and Damon slips in close behind me. Alex is across from us in a seat facing the back of the car. Swallowing the lump forming in my throat, I inch away from Damon — just slightly. His arm comes around my shoulders and pulls me next to him.

"As a family," he reminds.

Huffing, I cross my arms over my chest and his body shakes in silent laughter.

The remainder of the ride is quiet, especially since Alex has nodded off. As we ride, Damon rubs his thumb on my shoulder. It feels comforting, relaxing...just plain good. I want to hate it since he's already proved he would push this 'living as a family' arrangement to the max, but I can't.

When we pull up to a towering building, the car briefly stops before pulling into an underground garage. A speed bump just inside the garage wakes Alex. His eyes widen, looking at the darkened garage. He reaches for me, but the straps of his seat hold him back, frustrating him.

"It's okay, buddy. We're home." Damon leans forward, cupping Alex's face.

I scoot out from under Damon's arm and unbuckle Alex, who leaps out of the seat and into my arms.

Douglas opens the door for Damon and he climbs from the car, extending his hand out to me. Taking his hand, I stand from the car with Alex holding tightly around my neck. We both take in the cavernous garage.

"This way," Damon states, taking my hand. The thud of the trunk echoes around us and Douglas stands with our luggage.

Inside the silver elevator, Damon presses *P*. As the doors seal shut, a lump forms in my throat and knots twist my stomach. When the elevator begins its climb, Damon wraps an arm around Alex and me. I look up at him and he smiles down at both of us. For a moment, his eyes flicker to my lips and my stomach flutters. He leans his head toward mine. His breath washes over me and I lick my suddenly dry lips. The ding of our arrival to his floor pulls us away from each other. I adjust Alex to the hip between Damon and me as he motions for us to exit first.

Upon entrance, I scan his home. There's a dining room to my left with a dark table able to seat eight. Straight ahead is the open kitchen. My lips part in awe of all the stainless steel appliances and dark granite counter tops. Before I realize it, I stand before the L shaped island, running my fingers over the smooth, dark surface. A click sounds from behind me, lighting the open floor plan and drawing my attention to the large living area. An oversized dark leather couch lines a wall made up of windows, revealing the city skyline. A shiver runs across my spine as my overactive imagination pictures Alex pressing up to the glass and looking out. I pull him closer to my body. "What's the matter?" Damon moves next to me.

"Nothing." I shake my head and look over to the kitchen.

"Olivia, please. I want you to be comfortable here." Stepping in front of me, he uses his finger to lift my chin. Our eyes meet and for a moment, I'm lost in the color and resemblance to my son.

"It's nothing." I try to pull my head away, but he uses his hands to hold me in place.

"I'll fix whatever it is," he pleads.

"There's nothing to fix," I sigh. "The windows just make me nervous."

Confusion flashes in his eyes.

"No one can see inside. They are tinted."

"It's not that." I groan at my own overactive thoughts. "I just...it's just that...my imagination goes a little crazy and I can picture Alex falling out of one."

His eyes widen and he releases my face.

"They don't open," Damon assures. He walks over to a window and presses on it. "They're a solid sheet."

"I would hope they didn't open being this far up," I respond, sarcastically.

"Then why would you think he would fall out?"

He walks back to me.

"I told you. It's just my overactive imagination," I huff, annoyed with myself. I step around him and closer to the kitchen.

This large island is a dream. I run a finger over the smooth surface. *I wonder how often it gets used.*

A throat clears and I turn at the sound.

"Where would you like the luggage, Mr. Knyght?" Douglas stands a few steps inside the apartment, awaiting instruction.

Damon turns to me.

"Which bags are Alex's?"

"The green and blue bags are his."

"Take the green and blue to the nursery at the top of the stairs, first door on the left. The red bags can be placed in the master bedroom."

My breath catches.

"Yes, sir." Douglas nods, moving quickly with his orders.

"Damon, I'm not staying in your room," I argue.

"We are living as a family, remember? That is the deal we made."

"Yes, but that doesn't mean—"

"Some wives may sleep in separate bedrooms, but I assure you, my wife does not," he states, cutting off my further argument with a raised brow and half-smile. Simultaneously, I want to both lick and punch that eyebrow.

"Don't push your luck too far, Damon," I warn with narrowed eyes.

"I'll take everything I can get out of these conditions." He walks closer and leans his face mere inches from mine. "And I believe you like the way I push you."

I open my mouth to argue, but he pulls away and motions for me to follow.

"I'll show you the upstairs of the apartment. Come." He pauses at the bottom of the staircase, watching me and waiting.

As we ascend the staircase, Douglas descends, excusing himself.

"This is Alex's room." His hand presses to the small of my back, guiding me into a fully decorated nursery.

"How?" I walk to the center of the room and take in the light blue, green, and cream colors.

Alex wiggles in my arms and I place him on the floor. He wobble-runs to a corner full of colorful oversized blocks and begins to stack them.

Warmth covers my back just before Damon's arms wrap around my waist.

"All it takes is a decorator and a very helpful sister-to-be," he whispers into my ear, warming much lower body parts.

"You shouldn't have done all this. It's only for a week."

He turns me to face him, his expression hard. "Not if I have anything to say about it."

"Damon," I warn, "you promised to sign the annulment papers after this week."

A grin spreads across his face, melting away the hardness.

"I did."

I exhale in relief.

"But I will still be Alex's father and it's only right he have a place of his own when he is visiting me."

I tense at the thought of sending Alex away for lengthy amounts of time.

Damon pulls my stiff body against his. I raise my hands, pressing them against his chest. His cheek grazes mine as his lips whisper against my ear.

"Besides, if Vegas proved anything, it's how compatible we are physically." His tongue touches my lobe, causing a shiver to spread through my body. "Perhaps it will persuade you to stay."

"That..." I shake the lust away, "that's not going to happen."

He pulls away, a smirk on his face. "So you say."

Motioning toward the hallway, he says, "*Our* room is this way."

"I can't just leave Alex in here alone."

"That's what this is for." Reaching next to the door, he pulls a built-in gate out of a hidden space in the wall.

"Oh." I walk over, follow Damon out of the room, and pull the gate until it snaps shut.

"This way." Damon's hand finds the small of my back once more, edging me toward the double doors before us.

Entering the bedroom, I expect clinical and cold. Instead, the king sized bed covered in a sandy colored comforter, blue-green throw pillows, and hints of white, surprises me. With a king size bed, hopefully I'll be able to keep distance between us at night.

"Welcome home, Mrs. Knyght." Damon's arms circle me once more.

"Damon, you can't call me that."

His arms tighten.

"You promised you would—"

"You want me to lie to everyone?" I cut him off and pull from his embrace. "Why would you want to lie to everyone and make it that much more awkward when this is over?"

His chest heaves and his eyes narrow.

"Momma!" Alex shouts. "Momma!" Panic plagues his voice.

"I'm right here, baby," I shout back, quickly exiting the bedroom.

Alex is practically climbing the gate to get to me when I finally lift him into my arms. He buries his watery-eyed face into my neck and squeezes.

"What's wrong?" Damon looks over Alex. "Is he alright?"

"He's fine. It's unfamiliar to him. I'm sure he thought we left him."

I hug Alex tighter, assuring him.

"I'm sorry." Damon deflates a little. "I didn't mean for him to get frightened."

"He's okay. Really," I assure Damon.

"Hey, buddy. Are you hungry? Want to get something to eat?" Damon rubs Alex's back, just as his little head pops up.

"Eat!" he shouts.

"What do you want, buddy?" Damon smiles.

"Cookies," Alex cheers.

"I don't think so." I purse my lips. "Maybe cookies after you have dinner."

"How about pizza?" Damon offers.

"Pizza," Alex repeats.

"Pizza it is."

Damon puts his cell phone to his ear and then presses the *L* button instead of the *G* I expect. When we stop, the three of us step into the lobby of the building.

"Mister Knyght," a man greets. Standing up from his shiny black desk, his full uniform identifies him as the doorman.

"Peter." Damon gives a brief nod.

Alex tugs on my hand, wanting to get closer to a large water fountain. I pick Alex up and he struggles against my hold.

"Peter?"

"Yes, Mister Knyght. What can I do for you, sir?"

"This is my wife, Olivia, and our son, Alex," he introduces. At the mention of 'wife' — again — part of me wants to throttle him, while the other part, which I suppress, curls up cozy to the idea.

"It's a pleasure to meet you." Peter's wide eyes take in the sight of Alex and me, lingering on Alex a bit longer.

"Yes, a pleasure." I give an uncomfortable smile and start to walk around Damon. *I need a quick exit.*

Damon grasps my hand and matches my pace as we exit the glass doors. Once outside, I pull my hand from his and turn to face him.

"Will you please stop?" I beg.

"Stop what?" he asks, attempting genuine confusion. I don't buy it.

"You know what I'm talking about. Don't play with me," I growl low.

He sighs.

"He will see you here all week and needs to know who you and Alex are." His eyes shift to Alex. A smile spreads over his face and he reaches out, taking Alex into his arms. "Let's get that pizza."

"Pizza!" Alex claps.

Following Damon, we stop at a blue-silver car parked along the curb.

"This is your car?" I ask, surprised by the lack of flashiness. Not only is it a four door, it's not an import.

"No." He opens the door to the backseat and buckles Alex into an unfamiliar car seat.

"No?" I ask, confused.

"I just saw the car seat in this one and figured we'd take it." He stands straight and closes the rear door with a shrug.

My mouth hangs open.

He laughs.

"I'm kidding!" He shakes his head. "Your face was priceless."

"That wasn't nice." I try not to laugh.

"I'm sorry." He provides a faux pout and opens the passenger door for me.

I slide into the light gray leather seat. Damon closes the door, crosses in front of the car, and then climbs behind the wheel.

"I guess I expected a sportier car," I state once he starts the engine.

"I have a couple of those. This is the safer vehicle for Alex."

"What kind of car is it?" I ask, mostly because I can handle car talk more so than wife talk.

"Subaru Legacy WRX," he answers. "It should be available to the public in a couple of months."

"You aren't the public?" I raise a brow at him.

"Baby, *we* aren't the public. We're Knyght's. It has its perks." He grins widely and pulls away from the curb.

"When did you buy this?" I run my fingers over the super clean dash.

"While in Pittsburgh." He shrugs.

"When?" I urge.

"Um..."

"You got it before I agreed to anything, didn't you?" I exclaim.

"I get what I want, Olivia." His eyes lock onto mine briefly before going back to the road.

"You presumptuous—"

"Hey," he cuts me off, "there's a kid in the car." Thumbing over his shoulder, he smiles.

Taking a deep breath, I try to calm myself.

"And the car seat?" I ask.

"I picked it out when I got back last week," he states nonchalantly.

"Where are we going?" I try to change the subject.

"My favorite pizza place."

After a few more streets and stops, we pull up to a curb. Looking out the window, I shake my head. Damon is out of the car and opening my door before my final shake is finished.

"This is your favorite place?" I stand from the car. "Pizza Play Land?"

He doesn't step back when I exit, putting less than three inches between us.

"Yep." He grins, leaning closer.

I back against the car, but stop before falling back inside.

"It's so nice to have you here." He kisses my nose.

I turn my face away.

"Damon," I warn.

His lips press against my neck and heat blossoms across my skin, from neck to breast. I push him back, ignoring the large seductive smile on his face.

"Listen, Damon..."

I poke my finger into his hard chest and he grasps it, bringing it to his mouth and sucking. My body quivers as my breath catches. Before I melt into a pool of lusty goo, I yank my finger from his mouth.

"Will you stop it?" I put my hands behind my back.

"Nope."

I'm about to argue, but he presses his lips to mine. It's not erotic, but it's not a chaste kiss either. When he pulls away, my fingers hurt from knotting them behind my back in order to keep from grabbing him.

"Play nice, Olivia. It's family time."

Taking my hand, he pulls me away from the car and onto the sidewalk. I'm still lost in a mix of shocked yearning.

While I take a moment to collect myself, he retrieves Alex from the car. Slipping his hand into mine once more, he leads us across the street to the pizza shop.

Inside, there is an area with colorful tables sectioned off. Alex sees the rides and ball pits, immediately making him want down.

"I want ride!" Alex struggles in Damon's arms.

"After you eat." Damon finds an empty table while I retrieve a highchair.

"Now!" Alex screams.

"Alexander," I scold.

"Come on, Alex, eat some pizza with daddy. Then you can go play. Okay?" He slips Alex into the chair.

"Now," he screeches, kicking his legs and almost knocking over the chair.

"Alex," I warn.

"Play now!" he shouts.

"Do you want me to take you to the restroom, little boy?" I threaten.

Alex stiffens. He shakes his head, his eyes wide.

"Then settle it down." I point at him.

He obeys, but continues to pout.

Damon retrieves pizza from a large buffet style set up and brings it to the table. As we begin to eat, Damon sits back, giving me a curious look.

"What does the restroom mean?"

"No restroom." Alex shakes his head, stuffing a cut up piece of pizza into his mouth.

"You aren't going to the restroom. As long as you behave." I rub his cheek.

Turning back to Damon, I answer his question.

"It's sort of a mother's secret weapon for discipline."

Damon still looks confused.

"Children figure out quickly that most moms won't spank or discipline them in public, so by taking him to the restroom when he behaves badly, you have privacy to discipline."

"So, you spank him?" Damon's voice tightens.

"On occasion I have, but it doesn't always mean a spanking. Mostly, it's like a time out. We talk and he has to stand patiently for a few minutes before we return to the public area." I shrug.

"I don't believe in beating a child," Damon states firmly.

"I don't believe in beating a child either," I bite out. "However, if my son is misbehaving, I'm not above a swat on his butt to get the point across."

"It's not necessary to—"

"I don't beat my son, Damon," I growl low, narrowing my eyes.

"I didn't mean to imply you did."

"Then what did you mean to imply? You're making it seem as if I beat him. A beating and a swat are very different."

"But you have spanked him?"

"I've swatted him, yes. Not like bend him over your knee spankings. He's still young."

He nods, but sits quietly, eating, for a few moments.

"Play now?" Alex pushes his mostly empty plate away from him.

"Let me clean this up."

I start stacking the garbage onto a red tray. Damon takes the tray and heads to the garbage.

"Play," he cheers, trying to climb out of the chair.

Once he's unbuckled from the chair, I lift Alex and set him on his feet. He tries to dart off toward the games, but I grab his arm.

"No running or taking off from me. Stay with Momma."

We walk to the game side and begin utilizing the golden tokens Damon acquires from a change machine against the wall.

Two hours later, Alex is passed out and I'm trying to slip him into pajamas without waking him. Tucking him into bed for the night was harder for me than him. I only hoped waking up in a strange room wouldn't scare him. Sighing louder than intended, I exit the room.

"You okay?" Damon walks up behind me, wrapping an arm around my waist.

"Just tired," I respond, moving out of his grasp and descending the stairs.

In the living room, I sit on the couch and let the softness surround me. I don't want to even discuss sleeping in the same bed yet, but the argument would be inevitable.

"So, he's really started talking." Damon forces a smile as he sits next to me on the couch.

"Mmhmm." I nod, resting my head back.

"You're tired. Why don't you head to bed?"

I tense for a second. *I guess this argument will come sooner rather than later.*

"Nothing is going to happen that you don't want to happen. I promise." His fingers gently touch under my chin, moving my face to look at him.

"I would like to know the plan for this week first." I remove my face from his fingers and stretch a little.

Taking a deep breath, he leans back on the couch.

"Tomorrow, I need to stop by my office, but I would like for both of you to come with me."

"To your office?"

"Yes." He shrugs. "Then we will head over to my father's place for brunch or lunch."

"You're taking me to meet your parents tomorrow?" My eyes widen.

"You will meet my father, Damon Senior, and my stepmom, Heidi."

"Do they know about all of this?" I motion between us.

He nods.

"Yes, he is aware that I've remarried and of Alex."

"Does he know the details?" I prod.

"Everyone is very much aware of the details now. Hugh couldn't keep his damn mouth shut," he growls.

"Hugh?"

"My younger brother. You will meet him at the office, as well as his fiancée, Scarlett." Standing from the couch, he pauses and looks down at me. "Do you want something to drink?"

I shake my head.

"What about your mother?" I ask his retreating form.

He stops at the steel fridge and retrieves a beer bottle.

"We will meet with her for brunch the next day."

Upon his return, he sits back on the couch.

"I'm sure she will also want us for dinner at some point, but the evening after we have brunch with her will be our first date night." He smiles large before taking a long pull from his beer.

"What exactly are we going to do with Alex?" I smirk, thinking I finally have him. "There's no babysitter here."

"Taken care of," he quips.

"Taken care of how? You can't just leave him with a stranger. He won't like it," I argue.

"Heidi has graciously offered to watch him here. She is amazing with kids. They love her. He will be fine, trust me."

His hand finds my thigh. I narrow my eyes at him and push it off. He shrugs again.

"If he gets upset, I won't go."

"You agreed to two dates." Damon sits up straighter, his face intense.

"Yes, but I won't make Alex suffer just so you can have a date," I say, knowing he wouldn't argue once I used Alex as the main point.

Huffing, he slouches back into the couch.

"And you need to stop introducing me as your wife. You and I both know that at the end of this week—"

Damon sits back up and leans toward me.

"You are my wife and that is how you will be introduced."

"So, you won't have a problem later, after the annulment is finalized? Or are you trying to tell me that you won't sign the papers?" I raise a brow, challenging him.

"I will introduce you as what both you and Alex are to me. You are my family. Regardless of what some piece of paper says about our union." His intense eyes bore through me.

Suddenly, I'm too exhausted to fight.

"I'm going to bed." I stand before he can say anything else and make my way upstairs.

After quickly brushing my teeth and changing into pajamas, I slip into the massive bed, hoping to get lost in the covers. I try to stay as close to the edge as I can without falling off.

While my body is exhausted, my brain won't stop. After the conversation with Damon, I'm more nervous about the events of this week. I can't be sure he will sign the papers and I have no clue what he has up his sleeve. But if he thinks I'll back down from this, he has another thing coming.

Chapter nine — oh, new york, oh god
Olivia

True to his word, Damon did not take advantage of us being in bed together. He climbed into bed, without touching me, and we fell asleep on our own sides. I thought I would've been more relaxed at his distance, but I still couldn't sleep soundly. Waking alone the next morning makes me feel rejected, even though I do so every single day at home. And I do not like that one bit. Shaking off the unreasonable feeling, I focus on the scent of bacon in the air.

Reaching the kitchen, Damon is standing at the stove in a white t-shirt and pair of blue pajama bottoms. Alex is sitting in a high chair near the island. *He really has thought of everything.*

"Good morning, baby." I lean over and kiss Alex on the head.

"Good morning to you, baby." Damon looks over his shoulder with a grin.

Rolling my eyes, I slip onto a stool next to Alex.

Damon sets some eggs on a plate and turns back to the stove.

"Mon," Alex calls as he reaches for the eggs.

"They need to cool down first," Damon responds.

"Daddy will give them to you when they aren't so hot. I promise," Damon continues.

My eyes widen in astonishment.

"What?" Damon asks.

"Daddy?" I clip.

He shrugs.

"I already told you I wish for him to call me dad. With the paternity test confirmation, I didn't think you would fight me further about it."

"You don't think we should've discussed it before you decided to start?"

He shrugs.

I cross my arms over my chest and Damon chuckles.

"You look alike when you pout." Using the turner, he motions to Alex and me.

I look over at Alex and sure enough, he's pouting about his eggs. Realizing I'm acting like a two year old, I quickly stop.

"Here you go. All cooled." Damon sets the plate on Alex's tray, along with a sippy cup of juice. "Do you want some orange juice?" he asks me.

"I can get it. You don't have to serve—"

"Sit, I'll get it." He moves around the kitchen with grace and familiarity.

He's different here. Not better or worse, just different. Something has changed compared to the man I first met. I hate it. I hate it because I find myself drawn to him more.

At the completion of breakfast, Damon shoos me upstairs to prepare for the day of visiting his family. Just thinking about the introductions has my nerves on edge and I take a little longer in the shower than necessary. My only hope is his family feeling like this is madness. Mentally crossing my fingers, I pray they will be my allies in getting him to sign the annulment papers.

After I finish getting dressed, I get Alex cleaned up while Damon showers and dresses. Soon, Douglas is once again chauffeuring us. First stop, B.I.G., where Douglas parks in a cavernous garage below a tall building and escorts us to a silver elevator.

Upon arriving to the executive floor, we step into a wide marble floor lobby where designer labeled professionals bustle about. Even with Damon wearing dark jeans and a button down shirt, my black skinny jeans and blue blouse suddenly feel like a bad choice.

Damon takes my hand, leading us past a dark reception desk. He introduces us to executive assistants who look surprised, but are quickly fawning over Alex. Not to mention, fawning over Damon right in front of me.

"Is there anything I can get you, Mr. Knyght?" a sleek blonde wearing a barely appropriate pencil skirt practically purrs.

"I don't believe I've ever seen you dressed so casual, sir." Perfectly curled dark hair leans forward, showing ample cleavage from her button-up silk blouse. "It's a very handsome look on you." She extends her arm and fingers the cuff of his shirt.

Damon quickly steps back, discomfort wrinkling forehead.

I hook my arm around his and he relaxes, allowing me to press against him. I excuse us from the executive harem and provide them with an obviously fake smile. Laying my head against his arm, I walk us in the direction we were previously headed.

"You have quite the number of well-groomed groupies," I taunt, though I don't really care about them. It was mostly amusing. I move away from him and drop my arm from his.

"Jealous?" He wraps his arm around my waist, pulling me back against him.

"No," I protest a bit too quickly, trying to pull out of his hold.

"That has actually never happened. I'm not sure what's gotten into them." He tightens his arm to keep me in place.

"Yeah, right," I snort.

"I've never noticed that behavior before." His fingers apply pressure to my hip. "Quit fidgeting," he commands, looking down at me.

"Give me some room to breathe," I mumble, narrowing my eyes.

"Damon." An unfamiliar voice breaks our moment.

I look toward the voice and see a tall, lean man with brown hair and bright eyes approaching.

"I thought you were out for the week?"

"Sorry to disappoint you, Hugh," Damon chuckles, pulling me tightly against him.

I swear, if he squeezes any more, I won't be able to breathe.

"I need to take care of a couple things before we head to Dad's for lunch," Damon finishes.

"So, you're going to Dad's first?"

"Yes, I want him to meet Alex and..." Damon pauses and then frowns. "Shit, I'm sorry." Damon rubs the back of his neck. "Hugh, meet your nephew, Alex."

Damon takes Alex from my arms and holds him high.

"Alex, meet your Uncle Hugh." Damon smiles proudly at Alex before turning to me. "And this is my wife, Olivia." He takes my hand and presses his lips to my skin.

My jaw muscles tense at the label he places on me. I fight to provide a genuine smile.

Hugh stands silent and stoic. My nerves ping pong underneath my skin the moment his gaze meets mine. I stiffen. He smiles.

"It's a pleasure to meet you." Reaching out, he offers his hand. I take it.

"Oh my goodness. Who is this handsome little guy?"

From behind Hugh, a perfectly coiffed blonde with a glowing peaches and cream complexion appears. I can't help but assume she is another Damon Knyght groupie. My hackles rise.

"This is Olivia and Alex." Hugh introduces before turning an affectionate gaze upon the woman.

"Oh." She fumbles a moment, but quickly composes herself. "It's so nice to meet you both."

Her warm and genuine smile shows that she really means those words.

Stepping closer, she places a perfectly short-nailed manicured hand on Alex's cheek.

"You are such a cutie."

Alex, nervous at first, beams at her praise and affectionate cooing.

"This is Hugh's fiancé, Scarlett," Damon informs.

"Now I'm just Hugh's fiancé?" Scarlett raises a brow at him. "Last time I checked, I am your Vice President of Marketing and E-commerce." She crosses her arms over her chest.

I'm gonna like Scarlett.

"Scarlett, I didn't mean—"

"Mr. Knyght?" Another unfamiliar voice announces the entrance of a well-put-together brunette in a skirt and jacket set that suited her age and profession. She needs to pass styling tips out to the rest of the executive assistant pool.

"Yes," Damon and Hugh answer in unison.

"Um, Mr. Knyght, sir." She focuses her attention on Damon. "Your mother is on the phone for you." Her discomfort is obvious, given her fidgeting with the hem of her jacket.

"Tell her I will call her back—"

"I'm sorry, sir, but she insists you speak with her." She clears her throat and drops her voice. "In regards to the Proneau situation."

Damon groans low and hands Alex back to me.

"I will be right back." He kisses the top of my head and turns before catching my glare.

"She can keep me company in my office." Scarlett wraps her arm in mine.

Damon turns to leave, but briefly looks back at Scarlett with a warning glance before disappearing around a corner.

As soon as we enter Scarlett's office, she releases my arm and motions to a large leather sofa.

"Please, make yourself comfortable." She smiles.

The click of her office door draws my attention to Hugh.

I place Alex on his feet, walk to the sofa, and sit. Scarlett appears with a large legal pad and pens, handing them to Alex. He squats on the floor and begins scribbling.

"Thank you," I say. "I wasn't quite sure what I was going to do to entertain him."

"No problem." She sits next to me on the sofa.

"So..." Hugh hesitates, "how are things?"

The way he asks and the expression on his face makes it clear he's not trying to make small talk. He wants to know how things have been since Damon's crazy ass entered my life.

"It's a bit unusual, but things are okay. For now," I answer carefully, unsure of his motives.

"I'm so sorry for...for everything that's happened." Hugh's shoulders fall. His face expresses pure guilt.

Clearing my throat first, I answer, "It's far from your doing. In fact, I'm partly to blame for the situation I find myself in."

"Please understand that I love my brother very much."

I nod.

"I just don't believe he's going about things the right way."

I nod again.

"Frankly, I didn't believe he was in the right frame of mind when he told me about all of this."

"You didn't, but you do now?"

Fear pangs my chest. Would his family encourage this?

With a sigh, Hugh pulls a black guest chair over to sit before me. Before he answers me, Scarlett chimes in on the subject.

"It's not that we think Damon doesn't have *demons* that need to be dealt with—"

"But I've never seen him so...so different, Olivia," Hugh interjects. "I don't know what it is, but he seems better. It's as if he's the man I knew before..." He allows the sentence to trail off.

"Before the accident," I finish for him.

Scarlett and Hugh both look at me with wide eyes.

"He told you about the accident?" Hugh practically whispers.

"Sort of. I discovered information online when I was trying to...well, when you have a man stalking you, internet research is the least a woman can do." I shrug.

Scarlett smiles.

"He hasn't given me exact details of the event, but I know he lost his wife and son in an accident he blames himself for."

Scarlett places a hand on my leg.

"The accident was never reported as Rebecca's fault, but it was her fault, Olivia."

"Scarlett," Hugh hisses.

Ignoring him, she continues. "She'd been drinking. And with her medications, the alcohol wasn't a good combination to drive on."

"Medications?" I wrinkle my brow, confused.

"Scarlett, this isn't our story," Hugh warns.

"Well, who the hell is going to tell her the truth?" she snaps and narrows her eyes on him. "She deserves to know. This is probably the only time we will be able to talk without Damon around."

Taking a deep breath, Scarlett composes herself.

"Rebecca had depression issues. Apparently, she'd grown up with them, but Damon wasn't aware of her condition when they became involved. Rebecca was very embarrassed about the medications she needed to take and kept it very low key."

Scarlett pauses, looking to Hugh for what I assume is support. My already raw nerves send the prickly skin feeling over my body.

"Damon didn't find out until DJ was born," Hugh adds.

Scarlett's hand tenses on my leg.

"She suffered severe postpartum depression after his birth. Still, it wasn't until DJ was almost three months old before Damon found out. Years of practice made her good at hiding."

Having never experienced post-partum depression, I only knew what the baby books had told me.

"What happened?" I barely choke out the question.

"Damon arrived home early one afternoon to surprise Rebecca. He had taken over the company not too long before DJ arrived, so he often worked long and late hours." Hugh took a breath.

"When he got home, he heard DJ screaming. He rushed to the nursery, but DJ wasn't there."

My stomach knots.

"Damon scrambled around their home, trying to find him. He finally located him on the floor of a hallway closet."

Gasping, I cover my mouth.

"Momma?" Alex questions. He looks up from the ripped and scribbled papers around him, concern on his little face.

Getting myself back in check, I smile at him. "It's fine, buddy. What did you draw?"

He holds up two ripped pieces. "Draw dis."

"That's so wonderful. I'm so proud." I blow him a kiss.

He smiles and goes back to scribbling. I watch him for a minute before looking back to Hugh.

"Where was Rebecca?" I ask.

"After Damon picked DJ up and tried to calm him, he got concerned that something happened to her." Hugh pauses, his brow furrowed.

"He found her in their master bathroom taking a bubble bath and drinking straight from a bottle of Vodka. She had put him in the closet to silence the crying and screaming," Scarlett finishes.

"I assume they would have gotten her help though, right? I mean, they were married when she...was in the accident." I glance between Scarlett and Hugh, unsure of who would answer me.

"Yes," Hugh answers. "Damon immediately got her help, took time off from work to be with her and support her, but eventually he had to return to work. He runs the company. So, he hired a nanny to help Rebecca throughout the day and alleviate some of the stress."

"She seemed better for a while. I mean, from what I saw of her, she seemed perfect with DJ and Damon — happy and content. I suppose she was just too good at hiding things," Scarlett sighs, heavily.

"Rebecca did show improvement, but she didn't ever really get *better*. In fact, other conditions began to surface, like extreme jealousy and paranoia. Damon tried to speak with her doctors in hopes they could help her. And the doctors tried. Damon and Rebecca went to couples therapy where they tried to address the issue, but it never resolved anything. It was like she didn't want help."

"Then why were they still married? Why wasn't she hospitalized?"

"She was good at hiding it," Scarlett repeats. "It looked like she was improving, even Damon thought so. Then Damon discovered she was having him followed because she believed he was sleeping around. She fired the nanny because she was sure the woman was trying to steal her family. And Rebecca's drinking became worse. Damon hired a nurse to live with them, but Rebecca was good."

Alex climbs up into my lap and lays his head down. Soon, his little arm stretches out to touch the gold bangles on Scarlett's wrist. Just as I'm about to pull his hand away, she slips them off and hands them to Alex.

"Her medication and alcohol weren't a good mix," Hugh continues. "Damon was out with clients the night Rebecca decided to put DJ in the car and drive after drinking heavily. She was trying to track Damon and his *mistress* down." Hugh's eyes begin to water. "That's the night we lost them."

"DJ wasn't even supposed to be with her." Scarlett sniffs. "Damon always tried to secure DJ's safety when he wasn't going to be around. DJ was supposed to be with Heidi and Damon Senior that evening, but when they arrived to pick him up, Rebecca was already gone."

Rubbing Alex's back, I absorb the information — this tale of sorrow and pity.

"Olivia?"

My gaze focuses on Hugh.

"For years, Damon has been in therapy to deal with the loss and guilt. He became obsessed with what he could have done to stop the accident and how he should've taken more precaution and better care." Hugh drops his head. "Then he grew angry and repressive. There was nothing but work and home. He's lived like a workaholic hermit."

I open my mouth to speak, but Hugh beats me to it.

"Until now." His eyes meet mine and hold my gaze.

I close my mouth.

"He's different." Scarlett rubs my leg. "The deep sadness isn't there. He talks about a future, instead of being obsessed with the past. Damon is like the man I knew before."

"He's become almost like the man he was before Rebecca," Hugh adds.

"I feel horrible about his past and I am sad for your entire family, but I am not a bandage to be applied. So, I'm not sure what you are trying to accomplish here."

"Oh, Olivia, no," Scarlett protests. "I'm not trying to convince you to be with him. Hugh and I completely chewed his butt out when he told us about what was going on with you. We were shocked about the tracking down, the marriage, and the existence of Alex."

"I thought he was delusional about your son," Hugh interrupts. "That he was latching on to you because your son resembled DJ and you were his way to save them." He pauses.

"That's not the case, Olivia. This is," Hugh motions between Alex and I, "something completely different. He's different, better."

The opening of Scarlett's door stops me before I can argue further.

"Sorry, that took longer than I expected." Damon casually strolls into the room and surveys our expressions. "What's going on?" he asks, his eyes narrowing on Hugh.

"We were just talking," Hugh states without turning to look at Damon.

"About what, Hugh?" Damon growls.

"Nothing." I stand and walk over to pick up Alex.

"Hugh..." Damon warns.

"We discussed things you should have already told her." Scarlett stands and moves next to Hugh protectively.

"It's not your place to discuss anything with her." Damon stalks toward Alex and I, wrapping his arms around my waist and pulling me to his side.

I try to wiggle free, but he digs his fingers into the flesh of my hip. I quickly abandon the idea of getting free.

"She deserves to know about the events leading up to you invading her life, Damon," Scarlett snaps.

"Mind your own damn business, Scarlett," Damon snarls before walking us from her office.

Nothing is said until we reach the elevator.

"I'm sorry they dropped all of that on you."

I pull free of his embrace.

"It's fine. You had plenty of opportunity to discuss it with me, but you didn't."

The intensity of his stare could be felt without looking to confirm.

"Olivia, my past no longer matters. All that matters is my present and future." He moves to stand in front of me, cupping my chin.

"This will be over when I leave at the end of the week," I respond, a bit too breathlessly.

He smirks and the elevator dings our arrival to the lobby. The doors slide open to an immaculate glass lobby.

"Come," Damon takes my hand. "My father and Heidi are waiting for us."

Damon tugs us along to a silver four-door car waiting at the curb. We drive in uncomfortable silence for thirty minutes before entering a street lined with homes of grandeur tucked away behind gated entrances.

We turn at one particular wrought iron gate and proceed through after Damon enters a code. Once parked, we both exit the car and I retrieve Alex from the backseat. Damon gets the toddler bag before escorting us toward the large, stone house. Before we take more than two steps, the front door opens.

"Son," a handsome man with salt and pepper hair greets Damon. "I'm glad you've arrived. Heidi is going on non-stop about when to serve lunch and whether I think our grandson will like her."

He pulls Damon into a one-arm hug and then turns his attention to Alex and me.

"This is Olivia and Alex," Damon introduces. I silently thank the stars for not being labeled his wife this time.

"Welcome." Damon Senior smiles broadly. "It's quite a pleasure to meet the both of you. Please, come in."

Stepping back, he motions for us to enter. Damon guides me into the house with a warm hand against my lower back.

The house is large, open, and the mahogany staircase the focal point of the entryway. Hardwood floors shine so clean, I am sure I could check my reflection in them.

"Damon!"

I look up from the floor to see a tall, model-esque woman rushing toward Damon. Her long blonde hair shines like the floors and curls flawlessly around her picture perfect face and sculpted eyebrows. When she smiles, I immediately recognize Damon's half-brother, Hugh, in her features.

"I'm so glad you're here." Her long, thin arms wrap around Damon, squeezing him tight.

Damon returns the embrace, lifting her off her feet.

"Heidi," he coos, "it's always a pleasure to see you."

When they pull away from each other, she turns toward us. Her eyes stop on Alex.

"Oh my," she gasps, placing a hand on her chest. "You look like your daddy, don't you?"

Stepping closer, she brushes her fingers over Alex's cheek.

"May I?" she asks, looking to me as she reaches out for Alex.

"I don't think he—"

Just as I'm about to tell her about his shyness, Alex surprises me by going into her arms without hesitation.

"He usually doesn't take to people so fast," I mumble, mostly to myself.

"Heidi is a natural with children. Always has been," Damon Senior explains.

She carries Alex off into the next room and I follow slowly.

"Look, Damon, he has the Knyght eyes." Heidi turns, showing Damon Senior.

When he leans in for a closer look, Alex buries his face in Heidi's shoulder, causing her to snuggle him and Damon's father to laugh.

"He definitely has the same unruly hair as his father." His father looks to Damon with a smile.

Damon slides an arm around my waist and pulls me close to his side. Pride pours off him and contentment tries to creep through my body.

Heidi continues moving, leading us through a set of double doors to a dining room with seating for eight. The amount of food on the table can probably feed double that amount.

Damon's father pulls out a seat for Heidi, who sits with Alex in her lap.

"I can take him," I offer.

"Nonsense." Heidi shakes her head. "I am not giving him back until I absolutely have to." She smiles, warming my insides. *It's no wonder Alex took to her so quick.*

Damon pulls out my chair and tucks me into the table before sitting to my right.

"Are you planning on any more little ones?" Damon's father asks as he takes a seat.

I'm unable to respond, choking on my own saliva.

"Not at this time," Damon answers.

I snap my head to look at him and narrow my eyes.

"Damon," I hiss.

"I'd like three more," he continues.

My mouth pops open and Damon looks at me with a smirk.

Oh, he better be messing around with me.

"Three seems to be more than Olivia is planning." Damon's father chuckles as he hands his plate to Heidi. "I'm sure you'll be able to convince her, though."

What the...?

Heidi begins to make his plate, even taking food from the dishes right in front of Damon's father, before handing it back to him.

Without a thank you, he picks up his empty wine glass and holds it out to her as well.

Heidi pours his wine and hands it back to him, then does the same for his water glass.

What the hell is with this guy?

"Are you going to eat?" Damon's question pulls me from the feministic rant I'm about to spew forth.

"Sorry." I force a smile. "I spaced for a minute."

"Allow me." Damon takes my plate and begins placing food on it.

I can't help but catch the disgusted look on his father's face. Apparently, in the world of Damon Senior, women are meant to serve men and not the other way around.

When Damon returns my plate, I make sure to smile smugly before I start eating.

Yeah, take that you chauvinistic brat. My inner feminist does the running man.

Lunch conversation revolves around medical talk and investments. Heidi dotes on Alex, while *serving* her husband.

"So, have you thought about a proper wedding now that you have *things* handled?"

At Damon Senior's question, I look at him with wide eyes.

"I'm afraid we won't be having any more ceremonies," I respond quickly, hoping to deter the conversation.

Damon's hand comes to my thigh, lightly squeezing. *I wish his touch didn't affect my body.*

His father cocks an eyebrow.

"Really?" His attention turns to his son. "I would think you'd want to include your family in this, Damon."

Opening my mouth to speak again, a stronger squeeze to my thigh silences me. The rougher touch sends fiery sparks between my legs and I begin trying to peel his fingers off.

"Olivia isn't one for large ceremonies or being the center of attention. So, I'm afraid we've decided against the idea of another wedding."

"That's a shame. It would have been nice to get all of the family together again. We rarely have everyone in same place." His father shrugs and extends his empty wine glass to Heidi. Without batting a perfectly curled lash, she pours him more wine.

After lunch, we retire to a large sitting room. Heidi returns Alex to me and hurries out of the room. Just as I'm about to ask if she is okay, she returns with boxes.

"We picked up some things for Alex." Heidi places the silver wrapped gifts on the floor.

Alex slips from my lap onto the floor with her.

"You didn't have to do that," I say, trying not to sound unappreciative.

"Of course we did!" Heidi exclaims cheerfully. "He is our only grandchild..." She quickly stops and glances to Damon, apologetically.

Damon tenses for just a moment before giving her a genuine smile. His eyes move to Alex and the rest of the tension melts from his body.

"It's our job to spoil him." She offers Alex one of the gifts.

He eyes the shiny paper before pawing at the box.

"Mine?" he asks, sitting down to tear into it.

"They are all yours." Heidi scoots next to him and helps peel away the wrapping paper.

The boxes are stuffed with clothes, toys, and books. Of course, Alex seems to find the empty boxes more amusing than the gifts inside. Heidi, Damon, and Damon Senior all laugh, enjoying my little boy.

"You used to do the same thing," Damon's father announces with a broad smile.

I swallow the large lump of emotion forming in my throat.

We chat a bit longer, mostly about Alex, before Alex is fast asleep in Heidi's lap.

Damon leans over, bringing his lips to the shell of my ear.

"He seems to truly like Heidi. Don't you think?"

I grind my teeth and nod, darn well knowing what he's getting at with the comment.

"That should put you at ease about our date tomorrow." The warmth of his breathy words caresses my skin, causing a shiver.

He moves away, returning to his seated position. I look up at him, taking in his smug smile.

After visiting for a few hours, Damon and I give our thanks and head back to his apartment. Alex, worn out from his day of introductions and playing with Heidi, sleeps for the duration of the ride, waking in Damon's arms while riding up the elevator.

"Idee," he yawns, looking around.

His inquiry only cements the fact that I cannot back out on date nights.

"You will see her tomorrow, buddy," Damon answers, rubbing Alex's back. His smugness doesn't go unnoticed.

Clearly, I need another way out of this marriage. I see no sign of Damon fulfilling his end of this agreement.

Once in the apartment, Alex wiggles, wanting down. Damon sets him on his feet and he walks around the apartment, exploring and rubbing sleep from his eyes.

"You hungry?" I run my fingers through his sleep-mussed hair.

"Yep," he responds, more energetically.

"What do you want to eat?" Damon asks, squatting down to his level.

Alex scrunches his face in concentration and then looks up at me.

"What if I surprise you?" Damon pats his shoulder, stands, and walks toward the kitchen.

Alex watches him walk away for a moment before following after Damon.

The sound of cabinets and pans breaks my attention from Alex. My eyes shift to Damon, who is moving around the kitchen.

"What are you doing?"

Looking over his left shoulder, he answers, "I'm going to make dinner for you two."

"You don't have to do that. I can cook dinner."

I step further into the kitchen and he practically shoves me out.

"It's fine. Take Alex up so he can play."

Hesitating for a moment, torn between helping or letting Damon cook for us, I finally take Alex by the hand and lead him to the living room.

Digging out a couple of his new toys and turning on cartoons, I set Alex up on the living room rug to play. While he's distracted, I make calls to both Mercedes and Felicity to check in on things.

Mercedes is more interested in what Damon's place looks like, how his family reacted, whether we were humping good and properly, and if he has any single brothers. Felicity, on the other hand, focuses on whether he's being nice, if his family was accepting, if there are any signs of psychotic tendencies or mental illness in any of them, and whether I need money for an escape.

While Felicity's offer of escape is tempting, I knew he would only follow me wherever I went. And when I tell Felicity about Damon Senior's behavior with his wife, the conversation turns into a feminist rant, which only ends because Damon announces dinner is finished.

Damon made spaghetti, meat sauce, and salad, which tastes amazing. His ability to cook a meal both surprises and impresses me.

After dinner, he plays with Alex and helps to bathe and dress him for bed. While Alex had been shockingly easy to put down the night before, tonight he's giving me some trouble. I end up sitting in a rocking chair with him until he calms, and then stay in the chair after lying him down, just to be safe. It isn't until Damon lifts me from the chair that I realize I'd fallen asleep.

"I should stay with him tonight," I yawn.

"He will be fine," Damon argues, cradling me closer to his body.

"What if he wakes up and—"

"Then we will go to him." Damon sits me on the bed.

After taking a moment to orient myself, I grab some pajamas from a bag and go to the bathroom to change.

Mid tooth brushing, Damon walks in wearing only boxer briefs. In the large, full-wall mirror behind the sink, I can see how the cotton caresses his toned body. Amidst my ogling, Damon drops the briefs to the floor, giving me full viewing access to his sculpted back and ass.

Before climbing into the shower, he glances toward me. Our eyes meet in the mirror and he grins.

I quickly look away, spit the minty foam from my mouth, toss my toothbrush on the counter, and exit the room as fast as possible. One more moment with him in the confines of the bathroom and I would be a soaking wet mess. And not just because of the urge to.get in the shower with him.

Wrapped in the highest thread count sheets I've ever experienced, I'm about to drift off when the bed dips next to me. The smell of his freshly washed skin surrounds me, causing me to bite back a moan. The realization of how much he's affecting me and how much I am enjoying his scent has my eyes blinking open. His eyes are looking into mine as he grins, knowingly.

I curse my decision to lie facing away from the bathroom door, furrow my brow, and roll away from him.

His arm drapes over my side and his chest presses tightly to my back. My muscles lock up tightly.

"Relax," he whispers.

The scent of his fresh, minty breath crosses my cheek. I lick my lips because they are dry, not because I want to taste his whisper.

"I think we should discuss Rebecca and DJ," I state firmly, not giving away my nervousness.

It's his turn to stiffen. "Why?"

"You know why," I answer.

With a loud sigh, he rolls away from me.

"What did my meddling brother tell you?"

Rolling to my back, I try to summarize as much as possible, but end up giving him everything Scarlett and Hugh discussed.

"Damon, we are not a *cure* for your pain and loss." I stare at the ceiling after the words leave my lips.

"I know that, Olivia," he barks, but then his tone softens. "You make me feel better. I can't deny that, but there is so much more to all of this. More than I realized would be involved when I came looking for you."

"Why would you look for us? You had to know it would cause problems. What if I'd been married or had more children? What if I'd lost—?"

"There are a lot of what ifs, but I needed it. I know it's hard for you to understand, because you don't know what it's like to lose everything and feel so empty. It's as if a piece of you is carved out and nothing can fill it. It's just a bottomless pit."

I lock my jaw tight and will myself not to think about Isaac or his baby. Damon would be surprised if knew just how closely I could relate. A part of me wanted to sympathize with him, but the selfish part didn't want to share our common bond in sorrow and loss.

"Then this letter appears and there is confirmation that I may have a child out there in the world. There is a part of me, living and breathing, but I don't know what they look like, what their name is, if they are well. How could I not try to find you?"

He takes a deep breath before continuing.

"You think I'm using you both as a replacement. I understand why you think that, but it's not true. Not anymore."

Damon pauses and I open my mouth to speak, but he continues.

"At first, I was being selfish. I wanted to feel like a whole person again. I wanted to get back what I lost and fix all the mistakes I made. So, when I started looking for you and Alex...for anyone who conceived my child, it was in hopes to make me human once more — to feel alive."

He shifts, rolling onto his side. Bending his arm at the elbow, he props his head on his fist.

"I died with them in that car, but felt resurrected the moment I saw *him*." Damon's eyes blaze with intensity. The fingers of his left hand start a slow trace over my cheek and jaw. "And then, there was you. You were unexpected."

Furrowing my brow, I ask, "What do you mean?"

"The moment we were together in Vegas, the connection began. I know you feel it. I'm not blind."

I try to look away from him, but his hand turns my face back.

"How much I want you scares me and fills me with so much guilt."

"Guilt?" I whisper.

With our eyes locked on each other's, he nods.

"I never wanted Rebecca the way I want you."

I open my mouth to object, but he doesn't let me.

"I loved her, but I didn't know I could feel like this with someone — the way I feel with you. Pieces that were missing between Rebecca and I, things we couldn't quite do for each other, are not an issue with you. You are absolute, everything I never knew I needed, even when I knew I needed Alex."

Frozen silent with my lips parted and held hostage by his gaze, I can't process what he's saying. The moment his lips press to mine, the undeniable connection sizzles. The one I deny on a daily basis.

Terrified by both the physical and emotional feelings, I pull my lips away and turn my head.

His hand cups my neck as he rests his forehead on my left shoulder. No other words are said and neither of us moves. And when his breathing evens, I know he is asleep. It takes me much longer to fall asleep with the feeling of his body against mine, the words he just spoke circling in my head, and the lingering sizzle he left on my lips.

"Momma!" Alex wakes me with a shout.

I try to stretch, but Damon's body restricts the action.

"Momma!"

"Damon," I say while shoving at the restraining arm across me.

"Olivia," he groans in a husky whisper, causing heat to shoot straight between my legs.

He cuddles in closer, reflexively pressing his morning hardness against my leg. I shove at him again.

"Momma!" Alex's yell is more panicked.

"I'm coming, buddy," I yell back, shoving hard enough to move Damon off me.

"What's wrong?" Damon gasps, sitting up.

"Alex is awake," I answer without looking back as I exit the bedroom.

Damon

My body misses hers the moment she slides out from beneath me. The hard throb between my thighs burns for attention, but I climb out of bed and find Olivia calming Alex next to his bed.

"Is he alright?" I yawn.

Her eyes reach mine and my heart pounds. I look between them, standing in my apartment, in a nursery, and the rest of my life finally feels worth living. She will hate me, but I can't let them go. Not now. Not ever. This is right. Us, as a family, is right.

"Yeah, he's just adjusting to new surroundings."

Olivia will no longer meet my eyes. She smiles small and squeezes by me with Alex in her arms.

Sighing, I know last night's conversation is probably the cause. I'd hoped it would make her walls come down just a little; instead, it seems to have had the opposite effect. Maybe I should have told her the entire tale of the night my world crashed down around me. Would it make her hate me more? Would she believe me? Maybe she would blame me, too.

Stepping out of Alex's room, I stand in the hallway, listening to her move around the kitchen as she talks to Alex. My instinct is to run to her, beg her to understand, to accept us, but Olivia is stubborn and determined. Qualities I can admire, but not when I'm trying to get her to accept our unusual circumstances. Fighting the instinct, I go back to my room and get dressed.

Showered and dressed, I return to Olivia and Alex. They're both sitting at the kitchen island, eating.

"There's a plate in the oven for you." She motions toward the oven with her fork.

"Thank you."

Retrieving my plate, I sit at the island next to them. We eat in silence, Olivia still distant and my nerves about today's plan to visit with my mother weighing on me.

As I clear the breakfast dishes, Olivia goes upstairs to get Alex and herself ready. The closer we get to departure, the more anxious I become.

Mother had been supportive of the search for Alex. However, she does not approve of my impromptu marriage in Vegas. To be more specific, she is bitterly angry I entered a marriage with Olivia. But not going to see Mother isn't an option. Today has to take place under my terms and arrangements. If left to her own devices, my mother would ensure a meeting and it would not be in anyone's favor but her own.

"When are we leaving?"

"What?" I quip, snapping out my worrisome thoughts.

"For your mother's. When are we leaving?" Olivia frowns.

"Not for a few hours," I answer, still a bit distracted by my thoughts.

With a silent nod, she places Alex, who is freshly dressed in khaki pants and green polo shirt, onto his feet. He hurries over to the toys from Heidi and my father left in the living area.

"Will I be getting the silent treatment for the rest of your visit, or just today?"

"Sorry," she mumbles, wrapping her arms around her middle.

With a deep breath, I push off the island I'd been leaning against and approach her.

Her head lifts at my movement and she takes a step back.

"I didn't say those things last night just to say them. It was complete honesty. I meant every word."

I watch her swallow before speaking.

"I know you think you and I have a connection—"

"Damn it, Olivia," I growl low, not wanting to draw Alex's attention. "I don't think it, I know it."

"Mon," Alex calls out.

Taking a deep, calming breath, I turn to him.

"Yeah, buddy?" Smiling, I walk to him.

"Pay blocks." He tugs on the basket of multicolored cubes.

I help him pull out the toys and sit on the floor.

"Of course we can play blocks together."

Once settled onto the floor, I glance behind me to find Olivia gone — probably back upstairs.

After an hour of playing blocks with my son, Olivia returns to the living room dressed in a pair of black pants, which hug her legs, a long-sleeved, blue-green, flowing blouse that reaches almost mid-thigh, and a black belt that accentuates her thin figure. The color of her blouse compliments her fair, freckled skin and bright red hair. I could only wish we were alone and she was willing.

Turning my attention back to Alex, I ruffle his hair.

"You ready to go for a visit today?"

I pick up a couple blocks and put them back in the basket.

"No," Alex states firmly, pulling the blocks back out.

"We are going bye-bye to meet your grandmother," I repeat, cleaning up the blocks.

"NO!" he shouts. "Pay blocks!"

Wide-eyed, I stare at him, unsure of how to handle the outburst.

"Alexander," Olivia authoritatively warns as she makes her way next to him.

His body tenses, but he refuses to look at her.

"We are leaving, so let's clean up, please."

Squatting next to him, she starts placing more blocks in the basket.

He pouts for a moment before slamming each block into the basket.

"Be easy," Olivia orders.

Alex listens, helping to put the remaining toys where they belong.

At ten-thirty, we are received at my mother's home by her butler, Norman.

Olivia looks more nervous than she did at my father's, but the Banks Mansion can do that to people. She starts fidgeting and holds Alex closer.

"Norman," I greet with a nod.

"Mr. Knyght." He returns a brief nod. "Your mother is waiting for you in the breakfast room."

"Thank you."

Sliding my arm around Olivia's waist, I lead her to my mother.

"She has a room just for breakfast?" Olivia whispers.

I silently chuckle.

"It's just a fancy name for the room. I did mention I come from money, right?"

She looks up at me, annoyed. I grin.

"Well, my mother is born and bred money. It's her family with the high pedigree and old money."

When we reach the open French doors, I usher Olivia inside. We're the immediate focus of my mother's cold green eyes. She openly appraises Olivia and then Alex. Finally, she looks at me.

"Damon, come."

With a tap to her cheek, she prompts me to kiss her in greeting.

Slipping away from Olivia, I move to my mother's side.

"How are you, Mother?" I kiss her.

"Nothing new to report."

Her eyes bore into Olivia. I can feel the tension and Olivia's nervous fidgeting. Knowing my mother can exploit a weakness like a shark with the scent of blood, I move back to Olivia's side for support.

"Introduce me to my grandson, Damon. I've waited long enough to meet him." Straightening her already perfect posture, she looks expectantly at Alex.

Olivia hesitates, but I urge her forward. She complies, but only a few steps, so I take Alex into my arms and bring him to my mother.

"Mother, this is Alexander, your grandson."

Sitting in a chair beside her at the round table, I put Alex eyelevel with her. Alex grasps my shirt, hiding his face in my neck. *I feel your pain, little buddy.* I rub his back, hoping to soothe him.

"Let's have a look."

She shifts around in her seat and pulls his arm from my chest so she can look him over. Alex resists, but finally gives in.

"He has your eyes and that God awful hair." She turns to Olivia. "It should be cut shorter to keep it from looking so wild."

I shoot a look at Olivia, who is obviously trying to keep her anger in check.

"He also has a lot of his mother in him, I see." Mother's disappointing tone brings my attention back to her.

"Speaking of his mother, this is my wife, Olivia."

I motion for Olivia to take a seat next to me. She doesn't. My mother briefly glances to her before turning back to me.

"Olivia, this is my mother, Mildred Banks-Knyght."

"Yes, I see." Mildred forces a smile and then takes a deep breath. "Olivia, please sit. Your standing is making me uncomfortable," she states without looking at her.

"Wouldn't want that, now would we?" Olivia mumbles, taking a seat next to me.

Clearing my throat, I situate Alex in my lap so he can face the table, though he still won't fully acknowledge my mother.

"So, how long is he visiting?"

Mother picks up her antique teacup and sips slowly.

"Until the end of the week." There's no hiding the sadness at the mention of them leaving.

"I see." She places her cup back onto the saucer and sets the saucer on the table. "When will he be back to spend some time or to live with you?" she asks.

"Excuse me?" Olivia interrupts.

"Did you not understand the question, dear?" my mother patronizes.

"Mother," I warn.

She waves me off.

"Damon, I understand your need for *rebellion*, but your choice to marry is absolutely preposterous. And to top off this insanity, you didn't secure any of your assets before marrying this...this girl."

I quickly turn my attention to Olivia, wanting to calm the anger I know she will be feeling, but what I see is smugness.

"I completely agree, Miss Banks."

Olivia smiles at me before turning her attention to my mother.

"Excuse me?" my mother asks incredulously. "You agree with me?"

"Yes. In fact, I've offered your son an annulment, but he's refused me." Olivia crosses her arms over her chest.

I narrow my eyes at her.

"Is this true, Damon?"

"It's more complicated than that," I snap. "Think of Alex."

"Hmm..." my mother responds.

"Damon, I've told you we could make arrangements for Alex and for you to be in each other's lives. The annulment has nothing to do with him." Olivia reaches for a teacup and sips what I'm sure she believes to be a victory drink.

"Damon Patrick!" my mother exclaims, her body shaking from anger. "Agree to this immediately. Have the lawyers review the paperwork and sign the damn papers. Make visitation and custody agreements now."

"I'm not a child. I can make my own decisions."

Adrenaline causes my body to shake and anger boils in my stomach.

"Enough with this behavior. Do as I say!" Her hand slaps the table, causing the china to chatter.

Out of the corner of my eye, Olivia flinches, guilt flashing in her eyes. She has no idea what she's started or whom she has started it with.

"Are you listening to me?"

I meet my mother's gaze, knowing she's about to share her famous speech.

"You are my only child. The only heir to the Banks' empire and I have worked too damn hard for you to throw it all away on childish acts of insurgency. When we discussed your actions regarding this matter, I told you to seek out your child or children. Not once did I approve of marriage."

She begins to cough and wheeze.

"Damon?" Olivia scoots to the end of her seat, preparing to help my mother. "We should help her."

Ignoring Olivia's panic and my mother's act, I sit back in the chair.

"Mother, it's not going to work this time. Now, you can get control of yourself and visit with your grandson or we can go. Which shall it be?"

Mildred Banks immediately stops her theatrics and narrows her eyes on me.

"I don't know what's gotten into you," she grumbles, picking up her cup and sipping once more.

The look of disbelieve on Olivia's face is priceless. I have to suppress my urge to laugh.

"I've grown up. It would be quite nice if you would respect that and stop acting."

I grab a couple of finger sandwiches the maid just placed on the table and set them in front of Alex.

The remainder of the visit goes in the fashion it started. She ignores Olivia, dotes on Alex, and continues attempting to convince me to sign the papers.

After a couple of hours, I excuse us from my mother's presence. Olivia thanks her for her hospitality, which I'm sure takes great effort, and we get into the car, where Alex falls asleep and Olivia stays quiet.

"Penny for your thoughts?" I ask while maneuvering the car.

"Your family, they are...I mean, they are crazy." She shakes her head.

I laugh.

"I didn't realize I was being funny." She raises her brow at me.

"Oh, it is very funny. Straight forward and funny." My body shakes with silent laughter during the last few minutes of the drive.

Alex doesn't wake when we return, so I carry him to his bed. Olivia follows, helping to tuck him in.

"You should get dressed," I state as we leave Alex's room.

"Where are we going?

"It's a surprise." I wink.

"I need to know how to dress." She rolls her eyes.

"It's a well-known restaurant in New York. Exclusive." I grin slyly.

"Thanks for nothing," she teases and disappears into what I'm hoping will one day be *our* room.

I spend the next hour in my home office making calls and responding to emails. Just as I finish up and prepare to get ready for the evening, Heidi arrives to watch Alex.

"Good afternoon, Heidi."

We embrace briefly before she pulls back and looks around me.

"Where is that handsome son of yours?" Brushing by me, she takes a deeper look into the apartment.

"He's napping, but will probably be up soon, if not already." I shut the door behind me and walk toward Heidi.

"Oh," she sighs disappointedly.

"He's awake."

Heidi and I both look up the stairs where Olivia is slowly descending with Alex on her hip.

"Idee," Alex squeals in excitement.

"Come to Idee, my precious boy." Heidi snatches up Alex before Olivia has both feet on the main floor. The sound of the two giggling fills the room.

Heidi is acting more like the doting grandma than my own mother. I'm much happier Alex has Heidi to watch over him today rather than my mother, who repeatedly called Heidi a gold-digging child bride during my childhood.

"I'm almost ready. I just need to finish getting dressed."

Olivia's voice pulls my attention to where she stands at the base of the staircase in my robe. Licking my lips, I fight the urge to pull the loose end of the terry loops. My dick swells as I imagine what I would find underneath the terry cloth.

She clears her throat and I meet her eyes.

"Eyes up here." She motions to her face with one hand while fisting the collar of the robe together.

I grin. Reaching out and caressing her cheek, I take one step closer.

"My robe looks good on you, but it would look better tossed over the railing."

With a sharp intake of breath, she steps back from me and hurries up the stairs.

I follow.

While she dresses in the bathroom, I slip into dark jeans and a light gray, button down shirt. On the last button, the bathroom door opens.

Olivia emerges, wearing the tightest black jeans and a dark purple, sleeveless turtleneck. Every item of clothing clings to her slender body, revealing the soft curve of her waist and swell of her breasts. Her long red hair slicked back into a ponytail makes me think of naughty fist wrapping actions. Then, just to torture me, she topped off her please-fuck-me-on-the-restaurant-table outfit with tall, black, leather leave-them-on-while-you-bury-your-face-between-my-legs boots.

I'm pretty sure I groan out loud.

When she stands, fully dressed, I look at her beautiful face. One eyebrow raises before she shakes her head with an eye roll.

"What?" I shrug. "How am I supposed to react to your outfit?"

Still shaking her head, she exits the bedroom.

I grab a dark gray jacket from my closet door, slip into it, and follow her downstairs. When I reach the first floor, the vision of Olivia bent over at the waist kissing Alex on his head greets me. My body springs to life once again, making me regret wearing jeans in place of roomier cotton slacks. Being alone with her tonight, dressed as she is...it's going to be difficult to resist touching her.

"Be good for Heidi, okay?" She kisses Alex once more before straightening to her full height.

I nod, leaning down to kiss my son goodbye.

"Listen to Grandma Idee."

Alex smiles and from the corner of my eye, I see Heidi beam from being called his grandma.

In the elevator ride down to the car, Olivia fidgets nervously next to me.

Taking her hand, I try to soothe her nerves. "He will be fine."

"What if he freaks because I'm not there?" Biting her bottom lip, she looks up at me.

I cup her face with my free hand and rub at her lip until she releases it from her teeth.

"Heidi will call if anything happens, and it's clear he likes her."

"You promise you aren't going to have him taken from me while we're out?" Her brow furrows, but I can tell she's completely serious.

I drop my hand from her face and release her hand from my grasp.

"I can't believe you think I would do something like that."

I take a step back from her, feeling like someone just sucker punched me in the stomach.

"I-I'm sorry, but put yourself in my shoes. I'm nervous. You tracked me down to find him, and you…"

"I what, Olivia?"

My jaw tenses.

"You've dealt with some past issues…" she pauses, taking a deep breath. "Look, I'm sorry. I blurted it out before I thought about what I was saying."

I close my eyes and deeply breathe through my nose, trying to relax the anger and hurt coursing inside me. The elevator chimes, announcing our arrival to the lobby. I quickly exit, leaving her behind, but stop a few feet away and turn around. Through clenched teeth, I clarify something she needs to hear.

"I would *never* do that to you or him."

She steps off the elevator until she's just a foot away from me.

"Damon, you've done some things people would think were crazy, so I had that thought and spoke too quickly. But how can you blame me for thinking you may—?"

"Because, Olivia, I'm not a cold hearted monster who would strip a child away from his mother," I growl. Snatching her hand, I pull her out of the building and to my awaiting car.

Does she really believe I am capable of stealing our son away? Why can't she believe I want them both?

Chapter ten — oh god, yes, new york!
Damon

The drive to the restaurant is quiet and full of tension.

"I'm sorry," she whispers when I help her from the car.

"It's over," I mumble. "I'm sorry you got the impression I would do something like that."

Entering Masa, the hostess gives us a welcoming smile and seats us at the private table I reserved for tonight. The waitress is quick to get our drink order and run through the specials. Once the waitress leaves, Olivia and I lock eyes over our menus.

"I'm sorry," she whispers once more.

"No more apologies." I shake my head and smile. "Okay?"

She nods and forces a smile.

The waitress efficiently brings our drinks, takes our meal order, clears the menus, and departs.

"I think we should take this time to learn more about each other."

"Okay." She nods and sips at her water. "Did you always want to work for your mother?"

"You've learned enough about me over the past few days. It's my turn."

Her eyes widen in a brief moment of panic before she composes herself.

"Didn't you learn enough through your investigation?" She puts her water glass to her lips once more.

"It seems there are things not so easily uncovered by a private investigator. So, how about you tell me about Isaac?"

She chokes on her water and hurries to cover her mouth with the cloth napkin in her lap.

"How do you know that name?"

"Who is he, Olivia? And why is my son's middle name the same as his?" I narrow my eyes at her attempt to deflect.

"An ex-boyfriend." She shrugs and looks around the room, refusing to look at me.

"An ex-boyfriend whose things you just so happen to hang on to?" I ask, raising a brow.

The fact that I felt this jealously over the memory of a dead man should be cause for concern, but I can't worry about it right now.

"Please, don't do this." She closes her eyes and drops her chin.

Guilt tears through my jealousy.

"I didn't mean to upset you."

Her head jerks up, eyes blazing.

"Yes, you did. You knew exactly what you were doing. How much do you already know, Damon? Tell me."

"I know you used to be with him and he died in a motorcycle accident."

"Is that it?" she snaps, crossing her arms over her chest. "Is that really all you know?"

"Yes. It's all the P.I. could uncover."

She snorts.

"You should demand a refund then."

I notice her watery eyes as she takes a deep breath and releases it through her flaring nose. Her eyes meet and lock on mine.

"Isaac was the love of my life."

Her words hurt a little.

"I lost his baby after his death." Venom pours from her words. "Are you happy now, or is there more you need to know?"

"Is that why you sought out a donor to have a child?"

She stares angrily, nose still flaring.

"I chose a donor because I didn't want or need a man in my life." Her words are cold and practiced.

"You don't want to fall for someone else, do you?"

Her eyes widen just enough for me to notice before she slips her angry mask back on.

"Fuck you," she growls before standing. "Go to hell, Damon. Don't pretend to know my innermost feelings." Throwing the napkin on the table, she stomps away.

I watch her storm off, unsure of where she thinks she's going to go. I have the valet ticket in my pocket and she doesn't know the address to my apartment. At least, I don't think she knows. Relaxing back in my chair, I wait for her to finish her tantrum and return.

Twenty minutes later, ten of which her food has been waiting, she returns and sits in her seat.

"Welcome back." I fight not to laugh, but can't hide my smile.

"Shut up." She pushes her plate away from her. "You suck at dates."

No longer able to hold it back, I laugh — loudly.

"It's not funny! You do suck at them."

"Okay, okay." I put my hands up and try to squelch my laughter, but catch her trying not to laugh out loud, too.

"I'm sorry," I half say, half laugh. "Honestly," I compose myself, "I apologize for upsetting you. I'm just curious about him and about you. You are so unwilling to share your past with me."

"There's no reason to know the details of my life, Damon. We share a child and nothing else. My past doesn't play a part in your life any further than Alex."

I stiffen at her constant reminder of our expiration date.

"Please eat," I grumble, turning my attention to my own plate.

She hesitates, her hard eyes giving way to her annoyance at my request.

At the completion of the meal, she starts to fidget. As I pay the bill and we prepare to leave, she grows more anxious. I finally realize she's excited at the thought of ending this night.

Once in the car, I decide it's time for her to understand that I'm not through with her just yet.

"Did you enjoy dinner?" I pull away from the restaurant and into New York traffic.

"Yes." She nods. "Thank you. For dinner," she quickly adds.

"It's my pleasure. Now, we're on to the next destination." I try not to smile too wide or reveal my amusement.

I feel her wide eyes on me before she speaks.

"What do you mean? Aren't we going back to your apartment?" I can't miss the panic in her voice.

"Nope, but would you like to call to check on Alex?" Pulling out my phone, knowing she will say yes, I dial Heidi and hand the phone to her.

"Hello." She pauses. "Yeah, he's driving. I just want to check in on him." Another pause, this time a bit longer. "Really? That's great. Can I speak to him?"

As I maneuver through the traffic, I see her rub the palm of her free hand on her thigh out of the corner of my eye.

"Hey, little man. I miss you," she coos before giggling. "Are you being good?" She laughs once more. "Okay, baby, go have more fun and listen to Heidi."

She ends the call and hands the phone back to me.

"He's doing well, I take it?" Keeping my eyes on the road, I slip my phone into my jacket pocket.

"Yeah," she sighs.

Parking in a space near the French Culinary Institute, I climb out and round the car. I open her door and she unfolds her body form the vehicle. Confusion wrinkles her face.

"What are we doing here?"

"You'll see." I grin, placing my hand on her lower back and guiding her to the door.

She stops a couple feet from the entrance and turns to me.

"Damon, it's late and this place is obviously closed," she argues.

"Not to us." With a shrug, I turn her back around.

With the press of the button, one of the school board members greets us. She introduces herself and quickly leads us to a kitchen. Two fully supplied steel tables sit at the front of the room.

"What's going on?" She eyes me while I slip off my jacket and wrap an apron around my body.

I only smile and put an apron over her head, spinning her so I can tie the back.

"Good evening."

Olivia jumps at the unfamiliar voice.

"Good eve...oh my goodness," she gasps. "You-you're Jaques Torres," she stutters, her mouth gaping open.

"The last time I checked." The chef chuckles.

"Damon?" Her eyes still on Jaques, she grabs my sleeve and tugs. "Do you know who he is?"

"I hope he's Jaques Torres, since that's who I made arrangements with tonight."

She looks up at me, her mouth still open and eyes round in surprise. Closing her mouth, she releases my sleeve and steps toward him.

"You're Jacques Torres," she restates in a breathy voice. "You're amazing."

Her head slightly tilted, the lilt to her voice is amusing.

I move to stand beside her at the workstation facing Jacques.

"The work you've done with chocolate is unbelievable."

I can't help but laugh at her star-struck behavior. This earns me an elbow to my side.

"Thank you," Jacques laughs. "Now, let's get started on our lesson."

"Lesson? What Lesson?"

She doesn't wait for a response; instead, she double checks that the apron is secured around her while pushing past me to stand next to Jacques.

Part of me doesn't like sharing her with this man, but my ego is eating up the fact that I did this for her.

Olivia works diligently next to Jacques over the next hour and a half. I mostly stand back and watch her. Olivia is beautiful all of the time, but in this atmosphere — in her element — she radiates confidence and beauty. My heart aches, wishing she could sense how much I feel for her.

When Jacques and Olivia finish, I volunteer as taste tester. After all, it's the least I can do. Then we say our goodbyes to Jaques and the board member before returning to my car.

"That. Was. Amazing."

Olivia practically floats on air. When she wraps her arms around me, I freeze.

"Thank you. No one has ever done anything like that for me."

Shaking off the shock of her initiating physical contact, I circle my arms around her, holding her warm body against mine. She smells of chocolate. Before I can find out whether she tastes the same, she pulls away and slips into the car.

"You're very welcome."

I close her door before rounding the car to drive us home.

Before heading home to my father, Heidi fills us in on how wonderful Alex has been all evening and that he's been sleeping for about an hour. Olivia goes upstairs to check on Alex and head to bed. I have some emails and work to catch up on before I can join her.

Thursday morning, I wake with a smile. Olivia is lying stomach down, facing away from me. My arm rests across her lower back, rising and falling with her breaths. There is no tension or awkwardness. She is relaxed and at ease. I snuggle in closer to saturate myself in the scent of her, relishing the moment before she wakes and pushes me away.

The blissful moment ends too soon for my liking. She shifts and starts to stretch her limbs. Closing my eyes, I pretend to be sleeping.

Her muscles flex below my arm, letting me know she has twisted her body to look at me. A small sigh escapes her lips before she slips from under me and into the bathroom. I roll to my back, rub sleep from my eyes, and, with my own sigh, climb from bed to check on Alex.

With Alex still sleeping, I start coffee and go to my office for my cell phone. Two text alerts show on the screen. One from Hugh, apologizing for butting into things, and the other is from Scarlett. No apology, just a confirmation that we are meeting her and Hugh for lunch today.

Since Hugh is safer to speak to, I call to confirm with him instead of Scarlett.

"Good morning," he answers with a hint of surprise.

"I'm listening," I respond curtly.

"Damon, you know we care and love you dearly, but she needs to have her eyes wide open going into this. She has to know everything if you want a remote chance with her." He sighs heavily. "You need to tell her the rest."

"It's my business to tell, not yours."

"We understand that, but you are going to ruin things before you truly get an opportunity at a real relationship."

"Hugh..."

"She needs to know about—"

"If you even think about further butting into my life, I cannot be responsible for what happens between us."

He sighs once more, this time in defeat.

"You need to tell her about it before she hears it from someone else. I am telling you now, do it before she finds out the wrong way."

"You think I don't realize the edge I'm walking?" I growl. "Do you think I want to risk this over one almost indiscretion? I'll be damned if I get further into that night than necessary."

"But the guilt—"

"I'll deal with that. It's not yours to bear."

"How can you say that? I've never spoken about the details, not even to Scarlett, and it eats away at me. We don't keep secrets and I bear this burden every day...for you!" Hugh's voice rises.

"Keep your mouth shut," I order through clenched teeth.

"You need to handle this better, Damon. I won't say anything, but *if* the question is asked, I won't lie for you any longer."

"Fuck you," I growl and hang up.

Tossing my cell to the desk, I press my palms onto the mahogany top and try to calm.

Nothing happened, yet just knowing I considered—

"What was that about?"

Olivia's voice cuts my thoughts and draws my attention. She stands in the doorway of my office with a black coffee cup in her hands, her brow wrinkled in confusion.

"Nothing," I quip.

The look she gives shows her disbelief, so I attempt to change the subject.

"Hugh and I simply don't agree about something."

"Uh huh." Her lips purse tightly before she walks away from the door.

"Did you need something?" I question as I follow.

"Yeah, the truth, but it's clear I won't be getting that from you," she responds with her back to me as she keeps walking.

My lips twitch with the urge to confess my sins, my deepest, darkest secrets — where I truly was the night Rebecca and DJ died, who I was with, what I'd almost done, and even the truth about Alex.

"Momma!" Alex calls through the baby monitor sitting on the kitchen island. Olivia changes course to get him.

"I'm coming, little man," she responds, climbing the stairs.

My phone rings in the distance and I stomp back to my office. Scarlett.

"What?" I bite out as I walk to the kitchen for coffee.

"Don't take that tone with me Damon," she scolds, as if she were my mother.

"I'm sorry," I mumble, hating her ability to make me feel like a child.

"As you should be." A small giggle follows her response. "I want you to meet us for lunch at Tavern on the Green. I already made the reservation and won't take no for an answer, so meet us at twelve." She hangs up.

Groaning, I slam the phone to the marble countertop.

"Another nothing, huh?" Olivia asks, carrying Alex to his highchair.

"No, that was Scarlett demanding our attendance for lunch this afternoon. We don't have to go if you would rather do something else." Pushing away from the counter, and my phone, I move toward the coffee.

"Did you have something else planned?" she asks from within the refrigerator.

She straightens, pulling out eggs, milk, and butter.

"Which cabinet holds your pantry items?" She looks toward me for guidance and I point to the large cabinet behind her. She turns and stretches for a box of pancake mix. After two attempts to reach the top shelf, she braces her hands like she's going to climb.

I quickly move to grasp her waist to prevent her from falling. She starts a bit and tenses under my touch.

"Thanks." Her words are breathy as she slips down against my chest.

Olivia quickly moves away from me, busying herself with making pancakes.

I sit in a chair next to Alex and play a game of peek-a-boo until Olivia places pancakes on the breakfast bar. We eat in comfortable silence, discussing the warm October weather expected and decide we should get Alex out of the apartment.

While Olivia gets herself and Alex dressed for the day, I clean up breakfast plates and mixing bowls. When complete, I go to get myself dressed.

Once dressed, I meet Olivia and Alex in his room.

"I'm thinking we could take Alex to the Central Park Zoo."

They both turn to me. The wooden doorframe presses into my shoulder as I lean and wait for her to respond.

"Dad," Alex blurts, toddling toward me.

My eyes shoot to Olivia, both of us wearing matching expressions of shock. I finally find my voice.

"Yeah, that's right."

Stepping into the room, I lift him into the air.

"I'm your dad."

There is no fighting the smile off my face. Pulling him close to my chest, I look down to Olivia. A mixture of emotions play on her face.

"So, what do you think?" I ask, bringing the conversation back to the zoo.

"Yeah, sure." She shakes her head.

Obviously, she's settled on being annoyed by this stepping-stone between Alex and me.

"You want to go see some animals?" I tickle under his chin.

He laughs and then screams, "Anmahs!"

After Alex's day bag is packed and we have extra jackets, I hail a cab to take us to the zoo. Most of the animals are still outside and we haven't needed our coats yet. Halfway through our outing, my phone vibrates and dings. Pulling it out of my pocket, I find another text from Scarlett.

You had better show up.

I shake my head and slip the phone back into my pocket.

"Scarlett is adamant we join them for lunch."

"Okay." Olivia shrugs.

She helps Alex to stand on a stone fence to see the animal enclosure better.

"We should start heading back to the entrance if we want to meet with them on time."

"Okay."

Narrowing my eyes, I study her lack of reaction.

"Are you going to speak to me at all today?"

She helps Alex back into a wagon and we make our way back to the entrance.

"I've spoken to you." She leans down to give Alex a spill-proof cup.

"Hardly," I growl. "You're being very short."

She sighs.

"I don't appreciate being lied to."

We don't speak again or look at each other until we are secured in another cab.

"What if I said I was arguing with my brother because he and Scarlett can't mind their own business?"

"Is that the truth? Or has it taken you all morning to come up with this?" She raises a brow.

"The truth."

"Hmm." She turns to look out the window. She's obviously not sure whether she should believe me.

The ride to the restaurant is quiet, aside from Alex squealing.

When we arrive, Scarlett swoops in on Alex and Olivia. Hugh stands, calmly and apprehensively, gaging my reaction to his presence.

"Everything okay?" I ask.

He nods. "I've said my piece."

"As have I." I raise my brow and smirk.

"Come and sit down, you two." Scarlett rolls her eyes and waves us over to two empty seats.

During lunch, the previous tension between Hugh and I dissolves. We casually discuss business and family. Scarlett engages Olivia to learn more about her and Alex.

"Oh, Damon," Scarlett blurts across the table, "we got the box for the Yankees game. You two should come with us." It wasn't an invitation. She was making demands again.

"Scarlett, I've made some plans—"

"Cancel them. We have the box and it's the World Series. You and Olivia can join us. We'll have fun." She turns from me to Olivia. "Tell me you'll come?"

Scarlett doesn't pout, but she has this look that defies rejection. I almost feel bad for Olivia. She doesn't stand a chance.

"Well, I'm not sure. Alex will need a babysitter and I don't know if—"

"Heidi will watch him, I'm sure." I could've gotten us out of the invitation, but I'm now seeing the possibilities of this outing. An outing where Olivia and I can relax, have fun, and also have the buffer of another couple.

Scarlett smiles, knowing I'm completely onboard with the plans.

"Idee?" Alex looks around for her. "Idee?"

"You want to see Heidi, huh?" Scarlett coos.

A large grin lights up his little face.

"I guess. If Heidi doesn't mind, that is," Olivia hesitantly resigns.

"Since she's done nothing but talk about Alex since their night together, I'm sure she will be more than willing," Hugh reassures with a smile.

"We'll have to ask her." Olivia looks to me.

"Taking care of it now." Scarlett smiles, her phone already to her ear.

Scarlett is a force. And this is why she works for me.

"Heidi, it's Scar. We are out with Damon, Olivia, and Alex."

She pauses, and then tilts her phone from her face. Her eyes meet mine and then Hugh's.

"She says hello and she loves you both."

I smile. Heidi is a softer more loving force, but just as powerful.

"Heidi, can you watch Alex tomorrow evening?" Scar nods, listening. "I'm sure they can bring him to your house this time." Her eyes seek mine in a silent question.

I nod.

"Yes, they will bring him to you." Another pause. "Great, thank you so much!" A smile spreads over Scar's face. "Yes, I promise to start calling you mom, and I love you, too."

Scarlett ends the call, beaming. She's gotten her way — again.

"All set."

"I'm not so sure about leaving Alex in an unfamiliar house. I mean, he may get nervous about—"

"Olivia, he loves Heidi and she will spoil him rotten. You know how great he is with her."

She nods, reluctantly, looking at Alex and running her fingers through his hair. Pulling away from her touch, he shoves French fries in his mouth.

At the conclusion of lunch, we settle the final details of our night out. Scarlett calls it a double date and Olivia cringes.

"I'll have some Yankees clothes sent over to Damon's for you." Scarlett grins.

"My father would have a heart attack if he saw me in anything other than Pirates gear," Olivia giggles.

The sound is perfection.

Scarlett, a diehard Yankee girl, scrunches her face in distaste.

"Well, we'll remedy your penchant for black and gold tomorrow." She hugs Olivia as we part ways.

Alex fights sleep in the car on the way home, rubbing his eyes and sucking his fingers. He loses the battle just as we pull up to my building. Olivia leads the way to the elevator and to the apartment, as I cradle Alex in my arms. The curve and natural sway of her hips draws my attention.

She turns when we reach the door and catches me ogling her. I snap my eyes to her face, prepared for her annoyance. I'm surprised to find amusement glinting in her bright eyes. Shaking her head, she holds out her palm.

"Key?" she whispers.

"Left pocket," I respond in a hush, jutting my hip out.

For a moment, she hesitates, staring at my hip. Then she steps closer and slips her hand into my pocket.

Her fingers moving against me, so close to my groin, are enough to stir my lower body to life. I silently pray she finds the key before she finds me reacting like a teenager.

She fishes out the key and unlocks the door.

I calm myself, and my erection, while taking Alex to bed. On my way back downstairs, with the intention of going to my office, my body springs back to life at the sight before me.

Olivia lies across my couch, on her stomach, flipping through television channels. The curve of her ass is prominently displayed by the way she rests on her forearms.

Licking my lips and swallowing roughly, my fingers twitch to touch her, to glide over her curves and grip the plump flesh. Knowing she unwelcomes my touch, I turn quickly for my office and close the door behind me.

Groaning, I sit behind my desk and take deep breaths. No matter how much I try to fight the arousal, the image of her sprawled on my couch leads to memories of her naked body. It's been a month and I can still remember the softness of her skin, the way she molded against me, and how explosive the night had been. Reaching down, I adjust the discomfort in my pants.

Down, boy.

A crash and curse from the other side of the office door brings me out of my chair and moving toward the kitchen.

Olivia stands next to the counter with glass shards scattered around her sock covered feet. Her eyes move from the mess on the floor to me.

"I'm so sorry." She flushes from embarrassment and takes a step forward.

"Don't move." Throwing my hands out before me, I pin her with one look. "Stay there," I order and she obeys.

I turn, slip on the shoes I took off, and come back to the kitchen. Olivia still stands, unmoving. The glass crunches under the soles of my shoes as I step to her and lift her over my shoulder.

She squeals and fists the material on the back of my shirt.

After setting her down in a glass free zone, I move to the closet and retrieve the broom.

"Let me." She steps toward me. "It's my mess."

Waving her off, I sweep the glass into a pile. I reach for the dustpan, but Olivia grabs it first and crouches to help.

"Your feet," I object before noticing she slipped on shoes.

"All covered," she responds, emptying the glass into the garbage.

After returning the broom and dustpan, she looks up with concern in her eyes.

"I hope the glass wasn't valuable or of some sentimental value." She licks her lips in a nervous action. It doesn't help to quell the naughty thoughts swirling in my mind today.

Leaning against the counter, I grin.

"Olivia, until last week, I didn't even have glasses in the cabinet."

Her mouth pops open, closes, and then she laughs.

"In fact, just about everything was stocked right before you and Alex arrived. What were you trying to get?"

"The pitcher." She points to the highest shelf.

Reaching up, I hand it to her.

"Thanks." Blushing, she steps around me to a bowl of lemons I hadn't noticed.

"What are you making?"

"Lemonade."

I watch as she slices, squeezes, and tosses the juiced pieces into the sink. She continues by adding water, sugar, and stirs.

"What?" she asks in an annoyed sigh.

"What do you mean?"

"Why are watching me? It's making me self-conscious."

"I dunno." I shrug. "I was just watching."

Once she pours herself a drink, she returns to the living room and I walk back to my office.

After Alex wakes from his nap and eats a small snack, we play cars in the living room. The moment is quiet, casual, and, for me, so surreal. Crayons, cars, cartoons, and blocks are now more satisfying than anything else in life.

"What would you like for dinner?" I ask, my head buried in the three-foot coloring book Alex and I are working on.

When she doesn't respond, I look up and catch her in deep thought.

"Olivia?"

She blinks and focuses on me.

"I can cook something," she offers, standing from the floor and walking to the kitchen.

"I didn't mean you have to cook. We can call for delivery or go—"

"I can cook," she cuts me off with pots and pans banging.

Not wanting to argue this point, I return to coloring.

The evening remains quiet and casual. We follow dinner with a Disney movie, the three of us relaxing with Alex in the middle. With my arm stretched over the back of the couch, I can almost encompass both of them. When Alex falls asleep, Olivia carries him up to bed. As I follow, the doorbell rings.

"I'll get it."

I open the door and one of the doormen greets me, holding multiple bags in his arms.

"Miss Manson had these sent for Mrs. Knyght. May I bring them in?"

Stepping aside, I allow him to bring the bags in and set them to the floor. He quickly exits with a nod and a 'good evening'.

I stare at the multiple bags. *Just how much Yankees clothing does Scarlet think Olivia needs?*

"What is all that?" Olivia's question draws my eyes away from the mound of packages.

"I'm pretty sure it's your Yankees gear."

Reaching down, I pick the bags from the floor.

"All of this?" she asks, astonished.

"I'll carry them to the bedroom so you can go through them."

"I can take them," she reaches out.

Avoiding her hands, I step around and ascend the stairs.

"Thank you," she practically whispers when I set them on the bed.

"You're welcome." I quickly step to her and kiss the side of her head.

Before exiting the room, I turn back to her. "I'll be in my office if you need anything."

"Okay." She doesn't look up as she pulls clothing from a bag.

I hesitate a moment longer, watching her take shirts, shorts, a jacket, and other accessories from the bags. She mumbles about buying so much and how it probably cost a fortune. Keeping my amusement to myself, I descend to my office.

Friday morning, I wake alone in bed to loud screaming from downstairs. Jumping from the bed, I rush toward the loud voices.

"What the hell is going on?" I look between Maria, my housekeeper, to an annoyed Olivia.

"Please tell her who we are." Olivia gives me a pleading look.

"Maria," I grin and walk toward her, "this is my wife and son."

Her brow furrows. "Señor?"

"Yes, Maria." I move, standing next to Olivia and putting my arm around her. "This is my wife, Olivia, and our son, Alex."

Maria studies the three of us for a brief moment before relaxing her defensive stance.

Nodding my thanks in her direction, I turn to Olivia.

"Olivia, this is Maria, my housekeeper."

As the situation sinks in, I fight not to laugh.

"You're so intent on telling everyone about us, how about you make sure your cleaning lady doesn't think I'm robbing you with a baby on my hip?" She snorts and then laughs.

My laughter erupts and Alex even joins in with forced chuckles. As she goes about her weekly routine, Maria mumbles, "Loco."

We laugh harder.

After the unusual wake-up call, we eat a quick breakfast before getting ready for the day ahead of us. Olivia and Alex go upstairs to dress while I work in my office and Maria completes her three hours. Maria's departure makes me aware of the time. Needing to get ready for the day, I step away from the work waiting on my desk.

Stepping around the staircase, I see Alex sitting in his high chair with a wooden spoon and large white bowl. Walking closer to the open kitchen, I notice Olivia swaying around.

"Dad," Alex blurts, causing Olivia to spin around. "Bake cake," he says, his proud smile outlined in chocolate.

"I see that, buddy."

"Actually, we're making cupcakes," Olivia clarifies in an unusually shy manner before giving a small shrug. "I guess I can only stop baking for so long before the desire resurfaces."

"I'm not complaining." I smile wide. "This place has never smelled so amazing."

"Yum," Alex hums.

I move toward my chocolate covered son and kiss his head.

"I'm going to take a shower."

Olivia, having just placed a pan in the oven, turns at my statement.

"We should probably get going in about an hour. Preferably before Scarlett begins nagging me."

She smiles so warmly, my chest tingles and my arms ache to reach for her.

"Okay." She nods and waves a hand over the messy counter. "I'll clean this up and get Alex and myself ready to go."

Around noon, we pull into Heidi and my father's driveway. Heidi eagerly pushes their butler out of her way so she can scoop Alex out of Olivia's arms.

"There's my super handsome baby boy," she coos, placing kisses on his cheeks.

Giggling, he pushes her face away.

"Idee!" he exclaims.

We follow the two of them into the house. Once Heidi has convinced Olivia everything will be fine, we leave Alex and his things for the overnight stay.

Back in the car and on our way to the stadium, we fight the New York traffic. I figure this time alone is the perfect opportunity to ask some of the questions I have for her.

"I don't want to upset you, but I'd really like to talk while we are alone."

"Okay," she says, sounding hesitant.

"I'd like to know about your decision to have Alex."

Her head snaps in my direction. "No."

"No?" I furrow my brow, keeping my eyes on traffic.

"No," she affirms. "We are going to talk about why I had to hear about Rebecca and DJ from Scarlett and Hugh." From the corner of my eye, I see her cross her arms over her chest, her eyes planted firmly on me.

"They shouldn't have—"

"Well, they did and I want the whole story, Damon. All of it," she demands.

When I stay silent, her arms drop from her chest.

"Did they tell me everything or is there more?" she asks, her voice softer than before.

This is my chance, the chance to come clean.

"They told you what happened, and..."

"And what, Damon?" she presses.

"And it's the whole story." The words leave my mouth, my stomach flips, and instantly I want to take them back.

"Okay," she exhales, turning to look quietly out the window.

The rest of the drive is uncomfortably quiet. It's not until I'm leading her toward the company box that I obtain the courage I need.

"Olivia," I say, stopping us at the door to the box. "I need to—"

"You're here!" Scarlett exclaims, drawing Olivia's attention. She scans Olivia in her t-shirt, hooded jacket, and jeans. "Look at you all Yanked out! The colors are amazing on you." She winks, grabbing Olivia's hand and pulling her inside. "The drinks are over here."

"Oh, so it's going to be one of those games today?" I raise a brow, teasing Scarlett.

"Shush it, Patty! Olivia and I are going to have girl time. Go play with Hugh." She pulls Olivia away.

"You follow baseball, right?"

Olivia nods. "Yeah. My father is a big fan and we spend a lot of time watching together."

"Great," Scarlett sighs out. "It's so nice to be around someone who gets it for a change."

They huddle together next to the café style table lined with an assortment of drinks.

As I take a step toward Olivia, Hugh walks in front of me, holding up a beer.

"I'd leave them be." He glances toward Scarlett and Olivia as they move to the seating area. "Scarlett will verbally attack with more than your middle name if you don't."

Nodding my understanding, I raise the import beer to him.

"Thank you." I put the bottle to my lips.

"It's the least I can do since my fiancé will be monopolizing your...wife." He gives his head a small shake. "I'm still not used to that."

The two of us move to a set of cushioned chairs with a small table between. We're discussing the Proneau resolution when Scarlett interrupts us from across the room.

"Damon Knyght, do you have any idea who you married?"

Scarlett is twisted around on the couch, looking over the back, her wide eyes fixed on me.

"I'm pretty sure her name is Olivia." I smile, taking a pull from my beer.

From over the glass bottle, I watch Scarlett leap up and stalk toward me. She takes my beer, smacks me on the arm, and puts the bottle back on the table.

Hugh chuckles and I give him a quick glare. He covers his smile and looks adoringly at his fiancé.

"You are married to Olivia Harlow, smartass." She plants her hands on her hips.

Glancing around Scarlett, I look at a red-faced Olivia.

"Okay," I respond, still not understanding Scarlett's behavior.

"Harlow, Damon! As in, Harlow Cakes. Why didn't you tell me?"

"What does the bakery have to do with—?"

She smacks me again, adding a huff this time.

"I let the first one slide. I won't hesitate to retaliate if you hit me again. This is your only warning."

We stare at each other for a moment.

"Damon, she's famous. She makes some of the most amazing cakes. She's been featured in wedding magazines and on TV shows," Scarlett informs with a slight slur.

Glancing around Scarlett to Olivia, I mouth, "Really?"

She nods her crimson stained face.

"It's really not enough to make me famous, like Scarlett is insinuating."

Scarlett looks back at Olivia. "Don't be modest. Your work is quite beautiful. At least, what I've seen."

With a small shrug, I look back to Scarlett. "Her social stature isn't exactly my main attraction." I wiggle my brows.

"Behave yourself, Damon," Scarlett playfully scolds, glancing back toward Olivia. "You're lucky she didn't hear you," Scarlett whispers, "but I could always tell her all of the improper ideas you have." Grinning wide, she walks back to the couch and seats herself next to Olivia.

"You need to get her under control," I chuckle to Hugh.

"Like that is even possible," Hugh laughs. "Though, trying is quite fun." It was his turn to wiggle his brows.

We both laugh harder.

"The game is starting!" Scarlett cheers, pulling Olivia from the couch to the large, full-length windows.

Hugh and I stay seated, watching the girls drink, laugh, and yell through the glass. Olivia and Scarlett are not only providing entertainment, they are getting along so well, as if they've known each other for forever.

"Swing-batta-batta-swing," Scarlett yells, her hand smacking the glass. "What the hell was that?" she growls after the batter strikes out. Pouting, she moves toward the small bar. "We need more drinks," she declares.

"I really need to stop," Olivia argues.

"Oh, heck no, we are going to eat nachos, hot dogs, pretzels, and drink," Scarlett orders. "Speaking of nachos and hot dogs..." she turns her famous pout on Hugh, "honey, will you get us something to eat?"

"What do I get in return?" Hugh leans forward in his chair.

"You get to have your way with my uninhibited body." Twisting her body, she wiggles her ass at him. "And you know I'm up for *anything*."

"I don't want to know this," I groan.

"I'll be right back." Hugh stands from his chair, quick to run the errand.

"You're just jealous," Scarlett sticks out her tongue as she makes her way to get more drinks.

Olivia is bent over at the waist, laughing at the scene.

I can only stare at her smiling and enjoying herself. *Scarlett, you have no idea how jealous I am.*

Hugh returns in record time, placing baskets and plates on the table between us. Olivia and Scarlett join us, both of them clearly buzzing from the alcohol. They giggle like schoolgirls and laugh over the most ridiculous things throughout the meal and the rest of the game. Hugh and I have to pull the two of them away from each other in order to leave.

With Olivia in my arms, guiding her to the car, she looks up at me with sleepy eyes.

"I love Scarlett," she slightly slurs.

"I can tell she loves you, too."

Having had a few drinks myself, I help Olivia into the waiting car and slip in next to her.

"She loves you, too, Damon." Olivia curls against my side.

Instantly, my body ignites. I want to touch, caress, and grip. Keeping my urges in check, I only allow myself to place an arm around her.

"Who? Scarlett?" I ask.

"Mmhmm," she hums. "She speaks so nicely about you."

"Really?" I ask, genuinely surprised. Though I know Scarlett doesn't hate me, I never thought she would speak nicely about me to Olivia.

"Yes." She nods against my side. "She hates the sadness you've endured and wants you to be happy again." Olivia pulls her head away from me and looks up.

I look down and our eyes meet.

"She says it's been so long since she's seen you smile. Like truly and really smile." She gazes into my eyes for a moment longer before resting her head back against my side.

Every muscle in my body catches fire as her hand presses to my chest and slides to my opposite side. She's embracing me. Closing my eyes, I breathe in deep, only to become more aware of her scent and body surrounding mine.

Too soon, the car pulls up to my building. The driver opens the door. Assisting Olivia from the car, I'm a bit surprised that she is still awake. After all the drinks, food, and physical contact, I was sure she would have fallen asleep. Instead, she takes my hand and, with only a slight stagger, climbs from the car.

In the elevator, she leans against the wall and bends, taking each shoe off. The chime announces our arrival and, when the doors slide open, we walk the small distance to the apartment. As I work to unlock the door, Olivia catches me off guard — again. She leans against me from behind and presses her cheek to my back.

Taking a deep breath, I focus on the lock instead of the raging urge to ravage her body against the hallway wall. Twisting harder than necessary, I unlock the door and push it open.

Olivia pulls away and I want to yank her against me. She steps around me, walking into the apartment. I follow, closing and locking the door behind me. I continue to walk behind her, my attempt to keep her as close as possible, when she suddenly spins around to face me. Her hands plant against my chest.

"We should call and check on Alex." Her slight slurring reminds me of how much she's had to drink.

"I'm sure he's fine." I place my hands over hers, reveling in the feel of her touch.

"No, we need to check on him."

She slips her hands down my chest and into my pockets.

"What are you doing?" I ask, attempting to keep her hands from my full erection. Once touch and there is no telling what I'll do to her — drunk or not.

"I need your phone," she grumbles.

"He was fine when we called to tell him goodnight." Slipping my phone from my jacket, I hold it out to her.

"I just need to be sure." Her long fingers slip across the screen before she looks up to me, pouting. "I don't know your security code"

I want to suck her bottom lip into my mouth.

"6548," I breathe.

"What kind of code is that?" She twists her face, entering the numbers.

"O.L.I.V." I answer.

Her fingers freeze as her eyes widen and mouth parts on a sharp breath.

Taking the phone, I call Heidi and Olivia checks on Alex. Once she is satisfied, she stumbles toward the couch and lies down.

"I love Scarlet. She is so much fun." She throws an arm over her eyes.

I sit near her, pull her feet into my lap, and begin rubbing.

"Oh God," she moans, "that feels amazing."

My cock springs back to life. I move my hands up her calves, kneading the muscles. She moans and my dick throbs. By the time my hands reach her thighs, my jeans are the most comfortable item of clothing I could ever own.

Inching higher on her thighs, I quickly release her and move down the couch to calm myself.

"What's wrong?" She lifts her head from the couch, her large eyes focused on me.

"I...I just need to stop."

"Oh." Her lips press into a fine line.

She sits up slowly and tries to stand. Her balance wanes and she tips back.

Reaching out, I catch her before she falls.

"Thanks," she giggles.

Her hands grip my biceps and my breathing labors. Pulling her toward me, it's almost too much — too tempting. Her hip presses against the raging hard-on I've been trying to quell and I pull back.

"Oh." Her eyes widen.

I eye the round 'O' her mouth has forms, wanting to lick her lips, her skin. Reminding myself of how much she's had to drink, I step back further.

"You should go to bed," I growl, fighting the need to strip her bare and own every inch of her body.

"Okay," she whispers.

I must be delusional to think I hear disappointment in her voice.

Before she makes it to the stairs, I catch up, making sure she doesn't stumble.

"I'll bring you water and Tylenol." I leave her at the end of the bed, heading into the bathroom.

After retrieving the items, I step back into the bedroom. My hold loosens, causing the water and pills fall to the floor. She spins around when the glass clinks against the carpet.

She's wearing nothing but a thin, white, cotton tank top and panties.

In a flash, she snatches the black yoga pants from the bed and holds them in front of her chest as I stalk forward.

"I was about to—"

With my chest heaving and my breathing ragged through flared nostrils, I strip the pants from her hands.

"Damon—" She steps back, her calves pressing against the bed.

"Fuck, Olivia. You are absolutely beautiful." Dropping the pants to the floor, I grab her arm, pulling her back to my chest. My hands find purchase on her soft hips.

"We shouldn't—"

"Don't finish that sentence."

Sweeping the hair from her neck, I latch my mouth to her glorious skin. Fuck if the taste of her doesn't bring back memories of our night in Vegas.

She gasps.

Slipping my left hand from her hip, I cup her bare breast. I knead, sweeping my thumb over her hard nipple.

She moans.

Releasing her other hip, I slide downward. My fingers press against her cotton covered lips and rub.

She bucks her hips on another moan.

Turning her to face me, I capture her panting breaths with my mouth and press her toward the bed, laying her beneath me. Her weak protest is conquered by my tongue.

Our tongues thrust against each other, battling for dominance. Her hands caress my neck, slipping into my hair.

I hover over her body, tearing at my clothes. With limited space between us, I pull myself up to strip away my shirt and pants.

Staring down, Olivia's breasts rise and fall heavily. I climb over her once more, my mouth watering.

"Damon, stop." She uses her elbows to crawl back from me.

Grabbing onto her hip, I pull her underneath my naked body.

"Please, Olivia," I beg, kissing her neck. "You want this, too. I can feel it."

I run my hand from her hip, under her shirt, and feel her nipple pebble under my touch.

"This—" she presses at my chest.

"Is meant to be," I finish.

She presses against my chest harder.

"Stop!" she demands.

I comply, dropping my head onto her chest. Taking deep breaths, I try to calm the fire raging beneath my skin. Shifting my hips to move away, I briefly press against her.

She moans, thrusting forward.

"Olivia?" I look up, meeting her blazing eyes. "I don't know what you—"

Her hips press against me once more, her wide eyes full of confusion, lust, and desire. I flex my hand, brushing the pad of my thumb over her nipple. She tosses her head back with a whimper.

My hips press between her thighs, rubbing my bare flesh against the cotton barrier between us. Pushing the thin tank top up, I wrap my lips around her nipple — sucking, nipping, devouring her skin.

"Oh God," she cries.

Bringing my knees higher, I push her legs apart and steadily massage, cock to pussy.

"Fuck!" she wails, meeting my thrust.

Spurred by her response, I reach between us and push the cotton panties aside. Pushing the head of my cock inside, I press my forehead between her breasts. Slipping my hands behind her, I brace myself on my forearms and grip her shoulders.

Olivia pants and writhes beneath me, trying to push me further inside.

In a motion smoothed by her arousal, I'm buried to the hilt.

"Ah!" she exclaims, moving to meet me.

I pause for a moment, savoring the feel of her wrapped around me, pulling me deeper inside, before starting a slow rhythm.

Olivia, wanting more, drives her hips against mine — hard.

"Christ, Olivia," I growl, clenching my jaw, fighting the urge to pound into her.

She thrusts up again, breaking my restraint.

I grasp her left ankle and place it on my shoulder. Gripping behind her knee, I rock in and out of her, hard enough to press her thigh to her chest.

"Yes, shit, right there!" The fingernails of her right hand dig into my left bicep.

Pulling my right knee higher on the bed, I move faster. Raising my upper body just a little, I watch as the force of my thrusts causes her breasts to bounce. The sight almost undoes me.

"Oh, yes." Her left hand grasps the comforter.

"Right there, baby?" I angle, moving the weight of my body to my hands to get even deeper. "Is this what you want?" Rising up to both knees, I press both of her legs up and out, plunging inside the depths of her.

"Oh, yes, Damon. Right there, please!" she begs.

Chest heaving, she arches her back as her orgasm invades every part of her being. She cries out my name, wailing her release.

I look down as her pretty little cunt contracts around my cock. Watching the sheen of her come coat me with each thrust, I release with a roar of her name.

Allowing her legs to drop back to the mattress, I wrap her into my arms and roll us to our sides.

With our breathing labored and sweat coating our naked skin, we lie in silence, sated.

Soon, Olivia's breathing is even, her body lax. Cradling my head in my left hand, I gaze down on her, brushing her hair from her face.

"I can't let you go," I whisper, planting my lips to her forehead.

Chapter Eleven – goodbye, new york
Olivia

My head throbs and the soreness in my body immediately assaults me with flashes from last night. Baseball game, drinking with Scarlett, Damon helping me into the apartment, and then we...*oh, hell!* I slap my hand to my face and rub.

Not again, Olivia. What the hell is wrong with you? Why do you keep doing this? What is it about this guy that allows you to turn into a wanton sleaze in the matter of one evening?

Peeking through the fingers currently covering my eyes, I see Damon sleeping peacefully. In the relaxed state, I see more familiarity between Alex and him. Everything from his marriage trick in Vegas, to barging in on my life, to having sex last night rushes to the forefront of my mind.

Anger begins to simmer and knot my stomach. Yes, I drank too much in Vegas and last night, but that didn't stop him from getting me into bed either time. Anger grows to rage and I react. Reaching out, I roughly shove Damon away from me and climb out of bed.

"You asshole!" I scream, standing next to the bed, naked. The shriek reverberates throughout the room and I grab my head, trying to calm the hammer thrashing my skull.

"What the hell, Olivia?" he croaks, his voice still full of sleep.

"You had sex with me while I was drunk — again! What's the matter with you?"

Stomping to the bathroom, I slam the door. The sound echoes around my aching skull, causing me to wince once more as I lock the door.

As I turn on the shower, Damon begins knocking from the other side of the door.

"Olivia?" He knocks hard. "Open the door. We should talk."

"Go to hell!" I shout.

The knocking ceases.

Slipping into the shower, I try to let the water rinse away last night. The way he caressed my body, tasted me, took me, claimed...

"Stop it, Olivia!" I say out loud, shaking my head as I begin scrubbing my body.

As soon as I turn the water off, his knocking resumes.

"Please open the door!"

"Go to hell, Damon!" Grabbing the toothbrush holder, I throw it at the door. Brushes scatter in opposite directions as the holder breaks into two pieces.

"I'll break down the door if I have to!" he shouts.

"Go ahead, dickhead. Break down your own bathroom door! Cause that screams sane, you psycho!" I snort, laughing at his threat.

Wrapping a large towel around my body, I meet my own eyes in the bathroom mirror. A memory of us in bed pushes its way into my mind.

What did I do? This isn't just his fault. He stopped when I told him and then I...

I cover my face with my hands and a heavy thud begins against the door. Jerking my head to the door, I step back until I'm against the far wall.

The hinges give way after the third hit. Damon shoves the broken door out of his way.

"You are insane," I seethe, no longer caring who is right or wrong. "You need help, Damon. Serious fucking help!"

"I warned you," he growls. "You aren't going to run and hide in the bathroom this time."

He crosses his arms over his chest.

"I know you feel more than you let on. I could tell last night."

"That was the alcohol, jerk." I step forward, squaring my shoulders. "What does it say about this *relationship* if I have to be drunk to fuck you?" I raise one eyebrow in challenge.

Pain flashes across his face and I want to instantly take back the harsh words. I'd been drinking, but he'd stopped. I'd been just as weak.

"Yes, you had been drinking, but you seem to only let your guard down when you're drinking. You know, they say there is truth in *drunk talking*." He raises his own challenging brow.

Part of me wants to slap it off his face, the other wants to straddle his face and fuck it.

Shoving his chest, I maneuver around him and the broken door, making a beeline for the annulment papers. Once in my hand, I turn to find Damon's scowling face less than a foot from mine.

"Sign them," I order, shoving the papers into his chest.

He doesn't even look down, his eyes remaining focused on mine.

"Sign them, Damon. You promised. I came out here as you asked and I've lived with you *like a family*, now I want you to fulfill your part," I say, shoving the papers at his chest once more for emphasis.

He grasps my hand and pulls me to his chest. The papers crumple between us.

"I can't," he says on a sigh. "Can't you see how much I feel for you?"

His eyes search mine.

"Don't do this to me," I whisper, tears stinging the corners of my eyes.

His other hand comes up to caress my cheek.

"Olivia, I can't let you go. I need you."

Slapping his hand away, I shove him back.

"No, you need help. Professional help. You just busted down a door," I spit out.

"I know you feel more than you—"

"You're delusional." I step back from him.

His jaw clenches, the muscles twitching.

"I won't sign them, Olivia. You might as well throw them away."

"You bastard." Stepping forward, I slap his face. "I hate you," I growl.

He turns and calls back to me over his shoulder.

"I'll be in the shower." He stops at the broken door. "We need to leave in a bit to get Alex and meet my mother this afternoon."

He disappears into the bathroom.

Sinking to the floor, tears stream over my cheeks. Fighting to calm myself and not wanting to be in the room when he's done, I grab clothes and dress quickly.

In the kitchen, the smell of coffee fills the air. With a heavy sigh, I pour myself a cup and carry it to a large leather chair at the far end of the living room.

The blinds, still half shut, dim the morning light. Pulling my knees to my chest, I sip at the hot, black, liquid caffeine and reflect on everything.

Knowing there would be a risk to playing along to this family fantasy of his, I stayed strong to the task of getting the papers signed. Even when he brought up my painful past and I wanted to call it off, I pushed on toward the goal.

However, I hadn't expected a different side of him to emerge. There are moments, more and more each day, where I see *him* and not the stalker. His genuine desire to please Alex and me, to take care and make us happy, and the way Alex has bonded with him in return. For Alex to have someone to call dad...it feels better than I thought it would. It's something I hadn't realized was missing before.

And then there's last night.

Groaning, I rub my face. Yes, I drank too much — again — but I remember everything. I've been so focused on playing along, somewhere along the way, he's slipped in.

He didn't force me to cuddle against him in the car, allow him to massage me on the couch, or to slip his hands over my body next to the bed. Last night, the alcohol released all the repressed feelings — my attraction to him, how endearing I find him, and the security I haven't felt in forever. He wouldn't leave us and I find comfort in the fact.

How the hell did I let this happen? Did I really want him to stop last night, to sign the papers this morning?

The answer hits me so quickly, I almost dump hot coffee on myself.

No, I didn't.

This realization infuriates me, but doesn't stop the memory from my conversation with Scarlett.

"Olivia, he is so different with you. Hell, he wasn't this attentive to Rebecca — at least not when I was around. Things were so upside down with those two, not that I was privy to the details of their relationship. We weren't very close."

"What do you mean?" Looking at her, she shoves another drink at me.

"Rebecca didn't want to come around much." Scarlett shrugs. "You've met Mama Millie, right?"

The look on her face makes me burst out in laughter. I nod.

"Well, she was never a big fan of Rebecca, and with the way Millie is with Damon...I mean, you have to know that—"

"The way she is with Damon?" I ask, glancing over to Damon while sipping the delicious drink.

"Ah, you have yet to get the full experience. I'll just apologize now for what's to come." Scarlett smiles. At my confused expression, she huddles closer to me and continues.

"Mama Millie is a controlling bitch who has run Damon's life for him since he was a child. You know he started medical school, right?"

I nod.

"Okay, well, like his father, medicine was Damon's passion. Millie was not having that. He met Rebecca in college and she became his everything. This rebellion of Damon's, as Millie called it, was not taken lightly. However, she's smart. She didn't want to risk pushing Damon away, but when she wants something, she makes sure as hell she gets it." Scarlett sighs heavily. "Olivia, Millie basically forced Damon into taking charge of B.I.G."

"I thought she was ill and he stepped in to help?"

Scarlett snorts.

"That's what Damon thought, too. Hell, that's what everyone still believes."

"It's not the truth?"

"Hell no!" She snorts again. "She is an amazing actress. Didn't she put on a good show when you met her?" She raises her eyebrow.

"Sort of. She started coughing and Damon called her out for faking—"

"Oh, she's good." Scarlett grins. "That woman is something else." She shakes her head.

Before I can ask anything further, she jumps from the seat, pulling me with her. Next, we are pushing against the large glass windows and screaming toward the field.

Bringing the mug back up to my lips, I realize it's now cold. With a sigh, I set it down on the table beside the chair. My thoughts drift back to before the baseball game and the phone call I walked in on. He was clearly trying to hide something.

Had it been about Rebecca and DJ? Why would he keep more from me instead of being open when I gave him the chance?

The sound of Damon descending the stairs prevents me from dwelling on my thoughts any longer. Looking over my shoulder, he stands at the bottom of the stairs, eyes locked on mine. Unable to handle the weight of his stare, I look away from him. Anger boils in my stomach. All the confusion, lies, drama...I just want out.

"Olivia?"

I ignore his attempt for my attention. Instead of leaving me alone, he comes closer.

"Olivia, last night—"

"Last night is yet another example of how you take advantage of a situation."

Still not looking at him, I keep my tone level and cold, emotionless. Slowly, I take a deep breath and stand, facing him.

"Last night is not, was not—"

I don't allow him to finish.

"I don't know why you think I want to be with you."

This time, my words not only feel like acid on my tongue, they also act as another slap to his face. A small twinge of regret and guilt knot my stomach; regret for the words I just said and guilt for unleashing my frustration with myself and the situation on him.

"I know I said I would sign the papers, but I know you feel the change. You feel our connection, even if it's just a small one. But that is enough to try, isn't it?" His hands grab my shoulders, holding me tightly. "I'm falling in love with you and I can't just let you walk out of my life without a fight, Olivia."

Shaking my head, I shrug off his hands.

"You...how...you can't possibly be falling in love with me. You hardly know me, Damon," I stutter over my rebuttal.

"You're wrong and you know it." He grins. "I *am* falling for you and I *will* fight for you. I cannot sign you out of my life like you're asking me to do."

He reaches out for me, but I step away.

"Don't touch me."

Grabbing the coffee mug, I hurry around him toward the kitchen. Depositing the mug in the sink, I lean, press my hands to the counter, and breathe. Hating the fact that part of my feels a small amount of happiness at his confession, I focus on the over-the-top stalker and bullying behaviors he's displayed.

"Olivia—"

"We need to get Alex."

Not wanting him to see the tears forming in my eyes, I avoid looking at him when I exit.

"Shit," he growls low.

Slipping into a pair of shoes, I wait for him next to the door. When he gets close to me, I move away. Knowing his touch becomes a catalyst to the feelings I don't want, I'm sure to keep the distance between us.

The elevator descent and car ride are silent and uncomfortable. When we reach his father's home, I exit the car without acknowledging him.

"Are you going to give me the silent treatment for the rest of the day?" he asks with annoyance.

I don't look or speak when we reach the door; instead, I press the doorbell.

The Knyght's butler greets us, motioning for us to enter. Damon's hand grazes my lower back, so I walk a step faster. He sighs.

"Good morning," Damon's father greets from over his newspaper. "Heidi is gathering Alex's things." Folding his paper in his lap, he motions for us to sit.

I step to the lone antique chair and sit, taking my first look at Damon. His nostrils flare as he sits alone on the loveseat.

Heidi enters the room with Alex on her hip.

"How was he?" I ask.

"Perfect, of course." She smiles, setting him on his feet.

"Momma!" Alex runs into my arms, allowing me to hug him tightly. Fighting back the tears threatening to expose themselves, I kiss his cheeks until he's pushing to get away from me.

Once on his feet, he turns to Damon.

"Daddy!" He rushes to climb into his lap.

"Hey there, little buddy." Damon repeats my hugging actions.

Our visit is brief, since we are going to Millie's, so we collect Alex's things and Damon carries him to the car. Before I can leave, Heidi pulls me aside.

"Olivia, please give him a chance."

I open my mouth, but she puts up a hand.

"He is so...so...you make him Damon again. He's more himself than I've seen in such a long time. You both complete him, make him whole again." She hugs me tight. "And don't keep my handsome little angel away too long." Her smile is broad, dazzling.

In the car, Alex is the only one making any sound. Damon tries to talk, but I refuse to submit. My thoughts are all over the place and right now, I need to focus on lunch with Millie.

It's clear Millie doesn't want me in Damon's life, so, as crazy as it is, she's become my only ally. But, at the same time, I fight the urge to do things just to spite the self-righteous snob.

Pulling up to her home, a feeling of unease washes over me. After taking a few deep breaths, I finally exit the car and follow Damon inside. Her butler shows us to a large white and lavender room. Mildred Banks is sitting at a round table, facing the entrance of the room.

"Damon, darling," she gushes in an overly dramatic fashion. "I'm so happy you are joining me today."

Her eyes flicker to me and I feel Damon tense.

"Olivia, dear, you look lovely today."

I don't know her well, but it's clear something is going on.

I wonder if she poisoned my food.

"Mother." Damon nods, stepping forward and kissing her cheek. "Thank you for having us."

"And there's my lovely grandson." She leans toward Alex, rubbing his back.

That is one too many lovelies, if you ask me.

Alex burrows his face into Damon's shoulder.

I don't blame you, baby. I wish there was an armpit for me to hide in, too.

"He's so shy." She tries not to sound irritated. "You will need to bring him over as much as possible so he gets more familiar."

Unless as much as possible means twice a year, if you're lucky, not happening.

Brunch is served and conversation is surprisingly light. Mildred inquires about the things we've done to enjoy New York. She even offers an invitation for us to stay in her home during future visits.

I remain quiet, forcing polite smiles. Unsure of her overly nice and sweet behavior, I'm still suspicious.

"So, Damon, have you seen Dr. Strikner since you've returned?" Mildred casually looks at Damon.

His jaw tenses, the muscles flexing.

"Not recently," he growls through clenched teeth.

There's a weird glint in her eye, like she's enjoying his discomfort.

How can a mother purposely manipulate her son?

203

"So, he's not aware that you've remarried?" she asks, glancing to me, obviously looking for my reaction.

When neither Damon nor I speak, she presses her hand to her chest.

"I'm sorry, she does know about Rebecca and DJ, does she not?" Fake innocence oozes from her.

"Yes," he growls again. "She knows, Mother." Damon turns hard eyes on her.

She nods and turns to me.

"And you're still around after learning about the horrible night and all of the skeletons in my Damon's closet?"

This is my opportunity to choose a side, to work her distaste for my presence in my favor. With a glance toward Damon, my heart aches. The sick and devastated look on his face makes up my mind.

"Damon has been very open about the tragic loss of Rebecca and DJ," I respond, straightening my spine. "He's told me about it all."

I don't have to look at him to feel his eyes on me. Sure he's shocked by response, I turn my gaze toward him. My intentions are to reassure him, but the mask of panic he's wearing catches me by surprise.

"Hmm, is that so?" Millie's question pulls my attention to her smug face.

Oh no, what did I do?

"I'm astonished he was so open about his therapy, mental breakdown, and his little indiscretion. What astounds me more is you weren't scared off." She sits back in her chair. "I must say, I misjudged you."

"Mother," Damon warns.

My eyes shoot toward Damon and back to Mildred. She daintily picks up her teacup and sips. Once her lips are free of the porcelain rim, she continues.

"How *is* Vivianne?" She narrows her eyes on Damon. "She still works in your office, correct?"

Damon practically vibrates with anger. His face reddens and his hands clench the arms of the chair.

Vivianne? That sounds familiar. Who is…?

"You know damn well she does, Mother," Damon sneers.

Vivianne Lachlan. Miss Lachlan. The woman he sent to my bakery. Oh, to hell with this!

Having had enough of the games, the drama, the half-truths, I stand from my chair, drawing all attention to me.

"Thank you for lunch. I'll be going now."

The bastard lied to my face. I asked him specifically if there was anything else to tell me and he lied.

"Olivia, please, let me explain."

His pleas fall on deaf ears as I take Alex from him and hurry to leave.

"Olivia, wait!" he yells.

"Damon, don't make a fool of yourself. Let her go!" Mildred shouts after him.

"Shut up, Mildred!" he shouts, gaining on me.

As soon as I'm out the door, I don't know where to go or how to get there. All I know is I need to get away. I foolishly took a leap of faith, feeling awful for how his mother treats him, and chose his side. And it all just blew up in my face, with his mother holding the detonation switch. With Alex tight against my chest, I increase my pace down the sidewalk, hoping a cab would drive by soon.

Damon's car pulls up on the sidewalk about ten feet ahead of us and he jumps out of the car.

"Are you insane? What if you had hit us?" I scream.

"I made sure to be far enough away. Now, get in the car." He stalks toward us.

"Stay away from us!" I scream, causing Alex to jump.

"Olivia, the air is cold. Think of Alex and get in the car." He opens the back door.

Rational thinking finally sets in. Not wanting Alex in the cold air and not wanting to frighten him further, I calm enough to secure him in his car seat. When I stand and close the door, Damon is next to me.

"Let me explain." He cups my face.

Shoving his hand away, I step back.

"You had your chance. Instead, you lied and I end up being the fool."

Seething, I climb into the passenger seat. The drive back to the apartment is silent and once inside, I immediately retrieve the annulment papers.

Alex is on a blanket in the living room playing when I get back downstairs. Damon sits at the breakfast bar with his head in his hands.

Putting the papers on the counter, I slide them toward him.

"Sign them," I demand in a hushed tone.

He doesn't move or say anything.

"Sign them now."

"No," he whispers, shaking his head.

"Sign the damn papers, Damon," I hiss, quietly, slamming a pen down on the papers.

"No," he growls, pushing away from the bar so roughly, the stool falls to the floor.

With my attention on the stool, he's able to grab my arm and pull me against his chest.

"I won't let you go."

I try to pull from his hold.

"No, Olivia. I've made my mistakes, but let me explain."

Struggling against his hold, I growl, "Let go of me."

"I wasn't having an affair."

"I don't care. Let me go, Damon."

I attempt to get away once more. When my efforts prove useless, I look toward Alex. Thankfully, he's absorbed in his blocks.

"It was *that* night, Olivia. The same night I lost them," he croaks. "Vivianne was working with me on a large client project."

He sighs and releases me, but stays close.

"We were at dinner with the client that evening and ended up at the bar by the end of the evening, just the two of us. At first, it was innocent and nothing happened with her before this night. She was familiar with the business, so the conversation was easy. In the beginning, her advances were subtle and I brushed them off. But then a part of me, the part that needed to be comforted instead of comforting someone else's emotions, took over.

"So, you cheat on your mentally and emotionally unstable wife? That's awesome. I'm glad you were only selfish that one time," I sneer.

"You don't understand." He inhales sharply before continuing. "Yes, I encouraged Vivianne's attentions and I reveled in them. It had been so long since someone wanted me and my ego flourished under her attention."

I roll my eyes.

"I'm not proud of how far I let the flirtation go. She caressed my arm, wrapped a leg around mine, and the physical contact sent me into a lifetime of regret. It haunts me."

"Good," I spit the words. "It should."

"You don't understand. I didn't sleep with her."

"Yeah, okay."

"Olivia, we got a hotel room and things were out of control, but I stopped." His eyes meet mine, daring me to question his admission. "I couldn't do it. All I could think about was DJ and how disappointed in me he would be. So, I told her I couldn't do it and straightened my clothes. That's when Rebecca called and Vivianne answered my phone."

My stomach twists.

"And yet she works for you? You send her to *hire* me for a job? It's disgusting."

With quick movements, I get Alex and go upstairs. Damon is close on my heels as I start putting our things in suitcases.

"What are you doing?" he asks, full of panic.

"Packing," I snap.

Pulling the rolling luggage out of his room, he grasps the handle to stop me.

"Your flight isn't until tomorrow." He grits his teeth.

"I know when my flight is."

Tearing the handle from his hand, I roll the bag into Alex's room and set to work on his bags.

"I don't want you to go," Damon pleads from the doorway.

I don't bother responding.

"At least don't go like this." He arms wrap around my waist, surprising me.

"Don't," I warn.

"Daddy," Alex calls out from where he plays on the floor.

Damon releases me to go to Alex.

"Cars." Alex holds up a large red car before shoving it back and forth on the carpet.

Damon sits.

"You car." He hands the yellow car to his dad.

Damon pulls Alex into his lap, rocking him.

My body aches to console Damon, but I quickly remind myself of his ability to lie so easily to me. *What else has he lied about?*

Going into the master bathroom, I start collecting my toiletries. With the last item in my bag, I can no longer hold back my tears. Tears of frustration, sorrow, and hurt stain my cheeks. Soon, I turn on the shower to cover the sobs racking my body. After a moment, I climb under the warm spray.

How did he get to me? When did it happen and why can't I get rid of these feelings now?

After showering, the sound of laughter is like a balm to my bruised soul. Following the giggles, I find Alex laughing every time he and Damon crash cars together. Before I can leave them to their fun, Damon turns pleading eyes on me, his lips turning down in the corners. I pull myself away to prepare dinner.

The night passes with me lost in my own mind and Damon clinging to every moment he has with Alex. After Alex's quick bath, Damon tucks him into bed and lingers before descending the stairs. I collect the last of Alex and my things and pack them away for our trip tomorrow.

Knowing it's probably a lost cause, I can't stop myself from trying one more time to get Damon to sign the papers.

I find him slouched into the couch, his head back and eyes closed.

Dropping the papers into his lap, I stand over him.

"Sign them."

He doesn't open his eyes or move to catch the pen when it rolls off his lap into the crack between cushions.

"Please, sign the papers, Damon."

"No," he replies, his eyes still closed and no emotion in the one word response.

"You made a promise. I stayed the week. Sign the papers." The fight suddenly leaves me and I sound more whiney than intended.

As if in slow motion, his eyes open and he unfolds from the couch. He steps close, too close. My eyes widen from the intense look on his face.

"I will *not* let you get rid of me that easily." His right hand cups the back of my head, pulling our faces closer. "You are *my* wife. *We* have a son." He presses his lips to my forehead before releasing me. "Don't do anything stupid, Olivia." In one fluid motion, he walks around me, leaving me frozen in place. From behind me, he speaks once more.

"You've been warned."

A shiver runs up my spine from the coldness of his voice.

After getting ready for bed, I lock myself in Alex's room. Sleeping on a makeshift bed on the floor is anything but restful. There is no sound from Damon for the rest of the night. Not that I thought he was capable of hurting us, I just didn't know what lengths he would go to in order to keep us here.

The moment light illuminates the morning sky, I grab all of our bags and wrap Alex with a blanket to protect against the cold morning air. Using my cell, I call for a cab to meet us outside and with Alex on my hip, we slip from the bedroom and apartment without seeing Damon. Once we are shut away in the cab and pulling away from the curb, my stomach finally settles and I'm able to exhale my relief. Though, I won't be able to relax completely until we are back in Pittsburgh and our flight doesn't take off for another four hours.

After we've lurked around the airport, like criminals, for three hours, the calls begin. Damon's name flashes on the screen. Text message and voicemail alerts flicker one after the other. I disregard the voicemails, but his text are harder to ignore. I don't respond, but his increasing anger is evident.

My nerves are raw by the time we get to security. Hands shaking, I'm sure security is going to randomly select me for screening. Luckily with no interference from security, we make it to our gate. I choose to sit at the gate on the opposite side — just in case.

His messages are relentless, but I still find a free second to make an important call. Being that it's Sunday, I don't expect an answer.

"Alfonso Donovan," he answers professionally.

One deep breath, then I begin.

"Alfonso, it's Olivia." I fail to hide the nervousness in my voice.

"Olivia, are you okay? What's happened?"

His concern and familiar voice have me on the verge of tears.

"I'm fine."

I look to Alex, who is napping in his stroller.

"I...there's still time to process the divorce papers, right?"

"Of course." He pauses. "I'll file them first thing in the morning. Are you sure you're okay?"

"Yes, I'm fine."

"Where are you?"

"Still in New York, but on my way home."

"Did he do something to you, Olivia?" Alfonso's anger is evident.

"He didn't do anything *to* me. I'm fine, I promise. I just need to get him out of my life. You can do that, right?"

"We can try, but be ready, Olivia. He's got some of the largest New York lawyers on his payroll," Alfonso warns.

"I don't care," I counter with a sniff.

"I'll talk with the partners and call you this evening. I'll do everything I possibly can, okay?"

I'm about to respond when a muffled female voice comes through the line.

"No, I can't. I need to take care of something. Noelle, calm down. I have something to do for work," Alfonso pleas with the woman and I feel like an eavesdropper.

"Olivia, I'll call you, okay?"

"Okay."

"We'll figure this out. You just get home and give Felicity a call when you do."

"I'm not going to bother—"

"I am going to call her as soon as we hang up. You'll be lucky if she isn't waiting for you at the airport."

"Thanks."

We disconnect after our goodbyes.

Alex and I are finally called to board the flight. As we taxi out for takeoff, relief begins to wash over me. Enough so, that I'm able to nod off for most of the flight.

Groggy and exhausted from traveling, Alex and I step from the plane. He doesn't want to be in the stroller, so I practically drag him toward baggage claim. I want nothing more than to just be home.

"Olivia!"

Turning at the sound of my name, I see Felicity and Mercedes hurrying toward us. The moment their arms engulf us, tears pool in my eyes.

"Oh, Olivia." Felicity kisses my cheek.

"Cedee," Alex cheers, grabbing at her polka dot skirt.

Mercedes scoops him into her arms, snuggling him.

"I've missed you so much, little guy." She kisses his head.

Pulling from Felicity's lingering embrace, I wipe a stray tear from my face.

"It's so good to see you guys," I sigh.

"Alfonso called and told me a little, but he doesn't know much." Felicity gives sympathetic look. "I'm guessing New York didn't go well."

I shrug, biting my lip.

"Olivia?" Mercedes uses my name to press further.

"He..."

How do I tell them he's worked his way in, that he's gotten to me? How to you admit to your closest friends that things almost could've been good, but you're scared shitless at the thought of having feelings for your stalker?

"He lied to me," I blurt, unable to fully admit everything.

"What about?" Felicity inquires.

I keep my eyes on the turnstile, watching for my luggage.

"It's a long story." I rub the back of my neck.

"Well, you're stuck with us for the day, so we've got time."

Mercedes moves Alex to one hip before leaning to grab one of the bags we took to New York. She struggles until Felicity steps up and pulls the bag off like it's nothing.

"Jeesh, *She-Ra*, you just showed my weak ass up," Mercedes giggles.

Felicity shrugs. "Advantages of having a personal trainer."

"So, is she hot?" Mercedes wiggles her brow.

"Of course." Felicity shrugs again, a sly smile playing on her lips.

"I'm so jealous," Mercedes pouts.

"When you're ready to switch teams, let me know and I'll hook you up." Felicity wraps an arm around Ced's shoulders.

The familiarity of my friends warms me and brings a smile to my face. They are exactly what I need and it makes it easier to fill them in on the previous week's events.

"So, you slept together again?" Mercedes asks, looking over the back of the front seat.

"And you remember this time?" Felicity tosses out.

Mercedes smacks her.

"Ow, what?"

In the rearview mirror, I see Felicity fighting a smile.

"This isn't the time," Mercedes scolds before turning her attention back to me. "Liv, you've told us a lot and, honestly, I'm still processing it all."

"Me, too," I sigh, tilting my head against the cool glass of the backseat window.

Chapter twelve - good
Damon

"You've been warned."

The ferocity of my desperation courses through my veins. The thought of losing her and our son is unacceptable. I will not lose them.

Entering my office, I shut the door with force and throw my shaking body into the leather chair at my desk. I lean my elbows to the desk and place my head in my hands as a mental and emotional war rage deep inside me.

I promised to sign the papers.

If I sign them, she will be gone.

Isn't her loss inevitable anyway?

No. I'll fight. I have the resources.

Slamming my hands onto the mahogany desk, the fear and anger win. I clear the desk in one smooth motion, sending everything crashing to the floor.

Sitting back in the leather chair, I pull out my cell.

"Mr. Knyght?" he answers, his voice filled with sleep.

"I need you to be prepared for Olivia to file divorce papers."

I stand and walk over to the small bar built into the wall.

"Of course, sir, but the notice won't come until the end of this week. It will take time for the papers to process—"

"Damn it, Marcus," I growl. "I want to know the moment the papers are filed. Do you hear me? Be prepared to counter everything."

Opening the crystal decanter, I pour brown liquid into the tumbler.

"Yes, sir. I understand." He sounds much more alert now.

"Good," I snap before ending the call.

Tilting the tumbler to my mouth, the liquid fire flows down my throat. The burn is comforting, an old friend from my past life. The numbness will follow soon. Grabbing the half-full decanter, I throw myself onto the small brown couch in the corner and toss back another glass.

The shaking increases, sloshing the whiskey around in the tumbler. A sob tears from my chest. Dropping the glass to the floor, I cradle my head in my hands. Guilt, regret, pain, and fear assault me. Instead of pouring a glass, I drink directly from the crystal decanter until my body feels lazy, heavy, and my eyes close.

The sound of my cell startles me.

Christ, what had I been about to do?

"Hello?" Vivianne speaks.

At first, I don't realize she's answered my phone. When I do, I shove her aside and grab the phone.

"Where are you, Damon?" Rebecca screams.

"I'm on my way home, Becky."

Muffled car noises come from the phone.

"Who is she?" Rebecca sobs.

"Becky, where are you? Where's DJ?"

"Oh, now you care about us?!" She snorts just as a car honks.

She's driving.

"Becky, please pull over," I plead.

"Why? What does it matter to you?"

"Where's DJ?"

"That's all you care about, isn't it?" she cries. "Your mother is right. You only—"

I feel her presence before she speaks.

"Baby, you aren't going are you?"

Jerking away from Vivianne, I snarl and she steps back.

"Who the hell is she, Damon?" Rebecca yells.

"Becky, calm down, please. It's not what you think. I will explain, but I need you—"

"Fuck you, Damon! I knew it. I fucking knew it! Is your whore worth it, huh?"

"Becky, pull over," I demand. "I'll come get you and explain everything."

"You aren't coming near me or MY son!"

"Christ, Rebecca, I need you to pull over and turn off the car, please? Tell me where you park and I'll send anyone else but me. You don't have to be around me, just please pull over. Please, baby," I beg.

"You've ruined everything. You've let..." Her sobs make the rest inaudible.

Tears stream down my face while I slip into my jacket and shoes.

"I hate you, Damon!"

"You can hate me, just please calm down and pull over. I'll explain everything to you."

"You'll never see us again!" she screams.

"Becky—"

Screeching tires steal the words as my breath whooshes out of me. Crunching metal, a scream, broken glass, and a cry tighten my chest. The silence that follows feels like a death sentence.

"What happened?" Vivianne's voice wavers.

Unable to speak, I rush from the hotel room.

"Damon, wait—"

The slam of the room door cuts her off. I skip the elevator and run down the flights of stairs. Reaching the lobby, I bark orders for my car to the valet. Pacing impatiently while I wait, I pull out my cell and try to call Rebecca.

Voicemail. My stomach flips.

I dial again.

Voicemail.

This time, I call Hugh.

"Damon?"

"Hugh, has Rebecca been there at all tonight?"

Panicked, I don't know where to begin looking for her. I need a starting point.

"No. What's wrong, Damon?"

Running through the phone call as fast as possible, I keep my eyes on the drive, waiting for my car.

"Shit, Damon, what were you thinking?" Hugh admonishes.

My car arrives and I climb behind the wheel.

"I know, Hugh. I know. I was weak, but it didn't go far. I just—"

A beep interrupts me. Without a word to Hugh, I answer call waiting.

"Becky?" I gasp, feeling relief at seeing her number.

"Is this Mr. Damon Knyght?"

The voice is formal and male. Not Rebecca. My relief vanishes.

"Yes," I choke.

"Sir, I'm afraid your wife and son have been in an accident." He pauses and the lull in conversation terrifies me. "Mr. Knyght, we need you to meet us—"

"Where is she? Are they okay?"

The car swerves a bit.

"Sir, we'll need you to come down here."

He provides directions and I drive the short distance between my biggest mistake and largest loss.

Arriving to the scene, I run from my car, leaving it running with the door open.

At first, the mangled metal is unrecognizable. Then I realize it's Rebecca's car, or what's left of it. From the corner of my eye, I see paramedics pushing a gurney. I stalk toward them.

Hands grip at my arms, voices shout for me to stop, but the anguish propels me forward. Reaching out, I strip away one white sheet.

Looking down on the lifeless body of my son feels like a wrecking ball to my gut. Engulfing him in my arms, I hold him to my chest.

"Wake up, DJ. Please, wake up!" I squeeze harder. "Please, God, not him! Let him wake up." Screaming, I shake him.

Hands pull DJ's body from my arms and blackness takes over.

The next morning, I wake in a private hospital. Having been medically sedated at the scene and through the night, doctors speak around me to my mother and father.

I say nothing. I don't deserve to be alive, to be lying here breathing. I should be dead, not them. My unresponsiveness and overall state of being gets me placed on suicide watch.

After another day of the same, the doctors want to release me to an institution for medical treatment. Of course, my mother won't allow it, afraid of the family reputation. So, she hides me and my treatment well.

The day of the funeral, the doctors are reluctant to let me go — still unsure of my mental state. I bargain my sanity and promise to cooperate with treatment in order to say goodbye to the woman I loved and our son. The night after the funeral, I take all the pills from the cabinet in my temporary room at my mothers.

Three days later, I wake, still alive, in a private location. Strapped to a bed and routinely injected with unknown medications, I remember my mother being there once. It's the only time I see her and she looks nothing but disappointed and disgusted.

My father and Heidi routinely visit, along with Hugh. Hugh tries to pull me out of the comatose state, but there's no reason to come back.

Heidi arrives for a typical Sunday visit, but this time, she brings a photo album. She talks about them, about my life with them. My first words are to request the picture she has in her hand. She allows me to look, but won't give it to me until I prove I'm well enough to have the photo. She returns day after day, coaxing me from the fog I'd been living in.

Guilt and regret haunt my rehabilitation, shadowing me the entire time I stay with my mother for outpatient treatment and living inside of me every day I wake up breathing. Miserable most days, I live life for everyone else. Dead inside, I bury myself in work.

Until the letter from the clinic. The moment the letter is in my hands, I plan and plot. Three patients. Three women who received my sperm. The hunt begins until I have answers.

I stretch from a balled up position on the little couch, my back cracking in protest. Sitting up, my head throbs, my heart aches, and I feel nauseated from guilt and regret. I stand, groaning from the ache in my back.

When I open the office door, the apartment is quiet. Too quiet.

Slowly and carefully, I take the steps toward Alex's room. I push open his door and find it empty. Rushing to my room, I find the bed untouched. My stomach lurches into my throat and I begin a frantic search of the apartment.

"Olivia! Alex!" I shout, going room to room.

The throbbing in my head slowly subsides from the adrenaline coursing through me.

"Fuck!" I shout to the empty apartment. "I can't believe her."

Running, I retrieve my cell phone from my office desk. Picking up the device, I notice the time.

"There's only two hours until their flight." I shake my head. She snuck out without letting me tell Alex goodbye, without letting me explain everything to her.

Exiting my apartment, I call down to the doorman and learn that Olivia left for the airport early this morning. Holding my anger at bay, I request my car and hang up.

In the lobby, I stalk to the front doors.

"Mr. Knyght, the car has not yet arrived." His eyes widen, taking in my disheveled appearance.

"Christ," I curse, exiting the building.

I find a yellow car parked on the curb and hurry toward it.

"Hey." I flag down two people starting to climb into the car. "Wait!"

I reach the car as the man is helping his wife into the back.

"I need this cab, please. I need to get to the airport."

"I'm sorry, but you will just have to wait for yours to arrive." The lady sticks her nose in the air.

"I'll pay you," I blurt. Reaching into my wallet, the man starts to protest. "Five hundred dollars." I extend the money to him.

"Well, I never—"

"Shut up, Susan." The man hushes his wife, pulling her from the car. "It's all yours." He grabs the money from my hand.

"Frank, you can't be serious."

It's the last I hear from Susan before I close the cab door, toss him my credit card, and demand JFK airport.

"Yes, sir!" The driver smiles.

During the drive, I try to reach Olivia by phone. No answer, so I try texts.

How could you just leave?
No response. My anger grows.

You didn't even allow me to say goodbye to him.
No response. My anger sprouts horns.

I won't let you leave me.
No response. My anger boils into fury.

All of my calls go unanswered and my desperation forms into rage.

"Olivia, I swear to God, if you get on the plane without letting me see my son, I will make your life a living hell. Do you understand? I warned you."

Using my phone, I reserve a plane ticket.

My next attempt is the airport, trying to have them pull her from her flight. Of course, they won't do it unless the police or other authorities contact them. My further rebuttals get me hung up on.

"Bitch," I growl.

The cab driver glances at me curiously.

"Can't we get there any faster?" I bark.

"Dude, I'm going as—"

My rage unleashes.

"Don't ever call me dude! Get me to the fucking airport or I will make sure you regret every day you have left in this world!"

His eyes widen, his posture straightens, and the car shoots forward.

No longer in control of anything, I pull my phone out once more.

You will regret this Olivia! I'll make sure of it!

Enjoy seeing him now, because I will be taking him from you soon enough!

Don't get on that plane. You both are mine!

When the cab arrives to the airport, I leap from the car and rush toward the customer service desks. Lost in my anger, I push through the long line until I reach the desk. A man goes to argue, but with one look, I shut him up.

"Sir, you need to wait your turn," the attendant states with fake smile.

"Damon Knyght." I toss my ID on the counter. "Give me the damn ticket now."

Aware of my agitation, she pulls my information up in the system and prints the tickets.

"Do you have any luggage—?"

Grabbing the ticket, I rush away before she finishes.

Arriving to the security checkpoint, I shake with impatience.

"Fuck this." I push through the line again to reach the front.

"Sir, you need to get back in line," a man in a security uniform says, standing before me.

"I'm in a hurry," I snap, trying to walk around him for the metal detector.

"I'm afraid you aren't going anywhere, sir." His arm stretches out, blocking me.

"Get out of my way. I have a flight to catch," I sneer.

"You need to calm down, sir." Grabbing my arm, he guides me toward the cluster of security people.

Pulling from his grasp, I glare at him.

"I am calm!" I yell.

Suddenly, two more sets of hands land on me.

"You're going to have to come with us, sir."

"Let go!" I struggle, but they are large and easily restrain me.

"Calm down," guard one demands.

"I'll miss my flight." I struggle harder and manage to loosen one arm. Unleashing a fist, I hit the other guard and break free.

Hurrying for the shuttle that will take me to the gate, a large force crashes into me. We crumble to the floor.

"Get off me!"

The guard pulls my arm behind my back and shoves upward, causing jolts of sharp pain.

"That will be enough out of you," the familiar guard growls.

Guard two helps to pull me from the floor. He has blood from his nose smeared across his cheek. With both arms pulled behind my back, they click the cold metal around my wrists and lead me to a secluded security room.

"I need to get to my wife," I cry out.

"You're coming with us."

Passengers in line at security cheer for the guards.

Two hours in a holding room at the airport and the police finally arrive to take me. Homeland Security finished their investigation, so it's the local law's turn to take me to a jail cell.

"He's in here." The booking officer shows Hugh into the room.

"Damon," Hugh sighs, shaking his head.

"I need to get out of here. She left and took Alex." Gripping the bars, I plead with him.

"Son, you need to calm yourself." My father's voice surprises me. "We've come to take you home." He pinches the bridge of his nose. "Your mother is furious about the scene you caused."

"I don't give a shit what that vile woman thinks about anything," I snap. "She's a conniving, evil person!"

Both Hugh and my father look at me with wide eyes.

"Did he just—"

"Yes, he did," my father answers before Hugh's question is finished.

"Get me out of here. I need to go to Pittsburgh."

"Oh, no, you don't." Hugh shakes his head. "You are coming back to my place to collect yourself before you cause any more damage."

"I don't have time for—"

If you want out, then you'll do as I say." Hugh raises one brow, crossing his arms over his chest.

I glance to my father.

"I'm with your brother on this one."

With a heavy sigh, I concede. "Fine."

Upon release, the officer gives me my personal belongings as well as paperwork.

"Give me those." Hugh reaches out, taking my phone and wallet.

"What the hell are you doing?"

"You won't need these right now." He motions for me to follow to a waiting black car.

I follow, reluctantly.

The silence of the drive is cut by Hugh's phone.

"We're on our way now."

My eyes narrow, knowing he's talking about me.

"That's perfect. Of course. No. We'll see you shortly." He pauses for a moment before smiling. "I love you, too."

Furrowing my brow, I rub at the ache in my chest. Olivia and Alex are gone.

"Damon, I know you're hurting, but you need to calm down before you react." My father rubs his forehead. "I don't know what you were thinking."

"It doesn't matter now," I growl. "You let them leave and now there isn't anything I can do."

I glare at my father and brother.

"Do you realize the problems you already caused?" Hugh asks. "What would have happened if you had actually got to them? What would you have done?"

"I would never hurt them," I snap.

"No, but you obviously want to push her further away," he rebuts.

"What did your mother do?" my father asks.

At the thought of that harpy, I clench my teeth.

"She ruined everything."

My father nods, understanding.

"Did she tell her about—?"

My glare stops Hugh from finishing his question.

"Yes, but she insinuated it was much more than the reality of it all."

At Hugh and Scarlett's apartment, Heidi and Scarlett are waiting.

"Damon," Heidi cries softly.

Her arms wrap around me, pressing her cheek to my chest.

I don't move to return the embrace.

Once she realizes I'm not reciprocating, she pulls back and looks at me through narrow eyes.

"Don't, Damon," she states sharply. "Don't go back to that dark place."

"How about a drink?" my father offers the room, leaving to get one for himself.

"Come on." Scarlett tugs on my arm, pulling me into the living room.

Her goal is to get me to the couch, but I sit in a large chair instead. Scarlett kisses the top of my head and leaves the room.

My father enters, holding out a glass for me.

I take the drink and drain the scotch. Setting the glass on the coffee table before me, I rest my elbows on my knees and close my eyes.

"She told her about Vivianne," I whisper.

"Christ," Hugh curses. "I'm sorry, Damon. I never thought she would go that far to—"

"What about Vivianne?" Scarlett asks from behind me.

Still leaning on my knees, I look up and see Hugh's round eyes focusing on Scarlett.

"Um, it's just that..." he sputters, torn between being honest with her and loyal to his brother.

"I was with Vivianne that night," I state, dropping my gaze to the empty glass.

"What night are you...?" Her question trails off, having figured it out for herself.

The clicks of her heels are heavy on the wood floors just before she smacks the back of my head.

Jumping from the chair, I turn to face her.

"What the fuck, Scarlett?" I shout.

"Don't look at me like that," she yells. "How could you, Damon? Why would you?"

Scarlett turns her anger on Hugh.

"And YOU! You knew about this? All this time, you knew."

Her arms cross over her chest and her long legs carry her until she stands over my terrified brother.

"Scar, I'm sorry."

She smacks him in the head, too.

"You let me think I was completely honest with Olivia and then let me try to open her up to the idea of being with him, all while knowing he was with another woman that night?!"

Before Hugh can respond, she turns back to me.

"And how the hell can you work so closely with her every day? What kind of sick person does that? You know what? Don't answer. I don't want to know."

"I don't work with her by choice." My words are clipped and loud. "And I didn't sleep with her. I almost slept with her, but stopped. Rebecca called and Vivianne answered my phone."

Scarlett opens her mouth, but I cut off her argument.

"I was still wrong and unfaithful, but I didn't sleep with her."

Bile rises in my throat as I remember where I'd been that night — what I almost did and all I lost.

"What do you mean you don't work with her by choice?" Scarlett studies my face.

"My *mother* hired her and has the company locked in a ridiculous employment contract."

"So, you haven't taken it up with Human Resources?" Scarlett raises her brow.

"There's nothing I can do, Scarlett. I've gone to H.R., had lawyers go through the contract, and even talked to my mother. The contract is iron clad. I can't change her position and mother dearest told me it was my own foolish mistake and now I would live with the consequences."

"Wait a minute," Heidi interjects, garnering our attention, "you mean to tell me your mother knows what happened and basically told you to 'suck it up'?" Her face contorts in a mixture of disgust and anger.

"Not those exact words, but basically." Shrugging, I drop back into the chair. "She's been doing it my entire life."

"What kind of mother...no, woman, does that?" Heidi storms to the center of the room.

"Calm down, dear." My father reaches out a hand, but she pushes it away. Not used to this response from her, his eyes widen.

"I will not calm down. That...that...bitch doesn't deserve to be a mother." She loses her temper. "No offense, Damon, but I just can't believe she would do that to her own son. And what about Vivianne? What does she have to say for herself?"

I shrug again.

"She doesn't have anywhere else to go and needs the money." Groaning, I rub my face. "Look, I didn't choose her and my mother won't release her from employment."

"Even after you told her about the night?" Scarlett's voice drips with disgust.

I nod.

"I have no choice but to keep Vivianne around. She only deals with me when I absolutely find it necessary. She isn't privy to information. I didn't even let her in on why she had to go to Pittsburgh to get a baker. Though, I did love the look on her face when she realized she had to travel so far for a cake." The memory causes me to grin.

"I've always felt bad for that girl, given how you treated her." My father shakes his head. "Now I understand why you bark orders and snap at her. I'm surprised she hasn't quit."

"Me, too," I grumble, closing my eyes. In fact, I'd hoped my behavior would make her do that very thing. It hasn't, obviously.

"I wonder why she hasn't," Heidi concurs. "I wouldn't want to deal with that every day."

Opening my eyes, I focus on Scarlett. She's been quiet and deep in thought for a few moments, causing me to feel nervous. A movement out of the corner of my eye draws my attention away from a contemplative Scarlett.

Hugh makes it two feet from her before her head snaps, shooting a glare in his direction, and stopping him in his tracks.

"I'm still pissed at you." Her voice is calm, but sincere.

Taking her eyes from Hugh, she glances at me for the briefest of seconds before exiting the room. Hugh drops his chin and sighs.

"I just want to sleep," I croak.

"Of course," Heidi coos, stepping to my side and taking my arm. Leading me to the spare bedroom, she leaves me with a kiss to my cheek and some final words.

"Things will work out. Give it time." She smiles before turning away.

I toss and turn on the bed for an hour, my mind unwilling to let me rest. For the next two hours, I alternate between sitting and pacing. My mind is a swirl of Rebecca, DJ, Vivianne, my mother, Olivia, and Alex. Guilt and pain have resurrected from the depths of my black spotted soul, constricting my chest and making it hard to breathe.

Exhaustion finally claiming me, I fall onto the bed and my dreams are even more devastating than the night before. Not only do I relive the night of my biggest loss, but my subconscious recreates the night with Olivia and Alex as the stars of my nightmare.

Sweaty and gasping, I bolt up in the dark room. Once my physical self realizes it was just a dream, I collapse back onto the bed and steady my breaths.

After a shower, I dress and follow sounds and smells to the kitchen. Upon my entrance, the room falls silent.

"How are you feeling this morning?" My father speaks first.

Shrugging, I take the cup of coffee Heidi holds out to me and sit on the stool between Hugh and my father.

"Well, you look better." Heidi smiles and returns to cooking.

I sip at the hot black liquid and savor the way it warms my throat and chest. Surveying the room, I notice one absence.

"Where's Scarlett?" I direct the question to Hugh.

"She left this morning," he replies, his face drawn tight and sadness filling his eyes.

"I'm sorry." Guilt assaults me, knotting my stomach.

"It's my own doing. Not yours." Forcing a smile, he pats my shoulder.

"Eat up." Heidi slides a plate of eggs, bacon, and toast in front of Hugh, my father, and me.

We mumble 'thank you' in unison and eat in silence for a few minutes.

"Well, you look calmer, so I suppose you should go through your messages." My father slips my phone onto the counter next to my plate.

Excitement rushes through my body. I grasp the phone and turn it on.

"Thank you," I blurt as I start scrolling.

I find an unsurprising amount of voicemails, texts, and emails, but only one gets my immediate attention.

Olivia: We made it to Pittsburg safely.

A smile begins to spread on my lips, just knowing she thought about me enough to let me know they made it home okay. My smile drops when Marcus' name flashes across my screen.

"Hello?"

"Mr. Knyght?"

"Yes, Marcus."

"Sir, the papers were filed. You asked to be informed—"

"What?" I growl, teeth locking tightly against each other.

"Miss Harlow, sir, you asked we prepare, so I contacted a Pittsburgh associate to provide notice when the—"

"Damn it, Marcus, just get to the point," I grind out.

"The papers were filed with a rush order from her law firm this morning." He rushes the words.

Anguish tears through me, igniting a deeply hurt beast overflowing in sadness and anger.

I'm barely aware of the world as it falls away from around me, a haze of despair settling in. I toss my phone, shattering it against the wall as my pain roars out of me.

Rebecca.

Hands grip my shoulders. I spin and connect my fist to a jaw.

DJ.

Grabbing the stool I was sitting on, I throw it back.

My little lifeless boy.

Shouts fill the air, begging me to calm, but I'm too far gone. My mind is bombarded with the images of my past, my losses.

Guilt.

"Noo," I cry, dropping to my knees.

I cover my face with my hands, tears soaking through.

Guilt. Pain. Loss. Olivia. Alex. Pain. Loss. Guilt. White sheet covered gurneys. Pain. Loss. Too much loss.

More shouting swirled around me and heavy knocking filled the air.

Too much loss. Too much noise.

I drop my head to the floor and repeatedly hit my forehead against the hardwood, needing to get the images out.

Soon, dizziness takes hold and I slump to the floor in a heap of anguish. When I wake, the setting is familiar. White and mint green rooms, straps on my ankles and wrists, and the sound of whispers.

"Damon?" The familiar voice draws my attention. "Damon, can you talk to me?"

Blinking away my foggy vision, my eyes rest on Dr. Strikner.

"Talk to me, Damon."

"Leave me alone," I rasp.

"Well, at least I know you're there." He smirks down on me.

A throb settles between my eyes. I reach up to rub, but find my hands are restrained.

"My head hurts."

"Smashing it on the floor can cause that," he quips. "Do you know what day it is?"

"Monday," I croak, and then clear my dry throat.

"I'm afraid it's Thursday."

"What?"

I focus wide eyes on him.

"We've had you sedated for three days because of your reluctance to cooperate."

He pulls a chair next to the bed. The screeching of the metal legs against the floor sends sharp pain through my skull.

"You'll be coming to stay with me for a few days."

He settles into the chair.

"Just leave me alone." Groaning, I close my eyes.

"Don't you dare shut down on us again, Damon."

My eyes shoot open and land on Heidi.

"I won't let you…no, I won't let that conniving bitch, who doesn't deserve the title of mother, make you disappear again." Heidi's hand grasps my forearm and for a brief moment, I feel a maternal connection to Heidi.

All of the years I've been jealous of Hugh just because he has Heidi for a mother instead of a monster like mine, rush through my mind.

She places both hands on my face, putting us eye to eye. I hear my father scold her from the other side of the room.

"You are not *your mother,* Damon. You are so much better than that. Don't let that woman defeat you with all of her evil plotting. I love you and have seen such good and love from you."

Her eyes search my face and a strange sense of resolution settles in my chest, a determination I'd never quite felt in the past taking hold.

"Don't let her destroy you."

At her whisper, I smile. She returns it with one of her own.

After a week of intensive therapy sessions with psychoanalysts, who worked fervently to get into my mind and force me to deal with everything, I start to understand the effect my mother has had on me. It helped that my father kept her away from me. I also began to see the mistakes I'd made with Olivia and the regret I feel still lingers.

Due to my progress, I'm finally allowed to return home and work. With regularly scheduled appointments with Dr. Strikner and medications prescribed, I know I need to stick to the treatment this time if I want to attempt a real life again.

My first hurdle is Vivianne. Not caring what my mother says, or how much we have to pay to buy out her employment contract, today is the last day I'll deal with her. I step off the elevator, preparing for whispers and awkward looks regarding my absence.

On my way toward Vivianne's small office, not one person acts any differently. After the third person welcomes me back to work, I grow curious.

"Vacation," Scarlett states from behind me.

Turning around, just outside the door of my destination, I soften the look on my face.

"I'm so sorry, Scarlett."

She puts her hand up, silencing my apologies.

"Vivianne is also gone." She raises one sculpted eyebrow and crosses her arms over her chest, challenging me to argue.

"You beat me to it." I grin. "That was first on my list of things to take care of."

"Good." She returns a smile.

Worry tightens my chest thinking about the wedge I placed between her and Hugh.

"Have you spoken to Hugh? Please tell me I haven't ruined things between the two of you. I really couldn't forgive—"

"Of course I've spoken to him." She rolls her eyes. "I'm still mad at him and he has a lot of ass kissing to do, but for some odd reason, I love that man." She winks.

Relief relaxes my tense muscles.

"Do you still love me?" I playfully bat my lashes.

She narrows her eyes on me.

"I'm still angry with you. And it wasn't easy for me to remove that trash from the building either."

"I'm sorry I didn't handle Vivianne sooner."

"Damon, I know your mother is to blame for a lot of the past and present, but—"

"But I'm also to blame for my choices," I finish for her.

Her arms drop from her chest and she steps toward me.

"I spoke to Heidi and there's nothing I can say about her except your mother is unbelievably cruel."

She wraps her arms around me and squeezes. My arms come around to embrace her.

"Thank you," I whisper.

Leaning back, she looks up at me with confusion crinkling her eyes.

I give a small shrug. "I needed that."

The two things I dread most, but need to take care, happen the next day.

My personal cell rings, flashing the name of my lawyer's office, during a conference call. My stomach churns and I feel sick. What I'm about to do is going to take a lot for me to accomplish. Everything about it feels wrong for me, like the world will stop spinning and I'll fall off the face of the Earth. Taking a deep breath, I answer with a heavy-hearted hello.

"Damon, we will need to act quickly. We sent the petition papers to your office and will need them signed and back before the end of today in order to—"

"That won't be necessary," I croak, feeling as if the wind has been punched out of me.

"I'm sorry?" He's confused and rightfully so.

Closing my eyes, I take a deep breath and then another. I need to do this.

"I only need the papers to complete the divorce and petition a custody arrangement for my son." Swallowing the lump in my throat, a familiar pain rises in my chest.

"I don't understand. I thought we were countering the—"

"Things have changed." I choke on the feeling of loss stinging my heart.

"I see." He pauses for a long moment. "I will send a petition for paternity and paternal rights, along with the marriage dissolution papers we will need to complete." He hesitates to end the call, probably waiting for me to change my mind again. "Okay, well, I'll have them over to you within the hour. If you can have them back before the end of business today, I can get everything filed tomorrow morning."

"Thank you." I end the call.

I know he's confused, but I don't care to explain my errors, faults, and dirty secrets.

With the way it feels to put a pen to the legal documents, I might as well sign the papers with my own blood. At completion, I feel drained and exhausted. Of course, my mother chooses then to use my office line to get in touch with me.

"This is Damon," I answer.

"This is your mother," she snips. "Why haven't you contacted me? I've tried to reach out to you repeatedly. I'm your mother for God's sake!"

"My mother?" I snort, humorlessly. "Why would a mother destroy everything for her child? Why would you want to do that to me, *Mother*? Why make me work with Vivianne and then throw her in Olivia's face? What do you want from me?"

"Don't raise your voice, Damon Knyght! I am your mother and you will show me respect," she huffs. "What you did to Rebecca was of your own doing, just like I told you before. As for Vivianne, what is this rumor about her having been fired? Should I remind you that she is contracted to my company through—?"

"Here, in *MY* company, she no longer has a position!" I slam a fist to my desk, feeling the sting crawl to my wrist. "I'm well aware her contract is with you as the sole employer, so she can report to your house and do whatever you wish of her. She isn't welcome here."

"How dare you?" she gasps.

"I learned from the best. *You* taught me well." I slam the phone into its cradle, never having felt freer in my life.

Three weeks of therapy sessions, I distract myself with family to avoid charging off to be with my wife and son. Scarlett enters my office with Hugh, my father, and Heidi. I smile, but the greeting falls when I take in their grim faces.

"What's going on?" I narrow my eyes.

"Damon, we need to speak with you." Dr. Strikner's voice surprises me. I hadn't seen him enter.

"What's this about?" I stand to walk around my desk. "I've been following my treatment plan to—"

"This isn't about your sessions, Damon." Dr. Strikner puts his hands out in front of him, palms facing me. "You are doing excellent. I'm only here for support."

Pausing at the corner of my desk, I study his face for something, anything that will give away their intentions.

"It's best if you sit and keep a calm head about you."

I hesitate for a moment before retaking my seat.

"Now, remember all the progress you've made." The doctor moves to the wall on my right and leans against it.

"What is this about?" I growl from annoyance.

"It's about your mother," my father states as he takes a seat in front of my desk.

"What about her? Is she ill?" My spine stiffens. Not because of fear, but because I feel nothing.

Heidi places herself on the arm of my father's chair. Hugh and Scarlett mimic their position in the opposite chair.

"Damon," Scarlett's voice wavers, "your mother, she..."

Scarlett looks to Hugh. He gives her a small nod. With a deep breath, she turns back to me.

"Your mother knew Vivianne."

Her eyes search mine and confusion furrows my brow.

"I know that. Mother was very familiar with VMG, of course she knew her."

"No, she knew her before the night Rebecca and DJ died. They were very well acquainted before that night."

What she says isn't processing or making sense.

"What are you trying to say, Scarlett? I'm well aware my mother knew of Vivianne and may have met her before...that night. Why does that constitute some sort of..?" I pause and wave my hand toward all of them, "intervention."

I see something flash in Scarlett's eyes.

"Damon, she set you up that night. Your mother knew Vivianne very, very, very well. Well enough to set you up. To set you and Rebecca up."

Slowly, the realization of what my mother has schemed washes over me and I feel as if I'm drowning.

Chapter thirteen – home sweet Pittsburgh
Olivia

Alfonso calls the night I return to discuss my request and to get further details about the visit. After telling him about the texts and voicemails, he wants copies of my phone records. A shiver creeps up my spine as I begin to understand how ugly this could get with Damon.

During the week after my return, Alfonso stops by twice for signatures. Felicity and Mercedes take turns staying at my apartment with me to provide emotional and moral support if Damon were to show up. However, there hasn't been word from him since the day of my flight — no more texts, voicemails, or unannounced arrivals. As the days pass, I feel more and more confident he's leaving us alone. A smile graces my face while there is a small, painful twinge in my chest.

Two weeks since leaving New York, I find myself in a familiar routine — lying in bed, struggling to fall asleep, followed by restless and vivid dreams about Damon. What pisses me off the most is that they aren't angry dreams. These dreams are of us together as a family, sitting in his living room with Alex. Or of just the two of us in his bed, sweating, naked, and out of breath.

The lack of sleep, on top of unwanted dreams, has me tossing my alarm clock off the nightstand when it begins to announce four in the morning. Climbing from the bed, dizziness assaults me, causing me to flail my arms for something to hold onto. My butt hits the bed with a bounce and my stomach churns. Quickly lying back, I inhale through my nose to ease the queasiness.

My body is protesting my lack of slumber.

With my stomach calm, I slide from bed and to the bathroom. A hot shower helps to wake me. A quick braiding of my wet locks, oversized jeans, and t-shirt in place, I follow the scent of fresh brewed coffee.

In the kitchen, I grab my favorite mug and pour the caffeinated goodness. On my third sip, Mercedes appears in her full rainbow of quirk.

"You look like hell," she blurts as she reaches into the refrigerator.

"Thanks. Good morning to you, too," I reply, sarcastically.

"Still not sleeping well?" she asks, pouring a glass of orange juice before propping against the counter next to me.

I shrug.

"Is it anxiety, the bad dreams, the stress...?"

"I'm pretty sure it's everything."

I sigh, not correcting her about the dreams. There's nothing bad about them, other than I'm obsessing over my soon to be ex-husband.

"Hmm." She eyes me for a moment before finishing off the rest of her juice. "Alright, time to make the donuts." She giggles and gives a light nudge to my arm.

Groaning at her crappy joke, I follow her to the bakery kitchen, my coffee still firmly in my hand.

Damon

The moment they tell me my mother was the mastermind behind Vivianne, embers of fury begin a slow burn in my gut. My family's faces all hold the same expression — fear and expectation. And they have every reason to feel this way. Urges to scream, throw, rage, and strangle my mother lie right beneath the surface of my calm facade.

With a deceiving composure, I excuse myself from the group. In the restroom, I splash cold water on my face and breathe deep. Droplets of water spray from my nostrils with each forceful exhale. Patting my face dry, I stare at myself in the mirror. Angry eyes stare back, but this time, there is a control containing the rage.

Taking quick, determined steps, I walk through my office and out the door.

"Damon, wait!" Hugh's footfalls follow his shout.

"Son, don't do this!" my father calls.

"Kick her ass, Damon!" Scarlett cheers, causing a twitch of amusement to lift one side of my mouth.

Without knocking, I enter my mother's home. Her servants look alarmed at my intrusion and hurry out of my path. I stop before the large woman who raised me when my mother was too busy to interact with her own child. Now the caregiver to the woman I want to throttle stands at the mouth of the large living room she used to sneak me in to play when forbidden.

"Virginia." I nod.

She stares into my eyes. Unlike the rest of the staff, I only see curiosity and hope on her face.

"Damon," she sighs. "I suppose you are here to speak with your mother."

It's not a question and takes me by surprise.

"You know about—?"

She shakes her head.

"No, baby boy, I have no idea why you are here to see her, but I've known this day would eventually come."

"What day?" I swallow, touched by the childhood endearment but unsure of whether I really want the response.

"The day you finally figured her out. The day you entered this house as a man determined and not the easily manipulated boy she's worked so hard to force you to be."

"How do you know I—?"

"Don't you forget who raised you, baby boy." She smiles, knowingly.

I return the smile for the briefest of moments.

"Where is she?" The darker urges to shout and attack deepen my voice.

"The study." She motions toward the stairs before cupping my face and retreating into the living room, closing the door behind her.

I inhale through my nose and hold the air inside, hoping to bring a sense of calm. It only takes the edge off the anger. Turning, I take the stairs two at a time and walk in long strides until I reach her door. Without pausing or knocking, I propel my body through the door and to the center of the room.

Her head snaps up from her desk, shock painting her face.

"Mother," I seethe, every bit of the anger and repressed frustration evident in one word.

"What's the meaning of this outburst? You don't just barge into—"

"How could you?" Stalking forward, I lean over her desk, pressing my palms onto the dark wood of her desk. "Do you hate me so much you would destroy my life?"

"I have no idea what you're talking about. Calm yourself." She leans back in the tall back leather chair.

"You can honestly sit there and pretend? You're okay with all the pain and loss you've caused?"

Tears form in my eyes. The night I lost my family flashes through my mind. The gurneys, white sheets, ambulances, police officers...all the loss and tragedy is like a slideshow of anguish. Something buried deep down within me snaps.

In four long strides, I round her desk and grab her chair. Spinning the chair toward me, her body jerks first to the right and then the left.

"Damon!" she cries.

Leaning down, I grasp her shoulders in my hands and shake.

"How can you live with yourself? You killed my son, your grandson!"

"Damon, stop it," she pleads, smacking my hands from her arms. "Please, stop!"

"Give me one goddamn good reason why I shouldn't wrap both my hands around your neck and squeeze the last lying, manipulating breath from your body?"

My hands slide toward her neck.

"Stop!" she screams, grabbing my wrists.

The flesh of my hands feels the fragile paper-thin skin of her neck. My fingers flex and she stiffens. I drop my hands, running them through my hair.

She slumps into her seat, sobbing.

"I can't. Believe. You. Were. Going. To—"

"Shut up, you aren't hurt," I spit.

"Damon, I don't know what has caused this break, but I didn't kill your son. You're delusional and—"

"Don't you dare!" I shout. "I can't believe you can sit there still lying about everything you've caused."

"Let me call the doctor," she hiccups.

"I'm done. I quit this life with you and your company."

Her eyes round, panic flushing her face.

"You can't quit. This is our family's company! You are my legacy!" she shouts, standing with perfect ease, her fragile façade fading away.

"I hope you live forever in this lonely hell you've created for yourself, Mildred! I never want to see you again. And if you come near my family, I will make you regret it."

She gasps.

"Walking away from this company and our family is not an option, Damon! I'm your mother. My blood is in your veins." Her hands clench at her sides.

Shaking my head, I let the disbelief wash over me. All she cares about is her family's legacy, losing her son means less than nothing.

"I. Hate. You," I say, accentuating each word.

She blinks, pressing a hand to her chest as if she'll find a heartbeat there. We both know she won't.

"You don't mean that," she whispers, almost convincing me that she may actually feel something.

"Oh, Mildred, this is the first time in my life I've ever truly and irrevocably meant those three words." The admission slips through clenched teeth.

"I'm your mother." She hits the desk with a small fist.

"You are nothing."

With those final words, I turn and leave her standing there, mouth gaping.

She yells for me on what sounds like a real sob, but she's always been an amazing actress. I refuse to look back.

From the moment my driver closes me in the back of the car to the time we park in the underground garage, my phone rings non-stop. Without looking at the screen, I know it's my mother or someone calling on her behalf. I'm also sure it will be a scheme or manipulation to get me back to the house.

When I arrive to the executive floor and the small lobby, my phone finally falls silent. The security guard nods as I pass through groups of employees waiting for the elevator or at the front desk. Just outside my office, Mrs. Shaw's blue eyes lock onto me and her spine straightens.

Poor woman. I have not been easy to work for.

"Mrs. Shaw, please follow me."

I don't stop to make the request; instead, I walk into my office and take a seat behind my desk.

"Yes, Mr. Knyght?" Her voice wavers with nerves and her fingers tighten on the pencil and pad in her hands.

"As of an hour ago, I resigned from my position here."

Her eyes widen and mouth parts.

"I don't want you to worry about your job. I'll be discussing everything with my brother and ensure you will be kept on at current compensation and benefits."

Her mouth opens more, but nothing comes out. She snaps it shut and swallows.

"I'll need your help to finish a few things as well as to take some notes and get you up to speed with some situations. It will be for your benefit, so you are able to assist whomever replaces me."

When she doesn't move, doesn't blink, and doesn't appear to be breathing, I prompt her.

"Mrs. Shaw?"

She clears her throat.

"I'm sorry, sir. I'm just a bit surprised. Of course I'll assist you with whatever needs done."

"Good."

I exhale.

"Let's start by getting my brother in here as soon as you can, okay?"

"No need, I'm already here." Hugh enters, worry lining his face.

"Hugh, I'd like to review some things with you and Mrs. Shaw before I leave."

"Another vacation?" he carefully asks.

I smile, knowing he's overheard something or perhaps my mother has spoken to him.

"No. I've resigned."

His eyes widen and lips part in shock.

"You quit?" Scarlett exclaims, pushing by Hugh and charging to my desk. "Don't let that bitch—"

"Mrs. Shaw, I'll call you when we are to begin."

She gives a small nod and hurries from the office, closing the door behind her.

I turn my attention back to Scarlett.

"She didn't do this. It's my decision, for once."

Scarlett shakes her head fervently.

"No, Damon, she did do this. She's forcing your hand, even if it's not in the way she planned."

"I'm getting as far from the Banks family, from my mother, as I can. I want nothing to do with her again."

"Fine, then make her release all her stock and hold on the company. Kick her out. Don't let her change your life by her actions. It's time for you to change hers!" Scarlett smacks my desk. "You are this company, Damon."

"No, it's my mother's and she will always have a hold on it, and me, if I stay."

"Scarlett is right." Hugh steps next to his fiancé. "Damon, you don't see it and you think it's your mother, but you're so wrong. It's *you* our investors and clients believe in. They are not relying on an elderly woman who they all can see won't let go of the strings."

I open my mouth to protest.

"Wait. Hear me out." He puts up a hand.

"When there is a problem with our major clients, such as Baxtor Broadcasting, who do they reach out to?"

"Blanche and my mother go way back," I argue.

"True, but it's Vincent — her son — who contacts you. He runs the company, Damon. Blanche hasn't controlled things since Vince took on the role of CEO. She holds stock, much like your mother, but she is a silent partner. He listens to her input, but makes the decisions."

"And if his mother were to advise against our initiatives, then—"

"You are kidding, right?" Hugh's brow rises, disbelief wrinkling his forehead. "You believe he makes his decisions based on what his mommy tells him to do? Do you think so little of him?"

"No, of course not, but—"

"But nothing," Scarlett interjects. "It's the same here. Everyone knows you are the force behind this company. No one believes for one second your mother has any ruling authority. Not even the investors."

"Every time we end an investor meeting where your mother attends, the first thing most people want to know is when they will hear your thoughts and plans. They crave your input, Damon." Hugh presses his hands on my desk, his palms flat.

"Just think about this before you make any final decisions. That's all I ask," Scarlett implores.

Olivia

Another week passes without a word from Damon. I'm still not sleeping well and the lack of sleep shot my immune system to hell, causing me to pick up some flu bug. Between the bakery, Alex, and not feeling well, I think I may lose my mind. Luckily, Alex still takes naps, so I'm able to sleep when he does. It's still not enough to help, though. For the last two days, I've been confined to my apartment and restricted from entering the bakery. Mercedes spends most of her day with me to help with Alex, except for today. Today, my father picked him up to spend time with his grandson and to give Ced and I a break.

A knock at the door is the first thing to get me off the couch I'm sharing with Mercedes, aside from bathroom breaks.

"I'm sorry to just drop by, but..." Alfonso pauses, taking in my wrinkled pajamas, frizzy hair, and blotchy face. "You don't look so hot."

He drops his bag by the door before sitting in a chair next to the couch.

After closing the door, I curl back up on the couch. I notice that Mercedes has straightened and fixed her clothes for a better appearance.

"I caught the flu," I croak, snuggling back into the couch.

"That sucks." Alfonso shifts his gaze from noticeably checking out Mercedes to me.

If I were feeling better, I'd excuse myself to leave them alone for a moment. It's the first time I've really seen him more than nod at her in a friendly greeting.

"Did you come by to tell her how awful she looks or is there a point to your visit?" Mercedes snaps at him, uncharacteristically.

My eyes widen at her remark and his obvious unease.

"Yes, I have news about your divorce."

Instantly, I forget about the weirdness between Alfonso and Mercedes. My spine straightens and every muscle tenses, waiting for him to launch into Damon's return fire. Seeing the weary eagerness on my face, he continues.

"Mr. Knyght is not fighting your petition." A small smile plays at the corner of his mouth.

He's not fighting the divorce? He's going to let us go? He's not fighting for us?

A part of me feels like twerking, while another part, one which shall not be admitted to if asked, feels like crying, screaming, and yelling.

"Olivia?" Alfonso invades my mixed thoughts. "I thought you would be happy?"

It's more of a question than a statement. I shake my head and blink.

"I am," I blurt. "I'm just surprised by this turn in events."
LIAR! You're disappointed.

"I don't think surprised is the right word," Mercedes chimes in, looking at me and avoiding Alfonso.

Her hand links with mine and squeezes.

"I agree," Alfonso speaks, drawing my attention, but not Mercedes'. "There's something else I need to discuss with you, though."

"What?" My relief ebbs.

"Mr. Knyght is petitioning for paternity and joint custody."

Shock tingles across my skin and widens my eyes.

He wants to take him for half the time? Take him to New York, near his crazy, controlling mother and chauvinistic father? Oh, hell no!

"No!" Shaking my head, I reaffirm my objection.

"Liv..." Mercedes begins.

"I won't send my son off to New York for part of the year."

"Olivia, Mr. Knyght has already established—"

"No, Alfonso!" I snap. "I want you to do whatever you have to in order to object to the petition. He can see his son, but only in Pittsburgh and supervised. I can't trust what he and his mother will scheme and plan."

Throwing back the blanket, I stand, determination stiffening my spine. My attempt at showing strength quells from the churn of my stomach. Darting off to the bathroom with my hand over my mouth, I kneel before the toilet.

I'm lying against the cool tile floor when Mercedes enters, following a light knock.

"You need anything?"

Grabbing onto the edge of the sink, I pull myself to a seated position.

"I think it's time for a doctor." Mercedes purses her lips.

"There's nothing they can do for the flu, Ced."

I raise my arms to her and she grabs my hands. She helps me to stand. Noticing my wobbling legs, she stays close to my side as I brush my teeth.

"What's going on in here?"

The sound of Felicity's voice surprises me.

"When did you get here?" I ask around the toothbrush in my mouth.

"Alfonso let me in just before he left." She shrugs. "He said he will be in touch with you soon and hopes you feel better."

"Okay, thanks." I remove the toothbrush and rinse my mouth. *Suddenly, the mint of the paste was not a good idea.*

With Mercedes help, I reclaim my position on the couch and snuggle the cushions and pillows.

"I'm going to clean up the bathroom a bit and pee. Be right back." Mercedes steps away and Felicity replaces her, kneeling next to the couch.

"Can I get you anything?" Felicity asks.

"I'm good, thanks." I give her as much of a smile as I can muster given the state of my stomach.

She stands, looking around the apartment.

"Where's Alex?"

"Dad," I rasp, closing my eyes and breathing through my nose.

"Damn," Mercedes' curse is muffled by the bathroom door, but still audible. "Liv, do you have any tampons?"

"They're under the—"

"Already looked, there's nothing there," she responds before I'm finished.

"There should be a box..."

My stomach flips again, but this time for a different reason.

Heart racing and mind spinning, I push off the couch and trudge toward the bathroom.

"Liv?" Felicity follows closely. Her arms are out, as if I'll fall at any second.

Barging through the closed door, I fling open the cabinet under the sink.

"What the hell?!" Mercedes shouts from the toilet, her bright pink skinny jeans bunched around her knees.

No blue box.

Air rushes from my lungs. Standing slowly, I grip the edge of the bathroom countertop.

"Liv?" Felicity hedges.

"Check the hall linen closet for tampons." My voice shakes, sounding fragile.

"Okay." She disappears, but returns quickly with an unopened box.

My brain is in overdrive, calculating, adding, and trying to account for the unopened box.

"What is going on?" Mercedes asks over the flush of the toilet.

Felicity moves to my left, placing an arm around my shoulders. Mercedes stands on my right.

"Liv, you're worrying me." Felicity softly urges me to answer.

"I'm late," I whisper.

"What do you—?"

"Oh my God," Mercedes says, cutting Felicity off.

Her arms wrap around my middle and she squeezes close to my side.

"Oh. Oh!" Felicity catches up and hugs me from my left.

Tears escape my eyes, streaming over my cheeks.

"This can't be happening," I sob, full of fear, worry, and disbelief.

"I'll be right back." Felicity vanishes from my side and out of the bathroom.

Mercedes guides me back to the couch. We sit silently for a minute.

"Maybe I'm wrong." I look up, seeing Mercedes' face filled with pity. "It could be the flu, Ced."

"Maybe." She takes my hand.

I drop my head to her shoulder and close my eyes.

We stay silent for some time, until Felicity pulls us from my denial bubble when she bursts through my apartment door with a white plastic shopping bag in her hand.

She empties the contents onto the coffee table. Three different pregnancy test twin packs scatter over the dark wood.

Sitting forward, I pick up the white box and give it a distasteful look before dropping it back down with the blue and pink one.

"Someone get me a cup." I sigh at the end of my request.

"A cup?" Ced leans forward, poking the pink box.

"To pee in," I groan.

"Eww." Her face scrunches in disgust. "Make sure it's an old cup that we can throw away afterward."

Felicity puts a glass of water and an empty plastic cup in front of me. I toss back the water, hoping it will stay down, and take the empty cup to the bathroom.

After dunking one of each brand into the cup, I line them up on the counter. We sit on the edge of the bathtub, waiting to check results. My leg bounces in anticipation. Deep down, I know the results, but part of me still holds onto the idea of having the flu.

"Alright, the results should be in," Mercedes says, looking at her watch.

"Do you have to make it sound like the elimination round of a reality show?" I mumble, standing from the edge of the tub.

"Sorry." She blushes and looks over the sticks.

"Which one is the one-minute test?" Felicity asks Ced. "We should check that one first."

"I don't think it matters." Ced's tone is quiet, but resolute.

I look down at three positive results and lose all air from my lungs.

"Breathe, Olivia. Breathe." Felicity wraps an arm around me and helps me sit back on the edge of the tub.

Tears slip over my face. I want to scream. Scream in frustration and anger. Anger for being so stupid and careless. And my inability to control myself where Damon is concerned. A couple of drinks and all my walls tumble under his persistence.

I drop a hand to my stomach, feeling scared and worried. How and when do I tell Damon? Do I tell him at all?

Three days later, I sit in the exam room of the second closest free clinic, waiting for results I don't really need. However, I need the reassurance of medical tests and exams, as well as the anonymity of the free clinic.

When did I become such a paranoid person? Oh, yeah. Since Damon.

The walls of the little room are covered in posters about adoption, HIV, Genital Herpes, and safe sex. Suddenly, I feel like a fifteen-year-old girl sneaking to get birth control. A knock and twist of the doorknob pull me out of my throwback thoughts.

A middle-aged woman in a white coat enters, giving me a once over. Once she's had her fill, we start discussing what I already know. I'm pregnant. I try to stay focused on her lecture about options, prenatal care, vitamins, diets, and so forth.

A doctor delivering the result, rather than a plastic stick, puts me in a zombie-like state. I barely remember dressing and leaving the clinic, so finding myself standing just outside the bakery window, jars me. I glance around, trying to remember the walk here.

Did I forget anything at the clinic?

I pat my pockets and run my hands over my messenger bag. Relief settles my panicked heart rate until I recall my thoughts during my journey home.

Did he do it on purpose? Would he do this just to further tie himself to me? It's possible, right? Right. I shake my head and rub my temples. *How do I tell him without giving him more of a reason to fight me on the dissolution? I could keep it to myself.*

I fist my hands in the hair at the sides of my head.

No, I can't just keep it from him.

Then, for just the briefest moment, the thought of something I would never consider blips into my consciousness. Guilt instantly claws at me from within and tears blur one eye.

Never. I lost one child. How could I even…? Jesus, Olivia, quit being a fucking coward looking for the damn easy way out. But isn't that what you are also doing with Damon?

With a deep resolute breath, I push the thought far from my mind and will it never to enter again. With my hand on my stomach, I enter the shop and greet the patrons and Mrs. Dorn before stepping into the kitchen.

"Hey, Liv," Sarah greets, smiling over a large creampuff cake.

"I just need to run upstairs real quick. I'll be right back, okay?"

She nods, her attention remaining focused on the cake.

Moving fast, I toss the plastic bag with prenatal vitamins and care brochures onto my dresser. With a quick change of clothes, I'm back in the bakery and the familiar bustling sounds of pans, music, and conversation. Everyone is so involved in their work, they don't acknowledge my return. Instead of disturbing them, I go search for Mercedes.

Entering Mercedes' office, I find Alex seated on her lap in front of the computer. They both look up as I walk in.

"Momma." Alex smiles before returning to whatever has his attention on the screen.

"Hey, how did it go?" She chews on her bottom lip.

"Nothing I didn't already know." I shrug.

"Momma, look." Alex points to the computer monitor.

Reaching out, I twist the screen and see Sponge Bob dancing. Alex giggles. "Bob so funny."

Both Mercedes and I laugh, too.

And it feels good to laugh for a change.

After an update on the bakery schedule, I take Alex and place him in the play area before burying myself in work.

Two days pass before I hear from Alfonso. He tells me the date for the mediation, where Damon and I will discuss the appropriate terms of custody. I decide to keep my pregnancy a secret, even from Alfonso. I'll tell Damon, but I won't tell him until the marriage is dissolved. No way is he using this child to fuel his fantasy.

The weeks leading up to the mediation have my nerves on edge and stomach in knots. Kneeling in a public restroom at the courthouse isn't ideal, but what other options do I have? Coming face to face with Damon again, tears me up inside. No matter how hard I try, a battle between love and hate rages. I'm not in love, but feelings — unwanted feelings — still linger like burnt microwave popcorn.

"Olivia?" Mercedes taps lightly on the stall door. "Are you alright?" she asks, her voice dripping with sympathy.

"I'm good, just give me a minute."

I wipe my mouth and pull myself off my knees, brushing lint and dirt from the conservative black dress I'm wearing. Exiting the stall, Mercedes hovers while I wash my hands.

Our eyes meet in the large wall mirror over the sinks.

"Maybe you should tell him before—"

I shake my head. "No. Not until the divorce is final."

Drying my hands under the blower, I give myself a mental pep talk.

You can do this, Olivia. You can face him and when you do, you will realize it's all hormones and not really feelings of...

I stop my thoughts from continuing and turn to Mercedes.

"How do I look?"

I brush my hands over my dress one more time. It's more of a nervous gesture than anything else.

"You look beautiful," she replies too quickly. By the look in her eyes, I can tell she's lying to me.

I know I look drawn, tired, and pale. The stress intensifies the nausea and morning sickness. My doctor monitors the stress and has threatened to put me on bed rest if things don't improve soon. Hopefully, after today, things will be a bit better.

Alfonso is pacing on his cell phone when we come back to the small meeting room. He doesn't look worried, but seems anxious.

"But how did we get the information?" He pauses and I keep listening to the one-sided conversation. "No, it's great, but we can't submit something if we don't have the releases and—"

This time the pause is accompanied with a look of shock.

"Really?" he questions with disbelief before ending the call.

"What was that about?" Mercedes asks the same question I'm thinking.

"We got some information sent to us. I need to go get the papers sent over and talk with the clerk. I'll be right back."

Alfonso exits before we can inquire more.

Sitting at the small table, my thoughts become an abyss of fear, sadness, and...disappointment?

These damn hormones have me going crazy. How can I feel disappointment? I should be relieved. The end of all of this is so close.

The meeting room door opens and Felicity enters. Taking the seat next to me, she places a hand on my arm. My paleness is intensified by the natural tan of her skin.

"Are you okay?" Her eyes search mine.

"I just want to get this over with."

Looking away, I drop my head.

"You don't look well, Liv." She rubs my arm lightly. "Are you following the doctor's orders?"

"What doctor's orders?" Alfonso looks between Felicity and me.

I shake my head. "Nothing. Are we ready?"

He hesitates, eyeing his sister closely before putting a hand out toward me and nodding.

Alfonso leads us down a hallway and I come face to face with Scarlett Manson. My hands tighten on my purse.

"I'm so sorry," she whispers. "I didn't know. I had no idea."

I open my mouth to tell her that it's not her fault, but I'm cut off from responding by Heidi.

"Oh, Olivia." Her arms wrap around my shoulders and hold me tight. "I'm sorry it has come to this for you and Damon." She pulls back, her bottom lip quivering and tears in her eyes.

My nose burns with emotion and I have to stay silent for fear of turning into a blubbering mess of sobs.

"Excuse us, ladies." Alfonso gently pulls me along and into another room.

Immediately, I'm drawn to him. His head is in his hands and his elbows on the table. The way he slumps over the table pulls at my heart and sends a tear down my cheek.

The scrape of Alfonso pulling out a chair for me pulls my attention away from Damon. I sit and notice papers in a new folder on the table.

"Is this the information you received?" I touch the manila folder.

"Yes," Alfonso whispers to the side of my head. "This should ensure the custody arrangement you are seeking."

"What do you mean?"

Just as I'm about to open the folder, the mediator arrives and begins going through the motions of the dissolution of marriage.

"Miss Harlow, you wish to proceed with the dissolution?"

"Yes," I croak. Fighting back the urge to look at Damon, I stare at a portrait on the wall behind the mediator.

"Mr. Knyght, you are in agreement with the filing?"

No longer able to look away, I turn, meeting his eyes.

"Yes. She can have whatever she wants, if it makes her happy."

There's a hollowness to his voice and dullness to his eyes.

"Very well. Let me get a few things straight before proceeding to the next matter."

For the next forty-five minutes, our entire time together is laid out in black in white. Vegas, Damon being Alex's father, and my week in New York. The last few months of my life is questioned and commented on as lawyers interject with information and proposals.

"Okay," the mediator states, clearing his throat. "Let's discuss the custody of Alexander Isaac Harlow." He looks between both of us. "Mr. Knyght, you are seeking joint custody and Miss Harlow is requesting supervised visitations."

It wasn't a question, but both lawyers confirm.

"I see we have the paternity test results, so we don't have to wait on those. Let's start with Miss Harlow. Can you please tell me why you are requesting such a restricted custody arrangement?"

Alfonso straightens and answers for me.

"We have submitted the voicemails and texts from Mr. Knyght the day Miss Harlow and her son left New York. My client is concerned for the wellbeing of her son, given the way Mr. Knyght verbally attacked her."

"I would never—"

"Mr. Knyght was suffering temporary distraught. He woke up Sunday morning and they were gone. He didn't get to say goodbye to his son and wife. They also had not reached a final agreement. My client didn't know what was happening or if he would ever see them again. I think we all can relate to letting fear guide us."

"True." The mediator nods. "But your client blatantly threatened Miss Harlow. That's much more serious than simply afraid and distraught."

He turns back to Alfonso and motions for him to continue.

"We were okay to leave it at the texts and voicemails, but some new disturbing information was brought to our attention just this morning."

Damon's lawyer is quick to object.

"This information wasn't provided previous to the meeting."

"As I said, we just received the information today." Alfonso hands a folder to the mediator and Damon's lawyer.

Damon's lawyer scans the documents, pushes them to Damon, and glares at Alfonso.

"Those are private medical records and cannot be submitted." His fists clench on top of the table.

There's a rumbling noise from Damon. My eyes move to see what's wrong. He looks sick. Tears pool in his eyes and his jaw tightens so harshly, I swear I hear his teeth gnashing together.

Grabbing the folder in front of Alfonso, I flip open the file and begin to read.

Breakdown, subdued, and law enforcement are just a couple of the words blaring out from the pages.

Oh my God. What is Alfonso doing?

"If you look at the last page, you will see the file was provided with consent." Alfonso sits back in the wooden chair.

Flipping to the final page, my heart skips a beat, heat floods my face, and bile rises. There, in perfect cursive, is *her* signature — Mildred Banks-Knyght.

His own mother would do this to him?

Looking up from the folder, his rage filled eyes lock onto mine.

Tears spill from the corners of my eyes and his rage washes away into an expression of sorrow and pain. Guilt bubbles in my gut and bile reaches my throat.

"Mr. Knyght has a difficult past, experiencing great losses. Anyone would be challenged—"

"I'm taking care of it," Damon growls, his hands fisting the folder, causing it to wrinkle.

"Damon," his lawyer hisses.

Damon's eyes, filled with blame and disbelief, meet mine once more.

"These records only prove my client's dedication to become well enough for his wife and son." His lawyer swings the story almost perfectly.

He's not perfect. He's definitely out of his mind, but who wouldn't be with a mother like that? Who hasn't been through something so devastating you would do anything to feel something again? Didn't I do something similar when I decided to have Alex? The only difference is I didn't have a psycho obsessive mother going Mother Bates behind the scenes. She's using my son and me against him, tearing him down. Why?

"Alfonso," I rasp, trying to hold down the vomit.

"You now understand the request for supervision. Miss Harlow clearly—"

"Alfonso!" I try to shout, but it's more of a gurgle.

Covering my mouth, I shove away from the table, sending papers and my purse scattering across the floor. Grabbing the closest garbage can, I lean over and empty my stomach. Having not eaten since my last episode, my body is wracked with heaves.

A large hand rests on my back, rubbing. The other hand pushes my hair out of my face and holds it away.

"Why is she here if she's so ill?" Damon barks.

It's Damon comforting me. And hell if my body doesn't warm and relax at his touch.

"She didn't say anything about being sick." Alfonso sounds farther away than Damon.

Taking a deep breath, I wipe my mouth with my hand.

"I'll be fine."

I stand, keeping one hand against a wall for strength.

"Here." Alfonso hands me a glass of water and straightens my chair from where it tumbled to the floor.

"Thank you." I sip at the water and make an attempt back to my chair.

Damon quickly takes my arm and guides me.

"You shouldn't be here if you're sick." His hand cups my face. He jerks his hand away quickly, a frown marring his face.

I immediately miss his touch and am about to protest him moving away when he kneels down to the floor. With his back to mine, I can't see what he's doing.

"Damon," I gargle.

My throat burns from the vomiting episode. I sip the water again in an attempt to ease the pain.

"What is this?"

He turns, holding out the pink box of Morning Sickness lollipops Mercedes ordered for me online.

"I..." I don't know what to say. I didn't plan for him to find out this way.

"Please take your seats," the mediator announces.

Alfonso collects the rest of the items that had fallen from my purse and Damon tosses the box in my lap, a look of scheming in his narrowed eyes. Eyes I feel on me after everyone is reseated and throughout the rest of the meeting.

"I will take the new information into consideration with the judge. We will need to schedule another date to finalize the custody," the mediator dismisses. I hurry out of the room.

"Olivia," Damon calls.

I keep moving until I can duck inside a ladies room. I'm not ready to discuss this with him. Not yet. Leaning over a sink, I splash cold water on my face. Felicity and Mercedes follow and stand at my sides. The door opens again and I'm almost sure it's going to be Damon.

"Olivia, I know this is horrible timing." Heidi's voice draws my dripping face toward her. Disappointment once again gnaws at me.

I'm losing it! Really? I'm disappointed he hasn't barged in after me? What's wrong with me?

Grabbing some paper towels from a dispenser, I pat my face.

"Please, Heidi, I can't—"

"There are things you need to know." Scarlett enters behind Heidi.

"No." I shake my head. "I don't want to know anything else. Please, not right now."

"I owe it to you to tell you everything. Things I didn't know until a few weeks ago." Scarlett's pleading eyes and my exhaustion make me cave.

"Fine," I growl. "What do I need to know?"

I already know enough and hate what I know.

Scarlett launches into a tale of deception I wouldn't believe if I hadn't already seen what Damon's mother is capable of doing.

"Scarlett, I appreciate your love for Damon, and I get it. Mildred not only messed with his head, but set him up, too. However, she didn't force him to lie to me." I point at myself.

"We know." Heidi hugs me. "We just want you to know, to understand, exactly how she has manipulated him and his life. I only hope you see how you change that about him." She gives a sad smile.

"I think she's had enough," Felicity says, putting her six foot — in heels — body between them and me.

Scarlett steps up, almost nose to nose, with Felicity, but a knock at the door silences whatever she is about to say.

"Olivia? Felicity?" Alfonso calls through the door. "Is everything okay?"

Without taking her eyes off Scarlett, Felicity calls back a response.

"Everything will be fine, Al. We're just about to come out."

Heidi places her hand on Scarlett's tense shoulder.

"Come on, Liv." Mercedes wraps an arm around my waist, guiding me to the bathroom door.

My insides clench, sure Damon is waiting to pounce the moment I exit. When Mercedes pulls back the dark wood door, only Alfonso stands there. Disappointment makes another unwanted appearance, but there is also a spark of anger. The anger is directed at the only man waiting for me.

"How could you provide that information without telling me first?" I ask, low and harsh.

Alfonso's brows raise in surprise.

"I thought you would be happy to have a fighting chance against him." His words, too, are low and harsh.

"It's sneaky and low and you know it."

"Olivia, has something changed that I'm not aware of?" His face wrinkles in confusion.

My mouth pops open, but nothing comes out. I don't know what to say.

Nothing has changed. What would have changed? It's not like I've changed my mind. I'm not...I am NOT developing feelings for Damon. It's hormones.

"Olivia."

His cool, calm, collected voice sends a shiver down my spine.

Turning my head toward his voice, Damon nods, passing by with a suspicious line at the corner of his mouth and a faint twinkle in his eyes. With Heidi and Scarlett flanking both sides of him, they disappear into the elevator, his legal team in tow.

Relief washes away the tightness in my shoulders.

"Well, I didn't expect that," Alfonso muses, drawing my attention back to him. "After the way he looked during the arbitration, I thought he would be a bit more disgruntled."

He shrugs and my spark of anger flickers once more.

"Why wouldn't he be pissed off?" I snap. "You blindsided him with those documents."

Crossing my arms over my chest, I narrow my eyes on Alfonso. His shoulders fall in defeat.

"Olivia," he rubs his face, "you need to tell me what's going on. I'm using whatever methods I can to make this come out in your favor."

He looks at me, his eyes searching my face for an answer.

"I want to offer a custody deal."

"What? Why in the hell would you decide to do that? We are close to getting full custody and perhaps keeping him out of your life for good." An incredulous look replaces the confusion from before.

"I need this to end, Alfonso. You don't know everything and things could get—"

"What aren't you telling me?" he demands, cutting me off.

"Leave her alone, Al!" Felicity steps close to my side, glaring at her brother. "She's had a shit day and doesn't need more of it from you."

"I'm pregnant," I blurt out while I have the courage. "And he knows it."

"W-what? How did...nevermind, I know how it happens." He rubs his forehead and sighs. "Once his lawyer gets this information..." he trails off.

"I know, which is why I need to end this quickly."

"The elevator is here," Mercedes calls, holding the doors open.

We walk to the elevator, no one saying a word until we reach the car.

I look out the window of the backseat, not truly seeing anything.

"I won't agree to joint custody, but I will agree to long visits to New York. Occasionally." I swallow the lump forming in my throat. "He can also visit Alex here in Pittsburgh, as long as prior arrangements are made and he isn't just randomly showing up. No supervision will be required," I choke on the last words and a tear escapes.

"I'll prepare the change and submit it to his lawyer for review," he mumbles. "Olivia?"

Pulling my eyes from the window, I look at Alfonso in the rearview mirror.

"I'm sorry. If you need anything, let me know, okay?"

I nod, leaning my forehead against the cool glass and closing my eyes.

Alfonso drops us off, promising to let me know when the next meeting will take place. Since I'm changing the proposition, it may come sooner than later.

Damon

Having agreed to think about the decisions I need to make, I take a few days to myself. My mother still attempts to contact me, but I refuse to acknowledge her. She's already created rumors by crying on the shoulder of Blanche Baxtor and a few of the investors. Vincent has already contacted me to discuss gossip of my resignation, which I'm forced to explain without getting too personal.

Where the other investors are concerned, her plan is backfiring. Most have reached out to the office and spoken with Hugh. They want to hold a meeting, without my mother, to secure my presence in the company. A few even mention pushing my mother out altogether.

So many things race through my mind and I'm not sure what I'm going to do or how I'm going to officially resign from B.I.G. without causing a problem for the company. I could care less about my mother at this point, but the company and the employees are another story.

I don't protest the divorce petition, but counter with a custody arrangement I'm sure she won't agree to. Part of it is to piss her off, but it's mostly so there is a reason we have to see each other again. She will have to meet with me in order negotiate the custody terms. A piece of paper can dissolve the marriage if she so chooses, but she needs to understand that I won't be out of her life. We are connected until death do us part by the blood that runs in Alex's veins.

After weeks of contemplation about my life, I know one thing for certain — I'm moving to Pittsburgh. I can't be away from them — not this far, anyway — any longer. My career, family, and life in New York are still uncertain. With the move to Pittsburgh, I'll have no choice but to leave the company.

My mind is burdened when I arrive to the arbitration to discuss custody of Alex with my legal team in tow. Heidi and Scarlett insist on being at my side for support. I believe they are also sticking close in hopes of getting a chance to talk with Olivia.

Olivia avoids looking at me, but I watch her. She looks pale and tired. *Does she want to end this so badly she would come to this meeting sick?*

The moment her counselor presents the manila folder, insinuating it incriminates me, my stomach knots. Finding my mother's signature on the release form doesn't shock me. This is her way of punishing me, hurting me. The familiar rage simmers, but it's different this time.

My legal counsel spars with hers and I sit back, feeling both vengeful toward my mother and angry that Olivia would take this route. I never thought she would use something like this, something from my mother, against me. Not after the way she boldly stood against her in New York.

Her raspy cry for her lawyer and sudden movement toward the garbage quenches the angry flames. Rushing to her side, I swipe back her hair and rub her back. It's sick, but just touching her sends my body into an animalistic craving. The sudden need to possess everything — her body, soul, and heart — fills me.

The minute the pink box catches my attention, I focus on one string of words — *Mother's Comfort significantly reduces your morning sickness symptoms.*

She's pregnant. Olivia is pregnant! I want to roar my excitement and rage at her deceit.

Surprising myself, I put on a cool and collected mask. Tossing the box into her lap, I retake my seat. A full-scale plan develops, easing every burden I felt coming in here today.

At the conclusion of the meeting, I try to get Olivia's attention, but she rushes off to hide in the ladies room. Instead of talking things over with her, I decide to implement my newest plan. If she wants to continue deceiving me, then I'll play the game my way.

Excusing myself from the legal team, I step into an empty hallway to make a few calls. First, is to my realtor. Instead of an apartment, I'll need a house for a family. Second, is to my brother. I need a full-scale investor meeting. There will be changes to B.I.G., but it won't be my departure. And the last item to be handled will require a bit more thought, but now that another child is on the way, there is no possibility of her getting rid of me.

Chapter fourteen - reckoning
Olivia

Morning arrives and I go through the normal motions: eat, dress, bake, eat, nap, take care of Alex, bake, and nap again. My second nap is interrupted when Felicity and Mercedes come down the hall.

"Why are you on the couch?" Ced wrinkles her brow, setting a brown bag on the counter.

Sitting up, I stretch and give a small shrug.

"I brought muffins." Felicity slides onto a stool at the breakfast bar and begins unpacking items.

"From where? Downstairs?" I roll my eyes.

She shrugs and smiles.

"You need to eat," Mercedes says sternly.

"The doctor says I'm fine."

I grab one of the muffins baked this morning and slather it with tons of honey butter.

"She also says you could use some extra calories, given your daily schedule." Mercedes puts a hand on her hip, scowling at me.

"So, Felicity," I change the subject, "how's the new girlfriend, Lorna? You haven't talked about her lately. Are you still dating?"

"Yeah." Felicity shrugs. "She wants to move in together, but it's too soon for that."

"Are you kidding me?" Mercedes chokes on her orange juice. "If you feel connected to someone, I say go for it."

"Some of us are more responsible than you, my friend." Felicity smirks.

"So what if I've lived with a few different guys." She shrugs. "The point is, I take the chance. I live." With a proud smile, she stuffs a muffin top into her mouth.

"I kind of agree with Ced." I watch Felicity from the corner of my eye.

"Well, well, well, Miss Harlow." Felicity grins. "I guess getting knocked up by your stalker husband has loosened you up a bit."

"Shut up," I laugh, but then seriousness washes over me. "Am I an awful person?"

I stare at the marble countertop.

"Why would you think that?" Ced moves swiftly to my side.

"I mean, I didn't tell him about..." I motion to my stomach.

"That would have put his craze-omiter into overdrive. You wouldn't have even made it to arbitration." Felicity places her long bronze arm over my shoulders.

"But he knows now and hasn't done or said anything." I glance up at her. "Maybe I was wrong to keep it secret. It wasn't fair of me to just hold the information."

"What's really going on here, Liv?" Ced, too, puts an arm around me.

"Nothing, I just—"

"Yeah, right," Felicity interjects.

"Spill," Ced demands.

I groan.

"It's just hormones," I state, more to convince myself than them. "But..."

"But, what?" Felicity urges.

"There are these feelings. Like yesterday," I slip out from their embrace and off the stool to start pacing, "it killed me to read those documents and have his business put on display for strangers. I felt sorry for him."

I stop and look at my two best friends. They sit, nodding. There's no judgment to be found, so I continue to spill my deepest secrets.

"I'm not blind to everything crazy he's done and that does scare me, but not as much as it should. He used extreme measures, but I know what it's like to be at a point in life where extreme is the only way you can breathe...feel."

Isaac flashes into my mind, bringing a tear to the corner of my eye. I'm reminded of how hollow I felt when I lost him and our unborn child. Alex was my extreme moment. My chance to be whole, to breathe and function once more.

"I just can't help how I'm feeling and it's driving me crazy. Every logical bone in my body knows it's insanity and has to be these pregnancy hormones driving me to coo-coo town."

"Liv, stop and sit. You're making me dizzy with the pacing."

With a deep breath, I retake my seat as Felicity requested.

"I'm losing it, aren't I?"

"No," Mercedes blurts.

Our eyes meet and she smiles.

"I don't think it's just hormones either." She shrugs unapologetically.

"But—"

Mercedes moves to stand directly across from me.

"Look, Liv, I think you two connect on a level because of the pain you've both experienced. You both try to be strong, but the debilitating losses you've both experienced leave a mark. You recognize this in each other and connect on a level like no other."

"She makes a point." Felicity finally enters the conversation. "However, he definitely still has a lot of healing to do. I mean, think about everything he's done. The stalking, barging into your life, threats, scheming, and lying. Those aren't so easy to forget or overlook."

"Yeah, but think about the circumstances," Ced counters.

"I have and I acknowledge them. But still, I don't know how she could even deal with all that crazy without losing her shit, too."

"*She* is sitting right here," I break into the conversation, reminding them I'm still in the room.

"Sorry." Felicity blushes for a moment.

The ring of my cell phone ends the debate of my situation.

"Hello."

"Hey, Olivia, I wanted to let you know that the papers have been received by Mr. Knyght's team and the arbitrator," Alfonso provides.

"And?" I chew on my bottom lip nervously.

"Damon is requesting forty-eight hours to review the proposal."

"Okay, that seems fair."

Alfonso clears his throat.

"What?" I chew harder, flinching when I break through the skin.

"Damon has some business matters to tend to in New York and will need the upcoming week to handle it. And you have business the following week, so it will be about fifteen days before the next meeting can be arranged and terms finalized."

"Okay," I groan.

"It's the quickest I can get things moving."

"I know, Alfonso. I appreciate all you've done. Thanks." I end the call.

"Do we want to know?" Mercedes leans against the bar.

After a moment, I relay the information to both of them.

Damon

Back in New York, Hugh, Mrs. Shaw, and Scarlett work overtime to help prepare my proposal for the Pittsburgh location. All investors and board members confirm to attend the meeting. I'm sure most of them are concerned I'll be stepping down, when, in fact, I'll be making other adjustments.

My law team is quick to request a forty-eight hour review period for her new proposal. It's unexpected. I didn't think she would propose an arrangement as such, but it now provides me with more leverage to bring my plan to fruition.

Goodbye, New York. Goodbye to my mother's involvement with B.I.G. and farewell divorce decree. Pittsburgh looks to hold a bright future for my wife, our children, and my company.

Olivia

Two days pass and I don't hear anything from Alfonso about the custody proposal. On the third day, I call him to find out that he's been playing phone tag with Damon's legal team and isn't sure what's going on.

By the time the weekend arrives, I'm exhausted. Alex having been exceptionally energetic for the past few days, I'm thankful for the knock on the door. Thinking its Felicity and Lorna stopping by as planned, I swing the door open without checking.

"Thank Go—" I choke.

"Hello, Olivia." Damon's voice is smooth and sexy as ever.

"You can't be here." I try to shut the door.

"I don't think so." He pushes his way into my home, closing the door behind his entrance.

I step back, but can't help but notice the way his dark jeans and black sweater hug his body in a sexy caress. With a mental slap to my wacky hormones, I growl and prepare to demand his exit.

"Did you plan on ever telling me?"

His question shuts down my demand.

He turns, pinning me with fierce green eyes — eyes flaming with bottled emotions. My breath hitches, remembering him staring down from above as he lazily moved between my thighs.

"Don't lie, Olivia. I know I deserve it, but please don't lie to me."

I remain silent, unsure of what will come out of my mouth.

"You know, when I saw that box, I wasn't sure why you had it. When it finally sunk in, I was assaulted with so many different feelings." He shakes his head. "I wanted to pull you into my arms, kiss you until you couldn't do anything but stay with me."

I open my mouth to apologize, but he puts a hand up.

"Then I wanted to strangle you." His eyes blaze into my mine, the pain crystal clear. "I couldn't believe you would keep something like this from me."

"Damon, I—"

"Let me finish. Please." The plea in his voice silences me once more. "Thank you."

"I realize I wasn't honest with you and I've never been more sorry." He takes three strides and kneels before me. "Believe me, I'm sorry."

His forehead presses against my stomach and his hands grip my hips.

"I know you are." I keep my hands at my sides, more afraid of myself than him.

"Thank you."

He releases my hips and stands before me, invading my personal space. His eyes hold mine captive as he caresses my face.

"At first, when I received the new proposal, for just a moment, I thought perhaps you realized I would never do anything to hurt Alex or you. That maybe, just maybe, you realized how much I've fallen in love with you and this was your way of offering me the only thing you could."

"You should go," I whisper, feeling the tears pool in my eyes.

He steps forward and I step back. The motion repeats until my back is against the living room wall, his damn eyes burning through me.

"Answer me," he growls. "Were you ever going to tell me?"

I nod.

"But not until after you and your pathetic lawyer tried to tear me down, right?" he sneers.

"I didn't know about the medical information until it was too late. I would never have allowed Alfonso to—"

"Why?" He presses closer.

My hands come up, pressing against his chest.

"Step back, Damon." I turn my head, closing my eyes to fight the tears.

"Answer me."

"Because I wouldn't do that," I say in a harsh hush, trying to make sure Alex doesn't overhear.

He draws his lips in thoughtfully. "We have things we need to discuss."

"I'm expecting company," I blurt. "We can talk another—"

"Daddy!" Alex runs into the room. "Yous here." He wraps his chubby arms around Damon's leg.

Damon leans down, lifting Alex into his arms and smiling.

"Hey, buddy. I've missed you so much." Damon hugs him tightly to his chest.

With him distracted, I slip out from between his body and the wall. Damon reaches out, grabbing my wrist.

"We aren't finished talking." His eyes glow with a savage inner fire before turning back to Alex.

"You wanna go get your pajamas for me while I talk to Mommy? Can you show me what a big boy you are?" Damon sets Alex on his feet.

Alex nods furiously, running off to his room. He's learning so quickly how to do things, wanting to prove he's a big boy. I have to wonder if it's Damon's male influence that has created the sudden need for independence.

Damon pulls me back to him and I look up.

"No more secrets, Olivia."

"No more secrets, Damon."

A muscle twitches in his jaw before his lips crash onto mine.

His lips are soft yet hard, demanding yet giving. For a moment, I'm lost in the kiss, but then I push away from him.

He pulls us to the couch, sitting me down, before kneeling before me again.

I tense as he places a hand against my stomach and leans in close.

"Hello in there. I'm your Daddy." Both of his hands come to my stomach, caressing.

Tears of guilt, sadness, and mixed feelings roll over my cheeks.

Alex runs back into the room, wearing mismatched pajamas with the shirt on backwards.

"Did it," he announces proudly.

Quickly, I wipe the tears from my face. Damon turns to him.

"Such a big boy," Damon chokes out.

Damon, unwilling to leave, and Alex demanding his father's attention, is still in my apartment when Felicity and Lorna arrive.

"Sorry," Lorna apologizes upon entering. "Our dinner reservation got messed up, so we were at the restaurant much later than expected."

"Are you okay?" Felicity places a perfectly manicured hand on my arm.

Nodding, I open my mouth to tell her Damon is here.

"He fell asleep on the floor playing cars." Damon enters from the hallway and stops just inside the living room. "I put him in bed."

"Okay, thank you." I nod and step toward the hall.

"No need to thank me. It's what a father does." His eyes move from me to Felicity and back.

With his presence at my back, I know he's following me, closely.

Leaning down, I kiss Alex on his head before righting myself.

Damon's hands come to either side of the crib, caging me in front of him.

The heat of his breath warms the back of my neck, the side, and then the lobe of my ear.

"We will speak later about all of this, Olivia." He straightens, taking the heat of his body with him.

I bite my lip, so as not to call out to him.

When I step back into the living room, Damon is gone and Felicity launches question after question.

Two days later, after Alex is already asleep, Damon returns with a folder and determination on his face.

"Alex is already in bed," I say as I answer the door.

He half smiles.

"That's probably best, since we have things to discuss that need your uninterrupted attention."

Stepping further into the living room, he motions to the folder in his hand.

Suddenly, air can't fill my lungs fast enough. Anxiety grips my chest the way I imagine a demon possession feels.

"Damon, it's late." My argument sounds weak to my own ears.

He turns, facing me with hard eyes.

"Take a seat, Olivia, we have things to discuss."

Exhaling any fight I could muster, I take a seat on the chair opposite my couch.

Damon sits on the couch, laying the folder onto the dark wooden surface of the table between us. My fingers flex, wanting to grab the folder and tear through it.

"I'm aware you have been awaiting my response to your proposal regarding custody." He pauses, waits for me to nod, then continues. "Well, I have decided to counter your offer with one of my own."

I take a deep breath, holding the oxygen in my lungs.

"I propose a pausing in our dissolution of marriage."

"The filing has already been made," I interrupt.

"Yes, but it is not yet filed, which means we can place a hold on the filing."

I open my mouth, but he puts a large palm up, stopping the words from leaving my mouth.

"You agree to a hold and sixty days of relationship and marital counseling."

Unable to form words, I stand and go to the kitchen for a glass of water. My throat is so dry, I almost chug an entire glass. Wiping my mouth with the back of my hand, I place the glass in the sink and return to my seat.

Damon sits, forearms to knees. His head raises to watch me settle back into the chair.

SADIE GRUBOR

"And if I reject your offer?" I squeak.

He smirks.

"Then, given the newest development," he waves toward my barely there belly, "I will contest the divorce and can drag this out into something uglier than necessary. Neither of us wants that, do we?" He watches me with smug satisfaction in his eyes.

"You already agreed to the dissolution. It's documented that—"

"That was before my knowledge of our unborn child," he says, his words cool and confident.

"I could say I just found out." The words just slip out in defiance against his attitude and demeanor.

"And I can petition medical records from the clinic you visited." One brow raises over his bright eyes.

At the challenge, every muscle in my body stiffens.

"What exactly are you proposing?"

The determination on his face transforms to a satisfied smile on his lips and in his eyes.

"Dissolution is placed on hold. Sixty days of relationship counseling, living separately, visitation established with mutual agreement. You can think about it and bring your visitation suggestions to the next arbitration." He shrugs. "I don't think I'm asking for too much."

"Just two months more of marriage," I snap, harsher than intended.

"It's better than two or more months of court dates and legal fees, don't you agree?"

Furrowing my brow, I think of the first bill sitting on the desk in my bedroom. The amount won't break me, but it's enough to make his statement sting. He could afford a full team of lawyers and their support staff twenty-four hours a day if he so desires. I, on the other hand, am currently trying to buy the bakery and apartment from the owner.

Holding my head high, I meet the intensity of his stare. The warm tingling in my belly is unexpected. Unwilling to let him see the affect he has on me, I fight, trembling.

"Sixty days of waiting, not sixty days of living together as a family, correct?"

"Correct."

"And how many counseling sessions are involved?"

"We can let the counselor decide what they feel is best."

"What kind of custody agreement are you thinking?"

264

He smiles victoriously, knowing he's already won.

"I would like a couple days to determine my schedule and then discuss what works best for the both of us."

Damon places his long fingered hand on the envelope and pushes it toward me.

"A copy of my proposal is inside. Read it thoroughly. At our next arbitration, we can discuss and finalize."

"Our next—"

"It will be in three days. I've had my lawyers reach out to yours, but, given the hour, he won't be able to discuss it with you until tomorrow."

Damon unfolds from the couch, steps around the table, and offers me his hand.

Thinking he's going to shake on the deal, I grasp his hand.

Long, warm fingers wrap around mine, pulling me to my feet and to his chest. His strong arm secures around my back, holding me to him. My free hand presses to his chest, feeling the wild beat of his heart.

My body surges with hot, tingling desire. Tightening my thighs does little to counter the traitorous lust my body is pumping through me.

Releasing my hand, he cups my face.

"Please try, Olivia." His hot breath wafts over my face.

I open my mouth to respond, but his tongue silences me.

Our tongues battle for entrance and my fingers curl around the lapels of his jacket until my knuckles ache. He pulls us closer together. The feel of my breasts pressed so tightly against his chest is both torturous and exhilarating. Damon breaks the kiss, instantly waking me from my hunger-filled haze. Shock quells the lust, but leaves me in blank amazement and shaking.

Damon's thumb brushes over my flushed cheek.

Forehead pressed to mine, he whispers, "Ask me to stay."

And I almost do.

My body screams to claw at his Armani suit like it's Christmas wrapping paper.

Pressing my hands to his chest, I push six inches of space between us and take a deep breath.

"You should go," I puff out in labored breaths, keeping my eyes focused on the floor.

He stiffens before stepping back further.

"I meant what I said, Olivia."

Raising my eyes, his gaze of determination catches me once more.

"Please try."

Before I can respond, he is gone.

On weak legs, I cross to the door and lock it.

"The past three days went by too quickly," I whisper to Alfonso.

He nods, opening his mouth to respond, but is silenced by the entrance of the arbitrator.

"Good morning." He takes a seat at the head of the long table, spreading out folders, legal paper, and a pen in front of him.

"I've had an opportunity to review the new petition." His eyes rise from the open folder, focusing on me. "Miss Harlow, you are in agreement to stop proceedings in the case of your dissolution of marriage?"

"Yes," I croak.

"And, Mr. Knyght, you confirm agreement to this?" He turns toward Damon.

"Yes, sir."

"I see you both agree to marriage counseling while separated, which I'm glad to see, given the two children involved." Stern eyes make pointed contact with Damon and then me. "I suggest you both take the counseling seriously and the advice provided to heart. You have a young son and a baby on the way that needs you both to make a real effort."

A tingling sensation settles into my fingers and heat fans over my chest. *What am I doing?*

"As for custody during this time of separation, I suggest Alexander Harlow spend Sunday to Wednesday with his mother. And since Mr. Knyght has recently acquired a residence in Pittsburgh, he spends Thursday through Saturday with his father."

The second my eyes flash to the lock onto Damon's, my brow furrows with confusion.

Pittsburgh residence? When did he move here?

"Now, the arrangement is my suggestion. I realize you both have work schedules and some adjustments may be necessary. I'll require an adjusted agreement within a week or I'll file my suggestion. Do you both understand?"

He looks between us both and we nod in understanding.

I flex my fingers, feeling the edge of panic creep into my stomach.

"I would like a copy of the counseling schedule to include in the file if possible."

"Of course." Damon smiles.

"Any questions or objections at this time?"

"No, sir," is the united response.

"Okay. Well, unless there is a change, this is our last meeting. Best of luck to you both." He stands from the chair and leaves as quickly as he arrived.

Damon and his lawyers stand, shaking hands and speaking quietly.

Alfonso places a hand on my back and leans into the side of my face.

"Are you sure about this?"

"Yes," I whisper.

"Let's get out of here."

He stands, lightly grasping my arm and pulling me to stand. With a heavy sigh, I hold up my head and walk to the exit.

"Olivia," Damon calls, stopping me.

Tears sting my eyes and nerves flutter within my belly. Inhaling, I turn.

"I planned on telling you about my move the other evening. Things just didn't go exactly the way I'd thought."

"It's fine. Welcome to Pittsburgh." I force a smile. "Not sure how you can work in New York and live here, but that's your obstacle, not mine."

The words felt like acid on my tongue. I didn't mean to sound so mean.

"I'm sorry, I don't mean to—"

"It's fine," he replies, his voice terse. "B.I.G. is currently opening an office downtown, so I'll be overseeing the endeavor. It's also where I will base myself."

"What about New York?" I blurt.

He grins.

"Your concern is pleasing, but don't worry. Hugh will handle the New York office. I'm also not on the other side of the world, just a state away."

"Oh."

"We will need to discuss the custody arrangement. I don't think the arbitrator's suggestion is a good fit for either of us. Besides, I'd like to move slowly with Alex and allow him time to get familiar."

"I agree." A small flicker of relief calms the tingling. Knowing he's thinking about Alex and not his own desires quells the rampant fluttering, too.

"Can we grab a quick coffee...?" His eyes drop to my stomach before returning to my face. A small twitch at the corner of his mouth gives away him wanting to grin. "Decaf for you, of course."

"Right now?" An unwanted feeling of excitement zings through me.

"Yes."

"I really should get back to the bakery, and Alfonso is my ride, so—"

"Let me to drive you back. It will allow us time to talk in the car."

Between the late morning Pittsburgh traffic and road construction, allowing Damon to take me home could put me in a car with him for almost an hour.

"I—"

"Ready, Olivia?" Alfonso steps partially in front of Damon.

"Thank you, but I'll be driving her home." Damon moves aside and reaches for my hand.

"We have things to discuss in the car," Alfonso objects, his eyes following Damon's reach.

The warmth of Damon's hand engulfs mine, causing heat to rush over my skin.

"As do we." He keeps his eyes on mine, pulling me closer to his side.

"Now, listen—"

"It's okay, Alfonso. We need to discuss some dates and times." My voice sounds robotic. My eyes captivated by Damon's.

"Olivia?" Alfonso's question is laced with worry.

Finally pulling out of the trance Damon has on me, I turn to Alfonso.

"It's fine. Really," I reassure. "We need to talk about visitation and counseling. I'll give you a call later today to go over things."

Alfonso frowns, but concedes. With a curt nod to Damon, he strides toward the elevator.

"Thank you," Damon says, turning me to face him.

I shrug.

The finger of his free hand traces my jaw. I know I should pull back, but the thrill his touch stirs keeps me still. With a light squeeze around the hand he still held, he steps back, slowly pulling me with him.

"Shall we?" He motions to the elevator doors now opening.

Like a child in the old tale, I follow my pied piper.

Damon

Sliding into the limo after Olivia, her sweet and buttery vanilla scent surrounds me. I'm not sure if it's from working in a kitchen or if she is just naturally tempting. Closing my eyes, I take a moment to saturate my sense of smell to the point where I can almost taste her.

"How would you like to arrange visitation with Alex?" Her question pulls me from my sensory foreplay.

Before responding, I quickly provide the driver with instructions to take us out of the city and in the direction of Robinson Township to the bakery.

"I need to return to New York this evening, but I would like to start by seeing him when we arrive, if that's okay with you?"

"Sure." She nods her head, her eyes avoiding mine.

"Going forward, I'll need a bit of flexibility during my transition between there and here."

"That's fine, provided you give me some notice and not just show up unexpectedly."

She finally looks toward me, but I can tell she's keeping her eyes on my shoulder.

"I can agree to that."

Reaching out, I take her hand. Her gaze drops toward my touch and she noticeably tenses.

"Olivia."

Her eyes finally meet mine.

"Please relax. I don't want to stress or upset you. It's never been my intention to cause duress."

She purses her lips.

"I realize I've only caused duress," I quickly add. "And I am terribly sorry."

Something flashes in her eyes. I'm not sure if it's surprise or anger.

"I don't know how to convey just how sorry I am for what I've put you through. My acts have been selfish and, admittedly, they still are, but I vow to be gentler and subdued where you and Alex are concerned."

For a split second, her eyes narrow before she blinks.

"What about the counseling?"

Olivia slips her hand out of mine. I clench my fingers, trying to trap the warmth left behind.

"I've had some research done and contacted a Doctor Levingston. She is located in the city. She is well educated and recommended. I'd like to visit her and see how you feel about her."

"Damon, what do you plan to get out of these sessions?" A small tremor plagues her voice.

"We are having a child. I believe that alone is reason enough to try to make this work."

Her eyes boldly narrow on mine.

"You've wanted that before the baby," she argues.

"True. You and Alex are enough for me. Perhaps this baby will make our family worth it to you."

All expression erases from her face and I can't tell what she's thinking or feeling.

"Did you do this on purpose?"

"What?" I furrow my brow.

Her face drops and she watches her hands in her lap.

"The pregnancy. Did you get me—?"

"Of course not." Exasperation stretches my words.

Her body relaxes.

"I won't say I'm not pleased about it."

Her eyes jump up to meet mine.

"You can't ask me to be unhappy about our child. I'm just as thrilled about this one," the warmth from her body penetrates my hand as I rest it on her stomach, "as I am about Alex."

I smile. A small twitch at the side of her mouth gives away the smile she tries to hide.

"I'll be in New York for five days, at the least. What are some good days and times for me to coordinate our initial session?"

My fingers flex over her stomach and she tenses. Her hand covers mine. My heart thrums and excitement surges through my limbs until she pulls my hand away. Breathing out a puff of disappointment, I sit back in the leather seat.

"Tuesdays are usually best in the late afternoon or early evening. We'll need to talk about ongoing dates and times and I'll need to coordinate my schedule at the bakery."

She stares out the window, watching the scenery. It's going by too quickly. Soon, we'll arrive at the bakery.

"Thank you," she says in a broken whisper.

Looking back at her, she looks resigned and I hate it. I don't want her resigned. I want her to see the possibilities.

My silence pushes her to explain.

"For your apology."

"You deserve more than words." Taking her hand once more, I kiss her knuckles.

Too soon, we arrive at the bakery. Olivia is out of the car before the driver has a chance to shut his door. She's running away from me and it hurts.

Inside her apartment, Mercedes sits on the floor, playing with Alex.

"Dad," he squeals.

The smile spreading across his face and the way his eyes light up warms my chest. In my peripheral vision, I see Olivia watching his reaction as well. Alex stands and rushes toward me just as Olivia disappears down the hallway. Mercedes follows shortly after.

To my disappointment, Olivia doesn't appear again. Instead, Mercedes comes back and stays at the edge of the room, watching. I'm annoyed to have a babysitter, but she's there for Alex when it's time for me to leave.

I stand to leave and Alex cries his protest, breaking my heart into a thousand pieces. Mercedes comes to my rescue by distracting him with toys and television.

"Tell Olivia I'll be in touch soon."

"Okay." She bobs her rainbow-colored head.

"Thank you."

I exit the apartment and close the door behind me, thinking about how Olivia now hides from me. The running and hiding weighs on my mind as I descend to the waiting car. A lot of it is my own fault. The realization of what I've caused hangs over my head like a guillotine of guilt. Would I change anything? Of course. But I would never change making them a part of my life. Bringing them into my world is the only thing saving the soul that died years ago.

The driver maneuvers in traffic to get me to the airport in time for my flight back to New York, but I have plenty of time to make some necessary calls.

The first call is to my assistant. I need some local numbers for florists and such. Next, I call Hugh to check on the progress with all of the changes for B.I.G. We still need the final documents to remove my mother from any position of power, as well as final documents for the new Pittsburgh location. The last call I make is in regards to the mix up at the fertility clinic. I've had my legal team working their angle, but now I need to involve alternative methods. While my legal team uncovered many infractions and citations hidden really well within the division of the clinic where the switch occurred, there are rumors regarding the clinical director who suddenly left the establishment. These rumors are where my alternative methods will come into play.

"What can I do for you, Mr. Knyght?"

"Mitch, I have another job for you to handle." I settle back on the leather seat. "I'm going to need you to track down Dr. Phillipson. Seems he was the man in charge during the errors made at the fertility clinic and his sudden disappearance is rumored to have been accompanied with some monetary luck."

"You think it was a payoff to make the mix up?"

"I don't know, but I want to find out. Not just for my own situation, but for any others involved."

Chapter fifteen — Inner battle
Olivia

It's been three days since our conversation in the car, since I hid in the bakery until he left, and since the gifts started to arrive. Day one was imported extracts like Mexican Vanilla, Natural Apricot and Strawberry, aged Bourbon Vanilla, and others too expensive to buy in bulk in my line of work. Day two was a pregnancy themed basket — pregnancy books, baby name books, and a maternity clothing store gift card. Today, I stand at the island between my kitchen and living room, looking at a wooden box filled with foot scrub, lotions, creams, scented oils, and candles.

"Oh-mah-gawd," Mercedes drawls. "This smells fantastic."

She holds a small tube to her nose, eyes closed.

"It's supposed to be really good for stretch marks."

She pulls the tube away from her face and turns toward me.

"Lift your shirt so I can rub it on your belly."

She squeezes a small amount of oil into her palm.

"Put it back," I groan.

"Why?" She cocks the brow over her left eye.

"You know why," I scold. "I'm not accepting these gifts. As soon as I figure out how to return them, they are going back."

"You're so stubborn." She rubs her hands together and up her arms. The scent of warm, spicy, citrus fills the room. "He's obviously trying to be kind and make amends, but you just want to throw it back in his face."

Rolling my eyes, I push the gift away from the edge of the counter. Pressing my palms to the surface, I close my eyes and take a breath.

"Honestly, Liv, why can't you just be civil?"

"He doesn't want civil." I look up, facing her. "He wants married with children. You know if I give an inch, he'll push for miles."

273

Surprised by her sudden support of Damon, annoyance twinges my stomach.

She shrugs.

"I just think it would be nice to have someone pamper and help you with everything rather than shoo it away like it's infested with bugs."

Sighing, I turn and walk down the hall to return to the bakery.

"I have a cake to finish," I mumble.

Ced follows closely behind. "Are we still going to IHOP for dinner?"

My stomach grumbles at the thought of the yummiest pancakes ever.

"Of course."

With the start of one of the best mornings I've had in weeks, I decide to cook Alex some eggs. The knock at the door startles me and gets Alex into talking mode.

"Door," he calls before an even louder, "door, Momma!"

"I've got it, little man."

Wiping my hands on a dishtowel, I hurry to open the door so I can get back to the eggs. I freeze at the sight of an oversized bouquet of exotic flowers filling the doorway.

"You've got to be kidding me," I groan. "Can you please return them to sender?"

I'm practically whining and for a minute, I feel embarrassed.

"I'm afraid I will be extremely disappointed if I have to take them back." Damon's voice sends an unwanted thrill through me.

He steps forward, causing me to retreat and allow him entrance.

Annoyed he is taking the liberty to just enter my apartment, I bite out, "You promised you wouldn't just show up anymore."

Damon places the flowers on my living room coffee table and turns to me with a lopsided grin on his face.

"Now, it wouldn't be a surprise if I called ahead of time, would it?" His eyes move over me, lingering on my stomach.

"I thought you would be gone all week."

"Did you miss me?" His brow raises.

I narrow my eyes at him.

"I'm in town for the new location. I wanted to stop in and see the two of you. I also wanted to let you know that the appointment has been scheduled with the therapist."

Before I can respond, he turns to Alex.

"Hey, buddy," he coos, stepping toward Alex's chair.

"Dad." Alex smiles brightly.

"Is something burning?" Damon looks over his shoulder, his brows furrowed.

"Crap!" I exclaim, hurrying to scrape the ruined eggs out of the pan.

"I could take you out for breakfast," Damon offers.

"No thanks," I respond quickly. "I have things to take care of in the bakery."

"Are you sure I can't persuade you with IHOP?"

The pan slips from my hands, clanging in the metal sink. I turn to him.

"Are you following me around?"

He grins.

"No, I just like to know about the people in my life."

"So, you had someone else follow me?" I cross my arms over my chest.

"More like watch over."

No longer looking at me, he unstraps Alex and lifts him into his strong arms.

"What do you say?" he presses once more. "Allow me to take you to breakfast."

"I'm fine, but if you would like to take Alex…" I hesitate. Not because it's hard to say, but because it isn't as hard as I thought it would be. "You could take him for breakfast."

"Really?" Damon's voice is a mixture of excitement and shock.

I nod.

"Let me get him dressed."

Stepping toward them, I reach out for Alex, who slips into my arms.

Once he is cleaned, dressed, and packed for the trip, I return Alex to Damon. I've never seen this look on Damon's face before. His eyes are bright with excitement and his face slightly flushed.

"Thank you, Olivia." Damon smiles wide, taking Alex from me.

"Please bring him back," I choke back a sob.

Damon looks down at me, first with confusion in his eyes before the guilt flashes. His large hand cups my face.

"I would never do that to you. Never, Olivia. I swear it to you."

The intensity in his eyes convinces and gives me the strength to let them leave. Wiping a few tears from my eyes, I descend to the bakery.

After two hours of last minute touches and a large cake order, I'm exhausted but pressing on. Damon enters the bakery, getting everyone's attention. Alex is curled against his chest, sleeping. After brushing the flour and sugar from my food-color-stained hands, I reach for my son.

"If you don't mind, I'd like to take him up." Damon stops just a few steps from me, studying my reaction.

"Sure, thank you." I smile small.

Damon steps around me, his eyes penetrating mine with a deep, unspoken communication. My body flares to life, tingling and warming intimate places. I watch the broad width of his back until he disappears up the stairs. With a deep, shuddering breath, I return to work.

For the rest of the afternoon, I don't see or hear from Damon or Alex. It becomes so much of a distraction that I leave Angela to finish my cakes and go upstairs.

In the apartment, silence greets. Worried that something is wrong, I take quick steps down the hallway, stopping in Alex's room. It's empty. Worry turns to panic. Quickening my steps, I enter the living room and stop abruptly.

On the couch, Damon lays with his head on one arm and ankles on the other. Alex is sprawled out on his chest, both of them fast asleep; their breathing synchronized and faces so similar in the state of slumber. Unwanted emotions swirl through me again. I try to feel annoyed, but can't. Making dinner suddenly sounds like the best idea in the world.

Damon's schedule with the new location and business engagements keeps him busy. Part of me is happy that he's not around causing unnecessary feelings of warm fuzzies in my chest and hot throbbing between my thighs. The other part, the hormonal part, desires his dominating presence. It takes a lot of distraction to keep my thoughts from drifting to him and what he's doing.

"Are you listening to me?" Mercedes taps the kitchen island, drawing my attention back to my notebook and sketches.

"Sorry?" I look up from under my lashes.

She grins.

"I said I like the idea of the pineapple shaped and flavored cake. Alex loves pineapple cake."

A knock on the door interrupts the discussion regarding Alex's birthday cake and party planning.

"I'll get it." Mercedes slips off the stool next to me. "I think you need to scale back a bit. He's only going to be two and this is a kid's party. You know, we make fun of people who want to do lavish..."

At the dying of her words, I turn.

"Ced, what...?"

Damon stands just inside my door, his hair in disarray and his normal cool and calm demeanor replaced with something dark and filled with sorrow.

"Damon?"

His eyes meet mine. The pain and anger within them takes my breath.

"What's wrong? Are you alright?"

Slipping from the stool, I take hesitant steps until only a couple of feet separates us.

"My," he chokes.

Reaching out, I place one hand on his face. He nuzzles into my palm just before his arms wrap around my waist, pulling me against his chest. Burying his face in my hair, I hear him inhale. The tension leaves his body.

"Why don't you sit down?" I mumble against his chest, my hands resting at his hips.

Sniffing, he walks us over to the couch. I try not to trip over his feet, but fail. His arm, secure and strong, keeps me upright. When he suddenly stops, I know we've reached the couch.

"Sit down."

I gently place my hands on his shoulders and press.

The length of his body slides down mine. Once he's seated, he rests his head against my stomach, both hands on each side of the small bump.

"She's gone," he croaks.

"Who?" I move one hand to his head.

"My mother."

The response escapes him on a rush of breath. The heat of the words saturates my skin through my clothes.

"Your mother is gone?"

I pull back just enough to get him to look up. He does.

"Virginia found her this morning in the sunroom. She had a heart attack. No one was there."

His mouth twists unpleasantly as anger flashes in his eyes once more.

"Damon, it's not your fault." Cradling his face in both of my hands, I keep my eyes locked onto his. "It's a terrible—"

"Terrible?" he blanches. "How is the death of the woman you hate terrible?!" His voice rises.

My muscles tense and I snap my mouth shut.

"What's terrible is me, Olivia. I'm the terrible one."

A sob rips from his chest. He drops his head, resting it on my stomach again.

Taking his head into my hands, I step back. His head pops up, fear and confusion lining his face. Releasing his head, I take his hand and lead him to the spare bedroom.

I lead him to the bed and encourage him to sit. His blank expression and sorrow-filled eyes break my heart. I kneel and remove both shoes before standing and slipping his coat from his shoulders.

"Get some rest. I'll be in the kitchen—"

His hands grip my hips, firm and warm.

"My father told me she was dead and I only felt relief."

The rawness of his voice brings tears to my eyes.

"What kind of person feels better about the death of someone?"

His hands tighten, fingers flexing into the flesh of my hips. He raises his head, eyes wide, giving me access directly into his soul. The anger, guilt, shame, and sorrow completely bared to me.

"What kind of son doesn't feel sad at the loss of their mother? A monster. Me, the monster she's made me."

One tear escapes his eye, trailing over his defined cheekbone. That tear is the only one he allows, but it's enough. Wrapping my arms around his shoulders, I pull him to me. I press my hand to the side of his head, holding his cheek against my chest. His arms snake around and embrace me. He allows me to take some of the burden.

"You're not a monster," I whisper, dipping down and pressing my lips to the top of his head.

"I need you."

His arms constrict and pull me down to lie next to him. Burying his face in my neck, he curls his body around mine. His breath on my neck brings every hormone in my body to life, resulting in tingles, throbbing, and aching. The need for his touch almost puts me over the edge of sanity. When the rise and fall of his chest slows and evens, I know he's finally fallen asleep. I slide out from his hold and walk back to the kitchen where Mercedes sits, feeding Alex.

"Sorry," I apologize as she turns at my entrance.

"No worries. Everything okay?" Concern washes over her face.

I shrug. "Not sure."

She sighs.

"Do you need to get going? I know you were planning to take off about fifteen minutes ago."

"No. I'll finish feeing my little man." She ruffles Alex's hair and he giggles.

We finish our discussion about the birthday party before Mercedes leaves. After we say goodnight, I take Alex for a bath. He plays in the tub for about twenty minutes before we play a couple rounds of block tower build and destroy, and read two bedtime stories.

Entering the kitchen to clean up my papers, I find Damon sitting on one of the stools.

"Is this for his birthday?" he asks, his voice still flat and monotone.

"Yes."

I step closer to collect the notebook and sketches.

"Were you going to tell me about the party?" His eyes narrow on my face.

"Of course. I was just planning the idea for the party," I defend.

"But you didn't think I may want to help plan my son's birthday?" The furrow of his brow deepens.

"Damon," I take a deep breath, "you show up here upset and I try to comfort you. Now you're going to start an argument with me about planning my son's birthday? Unbelievable."

Taking the cake sketch from his hand, I fold it into the notebook. I pick the notebook up and hold it behind the arms I cross over my chest.

"Our son, Olivia. He is *our* son." He turns on the stool to face me. "I want to be a part of things. You know I do."

He releases a long, audible breath.

"I apologize for being harsh. Just please include me in these things."

"Fine," I quip, prepared to walk away from any further confrontation.

"When is your next doctor appointment?"

I freeze in place with my back to him.

"Are you serious?" I growl.

"What?"

I spin in place, coming face to chest with him. I stumble back, unaware he had been so close. His hands lock onto my arms. Pulling from his grip, I step back.

"You just lost your mother, grill me about Alex's party, and now you choose to start this conversation? Why are you trying to fight?"

"I'm not trying to fight. I need to leave for a couple weeks to take care of my mother's estate. I'm hoping I won't miss any more appointments." His face softens and eyes plead for understanding.

"It's not for two more weeks, but you'll miss the first session with the therapist." I rub my forehead, exhaustion settling behind my eyes.

"Christ," he grumbles. "I completely forgot. Do you think we can reschedule based on the circumstances?"

"I don't see why not." I shrug.

Damon stays for another hour and we talk about Alex's birthday party, days we can reschedule the therapy session, and the upcoming doctor appointment. He finally leaves with a promise to call with the details of his schedule.

Two days later, Damon calls with a request to visit Alex before going back to New York. I agree and when he arrives, it's not just to visit, but to drop his next bomb on me.

"The doctor feels like this is a good opportunity to meet with you individually." Damon shrugs.

"So, now I'm going to this alone? I'm going to a relationship counselor alone?"

"She says its common practice to have individual visits and help resolve individual concerns along with couple concerns."

"Fine," I bite out before going back to work on a cake.

The waiting room is modern and minimal with blonde hardwood floors, white walls, and gray trim. The furniture is a dark red and square shaped. It's very IKEA.

"You must be Olivia." A tall, dark skinned woman steps toward me, her heels tapping against the floor.

"Yes," I croak, my voice thick from not being used.

Standing, I reach out to the tall, sleek, and intimidating woman in her gray suit.

"Dr. Levingston?"

"In the flesh." She smiles and motions in the direction in which she arrived. "Please, follow me."

I follow, walking down a small corridor lined with enlarged photographs of the Pittsburgh city line.

"Please, have a seat." She waves to the tan loveseat opposite her glass desk.

I sit down and feel her eyes on me, examining.

"Are you feeling nervous?" Set settles into the black chair behind her desk.

"A little." I nod. "I've never been to a shrink before."

"Relax. We are just going to get to know one another today." She smiles warmly. "Would you like something to drink?"

"Water, please."

She stands, walks to a small black refrigerator, and removes a bottle of water. I take a few deep, cleansing breaths and try to relax. When she holds out the bottle, I quickly take it, twist the cap off, and drink greedily.

"So, let's start with why you are here." She sits back down.

"Because Damon refuses to just let go." I snort.

"Yes, I'm aware of your agreement with Mr. Knyght."

The shock of her knowing about our agreement must be clear on my face.

"I've already talked with Mr. Knyght. He's very open about the situation. I was actually quite surprised by it. Now, tell me your point of view." Her eyes roam my face, examining my reaction.

"W-what do you mean?"

She grins.

"Let's start with how you ended up married to Mr. Knyght."

"A great deal of alcohol and manipulation on his part," I huff.

"So, it's his fault you're in this situation?" One well-sculpted brow rises.

"I didn't say that, but he did orchestrate as much as he could," I defend.

"Miss Harlow, you aren't being accused of anything or judged. I want you to feel relaxed enough to answer with how you honestly feel. I may question you, but it's only for me to get a little deeper and gain perspective on your feelings. If I've made you feel defensive or wrong, I apologize."

I inhale deeply and hold the breath for a moment.

"Are you prepared to continue?" She smiles.

Exhaling, my muscles relax. I nod, my eyes focusing on my hands in my lap.

"Good. Please tell me about Vegas and please be as detailed and honest as you can."

The click of her pen draws my attention before I launch into my tale.

Once I finish, she asks about other situations. Occurrences like Damon showing up for the first time, the trip to New York, the dates, the night we conceived the child growing inside me, nothing is off limits. Surprisingly, my answers begin to come easier and easier. The rhythm of talking and unburdening myself is unexpected.

"Who is Isaac?" She looks up from the notes she's been taking.

The shock of his name catches me off guard.

"Wh-what?" I stammer, twisting my hands in my lap.

"You mentioned an Isaac a couple of times while talking. Who is he?"

She doesn't press or ask again. She waits patiently, allowing me a moment to process her request. I supply my standard response.

"He was a close friend."

Grabbing the water bottle, I drink a large gulp.

"How close?" This time, she presses.

Tears form, threatening to spill over my cheeks.

"It's okay if you prefer not to discuss him. I can see it's a very emotional topic. We could—"

"I loved him so much." Sadness thickens my throat, distorting my voice. "We were in a motorcycle accident. He was killed."

A tear finally escape as my body shudders from the million that want free.

Dr. Livingston pushes a box of tissues toward me. I take two and pat my damp face.

"So, you lost someone you loved very early in your life? That's a hard thing to overcome. Did you seek help at that time to cope?"

I shake my head.

"Not until after I lost the baby," I sniffle.

"You lost a child?" Her voice is gentle and soothing.

Unable to talk for fear of bursting into sobs, I close my eyes and nod.

"How did you cope with that loss?"

Swallowing down the tears and sadness, I open my eyes and look at her.

"It was like losing him twice." The tears now pour down my face. I grab more tissues and try to catch them all. It's impossible to contain them. "I'm losing him again," I sob.

Dr. Livingston's arms wrap around me in a cocoon of warmth and safety.

"Shh, it's okay. It's all in the past. You've built a nice and safe place to live."

"Safe?" I snort, wiping my eyes. "Look where I'm at now."

She pulls back and offers me a small smile.

"What?" I ask, curious about her smile.

"Did you hear what you said a moment ago?"

"That I lost him twice," I hiccup.

"You also said you are losing him again."

My eyes widen.

"Why do you feel like you're losing him again? What is causing you to feel this way?"

"I...I don't know."

Her hand rubs my forearm right before she stands up.

"Our time is up today," she concludes our discussion.

"But, I don't understand—"

"Only you can figure out why you feel like you're losing Isaac again. I cannot provide you the answers to how or why you feel."

Leaving her office, I feel cheated. I spill my guts to this woman and breakdown in her office, but she's helped with nothing. I want to call this whole thing off.

Days pass after the therapy session. Damon stays in touch by phone or text every day and evening. Before I realize it, it's been almost a week. I'm standing in the bakery kitchen working on constructing the pineapple cake for Alex's SpongeBob birthday party. After sliding the cake into the cooling case, I step into Mercedes' office.

"So, what's going on this week?" I sit in the familiar seat across from her.

"Well, you have your first consultation with Mrs. Manson tomorrow, late morning. Then you—"

"Who's Mrs. Manson?"

"The mother planning a wedding for her daughter who lives in New York." Mercedes looks up from her schedule book.

"That name sounds so familiar. Did we do something for them before?"

"No. This is a first time deal and they are a very wealthy family. Maybe you just remember when I first mentioned the appointment a couple weeks ago."

Mercedes shrugs and continues going over the schedule. Three consultations and a meeting with Felicity to go over the last of the hockey player's wedding are coming up.

Leaving Mercedes' office, I get to work on the wedding cake and have Angela work on the groom's hockey-inspired cake.

I lounge awake in bed, exhausted from the day in the bakery and Alex being as energetic as ever, but unable to sleep. I browse through the latest Bridal and wedding magazines. I'm halfway through the first when I realize I haven't even been paying attention.

Closing the magazine, I toss it on top of the pile next to me and rest my head against the headboard. My mind wanders back to my session with Dr. Livingston.

How can I lose Isaac again? He's gone, been gone. Why did I say that?

My cell phone vibrates on the nightstand before the ringtone begins. Without looking, I reach over and answer.

"Hello?"

My free hand grabs the previously discarded magazine and I start leafing through it again.

"Olivia." Damon's voice is soft and sad, but it stirs fluttering in my stomach.

"Damon?"

I sit up straight, ignoring the magazine as it slides from my lap to the floor next to the bed.

"Yes," he sighs.

"Are you okay?"

"No," he answers quickly.

"What's wrong?"

Silence lingers.

"Damon?" Worry turns the fluttering to knots.

"Olivia, please let me in."

"What are you—?"

There's a knocking sound from his end of the phone.

"Can I please come in?"

"You're here?"

As I ask, I slip from the bed and pad quietly down the hall. I pull the door open and take in Damon standing with his head leaning against the doorframe.

"What's wrong?"

The sorrow in his eyes tugs at me.

"Please?" He closes his eyes, clenches his fists, and breathes deeply.

Stepping back, I motion for him to enter.

His arms wrap around me the second he crosses the threshold.

"Thank you," he mumbles into my hair, tightening his embrace.

I lose the battle to remain neutral; instead, I encircle him in my arms. Running my hands over his back, my hope is to comfort, but it also makes me feel so many things I shouldn't feel for a man who's done creepy and manipulative things. He's stalked me, scared me, and made me feel.

"Let's get you settled into the spare room," I whisper and pull away.

Taking his hand, I lead him to the extra room and leave him to settle in for the night. Refusing to look back, I wipe rogue tears from my face.

Back in my room, I go to the bathroom to splash my face with water. After cleaning up the magazines, I curl into bed on my side. With absolute certainty, I know what's going to happen. So, when he taps on my bedroom door, I'm not surprised.

Chapter sixteen — Likes and dislikes
Olivia

The door opens and I pretend to be asleep. I fight to keep my breathing even and my eyes shut. Peeking out, I watch the shadow of him crawl until he lays low on the bed. With the top of his head almost reaching my breasts, he presses his face against my stomach. One hand grasps my hip and he whispers something I can't make out. His fingers flex into my cotton-covered flesh as his mouth presses against the small baby bump.

The nuzzling and caressing sends a jolt to my heart and causes my pulse to race. The anticipation of wanting more flushes my skin. I'm glad the room is too dark for him to see it.

Why does his touch cause so many emotions, so much feeling?

"Damon," I rasp.

I need him to give me space to gain composure.

"I'm sorry," he whispers. "I didn't mean to wake you."

"What are you doing?" The question is harsh, but I don't mean it that way. I'm just so frustrated from his touch, his presence, and my reactions.

"I can't sleep."

He rolls to his back, allowing me a moment to collect myself, but he misinterprets my silence.

"Please don't send me away."

Covering his face with his hands, he sighs.

"I don't want to be like my mother, having pushed everyone away to the point where I die alone."

"You aren't alone," I whisper, sitting up against the headboard. "You have Hugh, Scarlett, Heidi, and your father. Heidi is your true mother."

"You're my family."

"They are your family," I stress.

Rolling back toward me, he presses one hand to my stomach.

"You are family to me, Olivia."

His eyes look up and meet mine with the same burning desire I fight inside. I'm tired, frustrated, and oh-so-very scared of this man.

"Stop." I shove his hand away and slip from the bed, keeping my back to him.

The slap against the mattress causes me to spin around.

"Damn it, Olivia, why do you do this? Why can't you just try?" he growls in a low whisper as he climbs off the bed.

"Try what, Damon? To accept that I married a stalker obsessed with recreating a family he lost?"

The moment it's out of my mouth, I feel horrible and want to take it back.

He snorts.

"Don't forget you also slept with this obsessed stalker twice."

He holds two fingers up, staring at me with fierce intensity. The determination in his eyes causes me to take a step back.

"Yeah, I did. But it was under the influence of alcohol and manipulation both times." I mean for it to sound more ferocious, but the guilt from my previous outburst tempers me.

"It didn't take too much manipulation and you know it." He smirks.

In three long strides, he's backed me against the wall.

"You felt the connection in New York. We were connecting before you left."

His arms trap me against the walls.

"You're delusional," I snap. "It was all just to keep my end of the deal. You know, the deal you broke after you lied to me?"

"Stop running from me."

His face is so close, just one tongue lick away. The close proximity strokes the slow burning desire within me. This attraction to him, these feelings, are perilous.

"Stop running from me."

The heat of his breath caresses my lips. I lick them and his gaze slips to my mouth. He leans closer, running his nose against mine. My head falls back and eyes shut. His lips ghost over my ear.

"I want you."

He pulls back, but leaves less than an inch between us.

Desire engulfs my body. Instinctively, my body gravitates to his. His heat saturates me. His scent fills the air. I can hear my heart beat in my ears. Pushing away from the wall, I weave my hands into his hair and claim his mouth.

I pull back to catch my breath. His mouth drops to my neck.

"I love you," he mumbles against my skin.

His words are like a bucket of ice water. I freeze, dropping my hands from his hair.

He brings his head up, cups my face, and looks into my eyes. "What's wrong?"

"No." I shake my head.

"No, what?" His brow furrows.

"No to this." I shove at his chest.

"Stop fighting this. Stop running." His thumb rubs my cheek.

I push his hands away.

"I don't love you. I can't love you," I cry.

Tears blur my vision, but I still see the devastation on his face. My stomach turns and I rush for the bathroom. Locking the door behind me, I try to calm myself. But the sobs won't subside and there's no stopping the vomit.

Kneeling on the floor, my stomach now empty, my body shudders.

Why did he say it? How could I feel the words he so easily spoke?

My lie broke him. I saw it on his face.

New sobs wrack my body.

When I finally exit the bathroom, Damon is gone. I don't have to check to know he left the apartment completely.

Two days pass without a word from Damon. On day three, when I convince myself I'm only calling to discuss Alex's birthday, I dial his cell number. I pretend not to be hurt when my call is sent to voicemail after two rings or dwell on the thought that he sent it to voicemail when he saw it was me calling.

After a week, I'm sick and tired of thinking about, longing to hear from, and feeling rejected by mother trucking Damon Knyght. I never asked to feel this way. All I want is for my life to be as it was before, but...could I ever really go back to before Damon?

Sitting in the therapist's office, my leg shakes from nervousness. Waiting for our first joint appointment has put me on edge. Today is the first time we will speak in a week.

The sound of the door opening intensifies the raw, nervous energy coursing through me. His presence is all-encompassing. The business suit, with its clean, crisp lines and perfect fit over his leanly muscled body, causes my lower belly to clench. I close my eyes and take a breath, trying to calm my increase of body temperature and pulse resulting from just looking at him.

Upon opening my eyes, the spot where he once stood is empty. He's chosen a seat as far away from me as possible. Our eyes lock for a brief moment and a flash of something I can't read appears. However, the lack of emotion on his face sends a chill across my skin and tension thickens the air between us.

Dr. Livingston's office door opens, cutting into the silence.

"Hello," she welcomes. "Please, come in."

Holding the door open, she motions for us to enter.

Both of us standing, Damon holds the door open before guiding me into the room by the small of my back. This one small gesture causes tingles to erupt throughout my body.

"So," Dr. Livingston drawls, sitting behind her desk. "Damon and I spoke previously about the current disagreement between the two of you. I think we should first expand on the current cause of tension. Olivia, can you please tell me about the current dispute?"

"I wouldn't say it's a disagreement, but a moment of honesty he didn't want to hear." I fold, unfold, and refold my hands nervously in my lap.

Damon snorts from his chair on my right.

"I see." Dr. Livingston smiles. "Damon," she turns her attention on him, "you told Olivia you love her, correct?"

"Yes." He nods.

"And?" she presses.

"And she made sure to correct my misunderstanding by telling me she could never feel anything for me, besides disdain." He growls the last two words.

"What do you expect, Damon?" My anger flares. "After everything you've done—"

"I know what I've done." His hard eyes narrow on me. "I've apologized repeatedly for how I behaved, but if you need to hear it again, fine. I'm. Sorry. But I'm not sorry for caring, wanting, and loving you. Is it truly so terrible?" He sounds angry, but his eyes reflect nothing but pain.

"Do you even realize what you've done? You forced yourself into my life. Uninvited." Tears sting the back of my eyes. "I was happy, content with my life."

What I don't say, or ask, is whether he realizes how he's made me feel.

"Happy?" He snorts. "You've been hiding behind a secure routine and single mother label. If I were Isaac, it would—"

"Don't," I snap. "You don't know a damn thing about him, so don't you dare speak about Ifs."

You don't know how you've caused me to betray his memory with my feelings for you. I don't say this out loud, but it wraps around my heart like a vice.

"Let's calm down," Dr. Livingston interrupts. "This is an open and honest place to talk and things can get passionate given the topics addressed, but I would like to make sure we are being fair and keeping the arguing as minimal as possible."

Damon's eyes level on mine and soften.

"It wasn't my intention to make you feel this way. I know the mess I've made, but I cannot apologize for wanting to know my son and his mother. I also cannot control how my feelings have developed."

"Olivia," Dr. Livingston addresses me once more. "Damon feels you started to develop a connection in New York. Do you agree?"

I open my mouth to disagree, but close it. Damon's plea flashes through my mind. *Please try, Olivia.*

"Olivia?" she presses.

"Yes, I agree. We got closer, but it's not love."

"A friendship?" She sits back, resting into her high-back leather chair.

I nod.

"And the physical relationship?"

"Too much alcohol," I blurt.

In my peripheral vision, I see Damon shake his head in silent disagreement.

"You don't believe the alcohol was the cause?" she asks him.

"Of course he doesn't," I groan.

"I'm not saying it didn't play a part, but I don't think blame can be placed on that excuse. I believe the alcohol dropped her inhibitions enough to step out of her safety zone." He turns to me, a determined look on his face. "Allowing a connection beyond friendship to develop."

The savage inner fire lighting deep within his eyes forces me to look away. The tears threaten to spill over. He's calling me out on the feelings I thought I've been hiding so well. *It's not love. I'm not in love.*

"Let's try an exercise," Dr. Livingston interjects, straightening in her chair.

She weaves her fingers together, resting her hands on the desk.

"Damon, I want you to explain, calmly, why you felt the need to be so persistent in your pursuit of Olivia. I'd like to understand the reason behind the misleading and forceful nature."

"I couldn't risk her rejection," he practically whispers. "I knew she would run the first chance she could or would get the authorities involved. The risk of losing them after having just found them..." he inhales a shaky breath, "it was too much for me. It wasn't a risk I could take."

"And did you think about how your chosen path would make Olivia feel?"

"Not at the time." He pauses. "Now, I realize how crazy it all seems, but I needed them, had to meet them. I need to know my son."

"And Olivia?"

His hesitancy in responding draws my eyes to him. When he speaks, it's with so much emotion, his soul seems bare.

"The more I know her, the more I need her. She believes my feelings are based on my past, but she's wrong. The way I feel about her surpasses any past emotion I've felt for any other woman in my life. I've never felt this strongly, regardless of how quickly it happened."

He doesn't look at me. Instead, he closes his eyes and takes a shuddering breath.

My chin wobbles. I clench my teeth. A shiver runs up my spine, but it isn't from fear or annoyance. It's from the pleasure of his words.

"Olivia?" Dr. Livingston's voice pulls my gaze from Damon.

"Yes," I breathe out and clear my throat.

"Do you think you've built a wall or safe haven around you and your life?"

"Maybe." I bite my lip.

"Do you think it has something to do with your prior loss?"

The chin wobbling begins again and I choke out, "I don't know," but even I don't believe my own words.

"It's okay." She gives a warm smile. "I'm going to ask you a straight forward question. Are you afraid to love?"

My eyes swim in unshed tears.

"Maybe," I whisper.

"Thank you for being honest."

She looks down at the legal pad on her desk as I wipe away a stray tear. I can feel Damon's eyes on me, studying me. Refusing to look at him, I focus on the back of a picture frame on Dr. Livingston's desk. I distract myself by wondering if it's a picture of a husband, children, or perhaps a wife.

"Why did you allow Damon around once you returned from Vegas?"

Surprise widens my eyes. I thought she'd been done with me.

"I, uh," I stammer. "He was very determined and there were a few threats."

"How did the threats make you feel?"

"Scared. Worried."

"Why not go to authorities?"

"I thought I could handle it."

"So, you risked the threats?" Her eyes focus in on me and I shift on the small couch.

"It was a lot to take in, to process. I just acted on instinct and what my gut was telling me."

"And your instinct told you his threats were something he wouldn't act on?" She raises her brows.

My chest tightens and a knot forms in my stomach.

"No, not exactly. I definitely thought he would get lawyers involved."

"So, it was just the legal situation you worried about?" She presses further.

"I didn't want my son taken from me. I thought I could handle things on my own or through my lawyer," I defend.

"And New York?"

"It was a means to resolve the situation between us and then move on with my life." My temper flares.

"I apologize if I'm upsetting you." Dr. Livingston's eyes soften. "I promise, there is no judging. I am working to open up dialogue by discussing the past situation before we open communication regarding your current relationship."

Taking a deep breath and exhaling, I nod.

"Damon, why so many threats?"

With her redirection of questions, tension melts from my body.

"I would never hurt either of them," he quips.

"I understand. But, please, explain."

"Every step she took away from me, running from me..." he pauses, running his hands over his face, "I still had a few things to work on in regards to dealing with my past. It caused inexcusable reactions and I regret the words I said in anger."

"Are you still seeing someone to help with the loss of you wife and son?"

He nods.

"Good." She smiles.

Sitting back, she brings up her hands, forming a triangle with her fingers just below her chin.

"We're almost out of time today, but I would like for both of you to do something for next week."

Dr. Livingston stands, walks across the room, and returns with a set of small notebooks and a pen.

"For the next five days, I want you to keep an appreciation list. Try to write down one or two things, each day, of something you like about your partner, er...um...each other, or something you appreciate about them."

She holds a notebook and pen out to Damon and me.

"We aren't together every day." I take her offering.

She nods. "This is why I also mentioned 'like'. Since you are not living in the same home, when you are not together, try to think of something you like about the other person."

We sit in silence.

"This isn't a test." She grins. "It's just an exercise in appreciation and positive feedback. And I think both of you could use that from each other right now. Okay?"

We both nod before saying goodbye to Dr. Livingston and leaving her office.

The cool air outside the building reminds me to start wearing a heavier coat. I tighten the thin sweater jacket around me and wait for the bus. Warmth surrounds me and Damon's scent fills my nostrils.

"You should wear something warmer," he states, settling his suit jacket on my shoulders.

"I'll be fine." I move to take off the jacket.

His hands press my shoulders, stopping me.

"Please." His eyes are as pleading as his voice.

I nod, biting my bottom lip. My emotions are still raw and oh-so-sensitive. His kindness tugs at my heart.

"Did you get my message?" I blurt and turn away from his beckoning eyes.

"Yes. I'll be there." He removes his hands and takes a step back.

My body sways, just slightly, wanting to stay close.

"Do you need anything?" he asks, putting an air of detachment between us.

I shake my head.

"Can I give you a ride home?" he asks, his tone still cool.

"No, thank you," I choke out the words.

Pretending to look down the street for the bus, I hide the wobbly shake of my chin and tears threatening to spill. *Damn hormones.*

He stays next to me until the bus arrives. I hand him his jacket before climbing onboard. Our fingers touch briefly and heat zings up my arm. Quickly releasing the expensive clothing, I thank him once more and find a seat.

Once we pull away from the curb, I break down. All the held back tears and chin wobbles combine into a crescendo of sobs. I garner sympathetic and questioning looks from other passengers, but I'm left alone to expel my emotional turmoil.

Damon keeps his distance for five days. When he does visit, it's on the morning of Alex's second birthday party. Damon takes him to see his new place while I prepare for the party.

He's cordial and polite. I hate it. It's irrational and stupid to miss his all-encompassing and intrusive presence, but I do.

At night, I lie awake too long, going back and forth between the ridiculous part of me who hopes every sound is Damon barging into the room and the rational side, which is on repeat, listing everything crazy he's done.

The knock at the door pulls me from my thoughts. I turn to see my father enter the apartment.

"Hey, baby." He steps in close and kisses my head.

"Hey, Dad."

"Where's my little buddy?" He glances around the room, searching.

It's then I notice how much more my father's hair has grayed and thinned. He's still a strong, handsome man, but the signs of aging make me think about how much time we really have in life.

"Is he sleeping?" He furrows his bushy brows.

"He's with Damon."

My father's face turns to stone. "Oh."

"He's showing Alex his new home and keeping him busy while I get everything transported for the party."

Moving to the table, I start grabbing bags and packages.

"Let me get those." My father grabs the items. "I'll take them to my car."

"Thanks." I smile in appreciation. "I'll go ask Seth to load the cake."

He nods in acknowledgement, hauling everything out the door.

At the bottom of the stairs to the bakery kitchen, a wave of dizziness has me grasping for the wall. I prevent myself from falling, but not before twisting my left ankle at a funny angle. A sharp pain shoots up my knee and I sit on a step.

"You okay?" Seth kneels down, inspecting my foot.

"Yeah." I nod. "Just twisted it a bit."

Seth helps me stand and I wince slightly when I put weight on my left foot.

"Why don't you put some ice on it while I load up the cake?" Seth keeps hold of my arm.

"I can't. I need to get things loaded up and taken over to the pizza place."

Stepping away from him, I put weight on my foot again. It's sore, but better.

"See, I'll be fine." I smile at him. "Can you take the cake out to my dad's car?"

"Of course." He moves quickly to pull the cake from the cooler and boxes it up.

With everything loaded, my father drives us over to the pizza shop, which also houses a kid's play area and arcade.

Mercedes' car is already there when we pull into the lot and park. Inside, I hear Mercedes issuing orders and requests of the staff.

"This table needs to be wiped off. Could we get these two wiped down and pushed together?"

Shaking my head, but smiling, I join her in the designated eating area.

"What?" she asks. "They should have had this taken care of before we arrived. I called them twice yesterday and provided them a layout for the tables. It should've been ready," she defends.

"I agree," I reply, still smiling, thankful she's dealing with staff.

My father sets the boxes and bags on an empty table. I start unpacking, decorating, and setting out his gifts.

Thirty minutes later, Damon arrives. Alex walks beside him, holding his hand. The sight of them makes my heart skip a beat. I've started noticing more and more similarities between them. With a deep breath, I channel these warm and fuzzy feelings on Alex.

"Happy birthday, baby," I coo, picking him up into my arms. "Wanna see your cake?"

"Bob cake?" he asks with a giggle.

"Yep. It's a SpongeBob house." I bounce him a bit on my hip.

"Should you lift and bounce him?" Damon asks, brows furrowed and eyes filled with concern.

My confusion must be evident in my expression. He motions toward my stomach.

"It's fine," I say, giving him a small smile.

"Hey, little buddy." My father appears on my right, leaning in to kiss Alex's cheek. "Happy birthday."

Alex wipes the kiss away and presses into my side.

"Cake." He pats my chest.

"Okay, let's go see it."

I walk Alex to the table where the cake is on display.

After looking at the cake and presents, I sit at a table with him in my lap. We're watching Mercedes tie yellow and blue balloons to weights in the center of each table when Alex pushes out of my lap.

"Dorn!" Alex calls.

Looking up in the direction he runs toward, I see Mrs. Dorn extending her arms to him. She's just arrived, but being like a grandmother to him, she picks him up before worrying about setting any of her things down.

"There's my handsome boy." She kisses his cheeks and he giggles.

I missed having him around this morning, but I'm thankful for this moment to use the restroom.

Upon exiting the ladies room, I freeze. My father, wearing his serious face, is in what looks like a deep discussion with Damon. Swallowing my nervousness, I walk toward them as quickly as my ankle will allow.

"Sir, I understand and respect your concern for Olivia and Alex, but keep in mind, he is also my son and she's currently carrying my child. I wouldn't do anything to—"

"You've already done enough, son," my father cuts Damon off. "Liv told me about your loss and I'm extremely sorry about that."

Damon's shoulders tense.

"But that doesn't give you the right to implant yourself in my daughter's life the way you did. She allows you around, but I'm watching you. If you do anything to hurt her, or stress her any further, I will personally make sure—"

It's my turn to interrupt.

"Okay, guys. It's a birthday party not a sparring match."

I step between them, Damon on my left, my father on my right.

"Perhaps you should've mentioned that to your father before—"

"Don't *you* tell me what I need to do," my father says, his voice rising and causing multiple people to look at us.

"Enough," I whisper harshly, turning to my father. "Dad, I appreciate your chivalry, but please, this is Alex's birthday."

"Fine," he huffs. "I'm going to see if *my* grandson wants to play in the ball pit."

"Great," Damon quips and narrows his eyes. "Tell him *daddy* will be there soon."

For a moment, they stare at one another in a silent showdown. My groan pulls their eyes to me before my father walks away.

Turning, I face Damon.

"Try to behave."

"Me?" He gives me an incredulous look. "Your father approached me, not the other way around."

"Damon," I sigh, "if it was your daughter, what would you do?"

The harsh lines on his face soften.

"I apologize for creating a scene."

"Let's just not have another one, at least for today, okay?" I force a smile.

He nods. I step away, wincing from my ankle.

"What happened to your ankle?" Damon asks, his hand grasping my arm.

"I just twisted it a little earlier today." I shrug.

Before I can continue to walk away, he lifts me into his arms and carries me to a chair.

Sitting me down, he kneels to the floor. Taking my ankle, he props it on his knee. I press my hands to the skirt of my dress to make sure I'm not flashing everyone.

"It's swollen." He gives me an intense look. "You should have ice on this."

"I'm fine." I try to pull my foot away.

His long fingers wrap around and firmly hold it in place. My ankles have never been an erogenous spot, but the feel of his bare hands against my skin makes me shiver. I can feel goose bumps over by body and my nipples suddenly feel sensitive against my bra.

"Olivia, you shouldn't be walking on this."

I roll my eyes.

"Damn it," he growls low. "Stay here."

Releasing my ankle, he gently sets my foot on the floor.

Without further explanation, he walks away.

It only takes a couple of minutes for him to return with a white cotton towel in hand. Pulling a chair over, I hear the crunch of ice as he sits in front of me. Taking my ankle into his lap, he presses the towel to it. The cold makes me flinch, but it's a welcome distraction from the way his fingers and presence heat my body. Mentally, I curse the fact that he's given me something else to add to the appreciation list.

Damon

Olivia moves around the tiled eating area smiling and talking to the guests. I can't take my eyes off her. Her slight limp concerns me, but she's adamant about being a good host and won't sit with the ice pack any longer. The smile she gives her family and close friends makes me feel like a voyeur.

I'm a bystander to her happiness and I don't know how to become the active participant I desire to be. Our therapy session last week further opened my eyes, allowing me to fully realize the reasons for the strong as iron wall she puts up. Where I've mourned my loss and want to live with love in my life again, she's still holding on to her ghosts. Far from angelic, I'm a man used to having what he desires at his fingertips. However, I know the hurt she carries. The invisible scars left by such pain will always be there. Now, I must be something I'm not used to being — a patient man. At least while she learns how to heal and live with the scars.

Erik arrives, interrupting my internal musings. The look of surprise and uncertainty makes me uneasy. Standing, I slowly, but deliberately, make my way toward them.

"Rik!" Alex calls from his grandfather's lap. A bright smile lights up his little face and my jealousy spikes.

"Hey there, little man." Erik picks Alex up into his arms, hugging him. "Happy birthday, my man!"

"I didn't expect you—"

"Like I'd miss his birthday." Erik doesn't look at Olivia. "He's like a son to me."

"But he's not your son," I interject, crossing my arms over my chest.

Erik turns cold eyes on me.

"Surprised to see you here." One side of his mouth curls in disgust.

"Why would I miss my son's birthday?" I tilt my head just slightly.

"Maybe because you aren't truly family," Erik snaps.

"Dad!" Alex calls, reaching for me.

"You sure about that?" I ask, taking my son from his arms.

"I've known him since he was a baby. You just appeared out of—"

"Had I known about my son, I would've been here. I suggest you leave *my family* for me to take care of and worry about."

"Erik—"

"No, Olivia. He just shows up tossing paternity around like it's an excuse for being an overbearing asshole." Taking his eyes from me, he grasps Olivia by her upper arms. "You don't have to put up with it, Liv. We can get a life without him back."

When he pulls her toward him, I reach one hand out, pushing him back.

"Back off," I growl low, not wanting to worry Alex.

"Both of you need to stop," Olivia scolds.

"Hey, buddy, come here." Erik reaches for Alex and I pull him away.

"I'm a part of their life. Get used to it," he snaps.

Extending one arm, I stop Erik two feet away from Olivia and Alex. When he swats my arm away, I move another step in front of Olivia. Keeping narrowed eyes on him, I hand Alex back to Olivia. She takes him, settling him to her hip.

"You're pregnant," Erik chokes.

"Perhaps you should go now," I suggest.

"You fucked him?" Erik snarls low.

"That's quite enough." Olivia's father steps in front of Erik. "Come on, son."

Putting an arm around Erik's shoulders, her father leads him away from the watching eyes of the crowd.

Turning, I cup Olivia's face.

"I'm sorry."

"You're sorry?" She blinks a couple times.

"My temper gets the better of me."

"I understand," she says on a sigh.

"I don't trust him."

Brushing my thumb over her cheek, I stare at her lips.

"It's fine. He just needs to calm down."

Sliding my gaze up from her mouth, our eyes lock. There is a flash of desire before she blinks it away.

"Dad." Alex grabs my sleeve, pulling.

"Yes." Removing my hand from Olivia's face, I bring Alex back into my arms.

"Ball time." He claps, smiling.

"Okay."

With a desire-conveying glance, Olivia's cheeks flush a bit. Turning away, I take my son to the ball pit.

Alex's birthday continues without any further confrontations or arguments. In fact, Erik disappeared from the party altogether. Something to which I can say definitely pleased me. I know desperation and I can see it all over him. It makes you do things you wouldn't normally do and can push a person to extremes. The wild look in Erik's eyes at seeing Olivia pregnant worries me.

I sit in Dr. Livingston's waiting area and go over the appreciation list. I'm going over it a second time when Olivia enters.

She looks beautiful in a light blue puffy coat and scarf. The color compliments her bright red hair and porcelain skin. Her cheeks and nose are rosy from the cold wind outside. Her eyes meet mine as she unbuttons the coat. This time, her face flushes from warmth. She turns, undoing the rest of the buttons and hanging the coat up on one of the wall hooks.

When she faces me once more, it's like my heart bursts into a million bubbles. She wears a light gray long-sleeved shirt. It's long enough to come over her hips and, while it's not second skin tight, it fits her well enough to see her protruding abdomen. The black scarf around her neck coordinates with the tight black cotton pants and knee-high boots. She is breathtaking.

"I thought I'd be late." She smiles, taking a seat across from me.

"Why?" I ask once I'm able to speak again.

"The bus was running behind." She shrugs, pulling her hair over her left shoulder.

She starts twisting the hair into a braid and secures it at the bottom with a black band she had around her wrist. Then, she fans herself.

"Warm?" I ask, a small smile on my lips.

"A little." She grins. "That coat may have been a bad idea." She nods toward the puffy coat.

Before I can continue the civil conversation, Dr. Livingston calls us into her office.

"Good afternoon." She stands behind her desk, her dark hair pulled into a tight bun.

We exchange pleasantries before getting straight down to business.

"You both should have a list for me today, correct?" She looks between us.

"Yes," I answer a bit too quickly.

"Yeah," Olivia responds, a bit more hesitant.

"Okay, who would like to go first?" The doctor settles back in her chair.

"Go first?" There is a hint of panic in Olivia's question. Her body tenses on the couch next to me.

"I will." My offer instantly relaxes Olivia.

"Please, when you're ready." Dr. Livingston smiles warmly.

Clearing my throat, I begin.

"I like how you take care of Alex. And—"

"Sorry," Dr. Livingston holds up a finger, "you have started off very well, but I'd like for you to start with 'I appreciate how' and then use the other's name and continue."

With a nod, I straighten my posture and start once more.

"I appreciate how much Olivia cares for Alex. He is a happy, healthy, and very smart boy. I appreciate Olivia's strong independence and work ethic. I can even appreciate her need stay so strong she no longer knows how to be vulnerable." I inhale deeply before blowing out long and drawn air. "I understand this so well."

There is a small shudder in my chest, but I continue, this time turning my head to Olivia.

"I like the way you smell of sweet buttery vanilla."

She shivers. It's a slight movement, but my greedy eyes catch the motion. With a small smile, I keep my focus on her.

"I most appreciate you trying, really trying."

She looks at me from the corner of her eye. I hold them for a moment, but she blinks, interrupting the moment. We turn our attention back to the doctor.

"Very good." She nods, making notes on the pad in front of her.

Her head comes up from her writing, her eyes focusing on Olivia.

"Olivia?"

"How can I compete with that?" she blurts.

"It's not a competition," Dr. Livingston assures.

"But..." she pauses, looking at me quickly before turning back to the doctor, "but I...I don't have five things."

"Relax." The doctor smiles. "Take a breath and just give us what you do have."

I watch Olivia close her eyes, swallow a deep breath, and then, with determination, she opens her mouth.

"I appreciate how good he...I mean, Damon, is with Alex. I realize now that Alex was missing something two parents can provide a child. I am very thankful he now has it. I appreciate that Damon is accepting and cares about this baby."

Her hand goes to the small bump that seems larger each time I see her.

"And I appreciate Damon's willingness to help with anything he can. I know he's genuine in the way he cares."

The room falls silent. Not an uncomfortable silence, but anxious.

"Can I ask why you think it was so difficult to come up with five?" Dr. Livingston folds her hands together on her desk.

"You said it's not a competition."

"It isn't. Nor is it a test. I am curious, though."

"It's not like he's given me many things to appreciate. I cannot appreciate his previous actions, for obvious reasons, no matter how much he's trying to apologize and change."

Heaviness settles in my chest. Closing my eyes, I breathe in deep through my nose.

"I understand." Dr. Livingston's sympathetic response causes me to reopen my eyes.

"Okay, I'd like to try another exercise. This one will be a bit more intense and intimate."

Olivia tenses.

"Please shift on the couch to face each other the best you can."

Olivia and I both sit, unmoving.

"I typically have couples sit on the floor, but I'm not going to ask Olivia to do so. Now, face each other."

The doctor stands from her seat, walking around to lean against the front of her desk.

"For the next five minutes, you will simply look at each other. No looking away or past the person. If this happens, we will start the five minutes over again."

"Are we children?" I narrow my eyes on her.

"Not at all, Damon." She folds her arms over her chest. "But I am the doctor and this exercise only works if both of you participate fully." She cocks her right brow.

With our backs to the arms of the small couch, Olivia and I look into each other's eyes.

"Now, really look at each other. Focus on the other's eyes, small imperfections, twitches, and so forth. Starting....now."

Olivia focuses on my nose and then mouth for the briefest of moments before returning to my eyes. Her brow furrows just a little, but then we fall into a comfortable shared gaze. My chest warms, limbs begin to tingle, and breathes come quicker. The effect she has on me is astounding. Before we both realize it, the five minutes is up.

"Now," the doctor speaks soft and quiet, "share your thoughts with one another while considering your own reactions and thoughts."

"You are so beautiful," I whisper, reaching and taking the hand resting on her knee.

"Thank you," she breathes out.

"I am amazed by the way you make me feel without saying anything."

"Why do you affect me this way?" she asks.

For a moment, I'm silent — stunned. It's a question, but also a confession.

"I don't know," I answer, honestly.

"How can I feel like this for you, after all that's happened?"

"How do you feel?"

My hand tightens on hers in anticipation.

She shakes her head violently, breaking our trance.

"I don't want to do this anymore."

Her hand slips from mine. She turns back to face the doctor.

"That's fine. It was a very good start. I'm impressed with you both."

I'm unable to look away from Olivia. In a short moment of questions, she's revealed so much.

"You've done well with each exercise for such a short time," the doctor continues and I hear the sounds of her desk chair as she returns to sit. "Next, I'd like try something. This usually comes later in my program, but I think this is a good time in regards to your situation."

"Which is?" Olivia prompts.

"A date."

The two words bring my attention back to the doctor.

"A date?" I ask.

"Yes, I would like for you two to spend a couple of hours out in a neutral area with one another. No family or child. This should be as if you were taking a woman on a first date." She levels a look on me.

I nod.

"Why a date?" Olivia asks, finally having worked through the shock.

"It's a good way for you two to associate as a man and woman. This is essential to any relationship." The doctor sits back in her chair.

"You are not just a mother, a baker, a business woman, or his wife. You are, at your base, a woman." She turns her attention back to me. "And you are not just a business man, a husband, a father, or your past. You both need to see each other as one man and one woman. This will be a good start."

"A start?" Olivia presses, not missing the innuendo.

"Yes." The doctor smiles, almost slyly. "After our next appointment, I will be asking you both to spend a weekend together. Just the two of you."

"But—" Olivia tries to interject.

"We will discuss it at a further date, but don't panic. I'm not demanding anything to happen. I'll be asking that you two share a weekend together alone. Sleeping arrangements and so forth are established between the two of you and your comfort levels."

Dr. Livingston looks at her watch.

"I'm afraid we've reached our time. Until next week?"

Both of us nod before leaving her office.

After gathering our coats in silence, we exit the office building.

"Olivia?"

She turns, looking hesitant.

"I'd like to visit Alex tomorrow."

She nods. "Of course."

"Can I please give you a ride?"

She shakes her head.

"No, thank you. I need to think."

She gives me a small smile before turning to walk to the bus stop.

From inside the waiting car, I sit, watching, refusing to pull away until I see she's gotten onto the bus.

Chapter seventeen – dating your husband
Olivia

The ride home from the therapist is a blur. My mind awash in the memory of his confessions, the way he looked at me, and the way it felt. My feelings bubbling to the surface, flowed from my mouth like lava. It practically burned to ask him the questions, to make my own revelations known.

Entering the apartment, Mercedes sits at the small dining table, flipping through one of my magazines. Alex is in his highchair, eating.

"Momma." He gives me a food littered smile.

"Hey, baby." I smile.

"How'd it go?" She doesn't look up.

"Okay." I don't mean for my words to sound so desolate.

Her head pops up, eyes narrowing.

"What's wrong?"

"It's nothing." I shake my head.

Shedding my coat, I hang it on the coatrack and walk into the kitchen. I'd love a stronger drink, but know that's not an option.

"Liv," she draws out my name.

"Really, Ced, it's nothing. The sessions are emotionally taxing."

I shrug, open the fridge, and retrieve a bottle of water. What I wouldn't give for a super dark, strong cup of coffee.

"That's sort of part of the deal, right?"

Mercedes now sits sideways in the wooden chair, her arm resting on the back. I nod.

"Do you need to talk? Or are you all talked out?" Concern fills her eyes.

"Can we talk later?" Not wanting to push away her offer, I just need a bit more me time with these thoughts and feelings.

"Of course." She stands, walking to the kitchen island between us. "I'll call Felicity and we can do a girls take-out night. Sound good?"

Before I can answer, she's touching the screen of her phone and putting it to her ear. Smiling, I know how lucky I am. Not everyone has friends like mine, but everyone should.

Upon receipt of Felicity's text announcing she's arrived, Mercedes opens the door to let her into the apartment. Felicity sets the take-out bags on the table and the delicious scent of cumin and chilies fills the air. My stomach growls audibly, drawing a look of amusement from both Mercedes and Felicity.

"Get the girl some food," Felicity orders, slipping off her white down filled coat.

Tonight, Felicity wears dark blue yoga pants, UGG boots, and an oversized, bright pink sweater. This is uncommon for the normally put together Felicity. She catches my appraising eye.

"I came straight from yoga class." She slips off the boots, revealing perfectly white-tipped toenails.

I start taking containers from the plastic-reinforced paper bags.

"Since when do you participate in — and I quote — new age mat stretching?" Mercedes grins.

"Shush," Felicity responds with fake anger. "It's couples yoga," she mumbles.

The large helping of rice and beans I'm scooping onto my plate almost misses at her admission.

"Whoa, wait a minute." Mercedes puts her hands up, palms forward. "You are doing this for a girl?"

"Don't start with me, Ced," Felicity warns, playfully.

"The Lez-Ho is pussy whipped!" Mercedes shouts and falls into hysterics.

I join her, but shush her at the same time.

"Alex is sleeping," I remind on a laugh.

"I hate you." Felicity grins, taking a seat and reaching for the food.

"Ahh, our little playa playa is settling down." Mercedes tilts her head. "I'm so proud of you."

"Maybe we should talk about you and my brother?" Felicity counters.

Mercedes stiffens, the smile falling from her face.

"There's nothing to talk about," Mercedes shuts down, reaching out to prepare her own plate.

"Wait, what am I missing?" I ask around a mouthful of food.

"Oh, just the fact that our little Rainbow Bright lit up Al's night about a month ago." Felicity puts a forkful of chicken enchilada in her mouth, a satisfied grin on her lips.

Mercedes groans.

"How do I not know about this?" I ask Mercedes.

I drop my fork to my plate and begin searching for the enchiladas I unintentionally missed. Felicity pushes a foil container toward me, knowing what I am looking for.

"You've had a lot going on." Mercedes shrugs.

"And you didn't tell me?" I look at Felicity.

"I've only known for a little over a week. Her attitude with him at the courthouse didn't sit right with me."

"So, you told Felicity and not me?" My feelings are a bit hurt.

"No, no," Felicity interrupts my question. "I practically had to threaten my brother's life to get it out of him, but he caved."

Turning back to Mercedes, I furrow my brow.

"It was just one night and you had a lot going on. It wasn't exactly the most pleasant experience, so I just wanted to forget about it."

"What happened?" Felicity leans forward, concern on her face. "Al didn't say anything bad. Did he do something?"

"No, no. It's just…" Bringing her elbows to the table, she drops her face into her palms and sighs.

"It's just, what?" I press, concern ebbing away my appetite.

"He sucks in bed." Her response is muffled by her hands.

Silence lingers for about a minute.

"Oh my God!" Felicity bursts into a fit of laughter.

"Umm…" I'm not sure what to say.

Mercedes drops her hands.

"It's not funny, Felicity."

"Fuck yes it is!" She snorts. "Please, please, please let me tell him you said that!"

"NO!" Mercedes scowls.

"So, you're mad at him because he isn't...you know." I wave my hand.

"Because he's a bad lay!" Felicity giggles.

"This is your brother we're talking about," I remind her.

She nods. "It's the best ever! That arrogant Mister Perfect isn't so perfect."

"I thought if I was mean he would lose interest, but I can't get rid of him," Mercedes whines, taking a bite.

"I honestly don't know if I can keep this to myself." Felicity takes a deep breath.

"Well, you have to," Mercedes demands. "Don't be so cruel."

"Okay, okay." She puts her hands up. "I'll keep my lips as shut as your legs where his inept penis is involved."

Laughter bursts out and I cover my mouth to muffle the volume. Felicity mimics. Mercedes glares at both of us before joining.

After a few more jokes and almost all of the food, we lounge around the living room. The TV is on, but the volume is low.

"You ready to talk?" Felicity asks, putting her wine glass down on the coffee table.

She sits back in the oversized chair across from my seat on the couch. Mercedes pulls her legs under her, causing the couch cushions to shift briefly.

Sighing, I give them a recount of the exercises Damon and I participated in.

Felicity nods. "I can see why you would have a hard time with appreciating things."

"Liv, how does Damon make you feel?"

I shrug.

"No, come on," Mercedes pushes.

"We don't judge, Liv. You know that," Felicity adds.

"It's hard to explain because I'm still so unsure of it all." I focus on a nonexistent spot on the coffee table.

"Try." Mercedes voice is close and soon, her arm is around my shoulders.

Looking up, my eyes land on Felicity's and the kindness in them breaks me.

"How do I care about someone like Damon Knyght?"

Tears sting my eyes.

"How can I possibly fall in love with my stalker after everything?"

Mercedes' arm tightens, pulling me to lean on her.

"It's like those cheesy romances or news headlines: *Women who fall in love with their captors.* I mean, who does that?" A tear slips, catching on the side of my nose.

"Liv, no one chooses to feel." The sympathy in Felicity's voice is quickly replaced. "But it's about time you started."

"What?" I choke back a sob.

"You've been living in the shadow of the ghosts of loves past for so long," Mercedes adds, holding me tight.

"I don't—"

"You do."

Felicity stands, disappearing into the hallway.

"But I don't. I just—"

Felicity returns with a box on her hip and a stack of sketchpads under the opposite arm.

"You loved Isaac. Isaac loved you. Loving, caring, being happy again does not take away from what you had." She sets the items on the coffee table and I flinch. "You've put him in a tomb."

"It hurts," I whisper.

"I'm sure it does." Felicity takes her seat once more. "But do you really think Isaac would want you to hold on to him like this?"

She motions to one of the boxes containing dried up paints, pastels, and other Isaac remnants.

"I loved him so much," I hiccup.

"I know." Mercedes rocks me. "You know he wouldn't want you to hold back on life, Liv. I didn't know Isaac like you, but the times we were all together...Liv, he was so full of life and determined to live it."

A sob rips from my throat, a verbal confirmation of my heart tearing in two.

"We aren't saying to forget him, but it's time to let him go."

Felicity moves as she speaks, sitting on the table in front of me. Her hands take mine and our eyes meet.

"You feel like you're betraying him by feeling, but you're not. You've made him a ghost."

Hurt from her words sends a shot of anger through me. I furrow my brow and prepare to lash out.

"Liv, you love Alex. Does that take away from the baby you lost?"

My anger dissolves and I collapse against Mercedes. Sobs wrack my body, tears blind me. Felicity's arms encircle us.

I don't know how much time passes before we finally pull apart. Tears still burn behind my eyes, but the sobs seem to have exorcised the ghost.

Wiping my face with my sleeve, full of determination, I go to the hall closet — Isaac's tomb. Sitting cross-legged, I begin to pull out sketchpads, canvases, CDs, photographs, and all the things I'd locked away. I feel Felicity and Mercedes sit on each side of me, but don't look away from the portrait Isaac sketched of me. I sat on a large chair, magazines all around me, and my face looking down at the one in my lap.

"It's beautiful," Mercedes whispers.

For the next two hours, we sit on the floor of my hallway going through each box and work of art. They ask questions and I tell them stories about different works or trinkets. We cry and embrace, but we also laugh.

The emotional night is both a blessing and a curse, because the next morning, I am dragging. Felicity grumbles about the time Mercedes and I wake for the bakery.

"It's too damn early." She presses a pillow over her face.

Mercedes starts tickling her and gets a swat to the head for it.

Slipping into stretchy pants and a maternity tunic, I follow Mercedes out of the bedroom and into the kitchen.

My eyes avoid the closet, but catch on the boxes sitting next to the apartment door. Two will be shipped to Isaac's aunt for his family to go through. I've kept a few small things I can put into a scrapbook one day. And then there is the one to be thrown out. My heart pounds and there's a throb behind my eyes. The 'all cried out' throb.

"Liv," Mercedes gently calls.

Slowly, I look to her.

"Here."

She hands me a glass of orange juice and guides me to sit at the kitchen island.

I don't look at the boxes again, purposely avoiding the direction of the door when Mercedes and I head to the bakery kitchen.

Hours pass quickly in the bakery. There seems to be so much to do. And I feel like a horrible mother when Felicity brings a fed, clean, and playful Alex down to his play area. Distracted by the boxes this morning, I didn't grab the baby monitor.

"I'm so sorry," I apologize, wiping my hands on my *Keep your hands off my bun* apron and walking toward her.

"For what?" Her brow furrows with confusion.

"I just left him for you to take care of."

Felicity waves me off.

"I'm going to get moving. I have a couple appointments this afternoon. I'll grab the two boxes and mail them out, okay?"

She studies my face.

Taking a deep breath, I nod.

"You don't have to, Liv. This happens when you are ready, not—"

"No." I shake my head. "It's okay."

She kisses my cheek before yelling across the bakery to Mercedes.

"Should I tell Al to call you?"

Mercedes scowls.

Felicity disappears up the stairs, her laughter following her.

"Momma," Alex calls, waking me from a much needed nap.

Stretching, I grab my calf and begin rubbing the Charlie Horse out of it.

"Damn it," I curse to the empty room.

I had these during my pregnancy with Alex and I definitely didn't miss them.

"Momma." He's growing impatient and I hear the bounce of his mattress.

"I'm coming, baby," I call back, slipping from the bed and trying to walk off the remainder of the tense muscle.

A knock on the apartment door catches my attention. Grabbing Alex out of his crib, I carry him to the front door. I pull back the curtain and find Damon looking back at me. A rush of excitement courses through my body. Dropping the curtain, I take a breath and open the door.

"Good afternoon." He steps into the apartment, closing the door behind him.

"Dad." Alex reaches out and Damon immediately takes him into his arms.

"Be careful, he just woke up and hasn't been changed yet," I warn.

"I don't mind." Damon kisses Alex's head.

"I'm sorry he's not ready to go."

"It's fine."

"No, I mean, he still needs to be changed, to eat, and..."

The hormones and sleepiness make me emotional and my chin wobbles.

"Hey." Damon steps forward, cupping my chin. "It's okay. I'll help get him ready and I can take him to eat."

His thumb traces the side of my mouth, leaving a fiery path. I want to lick at it.

"I can take care of him," he reassures, releasing my chin. "Why don't you go nap some more?"

"I know you can." I sway, wanting to follow his touch. "But I need to get back downstairs."

"Please make sure you aren't overworking yourself." Concern wrinkles his forehead.

"I'm not. Mercedes won't allow me." I smile.

"Good." He grins.

"Let me put a bag together for him."

We both enter Alex's room. I gather items into a bag while Damon changes Alex's diaper and wipes him down with baby wipes. I finish before he does and just watch him caring for our son. Something I'm not ready to admit to fills me.

"There you go, buddy." Damon stands Alex up. "Ready to go bye-bye?"

"Bye-byes," Alex exclaims, excitedly.

Giving Damon the bag, I follow them out to the door.

"What's this?"

My eyes fall on the boxes.

"Just garb...things I need to throw out," I amend.

"I can take these down."

I open my mouth to object.

"I don't want you carrying boxes down the stairs. I'll feel better knowing you didn't."

He sets Alex on his feet.

"Hey, little man, we forgot a toy. Why don't you go get a car to play with?"

I smile, knowing he doesn't want Alex to think he's leaving without him.

"Come on. Let's get a toy to play with." Taking Alex's hand, I guide him to his bedroom and keep him distracted while Damon carries the boxes down.

A few minutes later, Damon appears in Alex's doorway, his face stormy.

"What's wrong?"

"You have a delivery," he quips and nods his head.

Squeezing by, I walk down the hall and freeze. Flowers. Lots of flowers. A supersized floor display sits next to my door.

"Olivia Harlow?" A guy stands just inside the door.

I nod.

"Can you sign here?"

He extends a clipboard to me.

My eyes still on the large arrangement, I sign and hand it back to the delivery man.

"Thanks. Have a good day." Then, he's gone.

Damon's footsteps give away his entrance behind me.

"Did you—"

"No," he growls low. "It seems you have an admirer."

Snatching the small white envelop on a thin string, I tear it open.

I'm sorry for how I behaved. Forgive me. Erik.

Briefly, I feel guilt, but then concern floods me. Erik never once bought me flowers or did grand gestures. We were never serious enough. He's never been the mature wooing type and we've been officially not a couple for months.

"I'm going to take Alex to eat." Damon's tone is so cold.

"Okay," I breathe.

On autopilot, I get Alex into his hat and coat. Damon opens the door and takes Alex, but pauses before turning to leave.

"Wait!"

He turns, surprise on his face.

"You can take those with you." I point to the flowers.

The corner of his mouth twitches. With a brief nod, he grabs the flowers and pulls them out the door with them.

I close the door and lean forward, pressing my hands against it for a moment.

When I hear the clash of the flowers in the large trash bin at the bottom of the steps, I straighten from the door and return to the bakery.

Damon

Alex eats with a flourish and is full of energy. It's too cold for the park, so I decide to take him back home to play. I also want to check on Olivia. She looks very tired. And I want to make sure Erik doesn't show up. He's grown brave.

Pulling out my phone, I place a couple of calls. Erik won't be able to breathe without me being informed. There will be a stop to this before it even starts.

Walking into the shop front of the bakery, I'm stopped right at the door by a large crowd of people. Mrs. Dorn and Mercedes work behind the vintage soda shop inspired counter and cases. They rush around, filling boxes and bags.

"Excuse me," I say, hedging toward the kitchen entrance.

"Wait your turn, buddy," a small, round woman snaps from two people in front of me.

"I'm not waiting on a turn." I smile, trying to stay cordial.

"Yeah, right." She snorts and nudges another person with her elbow. "This guy thinks he's going to budge in line."

The second stranger turns his scowl on me.

"You can wait in line like the rest of us," the man grumbles.

"Look, I need to get my son—"

"We all need something. You ain't the only one," a woman with a small child on her hip chimes in.

"Listen, his mother—"

"Don't care," the small, round woman grunts.

"Get out of my way," I growl.

For a moment, her eyes widen with fear and she takes a step back.

"How dare you speak to me like that," she says, loud enough for more of the crowd to hear. They all turn and gawk. "We all have to wait our—"

"Damon?" Mercedes calls out over the crowd.

"Yes." I wave above the heads.

"Let him through, please." Mercedes comes around the counter, helping to create a path.

I meet her halfway.

"You should come in through the back." She grins. "Especially at this time of the day."

"Hey! I've been waiting for fifteen minutes!"

I recognize the voice and don't need to look back to see the same woman from a few moments ago.

"They are insane," I whisper.

She giggles, nodding and releasing my arm at the kitchen entrance.

"Calm down, Mrs. Rhodes, he's not a customer. That's Olivia's husband."

At her announcement, all eyes shift and give me a once over. I've stood in front of thousands of employees, negotiated with foreign business associates, debated with multiple boards of directors, but this crowd intimidates me more.

"Next!" Mrs. Dorn exclaims and the group loses interest in me.

I slip into the kitchen.

Inside, I spot Olivia right away. She moves fluidly around a cake; her steps like a ballerina, her hands moving like a maestro over the cake. Golden swirls, twists, and intricate designs start to form on the dark red fondant.

"Momma!" Alex's shout takes Olivia's attention away from the cake.

"Hey, little man." Olivia smiles and it takes my breath away.

"Alex, my main man!" a woman I recognize from the New York job calls out.

317

Olivia sets down a stained cloth bag and wipes her hands on an apron that reads *I'd tell you the recipe, but then I'd have to kill you.* I can't help but grin as she approaches.

"What?" She tilts her head just slightly.

"I like your apron."

She grins, a slight blush coloring her face.

"I have a bunch of them." She shrugs away the embarrassment and reaches for Alex.

He goes into her arms, giving her a big hug.

"Did you eat good?"

"Num nums."

"Good boy."

"Down now." He pushes at her chest.

"Hold on." She walks to the far end of the kitchen. Placing a kiss to his head, she sets him down in his play area.

The minute he's loose, he runs off to a pile of cars and blocks.

"Was he good?" She turns to me.

"Of course. He's a wonderful boy."

"I can't disagree." She smiles.

"Olivia, I don't want to cause a fight," I watch her body tense, "but I would like you to let me know if Erik sends anything else."

My eyes search hers. I see her defiance flare.

"It's not about you. I just want to be sure I'm aware of his actions. They seem off to me."

Her body relaxes a bit.

"It's nothing, I'm sure," she states. "But I will tell you about any more deliveries."

"Thank you."

I set Alex's bag down next to the baby gate and straighten.

"I have a doctor appointment on Wednesday. There will be an ultrasound."

"Will we learn the sex?"

She fidgets for a moment.

"Do you want to know?" Her brow furrows.

"I...I don't know. I guess I didn't think about it until now. What do you want to do?"

"I'd like to know, so I can prepare the other bedroom accordingly. And so I know if I'll need to purchase girl things in place of the boy items I have stored away."

"You planned on another child?"

318

"No. I mean, I thought about it." She looks to Alex playing on his mat. "But it's mostly just because I haven't been ready to let go of his baby things yet. My plan was to donate them eventually."

She looks back at me, catching my grin.

"Can I be honest?"

She nods, her brow furrowing a bit.

"I hope it's a girl."

"Really?" She sounds genuinely surprised.

"Yes." I cup her face. "There should be another girl as beautiful as you in the world."

I don't miss the twitch at the side of her mouth. She's pleased by my words.

"Text me the time and address for the appointment."

I pull my hand away, enjoying the way her body sways toward me.

She nods.

"Also, our date."

She stiffens again.

"I'd like to get together Thursday evening for dinner. Is that okay for you?"

"I...I think so."

"Good. Dress casual and comfortable. I want this to be as relaxed and easy going as possible."

"Okay." Another nod.

With this being our most positive interaction, I don't want to leave. I want to cup her face, kiss her lips, and hold her so close that she sways into me. I want to squat on the floor with Alex and play cars.

I can only hope she responds positively to my surprise.

Stepping into the doctor's office, I'm not prepared for a room full of round bellied women. There are eight women, including Olivia. I take a seat beside her and settle into the chair.

"Hello," I greet her.

"Hi." She smiles small.

Her leg bounces and she fidgets in her seat.

"Are you okay?" I place my hand on hers.

She nods, leg still bouncing.

"Are you sure? You seem nervous." I nod to her shaking limb.

"Oh, no. I have to pee," she whispers.

"They don't have a ladies room?" My brow furrows.

She smiles wide.

"I can't go until after the ultrasound. I started drinking water too early and now I have to go every twenty minutes."

"Oh." Settling back into my chair, I think about this information. "Isn't that uncomfortable?"

"Can we not talk about it? I'm trying not to think about it. Distraction is key."

She winks and I swallow hard. I'm not use to this playful side of Olivia.

"Miss Harlow?"

Our attention turns to a woman in bright pink scrubs.

"Yes." Olivia stands, securing her bag over her shoulder.

I follow her lead.

"My name is Liz," she introduces herself to both of us, then turns to Olivia. "How are you feeling this morning?"

"Good, just overhydrated," Olivia jokes and Liz laughs.

"Let's see if we can get you taken care of quickly."

We enter a light blue and white room.

"Hop on up." Liz pats a beige padded table.

Olivia lays her bag and coat on a chair and slips onto the table.

"Can you unbutton or roll down the top of your pants?"

Liz clicks away on a keyboard and looks at a screen. Olivia pulls her shirt up under her breasts and pushes the stretchy pants low on her hips.

My eyes are riveted on the small bump — our child. Another child is growing in there. Before I can stop myself, I lay my hand on her.

Olivia's eyes widen and she bites at her lip. I want to lean down and take her mouth with mine. Instead, I smile wide.

"Excuse me." Liz smiles at me. "I need to put this gel there."

"Of course."

I remove my hand and stand closer to Olivia's side.

"This should be warm." Liz squeezes the light greenish gel onto Olivia's skin.

Seeing Olivia's hand lying next to her, I take it in between both of mine. Her eyes meet mine. She smiles and I can feel tension leave her.

"Do you want to know the sex?" Olivia asks.

"Yes," I answer on an exhale.

She gives one nod.

"So, that's a yes?" Liz holds a wide T-shape wand in her hand and presses it against Olivia's stomach.

"Yes," Olivia answers.

"Let me get my measurements done and then I'll turn the screen toward you."

Liz clicks some keys, rolls a ball-like object on the keyboard, and presses a few buttons with one hand while moving the wand around with the other. The longer she stays silent, the more tense I feel Olivia become.

"Everything is looking good, Olivia." Liz keeps her eyes on the monitor as she assures her.

Olivia audibly exhales.

"I was a bit worried for a minute."

"Sorry," Liz apologizes. "Everything is measuring on track for eighteen weeks."

A couple more clicks and then the monitor is turned toward us.

"Okay, you ready to meet your baby?"

Her eyes move from Olivia to me and back.

We both nod.

"Here's a hand."

She uses a finger to circle the screen before clicking some buttons.

"A leg and the little foot is here." Liz grins while pointing.

My heart constricts. It's suddenly hard to breathe.

"Okay, let's see if we can get a good angle."

The...*my* baby's leg kicks out.

"Do you feel that?" I ask Olivia.

"Not yet." Her eyes stay on the monitor.

"Ah ha!" Liz exclaims. "Say hello to your baby girl."

"A girl?" I whisper.

"A girl," Liz confirms.

I squeeze Olivia's hand, bringing it to my mouth and kissing her knuckles.

"Thank you," I speak against her skin.

Her eyes meet mine, but she stays silent. I don't need her to say a word.

In this moment, every crack in my heart heals, the darkest parts of my soul fill with light, and my chest swells. This little girl hasn't arrived yet, but I already love her the way I love Alex and Olivia.

During the remainder of her appointment, her doctor is happy with everything except her blood pressure, which is a bit high. She instructs Olivia to take it easy and avoid stress, but, for now, it looks good.

While I originally wanted a house, there wasn't anything on the market aside from a house still under construction. This leaves me in this three bedroom apartment for the next few months.

I thought this temporary apartment would be the location for our date night, but decide a neutral location will be best. To ensure we have privacy to talk to each other, I request a private dining room from the downtown steakhouse.

Dressed in dark jeans and a long, cream sweater, Olivia stares out the window of the car.

"Are you okay?" I ask, keeping my eyes on the drivers pushing and swerving before entering the Fort Pitt Tunnel.

"Yes." She nods.

"Please don't be nervous. I want us to relax and talk, that's it."

I break to avoid some idiot crossing into my lane just inside the tunnel. Olivia's hand moves to the dashboard.

"Sorry."

"Not your fault."

From the corner of my eye, I see her shrug.

We arrive at the restaurant after finding a space in the parking garage one block over. The lack of valet parking, and parking in general, is annoying. I should've used my driver, but I want this to be a normal man and woman going to dinner date.

After giving my name, we are immediately shown to a private dining table. It's set for two, but could easily seat four. The waiter takes our drink orders and leaves us to look over the menu.

"So, a girl?" I try to open up conversation.

"Yep." She grins at her menu.

"You wanted a boy," I say, mostly to spark a response from her.

Her head snaps up.

"No. I didn't care if it was a girl or a boy. Why would you think that?"

Her brow furrows.

"You just seem quiet on the subject." I shrug and look at my menu.

"May I take your order?" The waiter appears, taking both our orders and disappearing again.

There is a long, uncomfortable silence.

"Please tell me what's wrong?"

Our eyes meet and lock for a moment before she looks away.

"I don't know what to do," she whines. "I haven't *dated* in forever. I have no idea what we are going to talk about aside from visitations for Alex and the baby."

"None of that tonight," I state and take a drink from my water glass.

"What do you mean?"

"Tell me about your family. You know about mine. I think it's only fair you tell me about yours."

"Uh, um, you met my father. He lives in Beaver and works at the power plant. My mother lives in California, she's an acting teacher. They are both only children, I'm an only child, and my grandparents either passed away before I was born, or when I was too young to remember much about them."

"So, no cousins or stepsiblings?"

She shakes her head.

"My father never remarried and my mother would never risk her figure to another pregnancy," she giggles.

"Will I meet your mother?" I ask, curious about her absence.

She shrugs. "She doesn't come back East. She's more of a long distance grandmother, sending cards, gifts, and the occasional phone call. Though, the calls are typically when I'm in bed, since she waits until late in the evening West Coast time to call."

"I see."

"Have you and Hugh always been close?"

She finally settles back into her chair, relaxing.

"For the most part, yes. I was, of course, jealous of him as a child."

"Jealous?"

"He had my father and Heidi. Even at a young age, I knew my mother was different."

"Damon, I'm so sorry." Sympathy wrinkles her forehead and nose.

"It's fine. It's in the past." I smile, drinking from my water again.

By the time our food arrives, we are talking comfortably. We tell each other about where we went to school, first kisses, knowing what we wanted to do when we grew up, and things we didn't know about each other until tonight.

It's during dessert when I decide to confess a few things.

"I need to tell you a couple things."

I push away my dessert plate, resting my elbows on the table.

Olivia's eyes search my face as she settles back in her chair.

"What?" she asks, suspicion darkening her eyes.

"I want you to listen to what I'm about to say without getting angry. It wasn't her intention to upset you. She's just concerned—"

"She?"

Olivia's eyes narrow on me and for a moment, I think I see a hint of jealousy.

"Scarlett." I try to hide a grin.

Olivia's body relaxes.

"Her mother has visited your bakery for the upcoming wedding. You're making the cake for next weekend."

Olivia's eyes widen and her mouth pops open.

"Mrs. Manson…" she breathes. "That's Scarlett's mother, isn't it?"

She continues without giving me time to respond.

"I knew the last name sounded familiar, but I couldn't place it." She slouches back in her seat, shaking her head. "Why would I be upset about this?" Confusion wrinkles her brow.

"Scarlett knows your last interaction wasn't exactly cordial, so she didn't want to upset you further by coming into the bakery." I shrug. "I told her she was being crazy, but you know how you women are."

"Hey!" Olivia scolds, but a small smile gives away her amusement. "You're right, though. I wouldn't have minded her coming. In fact, it would've been nice to see her and apologize."

"Apologize?" I ask.

She nods. "Yes, I wasn't exactly nice that day."

Instead of commenting, I continue on.

"I'd like for you to consider going to the wedding with me next Friday and spending the weekend at my apartment."

"Spend the weekend?" she asks in a broken whisper.

"Yes, since we have the therapy exercise coming, I figure it's the perfect time. We will attend their wedding Friday evening, return to my apartment, and on Saturday, I'd like to show you the house I've purchased."

"You bought a house?"

"I purchased an under construction house. It's in the final stages." I nod.

She clears her throat.

"Where?" she asks, trying to sound nonchalant.

"McKees Rocks. It's a newer neighborhood. It will only be about twenty minutes, depending on traffic, from the bakery."

"Oh."

She picks up her water glass and takes a drink.

"I'd like for you to see it as well as the plans." I shrug. "So you can offer suggestions for child proofing and such."

Her brow rises inquiringly.

"Child proofing?"

"Olivia, I'll be completely honest."

Leaning forward, I place my forearms on the table and fold my hands together.

"I want you to see the house, offer your input, and make sure you like the house. It's my full intention for you to live in this house with me, our children to grow up in this house, and for you to share a bed with me every night."

Her lips part in surprise.

"You don't have to agree to anything now, but know I will do everything within my power to make it happen."

Her mouth shuts and she visibly swallows.

"Is that all?" she asks after recovering from my confession.

"No, there's one other thing I'd like to talk about. It's about the fertility clinic's mix up."

A twitch in her jaw betrays her nervousness.

"What about it?" she asks through her teeth.

"I'm having it further investigated. I'm not comfortable with all the unknowns. I just don't want you to be surprised about me looking into the situation more."

She exhales a breath.

"That makes sense. Thank you for telling me."

"So?"

I sit back in my chair once more.

"So, what?" She plays with the napkin on the table.

"Next weekend, will you accompany me to the wedding and spend the weekend?"

"I'll think about it," she answers quickly — too quickly.

"Olivia—"

"I said I'll think about it, Damon."

The drive back to Olivia's apartment is quiet. She keeps one hand on her stomach and the left on her leg. Before I can tell myself it's a bad idea, I reach out and take her hand in mine. She jolts, just a bit, in surprise, but doesn't pull her hand away.

"I didn't mean to upset you."

She sighs.

"I'm not upset, just thinking about everything."

Her head presses back against the leather seat, rolling to look out the window.

"Still, the night was going so well. I didn't mean to ruin the evening. I just wanted to be honest about things."

Lifting our joined hands, I kiss the back of hers. She gasps. I smile against her skin.

Chapter Eighteen – Letting go
Olivia

The minute the door is closed, I lean back. The tingling sensation from his touch lingers on my hand. The sounds of a drumming heartbeat fills my ears. Eyes closed, I take a deep, calming breath.

"Must have been a good time." The sneer in Erik's voice alarms me.

"What are you doing here?" I ask, straightening from the door.

Looking around, I find Mercedes seated on the couch. She puts a finger to her temple and swirls in the universal crazy motion.

"Apparently, Damon is bored with stalking you and has decided to follow me around."

"What are you talking about?" I furrow my brow and set my keys on the table next to me.

"I can't believe you're with him," he growls, loudly.

"Shh, Alex is in bed," Mercedes whispers harshly.

"You know what, Ced? You can go now." Erik keeps his eyes on me as he speaks.

"Who the hell—?"

"No, Erik, you can go," I say, cutting Mercedes off. I grab the doorknob and open the door.

"I patiently waited for almost a year. Almost a year, Olivia!" He steps close.

From the corner of my eye, Mercedes stands from the couch, putting her cellphone to her ear.

"Erik, I never made any promises. You chose to wait for something that I never — not once — said was going to happen for us."

I motion to the open door.

"You've become a whore, you know that?" he barks.

"Go to hell, Erik. I—"

327

Erik jerks backward out the door. Damon looms over him, his face red and chest heaving.

"What did you call her?" Damon growls, holding Erik by the neck of his shirt.

Erik stretches his neck to look past Damon. His angry eyes settle on mine.

"I can't believe you want a psycho! A stalker is who you can't seem to get enough of," he adds to the previous insult.

"Don't look at her." Damon moves, standing so I can't see Erik.

"Fuck you!" Erik shouts. "You can have the whore and—"

Erik's yelling is cut off by Damon's fist.

"Damon!" I shout, moving forward and placing my hand on his shoulder.

Erik moans, holding his hand over his nose and lip.

"You'll regret that."

Damon stiffens and prepares to strike again.

I grab his arm, stopping the next strike. Our eyes meet and the angry lines on his face smooth over. Turning to Erik, I narrow my eyes.

"Go home and don't come back. I don't want you around."

"I can't believe I wasted time waiting on a damn tease," he snarls through his swelling lip.

"Grow up. Name calling and temper tantrums are for children."

Guiding Damon inside, I slam the door in Erik's face and lock it.

I watch his shadow for a few minutes and wonder if I'll need to call the police. The whole time I've known him, he's never acted like this. For the short period of time we dated, he was laid back and easy going. When I ended our physical relationship and put more distance between us, wanting to just be friends, he understood and was cool about it. I don't know this Erik and I don't want to.

Damon's arms come around me, holding me to him. Each beat of his heart throbs against my chest. Soon, I swear our beats are synchronized.

"Are you alright?" I whisper against his chest.

"I'm sorry." His hushed apology confuses me.

"For what?" Pushing back, he allows me the room to look up at him.

"I didn't mean to get violent, but when he called you a—"

"He deserved the second punch, too. If you ask me," Mercedes chimes in and shrugs.

Damon chuckles before getting serious again.

"Do you want me to stay?"

I shake my head. "We'll be fine."

"I don't like the idea of you and Alex here alone."

Suddenly curious about him showing up at the apartment, I ask, "What made you turn around?"

"Mercedes," he responds. It's then that I remember her getting on her phone.

"Oh."

"Are you sure you don't need—"

"It will be fine."

A mixture of emotions plays on his face and I can see he wants to argue, but he gives a light nod.

"Promise you'll call the police and then me if he shows up again." His arms tighten around me.

"I promise."

He kisses my forehead before saying his goodbye and leaving.

"You okay?" Mercedes' hand touches my shoulder.

Turning, I step into her embrace. We hug for a moment before stepping back from each other.

"How was Alex tonight?" I ask through tears clogging my throat.

"Great, as usual." Mercedes sits on a stool at the kitchen island. "I tried to get rid of him, I swear. He just wouldn't leave."

"It's not your fault."

I shrug and walk to the fridge, retrieving a bottle of water.

"What is the matter with him? I've never seen Erik act that way."

"I was thinking the same thing." I exhale, suddenly feeling exhausted.

"Well, I'm staying in the spare room. I don't trust that bastard. He may show up again."

I nod.

"Thanks."

"What are best friends for?" She grins, grabbing a small bouquet from the counter in front of her.

"What are those?"

"Garbage now." She slips from the stool and throws them in the trashcan. "Erik brought them when he showed up."

"Was Alex awake when he got here?"

She shakes her colorful head.

"No, he'd been asleep for about thirty minutes."

"Good," I sigh in relief.

"Come on." She motions for me to come with her to the hallway. "We have an early morning and you look worn out."

"I am pretty tired," I confirm, walking to the spare room with her, side by side.

"I hope that's Damon's work and not because of Erik's behavior." She nudges me with an elbow.

"Ced," I hiss and then laugh quietly.

"Shucks." She frowns with disappointment.

"Go to bed," I playfully order before going to my door.

"Yes, Mommy," she responds in a squeaky voice, entering the room.

For the next three days, the bakery is so busy, Mercedes recruits some culinary students for some temp work. While my crew and I work on the finer details and construction, they roll fondant, mix batters, and bake. We've used one of the students a couple of times before, so he helps with some of the baked goods for the front of the shop.

Damon has called every evening to check on Alex and me. I've also receive texts telling me about the baby's development. The first being: **18 weeks. Our daughter's ears are now in position.** And the second, sent the next day: **You may start to feel her move. Please let me know if you do.**

Damon has been working late because of a new client. They're demanding his presence, so he hasn't been around very much. The longer he's away, the lonelier I feel.

I've never been one to feel lonely. In fact, I used to enjoy quiet alone time. I'd given excuses to people so many times, even my own father, so I could just stay home with Alex. Now, I get a fluttering sensation at the sound of Damon's voice. Disappointment stabs my chest when I realize he's not going to come over.

Today, day four, I've buried myself in work. Mrs. Manson, Scarlett's mother, is scheduled to come in for a final session regarding the wedding cake and I'm waiting for her to arrive.

"Olivia?"

The soft voice catches my attention. I look over the two-tiered chocolate cake to Scarlett and her mother standing on the other side of my table, looking nervous.

"Scarlett." I smile.

Coming around the table, I wipe my hands on my *I bake so I don't kill people* apron.

Taking in her perfectly put together blouse, slacks, high heels, and silk scarf, I stop myself from hugging her.

"How are you?"

"Good." She smiles, steps forward, and hugs me.

"You're going to get icing all over you."

"It's fine." She squeezes before pulling away and then focuses on my stomach. "Look at you," she coos, her hands hovering over my stomach. "Can I?"

I don't really like being treated like a Buddha, but I nod my approval anyway.

Her hands press and rub.

"Do you know what you're having?" She looks up from my stomach.

"Damon hasn't told you?" I furrow my brows, surprised he hasn't shared the news.

"No, he told me to ask you." She blushes. "I'm so sorry about how things—"

"You don't need to apologize. We were all in a tense and uncomfortable situation. Plus, I was a tad hormonal at the time."

"Still, I want to say how sorry I am. Heidi felt sick after everything."

"She shouldn't," I assure her. "Please tell her everything is forgiven, if you both can forgive me as well."

With a nod, she exhales, all the tension melting from her body.

"Let's go sit down." I motion for the women to follow me.

With the increased activity in the storefront as of late, Mercedes set up a small cubicle area with a table and four chairs at the far end of the kitchen. It's located close enough to the storefront entrance and far enough from the baking noises.

After taking seats, I grab the clipboard from the row hanging on the wall. This is another of Mercedes updates. The customers visiting each had a clipboard she hung on an even line of wall hooks, in alphabetical order.

"How are you feeling? Everything is good?"

"I'm feeling well. Tired mostly, but overall, *she* is doing just fine."

A grin spreads over Scarlett's face.

"It's a girl!" she squeals in delight.

I nod, laughing.

"Boys are wonderful, but a little girl is a precious gift." Mrs. Manson grins kindly.

"Ah, Momma. I love you, too." Scarlett looks to her.

"I was talking about your sister."

"You mean old lady," Scarlett grumbles just before they burst into unified laughter.

It seems Mrs. Manson is very much like her daughter, though they don't look much alike.

"I didn't know you had a sister," I say, grabbing a pencil and unclipping the order papers.

She nods. "Yeah, Amber is older than me. I'm the baby." Scarlett rests her head on her mother's shoulder.

"Any brothers?"

"Yep." Scarlett wiggles her brows. "You ready for this?"

I wrinkle my face in confusion.

"Hunter. His name is Hunter and he's the middle child."

My brow remains furrowed.

"She gave us all color names." Scarlett rolls her eyes. "Amber, Hunter, as in green, and Scarlett."

"They are very beautiful names," her mother defends.

"At least I got Scarlett out of the deal. Poor Hunter." She shakes her head. "He usually just goes by Hunt."

"His name is strong." Mrs. Manson playfully nudges her daughter.

"Mmhmm, sure it is, Momma." Scarlett winks at me and I smile.

After another minute of playful banter, we delve into the specifics for her cake...or cakes. Scarlett changes the stacked four-tier cake idea for a cascading cake. She wants four different cakes, all different flavors, and for them to be individually sat on pedestals at different heights. Around them, she wants a display of fresh fruit and small pastries.

After tasting different flavors of cakes, fillings, and frostings, compromising with her mother on having one normal white cake tier, and promises to stay in touch, the Manson women leave the shop.

Damon

The time away from Olivia and Alex is tearing me apart inside. The urge to hurry back to Pittsburgh is almost overwhelming, but there is something I need to do first. Something I've put off for so long, unable to bear the pain of my reality.

"Sir, we've arrived." The driver's eyes meet mine in the rearview mirror.

Taking a deep breath, I nod.

The driver exits the black car, opening my door. My shoes carry me from the paved road to the frozen earth. I pass so many marble markers in different sizes — mothers, fathers, sons, and daughters all around me. The large marble angel stands tall in the distance. She is tall, smooth, and white. In her arms, a small child clings. I stop before them, tears stinging my eyes.

Grabbing my chest, I drop to my knees. A quake of despair shakes my shoulders until the pain roars from my chest. The salty tears dip into the corners of my mouth before falling from my chin to the ground.

"I miss you," I rasp.

Walking on my knees until I'm a few mere inches from the stone, I trace the engraved name.

"I love you so much."

Pressing my forehead to the cold marble, I close my eyes and release my sorrow.

I'm not sure how long I stay this way. Warmth surrounds me and I feel a coat slip over my shoulders. I glance over my shoulder to see the driver already walking back to the car.

Wiping the dampness from my face, I move to sit on the ground. With my back against the stone, I talk to the family I lost.

"I'm sorry, Rebecca. I wish I would've been a better man for you. You were in so much pain and I didn't realize how much. Maybe I didn't want to see it. I regret so much, Bec."

Dropping my head, chin to chest, I sigh.

"But I love her, Rebecca. I love them so much. I hope you can be happy for me, even when I don't deserve it."

Turning back to face the stone on my knees, I press my right palm on the surface.

"You have a brother, DJ. And soon, you will have a sister." Tears pool beside my nose, the cold air chilling them until it's almost unbearable.

"Be a good boy for your mommy."

Bringing my hand to my mouth, I place my warm lips to the cold skin of my palm and press it back to the stone.

"Take good care of him, Bec. You are both forever with me."

Placing both hands to my thighs, I close my eyes and drop my head. After a few moments, I inhale the sharp, crisp air and stand.

"I love you," I whisper before turning back to the car.

Olivia

Stepping into Dr. Livingston's waiting area, I expect to see Damon. My stomach drops when he's not in one of the seats. My eyes sting and I blame my lack of sleep. Last night had been a restless evening. Tossing and turning, I couldn't settle myself. I was still awake when Damon's late night flight touched down at the Pittsburgh Airport. A feeling of relief had washed over me as I settled back into the pillows, but then I wrestled with the idea that he would show up at my apartment.

He didn't.

As I take a seat, the doctor appears.

"Hello, Olivia. Please come back."

"But Damon isn't—"

"He's already in the office." She smiles and waits patiently for me to follow her.

Inside her office, Damon stands at our entrance. His smile is wide, but dark circles tint the skin under his eyes.

"How are you feeling?" he asks politely as he studies my face.

"Just tired." I take a seat on the small couch beside him. "Restless night."

"How far along are you?" Dr. Livingston sits behind her desk.

"Nineteen weeks," Damon answers for me, causing the doctor to smile largely.

"A proud father." She turns back to me.

"Are you well enough for today?"

I nod.

"Okay, let's start with your date. Damon says you two were able to have a night alone together. How did that go?"

"It was uncomfortable at first." I shrug.

"Why?" she asks, pen hovering over her notepad.

"I haven't dated in forever." I feel heat flare over my cheeks. "I wasn't sure what to do or how to act."

"I think we worked it out," Damon adds, placing a hand on my leg.

"Did you learn anything about each other?"

We both nod.

"Tell me about it."

"We talked about our families. Some about our past, school, growing up, and things like that," I offer.

"Good." She nods, taking notes. "So, I'd like to do an exercise today to explore how well you really know your partner."

Standing from her chair, she walks to a filing cabinet, takes out some papers, and sits back down.

"This isn't a test. If you don't know something, just say you don't. This is only to open dialogue about sharing yourself with the other person. Alright?"

"Okay," I answer.

"Yes," Damon responds.

Dr. Livingston slides a paper toward each of us.

"These are what I'm going to be discussing. Read over them and take a minute to think about the answers for yourself, not for your partner. You will be answering the questions out loud about your partner."

She allows us a couple minutes before jumping right in to the first part.

"Can you name your partner's three best friends?"

"Hugh, Scarlett, and I don't know." Giving Damon a sideways glance, I wrinkle my nose.

"Hugh would be the closest I have to a best friend." Damon nods.

"And Olivia's friends?"

"Mercedes and Felicity." He grins.

"Yes." I nod.

"Can you tell me one accomplishment your partner is most proud of?" Dr. Livingston moves right into the next question.

Tensing, I know I can't answer this question. I open my mouth, but close it when Damon speaks.

"Establishing herself in her own bakery." Damon is quick to answer first. "And Alex, of course."

The doctor's eyes lock on me, expectantly.

I shake my head just a bit.

"I...I don't..."

"It's fine. Couples who have been together for years are not able answer many of these questions." She offers me a reassuring smile, but it just makes me feel worse.

Damon stays silent. From the corner of my eye, I watch him. He doesn't seem upset or concerned. It only makes me feel infinitesimal relief.

"The next question is about greatest losses, but I think you both know and understand one another's." She doesn't look up. "Next is about family, knowing about your partner's home environment as a child."

She looks up from the paper and between us both.

"Are you confident you both know this about each other?"

"Not completely, but I have a general idea," I respond. Knowing what I do about Damon's mother and father, and after our conversation during our date, I can put together a pretty decent idea.

"I agree." Damon nods, crossing his leg over the opposite knee. "I feel the same."

"Good." She smiles and continues through the list.

In the end, we know more than I thought about each other. But in the grand scheme of things, I am ashamed I don't know more.

"You both did very well." Dr. Livingston sits back in her chair. "I would like you to try the weekend together, or whenever you can arrange the extended alone time. If you need to go away somewhere for it to happen, then so be it. If you are unable to accomplish this before our next session, I'll prepare something different."

"My brother is getting married on Friday, so we've discussed the possibility of Olivia staying at my place for the weekend."

"Good." She smiles, standing. "Then I'll see you next week. Try to use the time together to have open discussions. Remember to let the other person have a minute to process things. Rushing each other into responses will only result in arguments and we want to avoid negative communication."

"Okay." I nod.

Damon stands, offering me his hand. I take it and allow him to help me to my feet.

The warmth of his skin and gentle pressure of his hand sends a pang through my chest. His eyes lock on mine. The twitch of his lip makes me wonder whether he knows how he affects me.

"Thank you." I pull my hand away quickly.

Outside the office, I pull my coat closed tight and fight a shiver. Snow has started coming down harder than earlier.

"Olivia?"

Damon stops me before I can step to the bus stop. I look over my shoulder.

"Please, let me give you a ride."

"It'll be—"

"Please. I'll feel better knowing you made it safely," he pleads with me, his jaw tensing.

Snowflakes pepper the exposed skin on my face, melting. Giving a nod, I allow him to lead me by my arm to his waiting car.

"Mister, Missus Knyght," the driver greets and opens the rear door.

I smile.

Damon takes my hand, holding it until I'm seated. He then slips in next to me.

"Thank you," he says softly.

"Thank you for the ride."

His hand finds mine, linking our fingers.

Heat rises from my belly, spreading across my thighs and up my torso.

"Will you join me for Hugh and Scarlett's wedding on Friday?"

His thumb rubs lightly against my skin. Each time the pad of his thumb touches the knuckle of mine, my heart rate spikes.

"Yes," I respond, huskier than intended.

"And you'll stay the weekend?"

He gently squeezes my hand.

"Yes," I whisper.

"Thank you."

Lifting and twisting our joined hands, he kisses the inside of my wrist. My eyes are drawn to the action and I gasp when the tip of his tongue grazes my skin.

"Please consider sharing my bed with me." His warm breath caresses the sensitive skin.

I swallow, preparing to scream, *Yes!*

"You don't have to answer me now."

Lifting his mouth, he brings our hands back to the seat between us. My eyes stay fixed on my wrist. I want to shout for him not to stop and press my wrist to his face.

"Just think about it, please."

His words bring my attention to his face again. All I can do is stare at his lips and nod.

The car pulls to stop.

"We've arrived," the driver announces.

"Thank you, William."

Damon opens the door and slips out. His hand darts back in and I take it. He helps me from the car, drawing me close to his chest.

Pressing his lips to my forehead, I melt into him. He pulls back and I'm about to protest.

"I'd like to take Alex for the afternoon tomorrow."

The chilled air swirls between us, waking me from my lusty reaction to him.

I nod. "Of course. Just give me a call and let me know what time you are coming. I'll have him ready."

A gust of cold wind blows pieces of my hair into my face.

"It will most likely be after his nap."

He uses both hands to gently capture my flailing strands and cups my head.

"Can you let me know when he goes down?"

"Yes," I breathe out.

"Until tomorrow."

He chastely kisses my mouth before taking a step back. My mouth stays slightly parted as he guides me to the door of the shop.

"Bye," I blurt, having finally shaken off the effect of his kiss.

With a half grin, he turns and climbs back into the car.

I stand in the cold, watching him pull away from the curb. My heart aches as I watch him go.

The next morning, I wake to a text from Damon.

19 weeks. Our daughter is developing senses and growing hair. Maybe it will match Alex's color.

I can't believe he's awake at four-thirty in the morning. With a large smile on my face, I get up and start my morning of baking. An hour later, Mercedes arrives, going straight to her office. The unusual behavior makes me pause in the middle of pouring blueberry muffins into the jumbo pans. Moving a couple steps to the office, I stop when she comes walking out with a smile on her face.

"You okay?" I tilt my head and furrow my brow.

"Sure am." She looks down at her cell phone and her smile widens. "I'm going to run out to the coffee shop real quick. I'll bring you back a decaf mocha hazelnut okay?"

"You just—"

She is out the back door before I can finish.

Frowning and unmoving, I wonder what is up with her. Breathing deeply, I exhale and go back to my abandoned muffins.

Slipping the pans into the large oven, I walk over to the speaker, holding an iPod. Touching the screen, I tap the music-streaming app and press play. Lipsyncing to Sia, I retrieve the pastry dough and premade cream cheese mixture from the cooler.

I coat the surface of my table with a flour and confection sugar mixture and then begin to roll out the pastry dough. Picking up the round pizza cutter, I separate the dough into squares. I collect the extra dough and ball it up, placing it to the side. I spoon a large tablespoon of cream cheese mixture onto one square and fold until it forms a sealed triangle.

Fingers trail the exposed skin on my neck. Jumping in surprise, I spin around and grab my chest.

"Damon," I gasp.

"I'm sorry for frightening you." His lips twitch.

"What are you—?"

His lips press to mine.

This isn't a chaste kiss. This is a hard, demanding, wanting kiss that has me parting my lips instantly.

His tongue takes dominance of my mouth. The kiss owns me. And I want it to. When he pulls back, I sway forward. Pressing my hands to his chest, I close my eyes, take a breath, and regain my composure.

"I wanted to see you and tell you good morning in person."

Opening my eyes, I focus on the grin he's wearing.

Recovering, I say, "Good morning."

He chuckles.

"I'll see you this afternoon."

Leaning in, he kisses the side of my mouth. Instinctively, I turn toward his lips, but he has already pulled away, walking backwards toward the door.

"Until then." He gives a slight nod and disappears out the door.

On autopilot, I finish the cheese pastries and clean up my work area.

When Mercedes arrives, with a smile still on her face and a mischievous look in her eye, I realize she was in on the whole thing.

"Does this mean you're team stalker now?" I ask, accepting the coffee she holds out to me.

She shrugs. "He needs a cheerleader."

With a wink, she spins on her heels and goes to her office.

I set the coffee on the table next to me, not ready to wash the taste of him from my mouth just yet.

Chapter nineteen - worth
Damon

"Hello."

"You ever thought about a career in private investigation?" Mitch taunts from the other end of my cell.

"You found something?" I place the client folder on the seat next to me.

"Oh yeah, and you ain't gonna like it." He snorts.

"My mother?" Nausea furls inside my stomach.

"Damon, are you sure you want to know this? I mean, this ain't some easy shit to tell you."

"Tell me."

"Damon—"

"Fucking tell me, Mitch," I growl, closing my eyes and waiting.

He sighs heavily into the phone and then launches into a cluster fuck of a primetime, award-winning show.

"Your wife, Rebecca, paid off a technician to get rid of the...uh, of the sample."

"Rebecca?" I choke.

"Yeah, man. She moved cash into the account of one of the techs. I got the tech to spill some information by promising not to share. Apparently, Rebecca wasn't too keen on the idea of having another child." He takes another deep breath. "But it doesn't stop there. Your mother is the source behind the doctor's involvement."

"Go on."

"Seems your mother paid the good doctor to switch up your supply. I'm afraid the reason why died with her, unless I can get a final location on Dr. Phillipson. Which, by the way, the money trail on him ran cold, so I'm trying some other angles."

I stay silent.

"Your mother offered him the money, he took it and handled the *mix up*. However, the tech wasn't aware of this, so the wrong samples were moved around. Turns out, there are at least three other mix up situations because of this."

I rub a hand over my face and roll my head on my neck. Each crack feels like my sanity snapping away.

"Do I have other children, Mitch?"

Panic seizes my chest. *This could be disastrous. Olivia would be lost to me forever. How could this be happening now?*

"No, Damon, you don't understand. It's not just you. There are couples out there with children who most likely aren't from who the parents think. When I say there are others, I mean other people completely unrelated to you or Olivia. They just happen to be bystanders."

"Christ," I growl. "Find Dr. Phillipson, I have questions for him. I also want you to collect as much information, legally, as you can."

"You goin' to the cops with this?" Mitch's voice deepens.

"If other couples or children are involved, I need to think about taking it to the authorities. They deserve to know."

"Think hard, Damon. A story like this will turn into a media frenzy," he warns.

"I know," I say on a sigh before disconnecting.

"Why am I so nervous? Should I be this nervous?" Hugh readjusts his tie for the fifth time.

"Stop messing with your tie." Setting my tumbler glass onto a small wooden table, I uncross my legs, stand, and walk to my brother.

"Everyone is nervous before getting married," our father offers from his leather seat across the room.

Stepping up behind him, I place both hands on his shoulders.

"You've been after Scarlett for years and now you have her. Hell, her mother made sure to plan the wedding quickly so you can get married sooner rather than later," I tease, drawing a small grin from him.

"Her parents love you and want grandchildren before Scarlett has the chance to wisen up and leave your ass. So, I'd say she's stuck with you now."

"Okay, enough teasing my baby." Heidi steps into the room, shooing me back to my chair.

Turning him away from the mirror, she adjusts his tie to perfection. Taking Hugh's head between her hands, she pulls his face close and whispers.

A part of me aches with a familiar jealousy.

Pressing a kiss to his forehead, she releases him. Turning to me, she scowls playfully.

"You leave him alone."

While pointing at myself, I mouth, "Me?"

"Yes, you."

With purpose, she walks over, leans down, and kisses the top of my head.

"Where's my favorite little man?"

"Dad is right here." Hugh pats our father on the shoulder.

My eyes widen before I choke out a laugh. Heidi joins Hugh and me by giggling. Our father looks ready to explode and I'm afraid Heidi will take the brunt of the anger.

She sways to him, sits on his lap, leans in close, and speaks too low for me to hear. Hugh, however, is close enough to hear. His face twists in horror.

"I don't want to hear those things." He steps away quickly.

Heidi sits up, smiling. Amused by Hugh's reaction, I'm sure, but also pleased with her ability to calm my father.

"Now, where is Alex?" Heidi asks, rising from my father's lap.

"He and Olivia are seated in the pew with you and Dad."

"Good." She smiles large and warm, the way a doting grandmother should. "Damon," she looks to my father, "let's get seated."

Setting down his drink, my father unfolds from the leather chair, gives Hugh a half hug, and escorts Heidi out of the groom's room.

I smile, knowing I get an evening of my wife and son among my extended family and having my wife in my home for the weekend.

When I approach the altar, I'm still plotting ways to get her in bed with me. Seeing Olivia talk animatedly with Heidi as we line up for the ceremony, warms my chest.

She looks beautiful. Her bright red hair, loosely braided over her right shoulder, compliments the blue dress. Her skin reminds me of moonlight. With its iridescent glow, her eyes are brighter and the smattering of freckles more prominent. She glances up, our eyes meet, and her cheeks redden. My desire to kiss each freckle — visible and hidden — must be obvious.

The ceremony is somewhat traditional, though short and to the point, just as Scarlett desired.

Now, with toasts, dinner courses, and first dances behind us, the reception cannot end soon enough. I'm happy for my brother and his new bride, but I have my own wife on my mind.

Scanning the dance area, I find her with Hugh. They sway to a slow melody and share a smile between them.

"A hundred dollars for your thoughts," Scarlett says close to my ear before sitting down next to me.

She had changed from the large traditional gown her mother wanted into a sleek, silky, white dress. This dressed hugged her body in a very Scarlett-desired, untraditional fashion.

"Isn't it a penny?" I raise my left brow.

She shakes her head.

"With the way you are looking at Olivia, I guarantee your thoughts are worth the extra pennies."

With a waggle of her brows, she grins. Chuckling, I shake my head.

"You look beautiful, Scarlett."

Her grin widens into a large smile.

"Thank you."

Leaning forward, she kisses my cheek. Then, she is back on her stiletto clad feet.

She pats my shoulder and walks away, saying, "I'm going to go reclaim my legally bound man servant before he tries to leave me for a hot, pregnant woman who knows how to bake some good shit."

Pushing out of the lavender silk covered chair, I follow her.

"I don't want to have to hurt my brother on his wedding day, so I better come with you."

Slowing, Scarlett waits for me to step next to her and places her arm in mine. Her head drops to my shoulder.

"You love her, don't you?" she asks.

"Yes," I reply, no hesitation in my response.

She squeezes my arm and sighs.

"Good."

"It could be better." I snort.

"What do you mean?" She lifts her head, looking up at my profile.

"Well, if she loved me in return, it would be ideal." One side of my mouth curls.

She stops, tugging on my arm. I turn to face Scarlett.

"Look closer, Damon. I can't tell you whether she loves you, but there's something."

I pull Scarlett into my arms and embrace her.

"Thank you." I kiss the side of her head. Her words are like a balm to my heart.

"Hey now, you have your own wife," Hugh calls out.

We both step back from each other and turn. Hugh is still dancing with Olivia, both of them laughing.

"But, yours does make some pretty amazing food," he teases.

"I told you." Scarlett smacks my chest before taking purposeful steps.

Hugh releases Olivia and puts his hands up.

"I'm all yours."

Scarlet presses to his chest and whispers in his ear. Hugh's eyes darken. His arms wrap around her and he claims her mouth.

Olivia walks toward me. Before she can step off the dance floor, I wrap my arm around her waist. It's time to dance with my wife.

The music is slow and sensual. Our eyes lock. With my right hand at the small of her back, I pull her closer, pressing her swollen belly against me. My left hand intertwines with her right and I curl our arms close between us. We move rhythmically to the beat and I mouth the next line in song.

"Now you know. Everywhere on Earth you go, you're going to have me as your man."

Her eyes widen and the parting of her lips draws my attention. Dipping my head, my mouth barely touches hers when the sound of her cell phone breaks the moment.

I growl.

She blushes, pulling away to take the phone out of a pocket hidden in the dress.

"Hello," she answers.

Pressing a finger to her other ear, she begins to nod and look around the room.

"I'll get him ready." She pauses. "Okay. Bye."

Slipping the phone back into her pocket, she looks up at me.

"That was Ced. She's almost here to get Alex."

She fidgets. I'm not sure whether it's from our moment on the dance floor or thinking about us being alone this weekend. Maybe it's both.

"I need to get him and his things together."

Olivia starts walking away.

"I'll help."

"You don't have—"

"I want to."

Taking her hand, we walk through the crowd, looking for Heidi, knowing she has Alex. She's had him most of the evening.

Olivia

The ceremony is lovely and the reception is wonderful, but exhausting. After making rounds with Damon to meet his family and their close friends, dancing with Scarlett, then Hugh, Damon, Alex, and a couple other men in the Knyght family, I'm spent.

However, knowing we will leave together, just Damon and me, in his apartment for the weekend, alone, I fight the sleepiness hovering. And, for the most part, I've been successful. That is, until the largest yawn of my life stretched my jaw so far, it cracked. Damon immediately gathers our things, excuses us from the gathering, and puts me in the back of a waiting car.

Damon settles into the leather seat, instructs the driver, and turns to me.

"You should have told me how tired you are."

"I'm fine," I say through another yawn.

He chuckles, placing his arm on the back of the seat. His fingers stroke my hair.

"You look beautiful tonight. Did I tell you?"

Taking a deep breath, I hope to inhale the courage to be stronger than the beating of my heart and throbbing between my legs. With a turn of my head, I meet his eyes. His beautiful eyes.

"Yes," I breathe out the word, "you did. But thank you."

His fingers press deeper into my hair until he's massaging my scalp. My body instantly relaxes against the car seat.

"Will you sleep next to me tonight?" he asks so quietly, my super relaxed brain barely comprehends.

"It's not a good idea," I mumble.

"Please?" His lips are close to my ear.

"Too soon," I slightly slur.

"Tomorrow?" He presses his lips after his question.

"Hmmm," I murmur just before closing my eyes.

The bed is different. The blanket smells different. It's not bad, just different.

Stretching, the sheets caress my skin and I curl back into them, my eyes closed. A sigh of relaxation passes through my lips.

Shooting straight up in bed, I gasp. I pull the blanket and oh-so-soft sheet away from my body, looking down.

"How?" I ask an empty bedroom.

Looking around, the room feels bare and unlived in. I slip from the bed, my long nightshirt dropping to my knees. I rub my hands down the soft worn fabric and walk to the door.

I jump when there's a knock.

"Olivia?" Damon's voice is muffled.

The knob twists and I step back, allowing him to open the door. "Olivia?"

He first looks to the bed before finding me standing on the other side of the door. His brow furrows.

"Are you okay?"

I nod.

"Yes, just a bit confused." I bite my lip, taking in the tight gray t-shirt covering his lean chest.

"About?"

"Is this your room?"

"No. This is one of the spare rooms."

"Oh." Licking my suddenly dry lips, I take in his messy bed hair. *When did I turn into such a horny person in the morning?*

"You preferred the spare room, remember?"

"Yeah, no, I did. I was just curious." Nodding, I step toward my bag leaning against the far wall.

"Your clothes are in the closet."

Spinning, I change direction for the closet.

"Did you..." I clear my throat, "change my clothes last night?"

"Yes," he responds, a small twitch at the right corner of his mouth.

"Thank you." I pull the double doors open.

"How long do you need to get dressed?"

Looking over my shoulder, I furrow my brow in confusion.

"I'd like to take you out for breakfast and then to see the house." He leans against the doorframe.

"Oh, um, give me thirty?" I respond, but it sounds more like a question. "I'd like to wash out the hairspray and the make-up off my face."

Pulling out my heather brown, bias-cut, cashmere sweater and black leggings, I hold them against my chest.

"Is that okay?"

In three long strides, he stands before me.

"You take as long as you need."

His hands grasp my upper arms and he pulls me close, pressing his lips to my forehead.

"Just come out to the living room when you're ready."

Without another word, he exits, closing the door behind him.

I'm ready in less than thirty minutes, but I take my time blow-drying my hair. If eating wasn't becoming such an immediate need, I would procrastinate further. Being alone with Damon, nothing to distract the feelings he creates, is frightening. *How does someone fall for a stalker?*

Fluffing my hair away from my face, I assess myself in the bathroom mirror over the sink. Taking a breath, I slip my riding boots on and head for the living room.

When I arrive, Damon is sitting on the couch, reading papers. He hears me enter and places the documents in file folders spread out on the coffee table. My eyes move from the folders to the plate of muffins and fruit.

"I thought you might need something to hold you over until breakfast."

He smiles, motioning to the plate.

At the sight and mention of food, nausea decides to appear.
"Thank you."

Walking forward, I take a banana to subdue my hunger.

"Would you like to take anything with you?"

Damon stands. I take in his full appearance and swallow hard.

"No," I shake my head, "I'm okay." I lift the half-eaten banana back to my mouth.

"Let's get going then."

Putting his cell to his ear, he turns to walk away. My eyes focus on the perfect fit of his dark pants. Shaking away my lustful thoughts, I follow closely behind, collecting my purse and coat.

Exiting the elevator, we're greeted by a doorman.

"Mr. Knyght." He nods, hurrying around the desk to open the door. "The car is second in line, sir."

"Thank you." Damon guides me through the door by the small of my back.

"Oh, sir." Damon and I both pause just outside the door.

"Yes?"

"A delivery from Frame Gallery arrived yesterday afternoon while you were out. They are in the safe room. Would you like for us to put them in your apartment, or hold them?"

"If you could put them just inside the entryway, I would appreciate it."

"Of course, sir. I just need you to sign something." The doorman rushes to his desk and brings back a clipboard. "If you would just sign here, giving permission for building maintenance to deliver inside your apartment."

Damon takes the offered pen and signs the release.

"Thank you, sir. Have a wonderful morning."

"Thank you." Damon hands back the pen.

"Have a good day, too." I give the doorman a small wave.

Holding my coat tight against me, I allow Damon to guide me to the awaiting black car. Once inside, Damon gives the driver instructions to take us to Market Square.

"Where are we going?" I ask, tilting my head and looking up at him.

"I'm not sure." He turns his head, looking down. "You're the local. I figured you could show me around downtown."

He grins and I smile.

After breakfast at Bruegger's Bagels, we walk Market Square and take in the history of the buildings. In the afternoon, we travel over to Station Square, taking in the historical railroad sites.

"I have an idea."

Taking his hand, I don't miss the way he rubs his thumb over my skin. The action keeps me warm as we walk through the chilled air.

"Where are we going?" I don't have to look to know he's smiling.

"The incline is a necessary visit."

We arrive to entrance *A* of Station Square and I pull him along until we are standing inside the lower station of the incline. The attendant gives a brief history of the incline as we wait.

There are more people than I thought in our group, so we are packed tightly inside the car. My left side presses against Damon's right. Lifting his arm, he puts it around me. I stiffen for a moment before settling against him and enjoying the dramatic sights of the city.

At the top, and back out in the cold air, I drag him to the Mt. Washington Observation Deck closest to us. We stand against the railing, looking over the city.

"This is amazing." His arm winds around me.

"It's beautiful." Instinctively, I drop my head against him.

"Thank you." He rests his cheek against the top of my head.

"For what?"

I try to pull back so I can look up, but he holds me against him snuggly.

"For trying, Olivia."

I swallow the emotion and urge to kiss him.

"We should get to the house before it gets too late."

He squeezes me one last time before releasing me.

My body protests the loss of his presence. I lie, telling myself it's just his body heat I miss.

"Okay."

Our journey back to the car is quiet, except for some questions Damon has about the city.

Back in the car, I realize just how tired my body is from walking and exploring parts of the city. I'm so tired, I drift to sleep, only waking when we stop in front of a newly built home.

"We're here." Damon brushes the hair away from my face, which is pressed to his shoulder.

"Sorry," I yawn the apology and sit up.

His fingers come to my chin and pull so I look at him.

"Never apologize for leaning on me, Olivia." His eyes search mine before dropping to my mouth.

The door opens and the cold air cuts through the lusty tension.

We enter the house and my breath leaves me. The foyer is open with a staircase leading to a small landing and hallways I believe would take me to bedrooms. From the foyer, I walk straight into an open kitchen, dinette area that could fit a twelve-person table and an oversized family room with a fireplace. The space is massive, open, and beautiful. Not to mention, the formal dining and living rooms. There is a full size laundry room off the kitchen, a two-car garage, full attic, four bedrooms, and four bathrooms. The master suite bathroom contains a large bathtub with jets, two-sink vanity, large windows for natural lighting, and a shower four people could fit inside. Then, there are the showerheads — one on the ceiling and three down each side. It's like a human car wash. A car wash I would sell my soul to enter.

"This is amazing."

I turn, finding Damon standing in the bathroom doorway, arms over his chest, leaning against the doorframe.

"I'm glad you like it."

Pushing off the door, he saunters up, takes my face in his hands, and kisses me. It's not chaste, but it certainly isn't long. It's just enough to flare lusty desires to life. He pulls his mouth away and I sway forward.

"Would you help me make some color and design decisions?"

His thumbs brush over my cheeks.

"Please?" His eyes focus on my mouth when I lick my lips.

"That's not fair," I breathe.

"What?" He grins.

"Softening me with kisses before asking things of me."

His grin grows.

"Probably not, but I don't play fair."

"No, you don't." I close my eyes, inhaling and exhaling deeply in an attempt to cleanse away the lust.

"Will you?"

His thumb moves to my bottom lip. I press my lips tight, so not to lick.

I nod, afraid to open my mouth and release my tongue.

After nearly two and a half hours of discussing colors, flooring, counters, tiles, and hundreds of things I never thought I'd be discussing with Damon, I'm wore out. Instead of the dinner originally planned, Damon and I stop for take-out.

Stuffed full from four pieces of Sicilian style pizza and two glasses of iced tea, I lean back into the couch, tempted to roll my pants down below my stomach. Damon pauses the TV just before Alex can give the next Jeopardy answer and turns to me.

"Done?" Damon asks, a piece of crust held between his teeth.

Even though it's completely common, something many other people do in their homes, my heart flutters.

"Yeah." I nod, rubbing my stomach.

His eyes follow the movement before focusing back on my face. "Everything okay?"

"Just full." I smile.

Suddenly feeling self-conscious about my stomach, I tug my sweater out and away from my body. He grins around the crust before tearing a piece off with his white teeth. Pressing play on the TV, he looks back at the screen. My eyes linger on his profile before I give the game show my full attention.

I'm so comfortable. My body protests any movement from the soft warmth surrounding me. I force my eyes open. Aside from the light of the television, the room and windows are dark. Stretching, I find my lower body is pinned to the luxurious cushions. My brow furrows and I remember where I am.

Damon's apartment. Damon's couch. Damon pinning my lower half with his body.

Propping up on my elbows, I glance down my body. Damon lies stomach down, his face buried against the side of my stomach, his arm draped across my hips, and his muscular left leg wrapped around my right. The way his body is flush against mine, I can feel every breath he takes — deep and even. My body reacts, flushing with heat. Swallowing the lust, I lie back down, letting my breaths match the rhythm of his.

Damon's left hand glides up and under my sweater. His fingers find the band of my cotton pants and dip inside. Pulling the material down over my belly, he splays his fingers over the now exposed skin. His hand warms my skin, branding it forever with his gentle, caring touch.

This is new. Doing it alone during my pregnancy with Alex, I never experienced this. The feeling of someone else loving the person inside you as much as you do. My family and friends had been supportive, but now I realize...it isn't the same.

A shuddering breath leaves me. Emotions swell and I close my eyes against threatening tears.

"Hey," Damon quietly rasps.

His head lifts from my side and angles up.

"You okay?" he asks when I don't respond.

I feel his eyes on me, watching me. Worry radiates off him and his hand tenses against my stomach.

"If you want me to stop, I will." He begins to pull his hand away.

I shake my head, finally finding the composure to speak.

"Alex didn't have this," I say, my voice cracking.

"What?"

His body presses closer. I rest my right hand over his on my stomach.

"I was alone." I swallow back tears. "And that was okay. But now, with you..." I rub my hand over his. "Alex didn't have two people loving him more than life itself. Not like this," I hiccup.

"Shh..."

His hand presses against me.

I shudder.

"It feels so unfair to him," I croak.

The couch cushion shifts and I open my eyes.

Damon straddles my legs, propping his upper body on his hands, which are placed on each side of me. With one hand, he pushes the sweater until it gathers below my breasts.

"You are a wonderful mother."

Bowing his head, he presses his lips to my belly button. Raising his head, his eyes find mine in the darkness.

"Alex is a wonderful and loved little boy."

His lips press a couple of inches above my navel.

"He has not lacked for love or care."

He kisses just below the bunched cashmere.

"Alex was loved more than life itself before he was born."

He brings his face above mine.

"He had you to give him all of that. And even before I knew of him, those feelings were in me. I am just now able to show him all the love I have."

Reaching up, I grip the sides of his face and pull his mouth to mine. This time, I claim his mouth, owning him.

He gives me some of his weight, dropping down onto his forearms for support. The feel of his entire body pressing against mine heats my body. Suddenly, the sweater is too warm and uncomfortable. My pants are too tight and constricting. The cotton bra feels like it's made of steel wool. I want every piece of clothing removed. I want his warm, toned skin pressed against mine and I will have it.

Fisting his shirt, I tug and pull at the material.

Moving his weight to one arm, his right hand slips under my sweater. Our lip mash together and teeth click. Our breaths are heavy through our noses, heat dampening each other's skin.

Damon curls his fingers into the cup of my bra and pulls. The feel of his fingers and the cotton scraping across my nipple causes me to break our kiss with a gasp.

"Damon," I moan.

His lips fuse to my neck, sucking, licking, and nipping. Shoving the cashmere up further, he moves, dipping his head down to take my nipple into his mouth. Arching my back, I squeeze my thighs together.

As he lavishes attention to my breast, his hand moves down my body and slips into my cotton pants. One finger instantly finds the thin elastic of my panties and slides under the material.

Faintly, I hear music. *Oh my God, he's making me hear music?* Wait, the music is familiar. Very familiar. It's not music. It's chiming.

Damon stops, pulling his head away.

"That's your phone," he pants.

I meet his eyes, darkened by lust, and prepare to pull him back down to my breast, until I realize why the chime is familiar. Mercedes.

"Alex," I whisper, eyes widening.

As a mother, I immediately think the worst. Erik.

My fear and panic written all over my face, Damon jumps from the couch and retrieves my cell phone.

Sitting up, I readjust my bra and sweater.

By the time Damon returns with the phone, it has stopped ringing.

"I'm sure he's fine," he assures, handing it to me.

Missed call. Mercedes.

I hit the call and redial.

"Liv," Mercedes answers, Alex crying for me in the background. "What's wrong?"

Panic wells in my chest.

"He's fine," she reassures. "His ear is bothering him. He keeps crying, pulling on it, and saying ear. I just need to know if I should give him Motrin or Tylenol."

"Does he have a fever?"

The couch shifts and Damon stands, disappearing from the room.

"It's only 99.9. Not too high."

"Give him the Motrin based off the dosage scale on the label."

Standing, I start pacing.

"Okay."

Unwilling to hang up, I keep Mercedes on the phone in silence.

"Liv?"

"Yeah," I blurt.

"He's fine. If it gets worse, I'll call. Okay?"

"Okay," I whisper and disconnect the call.

I take a deep breath and hold it for one calming moment before releasing.

A sound behind me draws my attention. Turning, I find Damon standing with my bag and another bag.

"What's all this?"

"I think I grabbed everything, but whatever I missed, we can get later."

"Where are we going?" I step closer, my brow furrowed.

"Alex isn't well." He walks to the coatrack and picks up my coat before holding it out to me. "You're going to be worried about him if we stay here. I'd rather you not stress. Besides, I'm concerned about our son as well."

I take the coat and slip it on, while Damon gets his own.

"But, this is the alone weekend…"

"We can do it another time." He shrugs into his coat.

My chest fills with warmth, heart skips a beat, and I swallow back emotion. Alex now has this — us.

Buttoning up my coat, we grab our things and leave the planned weekend behind.

Mercedes doesn't show one bit of surprise when we walk into the apartment. She gives a small smile as I sit down next to her on the couch and launches into the current state of Alex.

"He just went to sleep about fifteen minutes after the Motrin. I took his temperature before I called you but haven't since then. I figure the medicine has it down for now."

She speaks to me, but her eyes follow Damon and the bags he carries.

"You didn't have to come home, Liv. He really is fine."

Her eyes come back to my face.

"I can't be away when he's sick." I shake my head.

"Do you want me to stay? I can help if he wakes up during the night."

"I'll help her."

Both of our heads turn. Damon leans against the wall at the edge of the hallway.

"You're staying?"

I don't have to look at her to see the smile she's wearing.

"Yes, Mercedes, I'm staying."

"Okay, well let me grab my things and get out of your way."

She stands from the couch.

"You don't have to go," I blurt, feeling guilty with it being late in the evening.

"It's fine. I can—"

"Please, don't go on my account. You can have the spare room," Damon states, a twinkle of mischief in his eye.

Realizing, with Mercedes here, he plans on sleeping next to me, embarrassment heats my face.

"You sure?" Mercedes looks from Damon to me.

I nod, swallowing hard.

"Of course," I croak.

"I'll take the couch." Damon grins at me.

"You can't sleep on that thing all night," Mercedes implores, a trace of disbelief in her voice.

"I'll be fine." He straightens from the wall.

"You can sleep with me," I say with more composure than I feel inside.

His eyes meet mine, but he says nothing. We stare silently for a few moments before Mercedes breaks the quiet.

"Well, I'm going to head to bed. That little guy tired me out."

She steps to me, leans down, and kisses my head.

"Night, Liv."

"Night, Ced," I return, my eyes staying locked with Damon's.

In my peripheral vision, I see Mercedes brush by Damon and disappear down the hall. Once the spare bedroom door clicks shut, Damon speaks.

"Are you sure? I can sleep on the couch."

"The couch isn't comfortable enough for an entire night. It's fine."

"Olivia, I don't want you to be uneasy next to me all night. You need your rest."

"I'll be fine. I promise."

He studies me for a minute longer before striding forward and offering me his hand.

"Shall we?"

Without hesitation, I take his hand.

"We shall," I respond.

The corner of his lip curls and my heart thumps against my ribcage. He leads us to my bedroom where we change into pajamas and climb beneath the covers.

I settle onto my side, facing away from him. He slides his arm around me, spanning his hand across my belly. The heat of his body penetrates my back and the skin on the back of my neck warms from his breath.

Damon doesn't do anything else and I find myself more relaxed than I have in so long. So much so, I fall asleep quickly underneath the weight of his arm.

Crying pulls me from a slumber so deep, it takes me a few extra moments to sit up. When I do, I notice Damon is gone. As I realize this, he walks into the room with a bawling Alex.

"Momma," he sobs, stretching his arms out for me.

"Baby, come here."

Damon puts him in my arms. I pull him in close, cradling him to my chest.

"Is this the right medicine?"

Damon holds a small plastic bottle in one hand and turns on the bedside lamp with the other.

"It was on his dresser," he adds.

"Yes, that's it."

"Momma. Hurt ear," Alex cries.

I begin rocking him as Damon reads the back of the bottle.

A sucking sound draws my eyes from Damon down to Alex. His first two fingers are in his mouth. He gnaws on them and saliva covers his hand. Pulling them out of his mouth, he fusses. When I stick my own fingers in his mouth, he starts chewing again. Hard lumps from a tooth just beneath his gum press into my flesh. I remove my fingers and hug him tight.

"Poor, baby. Are those mean teeth bothering you?" I coo.

"Teeth?" Damon holds a dropper full of Motrin.

"Yes, he's not sick. He's teething. It feels like a molar."

Reaching up, I take the dropper and give Alex the medicine. I give the empty dropper back to Damon, pick the medicine bottle up, cover the opening with my finger, and turn it upside down. Placing the plastic bottle back on the nightstand, I work my finger into Alex's mouth and rub the pain medicine over the cause of his discomfort.

The bed shifts when Damon climbs back in. He moves close to my side, pressing his body to mine. Reaching over me, he turns off the bedside lamp. As he brings his hand back, he places it against Alex's back and rubs. We fall asleep together, the three of us, in my bed.

Loud banging wakes me to my light-filled bedroom.

"Who is that?" I grumble, shifting so not to disturb Alex where he sleeps between Damon and me.

"I'll check," Damon whispers, climbing from the bed.

He reaches the bedroom door when Mercedes calls out.

"Olivia." There's an urgency in her voice that worries me.

Hurrying, I slip out of bed and rush to the living room.

Emerging from the hallway, I see two cops standing outside my door, talking to Damon.

"Liv, they came here asking for Damon." Mercedes moves to my side, putting her hand on my arm. "They're here to arrest him for assault."

"What?" I exclaim, moving to the door and next to Damon.

"Can I make a call to my lawyer?" Damon asks.

"Sir, I'm afraid you'll need to do that from the station."

"What's going on?" I narrow my eyes at the officer.

"It's nothing, Olivia." Damon turns to me, cupping my face. "Get my phone, call Hugh, and tell him to get my lawyers involved," he instructs.

"For what?"

I pull my face from his hand and look at the officers again.

"Assault, ma'am," he informs.

"Who did he assault?" I bark.

"Me."

The sound of Erik's voice makes every hair on my body stand. Fury boils in my stomach. He stands smugly, a dark purple bruise under his eye and along his cheek.

"Sir, we told you not to come here. We have it under control." The second officer glares at Erik.

"My concern is for Olivia and Alex. Given *his* history, I feared he may harm them."

Without looking at Damon, I know he's angry. It pours off him in invisible waves.

"You're pressing assault charges?" I snort.

"Yep." Erik's brow raises in challenge.

That asshole!

"Okay, well, let me grab my purse and follow you to the station." I look away from Erik to the first officer. "I have my own charges to press."

"On Mr. Knyght?" The officer's brow furrows. "Ma'am, if you are in trouble—"

"No, not on *my husband*, but on him." I point to Erik. "He was in my home waiting for me the other night after I was out with my husband. He proceeded to grow angry and insult me. I've been receiving deliveries from him, unwelcome gifts, and I'm beginning to worry."

I put on my best face of concern and hold my stomach.

"Ever since he found out my husband and I are having another child, he's been pushy and threatening. I think I should press my own charges. Harassment, a restraining order, whatever you think would make me feel more secure."

"You're a liar!" Erik screams. "He's been stalking you and you did nothing!"

He stomps closer, pushing by the second officer.

"You bitch!"

Damon steps between us.

"Officers, do you see what I mean?" I look away from Erik to the first officer. "During his prior visit, he called me a whore. Mr. Knyght reacted by hitting him. I don't condone violence, but he was protecting me."

"Sir, I need you to step back." The first officer addresses Erik, placing a hand on his arm.

Erik jerks away.

"Don't touch me! You're here to arrest this prick for assaulting me."

"I'll grab my purse." I move to turn around.

"I can't fucking believe you!" Erik shouts, stepping toward me. I spin to face him.

"Don't." Damon pins Erik with a glare. "One more step and your good eye will match the other."

"Sir, I need you to calm down and walk away." The second officer steps forward.

"You're going to press charges against me, aren't you?" Erik has the nerve to sound surprised.

"If you want to go this route, Erik, I'll do the same. If you can't let go of this delusion you had of us being together, then I'll make sure the law erases any possibility for you."

We stare at each other over Damon's shoulder. The hardness starts to ebb from his dark eyes.

"Are we going to the police station, Erik? Or can I get back to sleep before my son wakes up for the day?"

Silence lingers uncomfortably.

"Mr. Knyght, I'm going to have to ask you to come with me," the first officer states. "Unless the charges are being dropped."

Silence.

"Sir?" The officer addresses Erik.

"Yeah. Fine. I'll drop the charges."

Taking two steps back, his eyes stay on mine.

"This is goodbye, then?" It sounds like a question, but I don't respond.

"Yes, it is," Damon answers for me — for us.

Erik's eyes flicker to Damon.

"To hell with you both," he snarls and descends the stairs to his car.

"I apologize for the disturbance." Officer number one nods.

"We didn't realize the situation with him." Officer number two motions to where Erik disappeared.

"You were doing your jobs and I thank you for doing them with class."

Damon offers his hand to both of the officers. They shake and say their goodbyes.

In the aftermath, I sit at the kitchen island, drinking a real coffee with caffeine. Damon sits next to me, sipping on his own mug.

"That one officer was hot as hell," Mercedes breaks the silence.

I burst into laughter, snorting and everything.

"Just saying." She lifts one shoulder and sips from her mug.

The day after the police showed up, Damon was called away on an unplanned trip. The new business deal he and Hugh were working required his attendance in New York. After getting some things from his apartment, Damon stayed one more night with us before leaving early Monday morning.

Damon asked me to cancel or reschedule our session with Dr. Livingston, but something made me keep the appointment. Now, the urge to run from the waiting room grows until I'm just about ready to bolt.

"Olivia," Dr. Livingston calls out, pulling my attention away from my escape route.

"Hello." I stand from the seat.

"Is Damon running late?"

"No." I shake my head. "He actually got called away for business. We also didn't get the full weekend together, but we are going to do that this coming weekend." I clear my throat and fight the desire to fidget. "I'd actually like to speak alone. If that's okay?"

"Of course it is." Smiling, she motions for me to come with her.

Instead of leading, she walks next to me.

"How's the pregnancy?" she asks, conversationally.

"Good." I touch my stomach reflexively. "Everything is on track and going well."

"That's wonderful."

We enter her office, but instead of her sitting behind the desk, she joins me on the two person couch.

"So, Olivia, what would you like to discuss?"

"Do I have Stockholm Syndrome?"

A small smile graces her lips as her hand comes to my knee.

"Stockholm is usually a result from kidnapping, abduction, hostage situations...those types of circumstances. And while I'm not an expert in that area, I don't believe you are afflicted with this syndrome."

"Are you sure?"

She smiles, but stays quiet, allowing me to purge my worries and fears.

"I mean, who does this?" My eyes search her face. "He tracked me down, followed me wherever I went, hired me to work for him, barged into my life, and just..."

I stop, trying to make sense of the words rushing through my head.

"You're going to need to ask me the question, Olivia."

Looking the doctor in the eye, I swallow any hesitation and ask, "How can I have fallen in love with him? For real, honest to God love?"

Taking one of my hands in both of hers, she leans close to me.

"I'll admit your relationship with Damon is of unconventional beginnings. And while some of the components are concerning, I will say that the time I've spent with both of you, I don't see cause for alarm. Bad decisions were made on Damon's part multiple times. However, I do believe they were emotionally driven circumstances where he tried to find healing in any way he could. He found that with you. What has surprised me is I think you've found healing in him as well."

She pauses, looking over my face.

"Love happens in the strangest of times and places. Some people fall in love during war, in a time when the world is being torn apart around them. Others find someone on the internet and fall in love having never met. Then, there are people who find love in a traditional fashion. Love is love, Olivia. It's a mysterious thing and I don't have the answers to everything. You will need to look inside and search your heart and soul for the answers to your question. It's not something I can give, but I will tell you what I've told many couples — you love who your heart chooses."

"But it doesn't make sense," I argue, lamely.

"Love doesn't make sense," she counters, releasing my hand and sitting back on the couch. Then, she adds, "Do you know how many couples come in her arguing about money, in-laws...anything you can imagine? And a lot of them have one thing in common. At least one of the people in the relationships loves the other, regardless of figure changes, money troubles, alcohol, or drugs."

"So, it can still be unhealthy?" I grasp.

"Sometimes." She nods. "But I'm not sure I see unhealthy with the two of you."

Dropping my head into my hands, I sigh heavily.

"Why are you trying so hard to fight your feelings?"

I snap my head up, tensing. She's calling me out.

"I'm not fighting."

She grins.

"Okay, maybe a little." I shrug. "If I allow myself to feel like this for him and it doesn't work, it will kill me." I swallow down threatening tears. "What if the insanity of it all is just too much? How can it work when we are built off so much deceit and craziness?"

"You work at it. If it's worth it, you fight to keep it." Dr. Livingston pats my leg.

"If it's worth it," I repeat, not as a question.

Returning home, I find Mercedes sitting on the living floor with Alex.

"Momma." Alex smiles, lifting two cars in the air. "Come home."

"Hey, baby." I return the smile, letting his happiness wash away my inner turmoil.

"You okay?" Mercedes' eyes narrow.

"Yeah."

Setting my purse on the table, I disrobe from my coat and move to the kitchen for a drink.

"You don't sound or look too sure about that." Mercedes leans against the island, forearms on the marble top.

I shrug and chug juice right from the carton.

"Spill it."

The stool screeches on the wood floor as she sits down.

With a sigh, I launch into my discussion with Dr. Livingston. When I finish, Mercedes sits there, just looking at me.

"Well?" I probe for a reaction.

"I don't know why you're being spastic."

"You don't know why I'm..."

I shake my head, not even bothering to finish. Instead, I look past her to check on Alex. He's still playing cars on the carpet.

"Okay," Mercedes puts her hands up, palms forward, "I understand your hesitation, but, Liv, come on. Give the guy a break."

"A break?" I focus back on her.

"Yeah. So, he fucked up." She covers her mouth, apology in her eyes for cursing. "He made some crazy decisions and if you wanted to have him locked away, I would be right there, retelling the whole tale to put him in a padded cell. But, do you realize how different you've been? Don't you feel different?"

I close my eyes, knowing I've felt different — alive and relaxed at the same time. Something I haven't felt for...well, in forever.

"He loves you."

My eyes snap open and meet hers.

"It's not obsession or crazy, it's love. And I'm pretty sure — at least, recently — you love him, too."

Tears pool, blurring my vision. I fight hard to keep them from falling.

"It's okay to love him."

Blinking, I fail. Tears drip from my lashes onto my cheeks.

"I'm so sick of crying." I wipe the wetness away.

"We'll blame the hormones." Mercedes winks.

"Okay," I laugh through the tears.

"So, when you move out, I get the apartment, right?"

I laugh harder, but she doesn't laugh.

"You're serious?"

She hesitates, but then nods.

"What about your place?"

She lifts one shoulder.

"I think it's time for a change. I'd pay rent for the apartment."

"Ced, it's not about rent."

Sobering, I realize I've been really self-absorbed in my problems and emotions over the past few months.

"I've been a crappy friend lately," I mutter.

"What?" Mercedes straightens. "No, you haven't."

"Yes, I have. We haven't talk about you or what's going on with you. I'm a jerk and I'm sorry."

She grins.

"Well, maybe it's been about you a lot," she playfully agrees. "I mean, it's not like you should be distracted by a Vegas one night stand, slash husband, slash baby daddy, slash another baby for the baby daddy, slash—"

"I get it," I cry out and giggle.

"Liv, I know you are going through a lot and I'm happy to have been here for you. Besides, you've always been the one for me to lean on. You're the dependable, put together friend who's needed a little crazy of her own. But, let's be honest, your time is up and I need some spotlight time."

We both laugh and I move, taking a seat next to her.

"Tell me how you've been, Ced."

"I've decided to be a bit more like you, since I'm growing up." She grins.

We sit and talk about Mercedes. She tells me about her night with Alfonso, the calls from him she's avoided until he finally stopped calling, and how she's been staying away from guys in general lately. Instead of going after every guy hoping to find love, she thinks maybe taking a break would be good for her. This brings us back to the conversation of her needing a change and moving into a new place. I discover that my carefree, crazy friend is at a point in lifestyle overhaul and I almost missed it. Mentally, I vow to be more attentive. I'm about to tell her this when my cell phone chimes. I'm prepared to ignore it so I can focus on Mercedes, but her phone pings as well.

While she checks her phone, I pull mine out of my pocket.

20 weeks: Not going to lie, this week is kind of gross. Something about meconium and sticky white substance on her skin. Good news, she gets eyelids and brows next week.

Grinning, I slip the phone back into my pocket.

"Felicity is losing it," Mercedes says, her eyes remaining on her phone.

"What's going on?"

Mercedes turns her phone toward me, showing me a text from Felicity.

Don't kill me. I couldn't help myself.

I shrug.

"I don't know what she's talking about."

Mercedes' fingers fly over the screen of her phone. When she's done, we both turn to watch Alex playing cars and discuss some of the things she's had on her mind lately.

Fifteen minutes later, there's pounding on my door.

"Do you think it's Erik?" Mercedes slips from the stool and starts for the door.

"Wait, maybe we shouldn't answer the door." I slip to my feet and step forward.

"Mercedes," a male voice calls from the other side of the door.

"That's not Erik," I state the obvious, relief washing over me.

"Oh no." Mercedes stops a foot from the door.

"Who is—"

"Mercedes, I know you're up here. Mrs. Dorn already told me where to find you."

Alfonso. I cover my mouth so not to laugh. Felicity's text suddenly makes sense.

"I'm gonna kill her," Mercedes snarls.

I snort, unable to hold the laughter in any longer.

"Cedie!" Alex shouts. A giggle follows his exclamation.

Mercedes glares at me over her shoulder.

"I didn't do it." I put my hands up in surrender.

"Mercedes, open the door." Alfonso knocks again — hard.

Groaning loudly, she steps forward and opens the door.

"What?" she snaps.

"You told my sister I'm bad in bed?" he growls. "You told that harpy I'm bad in bed. Do you realize she would take out ad space to tell the world something like that?"

"Not my problem." Mercedes shrugs.

"Not your...Jesus woman."

Alfonso looks and sounds distressed.

"Are you done?" Mercedes crosses her arms over her chest.

"No, I'm not," he states, his voice low and ominous.

Mercedes stands silent, waiting for him to explain.

"We're going to do this again," he demands.

"Do what?"

"Sex. I'm going to prove you wrong."

"Oh my..."

Mercedes looks back at me.

"Do you hear this?"

I nod, biting my lip so I don't burst into hysterics.

She turns back to Alfonso.

"You've lost your damn mind. Why the hell would I want to have bad sex twice?"

Her head gives a little swivel in emphasis.

"Listen, there are things...I was trying to be gentle and easy," he says, his voice dropping low, but I can still hear.

"Yeah, okay," Mercedes says in her best sarcastic voice.

"I'm going to pick you up after work tomorrow." Alfonso steps back, but keeps his eyes on her. "I'm not taking no for an answer."

"Well then, how about, drop dead."

Mercedes slams the door shut and locks it.

"Tomorrow, Mercedes. I'll be here at five o'clock. Be ready and well rested."

Unable to hold the humor back any longer, I laugh so hard, I'm having trouble breathing. Alex laughs from across the room and it makes me laugh more.

"This isn't funny," Mercedes growls, pulling her cell phone out of her pocket. "I'm going to beat the shit out of her."

Her fingers move fast and she presses the cell to her ear. Felicity is about to get a verbal smack down.

"I've missed you," Damon says against the knuckles he just kissed.

"It was only a couple days."

"Doesn't matter." He helps me into the back of his car while the driver puts my overnight bag into the trunk.

Slipping in behind me, the driver closes the door. We settle into the seat. His thigh presses to mine, causing me to be hyperaware of his every movement.

The car pulls away from the curb.

"Are you feeling well?"

Looking up from our touching thighs, I nod.

"Yes. The appointment is next week," I remind.

"I know." He grins.

"You're weekly updates are quite entertaining, by the way." I smile.

His grin grows into a wide smile.

"You haven't responded, so I wasn't sure how you felt about those."

The doubt in his voice, the fact that he is actually self-conscious, is unfathomable.

"They're good."

I place my hand on his leg. His larger hand immediately captures and holds it there.

We arrive to Monterey Bay Fish Grotto and the driver drops us off. Inside, we're seated in a room with the view of the skyline. The sky is dark, so the four towers of the PPG building flash, the headlights of the many cars moving through the city and the bridges. It's gorgeous.

Our waitress is professional, crisp, clean dressed, and can answer any question about the fresh fish of the day. Damon settles on the Swordfish Parmesan and I order Ahi Tuna Sesame, cooked well. The waitress convinces Damon to try the crab cake with remoulade sauce appetizer. As we wait for our drinks, I stare out at the Pittsburgh skyline.

"You love it here, don't you?" Damon asks.

Without looking away from the view, I answer, "Yes. The city is beautiful."

"You're beautiful."

My eyes meet his and I open my mouth to speak, but the waitress appears with our drinks.

"I'll be back with the appetizer."

"Thank you."

Damon nods to her before focusing back on me.

"I'd like to talk about something with you."

He lifts his glass and takes a drink.

"About?"

"The baby...and Alex."

His Adam's apple bobs.

"Okay..."

Staying vague with my response, I wait to see where he goes.

"Would you object to our daughter having my last name?"

It takes a moment to process what he's asking. I go with my gut.

"No."

"Okay." Damon sits up straighter. "This leads me to request Alex's name be changed to Knyght. I'd like our children to both have my last name. I know we didn't agree on this early on, but I hope we are now in a place where you will consider the idea."

"Yes."

"Yes?" Damon's eyes brighten.

I nod. He smiles.

"Would you be angry if I have the papers with me to start Alex's name change?" He lifts one brow.

I laugh, loudly, drawing attention from others in the restaurant.

"Do you have them?"

"Maybe."

He picks up his glass and drinks through curled lips.

"I wouldn't expect any less from you, Damon."

The waitress arrives with the appetizer. The crab cakes look and smell amazing. My stomach rumbles and mouth waters.

Being a gentleman, Damon serves me before getting some for himself.

One bite, and the crab melts in my mouth. I moan. Damon's eyes lock onto my lips.

"Do you have any preferences for the baby's name?" I ask before putting another bite into my mouth.

"What do you think about Harlow?"

"Harlow?" I furrow my brow.

"Yes. I think your name is beautiful, Olivia. For it to carry on as her first name would be nice."

"I don't know. Isn't that a bit odd?"

"I don't think so."

"Maybe." I shrug and sip my water.

"Do you have something in mind?"

"What about Rosalyn? I always lean toward traditional names."

"Rosalyn," he repeats, trying it out. "I like that."

"We have time. I was just curious about your thoughts."

"I appreciate you asking. I really do. Thank you."

"You don't have to thank me." I place my fork down on the empty plate.

"There's one more thing I'd like to talk about. Mind you, I've mentioned it before, but I just want to be open about my desires."

"Okay."

"This house isn't just for me and weekend visits, Olivia. I want us to be a family and live there."

"I need more time to think, Damon."

He nods.

"The house should be ready to move into two months from now. I won't move in without you."

"Damon, you paid—"

"The money doesn't matter to me," he says, his voice serious and definite. "What matters is when I enter that house, I want it to be with you. Without you, it won't be a home."

I open my mouth, but close it. Agreeing to move into the house is so much more than just living together. For Damon, this is my acceptance of our marriage, our family, of a life together.

"You don't have to answer tonight." His smile is obviously forced.

I know his hope was for me to agree immediately, but I don't. I need to think.

Dinner remains quiet with simple conversation over amazing meals. In the middle of our main courses, we switch plates. I honestly couldn't pick a favorite, they were that good. By the end of the meal, I feel uncomfortable. It's suddenly hard for us to find the easy rhythm we've recently shared. Even the car ride is quiet, making me feel the pressure of his question.

Swallowing my discomfort, I decide another topic may move us on from the silence.

"Anything new with the fertility clinic?"

"Actually, yes. The private investigator found some information I've been meaning to share with you and get your input."

"My input?"

He nods, going into the details of both his mother and Rebecca's involvement, and the fact that there are other couples who may have been involved.

"I'd like to make sure the other couples affected by the situation are aware. It's not fair for them to be kept in the dark or to find out some other way. I feel like it's my responsibility. But, I want your opinion, because taking this public will be a field day for the media. It could get crazy."

The feel of his eyes forces me to meet his gaze.

"Maybe being in the dark is better for some of those people," I offer.

"I thought about that, but my thoughts are to inform them. Perhaps it's selfish of me on some sort of level, but I feel like I need to do this."

Nodding, I look away.

"You don't agree."

Twisting my head back to him, I shake my head.

"No, it's not that. I'm just trying to think it through. You know, all the angles."

"I understand."

"Is there any way we could possibly tell these couples privately? Or at least try to keep it private?"

"I'm not sure. I suppose I could talk with my lawyers about a way to keep the information confidential."

"There are medical records and this does involve minors. I'd think there would be some law to protect them," I add to his thoughts.

"It's not a guarantee." His eyes bore into mine.

"I know, but we can try, right?"

"We?" His hand takes mine.

There it is. The ease and comfort settles between us.

"Yes, we."

He tugs, bringing me close to his side and wrapping an arm around me.

Stepping into his apartment, I kick off the heels I thought were a good idea when I picked out this dress for our date. One shoe smacks into a large item wrapped in brown paper. I turn to Damon with wide eyes.

"I'm sorry. I didn't mean to—"

"It's fine. Don't worry about it. They are facing away."

"Facing away?" My brow furrows in confusion.

I look back to where my shoe hit and realize it's a stack of wrapped artwork.

"You bought paintings?" I ask, stepping forward and placing my fingers on the edge of one.

"No," he answers, removing my coat from my shoulders.

"Are they from New York?"

My curiosity grows as my fingers dance along the brown-papered edge.

"No."

Looking over my shoulder, I give him an incredulous look.

"Why are you being evasive?"
"Because you're cute when you're curious."
Closing the gap between us, he places his hands on my hips.
"Jerk," I tease.
"See, I was going to let you look at them, but now..."
"Damon," I laugh.
His head dips close to my ear.
"You can look, but don't be angry."
Twisting my neck, I look at him.
He kisses my nose and steps away.

Turning my attention back to the secret art, I turn the first one around and tear the paper down.

My breath leaves me as tears well in my eyes. I swallow at the emotion trying to rip from my throat. Grabbing the next in the stack of three, I flip and rip the paper. The tears release, streaking my cheeks and dripping from my chin. Still with purpose, but slower, I grab the third and repeat. Covering my mouth, I stare at the portrait of me reading a cooking book.

On wobbling legs, I turn my body.

Damon leans against the wall behind me — tie gone, first three buttons of his shirt undone, hands in his pockets, and eyes riveted on my every movement.

I stride forward. His mouth is set in a grim line and his jaw muscle ticks.

Bringing my hands up, I grab his shirt.
"Why?" I croak on a whisper.
"For you, I welcome Isaac into our life and our new home."
"They're for the house?" I whisper.
He nods.
"I didn't mean to upset you. If you don't want them, I will—"
"You framed them? For me?"
He nods again.

Fisting the material until my knuckles ache, I yank him down so our faces are a breath apart. Damon's eyes search mine.

His lips part to speak again and I crash my mouth onto his with such force, it knocks us off balance. His hands come to my hips and firmly grip.

Sucking his bottom lip between mine, I lightly nip. He moans, sliding his hands up my back. Plundering my mouth, he forces his tongue against mine.

His fingers reach the back of my neck. They bury into my hair, fisting almost painfully. Pushing off the wall, he spins us until my back thuds against the barrier. Tightening his grip, he coaxes my head back. With my neck exposed, his mouth moves over my chin, stopping to lightly bite.

Damon sucks the sensitive skin of my neck. The anticipation of being skin to skin spirals out of control. Yanking in opposite directions, his shirt buttons pop open. I claw at the t-shirt he wears, hating the obstacle.

"I need to feel you," I moan.

I feel him hesitate for a split second before stepping away and pulling both shirts from his body.

Gripping his belt, I work the buckle and then the button of his pants. His hands rest on my hips, his fingers drawing the skirt of my dress higher and higher, until he can pull the jersey material over my head. Annoyed by the loss of contact, I growl.

The dress and his shirts gone, I shove at his pants and they fall to the floor. His mouth conquers mine and his hands return to my hips. I grip at his shoulders, pulling him close enough for my hard nipples to rub against him.

Squatting down, just a bit, he grabs the back of my thighs and lifts me against the wall. Wrapping one arm around his neck, I drink greedily from his mouth. I stretch my other arm down his back, digging my fingers into his flesh.

"Hold on," he growls against my lips.

"Always," I pant.

Pulling back his head, his eyes bore into mine. Something intense flares between us and whatever he sees makes his lip twitch.

Lifting me away from the wall, he carries me down the hall. Our eyes stay locked until he sits me onto the bed.

Kneeling on the floor between my legs, he grabs the straps of my bra and pulls them down roughly.

Leaning forward, I try to kiss him. He licks my lips, but won't give me his mouth. Narrowing my eyes, I pull my arms from the bra straps. I grab his head, pull him to me, and claim his lips. I wrap my legs around his waist, feeling his body press into me. His hard cock almost where I need it, I tilt my hips and rock. Our bodies meet and my head drops back.

Damon's mouth moves over my neck and collarbone. His tongue flicks over my nipple, eliciting his name from my mouth. His hands move over my thighs until they grip onto my cotton panties. Twisting and pulling, he tries to get them down my thighs, but I won't release him. Giving up, he grips one side with both hands and rips the fabric. The bite of the fabric into my skin intensifies my anticipation. His mouth moves to lick and suck at my other nipple, but he doesn't try to enter me.

"Damon, please," I cry out in frustration. "I need you."

"Patience, baby," he rasps against my breast.

Sliding my fingers into his hair, I grip and pull his head back.

"I need you, Damon. I want you to fuck me."

Heat lights his eyes and his nostrils flare.

Imitating him, I lick his mouth once and pull away when he tries to capture my tongue.

"Liv," he growls.

Bringing one thigh up onto the bed under my leg and then the other, he crawls us both further up the bed. With my toes, I grab the band of his underwear and push them down. His cock springs back, hard and ready against my thigh.

Resting his weight on his left forearm, he reaches between us, rubbing the tip of him over me. Rocking and angling my hips, I work to get him inside. The light hair on his legs rubs against the inside of my thighs, intensifying the throbbing in my clit. When he rubs the tip of his erection over it, I throw back my head and my arms fall to the bed.

"Oh my God, Damon!"

Bringing my right hand back to his head, I grab his hair and pull his face to mine. Our kiss is like drinking lava. The fire that lights between our lips spreads in a slow, deliberate heat across my skin until it collects between my legs.

"Are you ready, baby?" Damon pants against my mouth, his hand still taunting me with the evidence of his desire.

"You know I am," I snap, sexually frustrated.

"Like Vegas, so demanding."

I feel the smile against my mouth.

"What do you want, Olivia?" he asks, a teasing grin on his face.

Leveling my eyes on his, I put both hands on the side of his head. Lifting slightly, I stick my tongue between his lips and drop back to the bed.

"I want you inside me."

The teasing gone, he positions and slams inside.

"Oh yes, yes, God yes!"

Relief washes over me.

The musky scent of him, the way his hips piston between my legs, and how he hits the spot deep inside, build an erotic need within me.

His right hand moves across my skin, stopping to cup and squeeze my breast. My nipple between his lips, he sucks hard. Releasing the nipple, he rubs his thumb over the wetness left behind.

"You're gorgeous, Olivia," he rasps.

I'm unable to speak, my words drowned out by panting and moaning. My body coils tight, a hot ache grows at the core of me, and Damon thrusts harder, faster, as if he knows just what I need, what I want.

"Please," I beg on a gargled cry.

His hand slides down my body, over my belly, and between my legs. His finger joins where we are connected, gathering the wetness and rubbing it over my sensitive clit. One, two, three circular rotations and I explode beneath his body.

"Fuck, Olivia," he cries.

His hand moves from between us to beside my head on the bed. His hips thrust hard in an erratic rhythm that rides me through my erotic bliss.

Panting, Damon drops his head to my chest. Then he rolls, so that we are both lying on our sides, facing each other. I moan at the loss of him inside me, but I'm glad to straighten out my legs.

His left hand comes up, moving stray hairs from my face. I wrap my leg over his. He moves his left hand to my lower back and pulls me closer.

"I can't ever let you go," he whispers.

Placing my hand on his chest, I feel the rapid beat of his heart.

"Don't ask me to give you up."

He pulls me closer, trapping my hand between us. I can now feel that our heartbeats match and in that moment, I make a decision. It's time to be a little more like Mercedes.

Swallowing my nerves, I open my mouth.

"I won't."

Bringing his hand back to my face, he cups my chin so his fingers press behind my ear and his thumb on my cheek. Tilting my head, he looks down at me.

"What are you saying, Olivia?" he asks, his voice low and careful.

"I won't ask you to give me up."

"Olivia?" His tone becomes warning. "Don't play with me."

Working my hand out from between our bodies, I place my palm to his cheek.

"I love you, Damon."

His breath catches.

"I don't know how or why, but I do. I love you."

"Fuck, Olivia," he whispers before dipping down and kissing me.

This kiss isn't the lustful erotic type from earlier. This is gentle, loving, and caring. I close my eyes and bask in the emotions.

Pulling away, he rubs his thumb over my cheek.

"I love you, Olivia. I have loved you since I met you and I will love you always."

This feels right. He...no, we feel worth it.

Epilogue
Olivia

Oh my good Lord, my boobs hurt. They're so heavy on my chest, like I'm being crushed by cement blocks. Yawning, I stretch. My clothes stick to my damp skin and I groan.

"Damn sweating," I growl low, so not to wake the baby.

Glancing toward the bay window of our large master bedroom, it's still light out. I sigh in relief, knowing I haven't slept the entire morning away. I tiptoe to the basinet and look down on Rosalyn Harlow Knyght, or Princess Knyght, as I call the spoiled infant.

Tracing her soft, round cheek with my fingertips, a smile slides over my mouth.

"We need to talk about these late nights, princess," I whisper.

Padding quietly to the bathroom, the material of my sleep shirt rubs my over sensitive nipples. I grab my swollen breasts, my palms pressing to wet spots.

In the bathroom, I lean into the shower stall and turn on the water. I turn and look in the large vanity mirror above the double sink. Groaning, I pull on the hair band, releasing my greasy ponytail. Lifting the shirt over my head, leaving me in a pair of cotton panties, I can't help but stare at my chest. It's doubled in size. I place my hands against them and my palms become saturated with heat. My eyes move to the breast pump at the far end of the counter and then to the shower.

"I can hold those for you," Damon whispers from the door. His eyes are riveted to my hands covering my bare porno breasts.

"I need to pump," I whine, giving the shower a longing gaze.

He steps into the bathroom, closing the door behind him.

"What about Rosie and Alex?"

Releasing one boob, I point toward the now closed door.

"I can't hear her through the door and shower."

He smiles, walks to the stall, and shuts off the water.

"Hugh is playing with Alex. Scarlett and Mercedes are in the kitchen with the baby monitor. The minute Rosie makes a noise, those two will be fighting to get to her first."

"I didn't realize we had guests." I furrow my brow, thinking about how long I'd been asleep.

"I didn't want to wake you." His eyes drop to my chest and he grins.

"What?"

Glancing down, I quickly bring my hand up to cover my right boob. Looking back to Damon, I scowl. His grin grows into a wide smile.

"Perv," I mumble.

He laughs. Leaning over the large tub, he pushes the stopper and twists the knobs. Water surges into the basin.

I sigh with yearning at the tub.

"We have company."

"Yes, we do."

He straightens and continues.

"We have company who knows you are exhausted by a finicky infant and toddler."

Damon strides toward me, placing his large warm hands to my hips and hooking his thumbs into my panties.

"Which is why they are occupying Alex, listening for Rosie, and preparing dinner for you tonight."

His fingers dance along my backside, leaving tingles which travel straight between my legs.

"They don't have to—"

"They know that, but they want to, Olivia. And I want them to, so I can take care of you."

Leaning down, he presses his lips to my nose before claiming my mouth. His hands fist the sides of my panties and pull me close.

"Damon," I mumble against his lips.

He presses closer, harder. My hands grasp onto his shoulders.

I turn my head and gasp. "Damon."

His mouth moves over my chin and along my neck.

"We can't," I pant, fisting the long cotton sleeves covering his biceps. "Not for at least three more weeks."

"I know," he breathes against my flushed skin.

Moving down, his lips kiss and his tongue licks a path over my collarbone, to my chest, and between my breasts. Kneeling before me, he slowly pulls my panties down my legs and lets them fall to my ankles.

"Step," he commands huskily.

I comply, stepping out of the panties.

Standing before him, completely naked with swollen breasts and a pudgy stomach, I bite my lip. Remembering the tampon string between my legs, a wave of self-consciousness crashes over me. Just before he presses his face to my belly and kisses, I wrap my arms around his head, holding him in place.

His hands caress my skin from ankle to thigh, from thigh to hip, disappearing to cup my bare bottom and gently squeeze. Then, palms flat, he moves up my lower back, around my ribcage, until he cups a breast in each hand.

Dropping my head back, I revel in the feel of him worshipping my body.

"You're beautiful," he whispers.

Pulling his face back just enough, he swipes the flat of his tongue over my right nipple before repeating the action on the left. The sensation causes me to pull away, just a bit, but his hands come around to my back, pulling me to him.

"Damon," I gasp when he takes a nipple between his lips gently. "You can't—"

He releases my nipple as one hand disappears from my back and his tongue laves around my nipple. The feel of the plastic draws my attention to look down. With the press of his thumb on a button, the breast pump begins its task.

I run my fingers through his hair, touched and turned on, both making me feel weird. This shouldn't be a romantic or sensual situation, but he's made it one.

His mouth works against my other breast — small kisses to the underside, the flat of his tongue against the pebbled tip, and taking me into his mouth. The amount of time he spends on my breast drives me into lust overdrive.

After a few minutes, he pulls the pump away to place it against the breast he just lavished.

This time, he uses his fingers to draw patterns on the underside of my breast and occasionally swipes his thumb over the nipple.

Damon stands and my fingers fall from his hair to his shoulders. His eyes look into mine, as if he can see into my soul. His lips crash to mine in a searing kiss, claiming my mouth. When breath is needed, we pull away, eyes locking once more, and panting in unison.

Licking my bottom lip, I still taste him. His eyes drop, following the action.

The pump clicks off and disappears from my breast.

His hands on my hips, he guides me to the bathtub.

I'm not sure when or how, but the water is no longer on. He had me way too distracted to see him do this.

He helps me into the water and I sigh, settling against the side with my legs stretched out.

The warmth of the water washing away the sweat and milk from skin is almost as sensual as his mouth had been.

My eyes pop open when Damon steps into the tub.

"Lean forward," he commands.

As I move, he slips in behind me. Settling into the water, he pulls me so my back is against his chest. With his legs on either side of me, I get comfortable between them, placing my head back on him.

Soon, his hands are gliding up my arms. At my shoulders, he grips firmly and begins to massage the muscles of my neck.

I moan and melt against him.

Minutes pass, and soon, his hands become greedy, sliding over my collar and stopping at my breasts to play.

I squirm against him and tighten my thighs for relief.

Bowing his head, he presses open mouth kisses to the skin where my neck and shoulder meet. One of his hands continues a downward path over my belly.

Pressing my hands to his thighs, I close my legs tight.

He can't go there, I silently panic.

"Relax," he murmurs against my skin.

"Damon, you can't—"

"Shh…"

One finger, one long finger, slips between my wet legs.

"I'm still—"

The finger slips between my folds, pressing against my clit.

"Oh God," I gasp, dropping my head back once more.

"Open for me," he demands before licking from neck to earlobe.

Without protest, I part my thighs and dig my fingers into his.

The one glorious finger circles and rubs against me. Tingles grow into throbs. Throbs escalate to a precipice my entire lower body bucks to cross.

Water sloshes around us and Damon growls against my skin. My gasps and pleas for release fill the bathroom just before ecstasy explodes between my thighs and pleasure surges like an electronic current to each limb.

"You're stunning." Damon kisses my neck.

"I can't take anymore." I push his still circling finger from between my legs.

I don't hear him laugh, but I feel it against my back.

Closing my legs, I turn a bit and lean against his chest. His arms come around me and his cheek presses to my head, holding me tight — right where I should be.

 the End

acknowledgements

Sadie's BETAs – Marie Ruggiano-Parisi, Shea Murray, Kara Brooks Fuller, Tracy Gray, Stephanie Behill, Ruth Secrist, Bronwyn Winter, and Leeann Rednour Hohstadt – Thank you for taking time out of your busy personal time to read, critique, and encourage.

Grubor Groupies – Thank you for your support and feedback, and your entertaining posts. Special thanks to my group admins: Leeann Rednour Hohstadt, Kara Brooks Fuller, and Krista Savage Jones.
https://www.facebook.com/groups/GruborGroupies

Monica Black – Thank you for always correcting me and making me look like I know how to write. ☺

MY MINIONS: You are a source of inspiration and love. I cherish you!

Coming soon from sadie grubor...

Hidden in the Stars (Falling Stars 2)
  When your heart has been broken, shattered by deceit, how do you hide your pain from cameras and millions of fans? You dull the ache with gorgeous women who look nothing like the girl that tore you apart. You drown the pain with your two best friends, Captain and Jack D.
  All the bad boy behavior – super model girlfriend and major partying – splashed across the tabloids is the ultimate revenge. It's also the perfect way to hide among stars.
  Join Jackson Shaw, guitarist for The Forgotten and step-brother of Christopher Mason, as one small family of three discovers our hidden star. And, maybe, makes him shine like he did once before.
Tentative Release – Summer 2015

Susquehanna River Series (Book 1)
  A group of pontoon boat cruising, beer drinking, river camping, locals who find in a small town.   *Tentative Release – Summer 2015*

other books from sadie gruber

Falling Stars Series
Falling Stars
Stellar Evolution (a Falling Stars
novella)
Hidden in the Stars (coming soon...)

Modern Arrangements Trilogy

Save the Date
Here Comes the Bride
Happily Ever Addendum
Terms and Conditions

Stand Alones:

Live-In-Position

All Grown Up

about the author

To keep up to date on upcoming releases, sneak peeks, cover reveals, and inspirational music & images you can find Sadie Grubor on Facebook, Twitter, Goodreads, and her website.

Amazon Author Page: Sadie Grubor
Facebook: www.facebook.com/authorsadiegrubor
Goodreads: Sadie Grubor
Website: www.sadiegrubor.com
Twitter: https://twitter.com/SadieGrubor

You can also find me on Authorgraph.

about the Editor

It has been my pleasure to work with Monica, and I look forward to working with her in the future. She already knows all the crazy I have planned for her.

THANK YOU MONICA!!!

This is where you can find her, but she's really, really, really, really, really, busy, so she can't…. OKAY, perhaps I'm being a bit selfish. I'll still be pouty about it, just saying!

Monica Black – Freelance Editor
www.facebook.com/wordnerdediting
www.wordnerdediting.weebly.com

51455702R00217

Made in the USA
Lexington, KY
30 April 2016